The Dreamer 4

A.D. PLAUTZ

Note that all of the characters depicted in this story are purely fictional; any resemblance to actual living or deceased persons is merely coincidental. This story is dedicated to a patient spouse.

Author's Note: Please remember that anything can happen in a dream.

Olympus Story House

CHAPTER 1

ROBERT J. PARKER sat on the gurney, dressed in one of those stupid blue smocks that opened in the rear, waiting for the doctor to enter. The small square white room was brightly lit and was almost painful to his eyes. He was the chief engineer at an aerospace company and was presently midway through a detailed qualification test program. He was medium build, about 205 pounds and had blue eyes and graying hair. At the age of 57 he felt that he should still have some good years left, but the constant headaches and neck pain had forced him to check in with his doctor. He was also having some very strange dreams. Dr. Jack Simms was not only his doctor but a good friend and a close neighbor. What followed was a series of tests, the typical EKGs, X-rays and finally the MRI. He was hoping desperately for good news. His wife Sarah was in the waiting room and he wanted to tell her that everything was all right.

"Well, Robert, I got the results from the MRI." Dr. Simms walked into the room. He was not smiling and had a look of disappointment on his face. The formality of the announcement meant it was not good news.

"I wish I could tell you otherwise, but it is not good news. The MRI shows that you have a brain tumor." The doctor slowly sat in the only chair in the small room.

Bob was somewhat shocked by the revelation. "How b-bad is it?" he managed to stammer.

"As far as I can tell, it is way too deep to operate, but you can always go get a second opinion," he said, folding his hands helplessly.

Bob had known Jack Simms for over 20 years and had always trusted him. Jack lived down the street from him and was a good friend. They usually played golf together about once a month in the summer. Their wives were best friends. If Jack said the tumor was inoperable then it probably was. Jac was one of the best neurologists at the Cleveland Clinic.

"Jack, what can I do? Is radiation a possibility?" He asked desperately.

"Where this bastard is located, I do not think radiation will help. It would just cause more damage to your brain." The doctor looked at the floor in disgust. Bob Parker was a good friend of his and he did not like what he had to say.

"Is there any chance for chemotherapy?" Bob asked.

"Yeah we could try it, but this thing is so far advanced that it would probably make what time you have left even more miserable." Jack noted. "If you really want to do it…"

"I hear it makes you puke all the time and your hair fall out." Bob frowned.

"Yes…It could have some bad side effects. Based on the size of the tumor we would need to pump in the strongest stuff we have. And even then I doubt if it would stop it in time. You could end up in a vegetative state. I doubt if you want to end it that way."

"How much time do I have?" Bob asked meekly.

"Bob, I have to tell you that you might have 5 to 6 months left before it…" he did not continue.

"Shit," Bob whispered. He was looking forward to retiring and spending some time with his wife Sarah. She deserved something after 28 years of marriage and raising two kids. He had worked hard for almost 30 years and had often neglected his wife and kids, trying to get ahead. He was always working long hours and making business trips. He had finally made it to chief engineer only four years ago and had managed to save up enough money to retire early, maybe at 62. Now that was all for nothing. He felt betrayed by his body. He dreaded telling Sarah the bad news. Maybe he should just quit work and take her someplace she always wanted to visit, maybe Hawaii.

"Will it be very painful?" Bob asked looking at the floor.

"Toward the end it may get very confusing for you. You may lose control of your body. But there should not be a great deal of pain. The brain does not have pain sensors." Jack replied.

"What about this pain in my neck?" Bob asked.

"That is probably a delayed whiplash reaction from the car accident you were in a few years ago. Some people suffer spinal damage from getting hit from behind and it can take years to show up. I don't really think it is related. The X-ray shows you have a compressed disk," Jack said, standing up. "I'll give you a prescription for the pain." He offered to shake Bob's hand and said, "Angie and I will pray for you."

"Please don't let her tell Sarah yet. I need some time to get things in order." "Sure. I understand. It's just between you and me." Jack reassured.

Bob right then made the decision to quit work and put in his retirement papers. He would talk to the HR person at work tomorrow. His boss Marty, would not be happy but that was too bad.

He wanted to tell Jack about the strange dreams he was having about a college student, but decided not to. Jack would think he was losing his mental stability. Maybe next time.

He got dressed and joined Sarah in the waiting room. She looked up. "Well, how did it go?" she asked.

Robert looked at her. "Everything's good, just have a sinus infection that is causing the headaches." He lied to her. He could not tell her about the tumor yet. He needed to have some time to live normally yet. "He gave me a prescription for some pills to help."

They drove in silence on the way home. He knew she did not believe the lie.

CHAPTER 2

IT WAS THE FIRST day of the summer semester. Ronald Pritchard was sleeping beneath one of the large maple trees on the campus. He had been sitting against the tree in the shade and studying the dull hydraulic engineering text book, but the warm June air and the large breakfast he had before class made him drowsy and he had fallen asleep. A cardinal chirping in the tree above woke him up. He struggled up and stretched. The hydraulics book was interesting but it still put him to sleep. Looking at his watch, he had about an hour before his psychology class. He shrugged, picked up his books and walked toward the student union building. The student union building was a three-story green glassed structure with a full serve cafeteria on the main floor and student service offices on the second floor. A computer lab and meeting rooms were on the third floor. The building was surrounded by a park with several trees on two sides, a parking lot on one side and an outdoor terrace with tables on the other. A small bar that served beer and sub sandwiches was located in the basement for the older students. Ron thought that maybe a glass of iced tea would wake him up. Ron had just turned 22 and was six-foot-tall and only about 185 pounds with short blond hair and blue eyes. He was a senior, and after 3 ½ years of college he was looking forward to graduation. He had been offered a football scholarship at the college based upon his high school records, but had turned it down. He had decided to take engineering courses instead. He did show up for the football team in his freshman year, surprising the very coaches who had tried to recruit him. He only played that first year, having injured his ankle. So, he had dropped out of football in his sophomore year in order to concentrate more on his grades. The football coaches were all upset at him for quitting but he did not have a commitment to play since he wasn't on their scholarship. He felt he needed more time to study. Taking summer courses was not his ideal way to spend the summer but he wanted to graduate by the winter semester. Last summer he had worked as an intern in an aerospace company and really liked that atmosphere. He figured he had a potential line on a good engineering position at that aerospace company. They had asked him to apply there after he graduated. He only needed five more courses to graduate, so he was taking two courses in the summer semester, Hydraulics and Psychology. He figured to complete the remaining three courses in the Fall semester.

He entered the student union and ordered an iced tea from the counter. He was wearing his standard khaki pants, blue sports shirt and brown loafers. This was slightly better dressed than the typical college student, but he preferred the professional look. Ron saw his friend, George Coleman, Chief of the Campus Police Department, standing at the checkout counter. He knew George from an economics class they had both taken. Ron had been in his study group and helped him to pass the course. George had graduated that year with a degree in law enforcement and by good luck had landed the job of Chief of the campus police force. It was a small force with only about 4 officers. Occasionally Ron would invite George and his friend, Andy Hall, another police officer, over to play penny ante poker at his apartment. Andy was an African American coworker of George and soon became a fast friend of Ron also. Matt, the downstairs landlord of Ron's second-story apartment would usually join them for the poker games. Nobody really won much money at these games; Matt usually won and Ron usually lost. It did not matter to Ron; it was great fun just to get together and have a few beers with his friends.

"How's it going George?" Ron asked as he stopped to pay for an iced tea. "Hi Ron. Are you taking summer courses now?" George asked.

"Yeah, I need to get a couple of courses out of the way so I can graduate early by Fall quarter." Ron answered as they moved to a near table. George had his typical coffee, black.

"Is this going to interfere with our poker nights?" George asked as he sat down.

"No. It shouldn't. I am just taking a freshman psych class for a needed elective and an easy hydraulic engineering course. How about we get together this Friday?" Ron asked.

"Friday isn't a good night. We have all hands on deck for Friday nights now."

"Why, what's going on?" Ron was curious.

"Well, I'm not supposed to discuss it, but we have been seeing a few cases of young girls getting raped and then being dumped unconscious at their place of residence. When they wake up, they can't remember where they were or who they were with. And it is typically on a Friday night." George had a sad look on his face. "Boy, I wish we had a detective in our department." Friday was known to be a party night on Campus. The girls always remembered going to a party but not where or who they were with. George got up and headed toward the exit. Ron got up and walked with him.

"It sounds like they are being drugged." Ron stopped and turned toward the outdoor veranda.

"I think so. There is a date rape drug that someone may be using. I have read about it but didn't think it would ever be used on our college campus." George finished his coffee and tossed the empty paper cup in a nearby trash can.

Ron asked, "Did the victims have Rape kits performed so that there is a record of DNA?

"No. Our little hospital determined that there was indeed intercourse but they did not have any rape kits on hand. I have taken the action of ordering some for the hospital." George noted.

"Well, that is good." Ron replied.

"Well, I got to go, see you around." George walked toward the parking lot.

"Ok. let me know if I can help out." Ron decided to go out on the veranda.

Ron walked outside with his tea to the paved veranda where there were several tables set alongside the building. It was a very popular place on campus and most of the tables had umbrellas to block out the sun. Looking around he did not see any of his engineering buddies. He noticed a new girl sitting by herself at one of the tables. God! She was outrageously beautiful. She was a cute petite brunette with long hair parted down the middle and just touching her shoulders. She had bright green eyes and a tan complexion. She was wearing a smart blue conservative short-sleeve buttoned blouse and a white skirt. And she had a sexy figure. He observed all of this in just a few seconds. He wondered if she was one of the new nursing students. Most of the girls on campus wore shorts or blue jeans. He was a recently unattached bachelor and found himself immediately attracted to her. But he was way too shy and reserved to just go over and hit on her without any introduction. His experience with really pretty girls was that they were usually snobbish and rude. He picked an adjacent table and sat so he could face her. She looked up from her book and smiled at him. Wow! She smiled at me! He smiled back but did not move and pretended to open his engineering hydraulics book to study it.

A couple of sophomore preppy type guys with long hair and wearing button-down shirts and jeans came out of the student union, looked around and then walked over and sat down at the pretty girl's table. He had seen these guys around campus but they were not engineering students. They were probably business student weenies. They both attempted to engage the new girl in a lively conversation but she apparently was not interested and told them so. She talked to them quietly and they looked startled. He did not hear what she said to them but they reluctantly got up and left her alone muttering to themselves about unfriendly little twats. He was a little upset to hear that comment, but they were leaving so he did nothing.

Three tables away a heavyset football player wearing a football jersey and blue jeans named John Turley sat and watched the pretty girl. He licked his lips. Boy, she would be delicious, he thought to himself. He considered walking over and asking her out but saw her reaction to the two preppies. He would have to plan his attack carefully.

A few minutes later, Jean, one of the nursing students Ron knew slightly, came over and sat at Ron's table next to him. He had seen her on campus a few times. They had both attended a sophomore social studies class, but he never really got to know her that well. She was not that attractive and he had never been motivated to talk to her. She was a short-haired blond, wearing blue jean cutoffs and low-cut tight T-shirt. He noticed that she apparently did not wear a bra during the summer. She was also a bit on the chubby side. She leaned over and pulled a cigarette out of her purse and asked him if he had a light. Smoking was forbidden on campus except for places like the outside veranda at the student union. He really did not want anything to do with girls that smoked.

"Sorry, I don't smoke' he replied," and continued to study the hydraulic diagram in the book.

"Are you going to the concert tonight?" she asked, pulling a lighter out of her purse and lighting up. He actually pulled back away from her as she blew smoke toward him.

"What concert?" He hadn't heard of a concert.

"There is a rock group playing at the central auditorium tonight. Everyone is going to it." She sounded exited.

"I wasn't planning to go. I have a study project to work on." He said, hoping she would just leave. He noticed that the pretty brunette at the next table was watching them closely.

"Well, I have a spare ticket if you want to go." She leaned over, showing off most of her cleavage.

"No, no thanks, I really have other plans," he said trying not to look at her display.

"Well, OK then. Maybe some other time?" she started to get up to leave.

"Yeah, sure" He concentrated on the book as she walked away. He looked up and saw that the new girl was laughing quietly. She then smiled at him and then got up and walked back into the student union with her books and purse. He mentally kicked himself for not going over to say hello to her. But from the way she turned off the two other guys, maybe she was not interested in any male company. He looked at his watch; it was almost time to go to the freshman Psych class. He finished his tea and got up to walk to class.

Bob abruptly sat up in bed. The dream seemed so real; he could almost feel it was reality. He was seeing everything through Ron's eyes but had no control of what was going on. It was like watching a movie. He could smell the air, taste the tea, but he could do nothing but observe what was going on.

"Are you ok?" his wife whispered to him close in bed. "Yeah…I just had a dream."

"Wel…go back to sleep." She mumbled as she drifted off herself."

CHAPTER 3

" *J*ACK, IT WAS SO real! I could see colors and feel and smell everything as if I was actually there." He explained to Dr. Simms. He had returned to Jack's office a few days after getting the MRI news. "How do you explain it?" he asked.

"Bob, it was just a dream…It probably has something to do with the thing in your head." He was looking out the window at the falling snow. The weather service had predicted a major snow storm and it looked like it was starting. He knew that a brain tumor could cause vivid hallucinations. That was what Bob was probably experiencing.

"I know…but…" Bob was despondent. The dream was so real to him it seemed like he had completely transitioned into a different life. He was simply obsessed with it and had to tell someone. "It sure seemed so real," Bob said to himself.

"Look: I will give you some pills for the neck pain and headache; they will help you sleep better. The tumor could be making you hallucinate." Jack looked at him earnestly. He wrote out a prescription and handed it to Bob. He was worried that Bob had started to hallucinate because of the tumor.

"Yeah…Ok." He did not want to tell Jack that the headaches had stopped after the dream. Maybe he was getting better? Anyway, the pills couldn't hurt.

"So how is work going?" Jack wanted to change the subject.

"I told them I was retiring in a couple of weeks for health issues. They were shocked because we are just in the middle of a new program that I was doing the qualification procedure for." He looked at the floor. He knew his boss Marty was really upset with him, but it didn't seem to matter now.

"Did you tell them about your health issue?" Jack asked.

"No. It is none of their business." They would immediately review and waste a lot of time re-writing all the work he had done in the past six months if they possibly thought he had a mental-related problem.

"Well, have you told your wife yet?"

"Not yet. I am going to…in a couple of weeks. I want to live normally as long as possible without getting all the feeling sorry bullshit." Bob got up from the chair to leave.

"OK. Let me know if you need anything, anything at all. I can prescribe morphine for the pain and it will make you feel good. You will probably have some really good dreams then." Jack tried to smile.

"I guess you aren't too worried about me becoming addicted." Bob said as he headed for the door.

"No. You won't…" He stopped, didn't want to say that Bob wouldn't be around long enough to get addicted.

Bob left the office and walked through the 2-inch snow that covered the walkway to the parking lot. It was snowing heavily and was about 25 degrees, which was not too cold for February. As he neared his 5-year old Buick, he slipped on some hidden ice and almost fell, catching his balance at the last second by grabbing the door handle.

"That would have been a good way to go, falling and cracking my head open," he said to himself as he got in the car. It was rush hour and the drive home was slow. People were afraid to drive through the falling snow and traffic was bad this time of day. The roads to Strongsville were crowded and bumper to bumper. He finally pulled into the driveway of his split-level home. He could not park the car in the garage; Sarah's minivan and his mowing tractor were in there, along with most of his son's junk from when he had an apartment. Dave was an accountant, 30 years old and had recently gotten married to a girl named Elizabeth who had a seven-year old daughter named Susan from a previous marriage. When Dave left his apartment to move in with her in Columbus, he needed some place to store his apartment stuff, so naturally it was in Dad's garage. He had met Dave's new spouse at the wedding but did not remember meeting the stepdaughter. He had not seen them again since he'd had to travel to Taiwan on business over Christmas when they last visited. Dave had gotten a job in Columbus and had to move there to be with his new wife. Dave had met Liz at his new workplace and they had hit it off immediately. Liz had a difficult previous life. She had gotten pregnant in high school and dropped out. She eventually married the father of her child but after the baby came, he could not tolerate being around the newborn. He got a quickie divorce and abandoned her. She had to move back with her parents, got her GED and applied for loans to go to a community college to get an Associate's degree while her parents took care of the baby. She got a job at an accounting firm and worked hard to advance herself. Then she met Dave and found they had a lot of things in common. Within a couple of months, they were married. Dave, like his father, worked a lot of weekends and they had not been able to visit since Christmas. He wondered if Dave could get time off to maybe go to Hawaii with them.

He got out of the car and went inside saying hello to Sarah, and that he was home. He hung up his coat, grabbed the newspaper off the table and sat in his Barco-lounger in the family room. Sarah came in with a worried look.

"How did it go with the doctor?" She asked, obviously upset.

"Everything is ok," he lied. "The headaches have stopped and I feel a lot better." That at least was the truth. He did not like lying to her but was not ready for the pity routine yet. If she found out he was dying she would go bananas.

"They called from work." She had her arms folded with a stern look on her face. "Marty said you quit your job in the middle of the project."

Damn him! He thought. "No, I told them I was retiring in two weeks." He had his innocent look on his face. "You said you wanted to go to Hawaii, I thought this would be a good time to go."

"Robert, what is going on? This is not like you! We haven't discussed this —and you always plan things so far ahead." Her eyes were starting to tear up.

"Look…nothing is wrong. I was getting a lot of pressure on the project and I was fed up with it. The young guys can take over and do it, probably better than me." He was lying again but maybe she would believe this.

"You were telling me a week ago that you loved working on this project. What happened?" She was becoming calmer.

"They brought in a new customer representative and he is such a bastard to work for." He lied. "He doesn't like the way I do things so I said he could stuff it." He paused then added, "Anyway, I might be able to go back to the old landing gear company and work as a consultant part-time." This seemed to appease her. The landing gear company had been after him to return to work after he had been there eleven years. The reason he left there was because the new management did not know how to run an aerospace company. He had no real intention of returning.

That seemed to satisfy Sarah. "You really want to go to Hawaii?" she brightened up. "Can we really afford it?"

He smiled, "Sure we can. We have enough cash in the 401K fund that I don't even have to work anymore." He paused, "We can even take the kids with us, make it a family vacation."

"We can really do this?" she was cheerful again, already starting to figure how the kids would react.

"Yes, we can, and go first class too." He was thinking that it would really put a dent in the retirement money, but that would be fully recovered with his hundred thousand dollar life insurance policy after he died. Sarah would not have to worry about her future. He just wouldn't be there for her anymore.

Sarah ran to the phone, "I have to call the kids!" she was happy.

He still did not want to tell her about the tumor. He was feeling ok and wanted to enjoy what normal time he had left. Going to Hawaii was a spur of the moment suggestion but as he thought about it, a nice vacation to a warm environment couldn't hurt. Sarah had always wanted to go and it was a good way to steer her away from the topic of his health. He had to admit that he had always wanted to visit the Arizona Memorial. One of his uncles had been on the Arizona and died in the Pearl Harbor attack. He took out the new pills and took a couple of them. Then he went to bed early rather than watch TV. Sarah was on the phone and talking to his son David about the trip to Hawaii. It turned out that he had not taken any vacation this year so he was available to go and also bring Liz and her daughter Susan.

CHAPTER 4

*R*ON HAD FINISHED HIS *iced tea and was walking toward his Psychology class. He was a senior at the college but did not have enough electives to qualify for graduation. He had spent most of his freshman year taking Physics, Calculus, Statics and Thermodynamics classes. If he had not dropped out of calculus the first time he would not have had to take it over, but the first teacher really sucked. He had almost enough credits to graduate, but his advisor had told him he needed one more elective. The choice was either freshman psychology or one of the other social studies courses mostly dominated by the nursing students. Rather than spend time with a lot of nursing students and be one of the few boys in the class, he decided to try Psychology. So now he was taking Psychology 101. It should be an easy class, most of the social studies classes were. He fully expected to be bored to death, but it would be an easy 'A,' he figured. He had already made the Dean's List four semesters in a row. No reason to let up now. He was taking the hydraulics class since it was directly similar to the potential aerospace job he was hoping for. He had that class early in the morning. It looked like it might be interesting but would require a lot of problem-solving work. He was only taking two courses for the summer semester but that was enough. He didn't want to spend all of his time during the summer with college work. He would have enough credits to graduate winter quarter with three more courses. He walked over to the Hess building where the Psychology course was being held.*

It was an old brownstone four-story building with no opaque windows. Upon entering, he walked down the hall looking for room 126. It was an old building without air conditioning but it was not that hot yet this early in the day. As he walked into the room he surveyed the layout and the people. He usually liked to sit in the front so he was not distracted by the other students. As his eyes crossed the middle row...There she was! The pretty brunette from the student union was sitting about half way back in the middle row of desks. She was talking animatedly to another girl sitting to her left. The seat next to her on the right was open! He could not resist the chance to meet her in an innocent class room environment. He walked up the aisle and sat down in the desk on her right side. She did not notice him at first, but the girl she was talking to motioned to her to look. She looked over and blushed.

"Hello." She managed to say. Her voice was light and pleasant.

"Hi." He managed to say as he rearranged his books. "This seat isn't taken is it?" "No...not at all." She was smiling at him again. "My name is Sue, Sue Conner."

"Oh. I'm Ronald Pritchard. But you can call me Ron," he managed to say, returning her smile. He sat down and turned toward her.

"This is a freshman class, aren't you a senior?" she asked.

How did she know that? he wondered. Was he that much older looking than the freshmen boys? "Yes, but I needed one more elective to graduate so I picked this," he answered honestly.

"Oh, that's good. I mean...it's good that you can graduate with this class." She smiled and said "I see that your girlfriend asked you out to the concert tonight."

"She is not my girlfriend." He gasped. "I barely know her... Anyway, I don't have a girlfriend." This was a partial truth. His last affair had ended badly. Monica Martin had broken off their relationship about six months ago after she met a guy at her workplace. She really wasn't a keeper anyway, he told himself. Monica had used him and then thrown him away for some other guy. He realized that now. He needed to change the subject.

"Besides, she's a smoker." He looked at her. "You don't smoke do you?" he asked. "No. It is about the most disgusting thing a person can do," she frowned.

"So, what did you tell those guys who stopped at your table?" He changed the subject. "They left in a big hurry."

"Well, I asked them if they knew where the gay girls hang out since they were obviously gay," she replied. "They did not take it very well."

"But you're not really gay, are you?" he said hopefully.

"No, of course not," she said, laughing. He laughed along with her and noticed her friend who she had been talking with. She

was a brown-eyed brunette with her hair pulled back in a ponytail, wearing a pink sweatshirt and jeans with holes in the knees. She looked vaguely familiar.

"Do I know you?" he asked. "You look familiar somehow," he asked the other girl.

The girl smiled and said "I was a freshman at South High when you were a senior. You were one of the big football stars that year. Our school went 10-0 behind your catches. You might not remember me...I'm Joan Rivera. I was on the freshman cheerleading team"

"Oh...yeah, that was a good season. I don't play football anymore, though," he said pensively. "I keep hurting my ankle so I quit football."

He remembered seeing Joan now, a cheerleader, but there were a lot of kids at South High, it had about 2000 total students attending when he was a senior. He barely graduated with a 'C+' average, mostly due to all of the time he spent in practice and playing football. His academic score had improved greatly when he went to college.

Sue spoke up, "I was a freshman there that year too. I remember watching you play."

"I think I would have remembered you." he said in wonderment. That was how she knew he was a senior in college, he guessed. He sure did not remember seeing her at all. He would have remembered someone so pretty.

"No, I've always been a shy, wallflower type," she blushed slightly.

"I don't believe that," he shrugged.

This was already more conversation with this beautiful girl than he had expected. He figured that she would treat him like the two bozos at the Student Union. Wow! This was turning out to be a good day. Then the instructor walked in. Oh no! It was one of the assistant football coaches who was fulfilling his teaching contract requirement by teaching an actual class. Ron had previously played for the team in his sophomore year and they wanted him to play as starting wide receiver. He did pretty good as a receiver that year but his grades were not that good. After seeing that the practice time was interfering with his studies, he dropped the football gig so he could concentrate more on his studies. The football coaches were really upset about this since he was considered their best receiver. Oh well, maybe this coach would not remember him.

The coach scanned the class and saw Ron.

"Pritchard, what the hell are you doing in my class?" The coach shouted.

Robert sat up in bed with a start. The dream was so real. He wondered why this was happening to him. He had some football experience, had been a kicker in college but was never that good. He usually only played when someone was injured or if the team was ahead by several touchdowns in the fourth quarter. The thing in his head must be doing this to him. Maybe Jack was right about the hallucinations he thought.

CHAPTER 5

*T*HE NEXT TWO WEEKS at work were horrible for Bob. Marty, his boss figured that he was leaving them at a critical time to go to another company. All of the younger engineers were busy pumping him for information. The project was almost 90 percent done but they needed to complete the last tests. Joe Ross came up to him with a test procedure and asked, "Bob, the parameters for this test don't match the requirements. What gives?"

Bob looked at the document and glanced at the documentation requirements. He walked over to the workstation and picked up the customer performance specification. He turned a few pages and turned to Joe and pointed to the requirements page and said "Look here. This is the standard you are supposed to use for this test."

Joe looked. "Oh…Ok, I guess I missed that. Thanks Bob." He ran off to show the technicians.

Typically, an integrated engineering team would know all of the facets of a project but everyone was used to Bob running and directing things and everything always turned out good. Now that he was leaving, they all had to do some actual planning and work. Marty had called him into his office. Marty was the vice president of engineering but Bob actually ran things in the shop. He walked up to the office area and went in Marty's office.

"You cannot just get up and leave in the middle of the project." Marty screamed at him. "You are the one that set up all of the programing, sensors and test parameters. No one else knows what you did."

"Marty, I have given Joe my notebook—it has everything you need to know in there." Bob answered calmly. Joe Ross was a lot younger but very eager and ambitious. He had wanted to learn the ropes from Bob.

"Joe is an idiot," Marty slurred, "and you know it. He will need at least four months to get to the point where you are. Our deadline is the end of next month. We don't have a chance without your help. You know the customer, have worked with them intimately. You know what they want better than the rest of us. If you want a raise, name your price!"

"You don't understand, Marty. I just cannot be here any longer. I have already put in my paperwork with HR and they are setting up my retirement." Bob talked low, trying to defuse the conversation. "The customer is having problems with their turbine interface anyway. So, there is bound to be a delay." Bob tried to smooth Marty's feathers. "Marty, Joe is a bright kid, give him a chance, he may surprise you."

"Yeah, maybe you are right, but it sure would go a lot better for us if you stayed on another month." Marty admitted. "By the way, their program manager mentioned that they may increase the maximum design point."

That did not please Bob. "Boy, if they do that you will have to reevaluate our entire system." Bob thought about the drive shaft. It was from another assembly and was only marginal for the loading for this mechanism. He would have to tell Joe about it. He made a mental note to check the loading on the shaft.

"Just where are you going, anyway?" Marty asked calmly. "Hawaii," Ron answered as he walked out the door.

He went back to his desk. He took out the Failure Modes and Effects (FMEA) document and looked at the drive shaft. It showed that it had passed the analysis but was marginal. He marked the entry with a question mark. He hoped that the higher loading condition Marty had mentioned would not occur.

Bob started to daydream about the Hawaiian trip. He had Sarah set it up with the Triple A travel Bureau. It was going to be an expensive trip since they were going first class. He also asked that she sign up for as many shore excursions as possible with the cruise line they were going to use.

He got up and decided to leave early. What were they going to do? Fire him? He laughed at his own joke.

CHAPTER 6

*B*OB AND SARAH HAD made all of the plans for the March trip to Hawaii. They were lucky in getting a couple of cabins on a cruise ship that was not entirely sold out. They would fly from Cleveland and change planes in San Francisco and then fly to Hawaii. They were all set up with reservations at the Waikiki Hilton in Honolulu for a couple days and then get on the cruise ship, 'The Island Princess' for a cruise around the islands. Plans were to visit the Big Island with the volcano, travel to Maui and then Kawaii. Dave and his wife Liz were able to join them along with their daughter Susan, but Bob's daughter Lauren could not make it. She was in the military and stationed in Germany. She did not have enough leave time left to take off for two weeks. She was a captain in the Air Force and was in charge of an entire maintenance depot. She was engaged to be married to some guy named Steve, but they were waiting for her current deployment to be over. So, it would just be the five of them on the cruise, he and Sarah, with Dave and Liz and their daughter. It worked out pretty well. He and Sarah would take one cabin and Dave and his family would be in the other. So, he only had to book two rooms at the hotel and on the cruise ship.

Dave and Liz arrived at the airport 'Park and Fly' where they all were meeting. Bob had parked his Buick in row H and had just gotten his and Sarah's luggage out and was waiting for the shuttle bus when Dave drove by in his new SUV and parked a few spaces away.

"Good timing" Bob said as he and Sarah walked over to greet them.

"Yeah, we left Columbus early but still got stuck in the traffic jam at Pearl Road," Dave remarked as he opened the sliding door to let his daughter out. She was small for a seven-year-old; she was wearing a blue jumper and had brown hair and bright green eyes. She walked over to Bob and said: "Are you my new Grandpa?"

Bob was somewhat taken back by this, but bent over and said: "Why sure, if it is alright with you." "Ok." She smiled. Something about her was very familiar but Bob couldn't place it.

They had tickets for first class on the flight out of Hopkins Airport. The flight was uneventful and they arrived in San Francisco in time to make their connecting flight to Honolulu. For some unknown reason, none of their luggage was lost by the airlines, something that always worried Bob. This time, though, he really did not care.

They had a great time and everyone enjoyed the trip. They even got to visit the Arizona Memorial and the Battleship Missouri in Pearl Harbor. After several luaus arranged by the cruise ship, they even went on a small commercial tourist submarine to view an underwater coral reef. Bob was relieved that along with the headaches the vivid dreams had stopped, but found that he was getting tired a lot quicker and sometimes lagged behind the group as they hurried from place to place. Sarah noticed that he was becoming fatigued but did not say anything. She insisted they stop for pictures often so that he could recover a bit.

When they were on Oahu, they took time to see the Polynesian Cultural Center and watched a show and attended a Luau. Bob sat next to Sarah and Susan and watched the show. It was quite amazing with fire throwers and hula dancers. Robert actually felt good. He had no pain and the dreams had stopped.

Dave's stepdaughter Susan was amazed and excited by all of the new sights but she was always reserved and shy and did not pester her parents like most seven-year-olds. If offered a treat she would gratefully accept it but she wouldn't come out and ask for one. Bob made a point of taking her hand when they walked and paid her special attention since her parents seemed to ignore her most of the time. She was very happy to receive his attention. They talked a lot about her school and her teachers. Little Susan was a precocious child and impressed him with her vocabulary and her ability to concentrate and focus on topics. Not at all like almost all of the kids he had previously known. He could talk to her like an adult and she always seemed to understand what he was saying. She was definitely different than his son and daughter. He really enjoyed her company, something that surprised Sarah, but very much pleased her.

They spent one day on the big island and visited the Hawaiian Volcanos National Park. They walked through the lava tunnels in the park. Little Susan was amazed at how the lava flow created the tunnels. The volcano was inactive but was known to have small eruptions every few years. They then visited the Botanical Gardens and were amazed at the wide variety of colorful plants. Little Susan used her camera to take pictures of all of the flowers. She intended to use them in an art project for school. Bob was able to keep up with them without looking too exhausted. They got back to the ship in time to attend the scheduled dinner.

One night as the ship was traveling to the next island; Dave came to their room and asked if they were going to the show. It was a comedy act and looked like it would pretty much have adult content. Bob was dead tired from all of the walking they had done that day. They had been to see the 'Grand Canyon' of Hawaii. It was pretty spectacular. Bob had walked with them and tried to keep up but it really exhausted him.

"No, I'm going to rest up," he told Dave.

"Well, we want to go. Can you watch Susan?" Dave asked.

"Sure. No problem." Bob said. Sarah looked at him funny. He was not one to typically babysit children. He had very little patience for small children.

"I suppose I should stay too." Sarah sighed. She knew Bob could not tolerate small children very much.

"No, go along with them and have a good time." Bob replied. "We'll be alright. We can go over to the Arcade and I can watch her play some games," Bob asserted.

"You are sure?" Sarah asked.

"Yes. Go and have a good time." he reassured her.

Well, OK then." Sarah was surprised but she brightened up. She really enjoyed the shows on the cruise.

Little Susan was somewhat disappointed at not being included for the show, but she happily agreed to go to the Arcade with her step-grandfather. He sat and gave her his cruise card to pay for the games. She won almost every game she tried the first time. The little girl was a master at most of the arcade games and won most of the time.

"How did you get so good at these gaming devices?" Bob asked her.

"Mommy and Dave bought me a bunch of video games and I play them a lot at home," she confessed. She did not add that her parents typically ignored her most of the time.

"Doesn't that interfere with your school homework?" he asked.

"No, school is boring and way too easy," she replied, going toward a different game console.

He had heard that she got straight A's and that all of her teachers loved having her in their classes. He was amazed by the way she played the games. She seemed to be much older than her age. Later they went up to the Lido Deck and got an ice cream cone from the shop that was open 24 hours a day. She did like chocolate ice cream a lot. They sat at a table and ate ice cream and watched the waves. It was twilight and the temperature was perfect. Little Susan did not pester him with a lot of questions like most kids.

"So you think school is boring?" He asked her while she was eating her ice cream. "Yeah, the kids talk too much and don't pay attention. I like the teachers."

"What part of school do you like the best?"

"Art class is my favorite. We do all sorts of neat stuff in there." She smiled. "Maybe you should become an artist." He teased her.

"Yes, I would like that," she said seriously.

A couple of times, when the ship was traveling between ports, he would take Susan to the pool or to play shuffle board. He and Susan could play shuffle board for hours. At first, he would always win but she caught on very quickly and started beating him regularly. He didn't mind; she was having so much fun that he really enjoyed it. They always celebrated by having ice cream afterward. She said he was the best grandpa she ever had. Being with her took his mind off his condition and he really enjoyed her company.

He tried to interest Susan in chess. There was a set in the ship's library, so they sat down to play a few games. At first, he had to show her the moves and the basic strategy. He won the first couple of games easily but she caught on really fast. After about ten games she started to beat him. He was amazed at her concentration. She had a good mind, he thought, and would make an excellent engineer. When he asked her again about what she liked, she remarked that she really liked to draw pictures. Maybe she could be a designer.

Towards the end of the trip Bob noticed that his hands were sometimes feeling numb and he rubbed them together a lot try to get some feeling in them. Sarah noticed this but again did not say anything. Bob also noticed that his legs seemed heavier, and more effort was needed to walk. But he kept smiling and everyone was having a great time. During the flight back everyone was happy and relaxed. Bob was clearly exhausted and slept most of the flight home. That was unusual for him, since being an aerospace engineer, he knew what things could go wrong on an airplane. He was typically nervous about flying but he would readily admit that it really was the safest way to travel.

When they were departing the airport gate, Bob looked for a place to sit down. He was clearly exhausted and needed to catch his breath. Dave stopped as he sat down in the gate seating area.

"Dad, are you alright?" he asked.

Bob turned and replied, "Yes, I just need to sit a minute, all that walking aggravated an old football injury in my knee," he lied.

Sarah and Liz had stopped nearby and were chatting away about something on the plane. Apparently, Liz did not like the meal she was served in first class. Little Susan came over and sat next to him. "Are you ok?" she questioned.

"Yeah, it was a long trip and I'm tired. I hope you enjoyed the trip." Bob looked down at her. "It was the bestest time I ever had." She hugged him hard. "Good," he said, barely holding back the tears.

They said their goodbyes and went on their way. He made them promise to visit on a weekend in a week or two to review all of the photos they had taken. He really just wanted to see little Susan again. When he and Sarah got off the shuttle bus in the parking garage, Bob turned to her and said, "Why don't you drive home. I am really tired." His hands were totally numb and he did not trust himself to drive.

"Sure," Sarah replied. She knew something was wrong; he was always the driver when they were together. She was a very good driver but he usually got nervous if he wasn't driving.

"I'll be better with some rest at home," he murmured to her. He managed to get the luggage into the trunk of the Buick, but it took a lot of effort to make it look easy.

As they were driving home Sarah kept talking about the wonderful time they had on the trip. He listened and said yes when she expected a response but he really did not feel like talking. He wanted to get home to bed.

They got home and Sarah started to unpack everything in the bedroom. Bob let her. He managed to find the couch in the living room and was asleep almost immediately.

Dave and his family visited a week later. Bob was happy to see little Susan again. They stayed the weekend and on Saturday Dave and Liz wanted to take Bob and Sarah out to dinner. They asked if Sarah knew of any baby sitters they could call for Susan. Sarah did not know of anyone but one of her friends at church had a couple of older daughters, maybe one of them might be interested. Bob said that he was not feeling like going out to dinner and that he would stay with Susan. Sarah thought that was strange that he didn't want to go out but he had been rather inactive ever since they had returned from the Hawaiian trip. Dave asked if his Dad was feeling ok and Bob replied that he had an upset stomach, probably from the medication Jack Simms had prescribed for his constant headaches. Dave asked if he had seen the doctor about the headaches and Bob replied yes, that was why he was taking the medication. Sarah finally agreed to go with them out to dinner. Little Susan was not unhappy to be with her grandpa. They had some frozen pizza that he cooked in the oven, then they played some chess and then watched a Karate movie. Susan was impressed at how the little skinny kid could protect himself from bullies with his karate training. She knew first-hand how the bigger kids picked on the smaller children like herself. She had been picked on a lot. Bob asked her if the kids in school picked on her. She said yes but she had learned to stay away from them as much as possible and was smart enough not to get in fights. She had learned to always be close to one of the teachers whenever possible. He asked her if she would like to have karate training. She replied that she would be happy to do so but did not think her mother could afford the lessons. Bob made a note of this and said maybe it could be worked out. He then asked her if she wanted some ice cream. This brought a big smile to her face.

CHAPTER 7

GARY JOHNSON WAS THE assistant football coach in charge of the defensive line. He had majored in Sports Therapy in college but had a minor in Psychology so he was stuck teaching freshman Psych. It was not so bad he thought, freshman kids didn't know much and he typically bullshitted his way through this class. Thank god for the study guide one of the professors gave him. Without that he might actually have to read the textbook. As he walked into class he looked around. Not too bad, there were only about 15 kids. His eyes landed on Ron Pritchard. Son of a gun! That kid had real football talent. He was nominated for All-American in High School but missed out on that. Ron was really smart and could remember all the pass plays, had good timing and great hands. If he had stayed on the team and they made it to the playoffs, he could have gone all of the way to the NFL. Instead, he is wasting his time on an engineering degree. He noticed that Pritchard had sat next to the prettiest girl in the class. At least he has some taste, looking at the girl. Wow, she was a real looker. He thought of the assistant coach, Richard Bass, who was always dating co-eds from the college which was a major infraction for faculty and staff. Not Gary. Gary was happily married and his wife was expecting their second child. There was no way he was going to screw that up.

"Pritchard, what the hell are you doing in my class?" The coach shouted. Ron looked up and blushed. "Hi coach. I just needed another elective."

"We could have used your receiving talent last fall." The team went 8-3 with three of the games lost by less than 3 points.

"Sorry coach, my ankle injury still bothers me." Ron looked at the floor.

"Well...ok, but you better do really good in this class. I saw you were on the Dean's List four times in a row. Not bad for a jock majoring in engineering," Coach noted. The rest of the class looked at Ron.

How did he know that? Ron wondered. Still, it did not hurt that the class, and especially the girl sitting next to him, knew he was a good student. He looked over to her and she smiled at him again. Wow! Maybe he should ask her out. They could study Psychology together or something.

The first class was mostly boring stuff about what chapters they had to read and that at least two term papers would be required. The two papers and the midterm and final each counted for 25% of the grade. The coach noted that they did not have to attend class but if they didn't, they would miss what was going to be on the midterm and final.

After class ended Ron turned to Susan and Joan and asked," Hey, would you girls like to join me in the student union for a cup of tea?" He blushed. Boy, did that sound really lame.

"Sure." Susan replied softly, picking up her books and purse. Her friend Joan declined and said she would see her later and winked as she left them. They walked down the hall together.

"So, what is your major?" He sounded as if he was actually interested.

"Oh...I am going for an Art Education major." She replied.

"How come you are taking summer classes?" he asked.

"I wanted to get a head start before the Fall Semester. It is a lot easier to get a dorm room in the summer and they let you keep it for the next semester. Joan is my roommate."

"What dorm are you staying at?" he asked, trying to be casual.

"I'm in Fredrick Hall, which is right next to the student union," she replied. "It is very convenient and close to all my classes."

"Yeah that's one of the nicer ones," he noted. "Which hall are you staying in?" she asked.

"Oh...I live off campus. I have a small apartment over on Center Street. It's not quite in walking distance but there is plenty of parking near the student union."

"Wow. Isn't that pretty expensive?" she asked.

"It's not that bad. I have a walk-up in a duplex with the landlord living below. I like my own quiet place to study. When I was here living in a dorm, I had to spend most of my free time in the library where it was quiet." Only after your sophomore year were students allowed to live off campus. He could afford to live off campus now so he did.

They each got a cup of tea and sat down again on the veranda but this time at the same table. "I would have taken you for a coffee drinker," he remarked.

"No, we always had tea when I was growing up...I don't even like the taste of coffee." He was amazed that she had the some of the same likes as he. "Well, tea is better for you—it has a lot of anti-oxidants in it." He stopped; she would think he was an idiot.

"So, do you have a job to help pay for the apartment?" she asked, changing the subject. "Well...I was a summer co-op last year for an aerospace company and they asked me to return when I graduate. It didn't pay a lot but it was ok." He felt uneasy about talking about himself. "I also get a monthly payment from my trust fund."

"You have a trust fund?" She appeared to be impressed.

"Yeah my Dad was a VP of a big company and when he and my mother were killed in a car accident, I inherited his estate but it was set up as a trust." He looked down.

Oh...I'm sorry," she stammered.

"It happened a long time ago when I was just starting high school and I ended up living with my Grandmother. Dad always wanted me be a football player so when I had a chance, I put all of my effort into being the best football player possible for him." He started to tear up. "I grew out of that when I graduated from high school and figured that I could maybe make my living in engineering. I tried football here in college but it was just taking away too much time from my goal of getting a degree."

He decided to ask her out. "Say, what are you doing..."

"Oh my! I am going to be late for my next class!" she interrupted as she looked at the small watch on her right wrist. She hurriedly picked up her books and purse and dashed off, smiling at him as she left. She was taking an economics class on the same days as the psychology class.

"Ah...ok." He got up as she ran for the exit. She hadn't even touched the cup of tea. I guess I blew that, he thought to himself. Oh well, maybe he would see her in Psychology class again.

Bob awoke again. This time he did not sit up in bed but just lay there. The dreams had started again now that he was home. During the dream he was Ron. He could see and feel everything that Ron could see and feel, but he had no control over anything happening in the dream or even the conversations. It was as if he was an observer in Ron's body. He did not know what Ron was going to do or say. The girl was very beautiful, probably 18 or 19 years old. That would probably make Ron 21 or 22. He was Ron in the dream, but he had never experienced what Ron went through. Boy, in the dream it did feel good to be young again. But he kept waking up in this old body. His traitorous body was slowly losing control and there was nothing he could do about it. Damn! It was frustrating. He would not be able to keep it a secret from Sarah much longer. He would have to tell her about the brain tumor soon.

CHAPTER 8

BOB JUST HAD TO do some research on his dream. He knew there was a South High in Cleveland but the scenery in the dream did not look like the Cleveland area. So, he went to the web browser on his computer and typed in 'South High'.

Bingo. About ten or more high schools were named "South High". One was in Denver, one in Minneapolis, Oregon, Oklahoma, Columbus, Willoughby, and of course one in Cleveland. Next, he typed in "Sue Conner". Bingo. Over 200 pictures of women named Sue Conner appeared. None of them looked like the girl in the dream. Boy, that must be a very popular name he thought. Then he typed in "Ron Pritchard". Bingo. About 20 names appeared including a famous linebacker who had played in the old AFL. Nope; couldn't be him, he would be too old or dead by now. He gave up on the computer research and turned it off. Apparently, the people in his dreams were not real.

Sarah had just come in from her choir practice. She was a soprano in the church choir. He did not care much for the church service, but she always wanted him to go and it was ok. He would go and listen to the sermons. Sometimes the sermons were pretty good. The church had just gone through two different ministers recently and the present preacher, Reverend Morton, was not bad. At least his sermons did not put you to sleep and were actually interesting.

"How are the roads?" he asked as she was taking off her coat.

"They're not bad. The snow plows are out tonight and it's pretty much cleared up," she noted. "They say we will get more snow tomorrow."

"What'cha doing?" she asked, entering the family room.

"Oh, just looking at some computer files," he replied. He went to get up, but his left leg was not working and he fell down on the floor.

"Oh my God!!" She shouted, "Are you OK?"

He struggled to get up and was able to by putting all his weight on his right leg. "I'm ok, just lost my balance." He sat back down in the chair. He would sit for a while, maybe it would recover. "My leg just went to sleep," he lied.

She looked at him with doubt on her face. "I saw you stumble when you took out the garbage yesterday. Are you sure you're ok?"

He really was not ready to have this conversation yet. "I think those pills Jack gave me are making me dizzy. Maybe I should get a different prescription."

She looked at him hard but appeared to buy it for now. He was going to have to tell her eventually. Jack said maybe 5 or 6 months but it had only been three weeks. God. I wish I had more time. It just wasn't fair. He had worked hard all of his life and this was his reward? The feeling was returning to his leg and he was able to get up and walk to the bedroom. He did not usually go to bed this early but he was really tired. She would come to bed later. He did not worry about having to perform in the bedroom any more. They had not had any sexual relations for over two years. He had a bad case of ED which the stupid blue pills did not seem to help, and she had a rough time with menopause and claimed that it hurt too much. He missed the close intimacy but he had gotten used to it. She seemed not to care anymore but often took long showers. Sex was never that good when they were both young anyway. It seemed like a lot of bother to go through for a few seconds of pleasure. They had successfully had two kids; Lauren was first and Dave came along later. He was not a prude though. He often looked at the pretty girls in the office but was never tempted to have an affair. He knew he was not very good looking. He could not even think how he would be able to have an affair and not be able to tell Sarah. Now the gray hair made him look grandfatherly, but that was ok. When he was younger the girls in high school had always ignored him and he was never much of a romantic. He dated around when he was in the fraternity in college but never anything serious. He was lucky that Sarah had accepted his proposal when they were both in college. He got ready for bed, went into the bathroom and took a sleeping pill, and hoped the dreams would not come back.

As he sat in bed he was thinking, maybe his ED was caused by the tumor in his head. That could explain a lot. He would have to ask Jack about that the next time he went to the doctor.

CHAPTER 9

*H*E HAD BEEN SITTING *against the maple tree in the shade again and studying the dull hydraulic engineering text book, but the warm July air and the large breakfast he had before class made him drowsy and he had fallen asleep. A cicada began its boring noise above his head and woke him up. He struggled up and stretched. The hydraulics book was interesting but it was still putting him to sleep. Looking at his watch, he had about an hour before his Psychology class. He decided to go to the student union for an iced tea.*

Ron was whistling when he walked into the Student Union. It was Thursday and he had Psychology class on Tuesdays and Thursdays. He was looking forward to seeing Sue again. He got an iced tea and a bagel and walked out onto the veranda. He looked around but she was not there. Oh well, he was early. He sat down and munched on the bagel. Jean was sitting with a group of nursing students but did not pay him any attention. She was probably mad at him for being turned down for the concert. He did not care. She was a smoker and that made her a non-person in his book. He waited until almost class time but Sue never showed up. Maybe she just went directly to class? Disappointed, he got up and walked to class. As he entered the classroom, he saw that Sue's friend Joan was sitting in the same seat as last time, but Sue was not to be seen. He walked over and sat in the seat he had used in the previous class.

"Hi," he said to Joan. She looked at him and smiled. "Where's your friend today?" he asked quietly.

"Sue? She was not feeling good today. I told her I would take notes for her."

"Oh," he said, not hiding the disappointment in his voice. He knew that girls did not feel good for a few days about once a month. His ex-girlfriend Monica always had bad problems with that and never wanted him around at those times.

Class was boring but he tried to follow along as best he could. The coach was trying to describe different aspects of psychology but not doing a very good job of it. He had done the chapter reading, so he already knew all about the Ego, Id and Superego but apparently the coach was somewhat confused about this. Finally, the class was over and as they were all getting up, he turned to Joan.

"Tell Sue that I hope she feels better."

"Sure," Joan said as she got up to leave.

Ron walked down the hall and out the door. He went into the student union. They had a bar in the basement for students 21 and over. He showed his ID, went in, sat down at the counter and ordered a beer. As he drank it, he thought about his upcoming graduation. He had no one to celebrate it with. His parents were long gone, he had no siblings and his Grandmother had passed away a year ago. He was feeling downright lonely. He had always been a loner, not making many friends. He had some engineering friends but they were mostly nerdy. He had been recruited by several of the campus fraternities but the pledge program they all described did not seem that attractive.

He still hoped that the company he was an intern with last summer would remember him. It was hard to find a good position right out of college and if he could get a position with that company he could gain some valuable experience. Once you had experience it was a lot easier to find a better position. He finished the beer and walked out of the student union to the parking lot. His car was parked way in the back row where hardly any other cars parked. His car was a red Corvette convertible. He got in and put the top down. It was his summer car; his winter car was a Jeep Wrangler. He rented a storage garage by the year and rotated the vehicles as needed. The Corvette was by far much more fun to drive, but the rear wheel drive with a lot of horsepower did not handle well on wet or snowy streets in the winter time. He drove home to his apartment. He would try to work on his hydraulic homework problems, fix a frozen dinner and maybe watch some TV. He waved at his landlord Matt Posey, who was working at trimming the bushes in the front yard. He parked the Corvette next to Matt's Chevy pickup truck in front of the garage. Matt was a full—time auto mechanic and was always asking Ron things about his Corvette. Matt never used the garage to store his truck. Ron wondered what was in there. Matt would at times spend hours in there but Ron did not inquire. He felt it was none of his business what Matt did in there. He probably just needed to get some time away from his wife.

"Hi Ron, how's it going? Matt inquired.

"Not bad. I'm taking summer semester courses this year."

"You've been very quiet lately. The wife and I really appreciate that." "Well, I do study a lot" Ron said as he mounted the stairs.

"When is the next poker night?" Matt inquired.

"I'll let you know. It depends on George and Andy's schedules."

"You sure have a lot of cop friends."

He entered the apartment and sat on the couch. He could not get the new girl out his mind. He really wanted to see her again. He took out the Psych book and thumbed through the chapters. He needed to go to the library to research a topic for the first term paper which was due in a week. He had to be careful to write his own paper. The college had a big scandal last year when some students had copied the previous year's papers and were suspended. Now the college had a computerized system that checked for plagiarism. He thought about Sue and hoped she would be in class next week. Maybe they could do research together. Probably not. A pretty girl like that probably had a steady boyfriend and would not be interested in him. Still, if there was a chance, he would try to ask her out.

CHAPTER 10

*B*OB WOKE UP WITH a throbbing headache. He got up and went into the bathroom and took one of the pills Jack had prescribed. Everything appeared to be working this morning. Even his hands felt normal for a change. It was really strange not getting up early and going to work. He had been typically the first one in the shop and one of the last to leave. Now he really did not have anything to do. Maybe he would work on one of the

several honey-do projects Sarah had for him. He got dressed and went outside to get the paper. It was a nice spring day for April. It was cloudy but not too windy. He started to think about the garden he typically put in every year. Probably would not plant anything this year. The last frost before planting was typically May 15th. He wondered if he would still be around by then. That thought was depressing. He got the paper and went inside to read it. Sarah was just getting up, maybe he would surprise her with breakfast. He went into the kitchen and got out the eggs and the pan. He reached up into the cupboard to get the glasses for the orange juice and everything went black. Off in the distance he thought he heard a scream but then lost everything.

He woke up but could not see anything. His eyes would not open. He heard sounds but could not move. It felt like he was laying down, but where was he?

He heard his wife's voice. "Doctor, what is wrong with him?"

"I don't know yet. It appears to be a stroke. But he is not showing typical stroke symptoms," a different female voice said. "We'll have to do some tests, maybe an MRI to see the extent of what is going on." The doctor's voice was female.

No, he thought, I am not ready for this yet. With some difficulty he found he could open his eyes slowly. He tried to talk but it came out a groan. "Where am I he?" finally asked.

The doctor came over and asked, "Can you hear me, Mr. Parker?" "Yes," he managed to say.

"Well, you passed out at home and the ambulance brought you to the emergency room here at Southwest General," she said as she looked in his eyes to see if his pupils were differently dilated, which might give some indication of a stroke. "Can you see me Mr. Parker?" she asked.

"Yes." He was slowly getting the feeling back in his arms and legs. He saw his wife at the other side of the room. Sarah looked worried. The doctor was a young black-haired African American woman about 30 years old wearing the typical white doctor pants suit with an impressive ID badge over her breast pocket. He thought, she is very pretty for a doctor.

"Let me try to get up." He struggled to sit up but the doctor held him down.

"Just be still. I need to examine you." The doctor motioned for a nurse to assist her. They went through several tests but were then satisfied he was ok.

"I think we should schedule you for an MRI just to check things out." The doctor said.

"No need for that." He said, almost feeling normal again. "I just had one eight weeks ago; You can check with Doctor Simms at the Cleveland Clinic. He gave me some medicine and it sometimes makes me dizzy." He lied.

"Ok, Mr. Parker." The doctor said. "I will give him a call." She left the room with the nurse and pulled the privacy curtain closed.

Sarah came over to his bed and said "You better tell me what is going on Bob." She had been crying and now appeared to be upset.

"Okay, okay." He tried thinking how to deflect he question but was tired of lying to the woman he loved. He finally agreed that she should know. "Jack found something on the MRI. It appears that I have brain tumor."

"Oh my god!" Sarah sobbed. "Why didn't you tell me?" she asked.

"I didn't want you to worry. I was hoping to live normally for a little while longer," he confessed.

"What are you going to do? Can it be removed?" she asked.

"Well…it is inoperable and I didn't want to do the chemo Jack said it probably would not help anyway." He held her hand in his.

"So, what can we do?" she asked.

"Basically, nothing." He said. "Jack said I had maybe 6 months…" he did not finish.

Sarah looked at him, shocked. "That's why we did the Hawaii trip. You wanted one last vacation with your family."

"Yes," he admitted. "I missed not seeing Lauren, but she has her own life to live." He had never been very close with his daughter. Lauren always ended up arguing with him about something unimportant. She was always a rebel in the household, always challenging him and Sarah, always pushing the boundaries. She was a bright, intelligent young lady but found her parents oppressive, and had joined the military when she graduated from high school. The house was much quieter after she left, but they still missed having her with them. She had scored very high in her placement tests and was given a chance to go to OTS (officer training school), sort of a college in the service. Again, she scored highest in her class, and was commissioned a second lieutenant. He was really impressed with her progress and choice of career. How could someone that smart come from him?

The doctor came back into the room. "I had a chat with Dr. Simms. If you are feeling ok now, I can let you go home, but I recommend that you should get some rest, and I would suggest that you get a wheel chair and use it."

The trip home was uneventful, Sarah was very quiet, concentrating on driving. He felt almost normal, but had some residual numbness on his fingers and toes. When they got home it was after supper time. He found he was starving.

"How long was I out?" he asked Sarah. "About five hours," she said quietly.

"Can we get a pizza or something? I'm really hungry," he asked.

CHAPTER 11

JACK SIMMS AND HIS wife Angie came over to visit Bob and Sarah. Sarah had invited them over for dinner. She was serving her renowned lasagna dish and nobody ever turned that down. The girls went off to the kitchen to talk and Jack sat down in the family room with Bob.

"How is it going?" Jack asked, eying the wheelchair folded in the corner.

"Well, sometimes I feel normal, other times everything goes black and I lose the feeling in my legs and arms. Other than that, everything is fine," Bob said sarcastically.

"It is going to get worse," Jack said. "I wish there was something I could do."

"I know. I don't blame you. It's just so frustrating," Bob said. "Do you want a drink? I think we're having wine with dinner. It's a California Cabernet."

"Yeah, but I can wait for dinner," Jack said, noticing that Angie had entered the room. "Would one you guys like to go and open the wine for dinner?" She looked intently at Jack. "Yeah, I can do it." Jack got up and went to the kitchen before Bob could protest.

When he got to the kitchen, Sarah was waiting for him. "Jack, isn't there anything we can do for Bob?" she asked. "I can't stand to see him suffer this way."

"Sarah, if we operated to remove it, it would kill him. He didn't want to try chemo since he would basically be puking all the time." So, no…there is nothing to do but let it run its course."

"But…there is nothing?" she implored.

"We can hope and pray for a miracle but I don't think that will happen. I have seen these things before and unless you catch it early it's usually fatal." Jack walked over to the wine bottle and started to open it with the corkscrew.

Sarah thought about it. About eight months ago he had started having some headaches. He attributed it to the long hours on the new project. He would take a headache pill and it would typically subside. Maybe if he had gone to have it checked then? Now it was too late.

Angie was sitting with Bob and started talking about the Cleveland baseball team. "They look pretty good in spring training, don't you think? she asked.

"Yeah, a lot better than last year." Bob knew she was trying not to talk about his condition. She knew he was a big sports fan, typically attending several home games a year. Not this year. He would not be going anywhere anymore. He did not know when a seizure would start—there was no warning. He did not care for another ambulance ride if he could avoid it.

"Come on you two, dinner is ready." Sarah shouted from the dining room.

Bob got up and walked to the dining room without any issues. At least he was eating good. Sarah had been fixing all of his favorite dishes lately. He was liable to put on few pounds…oh shit, who cares about that now, he thought. The dinner was excellent, the wine good and the bread fresh. For dessert Sarah brought out one of her famous freshly baked apple pies. He managed to be a good host without having any issues.

Jack got him alone in the family room after the dinner and asked if he was still having the dreams. "Yes", Bob confessed. "Do you think I am hallucinating?" he asked.

"Probably that thing in your head is probably causing it to occur. I really do not have much information on tumors like this. Most people die before the tumor gets as big as yours." Jack remarked.

"That's reassuring," Bob grimaced.

"I am sorry. I wish there was something we could do."

After Jack and Angie left, Bob even helped Sarah clean up. He felt much better today for some reason. Except for some numbness in his shoulder, he actually felt normal. After dinner, Sarah asked him if he minded if Reverend Morton came over for a short visit. He said sure, that would be ok. She had asked the Reverend to stop by tomorrow for lunch so he could talk to Bob. Bob did not mind; for a preacher, Craig Morton was pretty much down to earth. Later they went to bed. He did not take the pill Jack had prescribed for him. He hoped he could sleep without the dreams tonight.

CHAPTER 12

ON WAS AGAIN SITTING under the maple tree in the park next to the student union. The summer weather was actually hot today. He was starting to perspire. This time he was reading the next chapter in psychology. It was on abnormal human behavior, different types of mental disorders and such. It was much more interesting than the chapters on the id and ego. After reading the chapter on autism, he began to think maybe he was slightly autistic. He had many of the same symptoms. He always thought he was slightly off a bit, but had attributed that to the severe traumatic experience due to the death of his parents when he was a teenager. The book said a mild case of autism was called Asperger's. Some famous people had that condition and it sometimes allowed them to make fantastic discoveries. He wondered about that; maybe that is why he was so interested in engineering.

He got up and decided to walk to the student union. He got his typical iced tea and looked around on the veranda. He spied Sue sitting at the same table as before. She was dressed nicely again in a blue dress but had her hair pulled back in a ponytail. He started to walk over to see her but when she saw him, she just got up to leave and walked by him without saying anything.

"Hey..." he started to say but she kept on walking. What the heck? Was she mad at him for something? He wondered, but he didn't follow her. He sat down and drank his tea. When he finished, he walked over to the Hess building and went inside. He entered the classroom expecting to see Sue sitting in the same seat as before but now she was sitting on the other side of her friend Joan. He took the hint and sat where he did before. The two girls were talking to each other and not paying any attention to him. The class was hard to endure. Mr. Johnson apparently did not read the chapters in detail but must have just skimmed through them. Half the time he got off on a tangent about some football story totally unrelated to the study material. He had a bad habit of using the phrase "You know..." a lot.

Ron looked over at Sue a couple of times but she was paying attention to the instructor and did not look his way. Joan looked at him a couple of times but did not smile either. As the class ended, he got up to leave as the two girls got up talking together animatedly. He rushed after them and when he caught up to them, he interrupted their conversation.

"Hey Sue, can I talk to you?" he asked. She stopped looked at him and motioned for Joan to go on without her.

"What do you want?" she asked.

"Are you mad at me for some reason? Did I say or do something to upset you?" "Yes, you did." She turned to walk away.

"Wait...please," he begged.

She stopped and looked at him, "Four years ago."

"Four years ago?" That would have been high school. "What did I do to you four years ago?" She stopped and turned towards him. "You don't remember, do you."

"I guess not. But, please tell me." He looked into her eyes, hoping for some clue.

"Ok...I guess I should tell you. I was just now trying to hurt you as you hurt me back then." "Please...let's go to the Student Union and talk," he replied.

They walked to the Student Union in silence. They sat down on the veranda at one of the tables away from the crowds.

"It was back in high school. I was a freshman when you were a senior." She began. "I had this big crush on you, the big football hero." She was squirming in her chair slightly. "It was the last home game of the year and you had just made the winning touchdown at the end of the fourth quarter."

He remembered that play. There were 2 minutes left in the game and his team was ahead 35 to 33. They were at the 50-yard line facing a 4th down and 10 yards to go situation. This was typically a punting situation. But the coach knew his defense could not stop the other team. Every time they got the ball, the visiting team simply picked apart the defense and marched down the field, scoring either a touchdown or a field goal. The home team defense was really tired, and the coach knew he could not rely on stopping the other team from getting the winning score. He called a time out and had Ron and the quarterback, Jim Tuttle, huddle with him. 'We can't stop these guys. I don't want to punt it to them.' So, he called an 80Y-cross. It was a post pattern pass. He looked at Ron and said don't drop the ball. It was basically a suicide play for Ron. Ever since he had caught two touchdowns in the first half, they were double teaming him. They got back on the field. The other team was in a punt reception formation. When Jim joined the huddle, everyone looked incredulous when he called the 80Y-cross. The other team was caught off guard, and Ron managed to get through and run toward the end zone. The safety and middle linebacker were both covering him. Jim threw the ball up high. It was too high. Ron had to jump in the air and just caught it by his fingertips but then fell heavily in the end zone just as the two opposing players crashed into him. Ron landed, still holding on to the ball but the 200-pound middle linebacker landed on him and during the impact his ankle was twisted almost perpendicular from normal. The official saw that it was a catch and signaled a touchdown. Ron thought his ankle was broken it was so painful. Jim came up to congratulate him but he barely got up. The roar of the home team crowd was deafening. The score was now 42 to 33 with less than 2 minutes on the clock. Jim helped him as he hobbled over to the bench and sat down. He watched as his team kicked off. The other team then methodically moved down the field and scored another touchdown. Then time ran out and the home team won 42-40. Ron limped off the field toward the locker room in great pain. Jim asked if he was ok but he could not talk to anyone.

"Yeah, I remember. I got really hurt on that play and could barely walk."

"When you were walking off the field, did you see a girl by the locker room door trying to talk to you?" she asked.

He searched his memory. "Come to think of it, there was this skinny girl in a fuzzy pink sweater wearing glasses," he remembered. "With all the crowd noise and all the pain I was in, I probably did not hear her." He looked at her. "Was that you?"

"Yes. You totally ignored me as if I wasn't there," she sobbed.

"Wow. I am sorry. Funny thing. My ankle was only a bad sprain. I thought it was broken. After they taped it up and I changed, I went out to see if that girl was still out there, but she must have left." He looked at her. "I had to use crutches for the next two weeks."

"You actually looked for me later?" she asked. She remembered that he was limping badly.

"Yeah, not that many girls actually talked to me in high school." This was true. He was a 145-pound skinny but tall kid and not that good looking in high school. He was a loner and usually hung out with the 'nerds.' This was very unusual for a 'jock'. He did not even go to the prom. He did not seem to have time for dating, and could not afford much in the way of entertaining a girl anyway. He usually would be busy with football practice, studying or taking care of his grandmother. He also had a part time job at a dry-cleaners on Saturdays to get some spending money. The trust fund money from his father went directly into a savings account for college. He did not get control of the money until he turned 18. He did date a few girls in college, but never really got serious with anyone until he met Monica, and that was now over.

"I'm sorry...I didn't know." She was blushing again.

"You wear glasses?" He looked at her.

"Contacts," she replied.

"Wow. I bet you even look good with glasses, too." He reached over and took her hand. "I am really sorry that I hurt you. I didn't mean to." He needed to reassure her. "Can we start over?" he asked.

"I guess so...I feel sort of bad now." She was looking at the ground. "Well, then...can I take you out to dinner tonight to make up for it?" "I suppose...," she reluctantly agreed.

Three tables away, John Turley was talking to his buddy Reggie Jones. He looked up to see Ron and the pretty girl sitting together talking in low voices. Damn that Pritchard! he thought. This could complicate things if she started dating someone else.

CHAPTER 13

*T*HE REVEREND CRAIG MORTON was a somewhat younger man, in his forties. He was married and had two kids in college. He was what some would call a liberal but he thought of himself as a progressive. He recently had replaced the minister at Sarah's Church. A lot of the people did not like the previous minister and when she left, he had been selected by the pastor nominating committee. He had been at the church for almost 8 months now and was still in the process of meeting all of the families. Sarah had told him about her husband. He had wondered why she had been attending alone the last few weeks. Since she sang in the choir, she did not have to sit in a pew alone. He could understand that Sarah and Bob were going through a tough time. He rang the doorbell.

"Hello, hello," he said to Sarah as she opened the door. It was raining outside and the Reverend had a raincoat that was dripping wet.

"Here, let me have that." Sarah said as she turned to hang up his coat. "Bob is in the family room. I'm making sandwiches for lunch."

The Reverend looked around the house. It was the first time he had visited the Parker residence and he thought to himself, looks like a typical upper middleclass family home. He walked into the family room and saw Bob sitting in a wheelchair, reading the paper.

"Hello Bob," he started. "It surely is raining outside today."

Bob looked up and smiled. "Hi, preacher." The preacher was dressed all in black except for his white collar. Bob found that he had better mobility in the wheelchair since his legs sometimes refused to move anymore. "I suppose you are here to cheer me up."

"Well…Sarah has put your name in with our prayer group and I thought I would stop by to say hello."

"Well, that's nice of you. I'm not even a member of your church. I am an ex-Catholic, was schooled in a parochial school until the age of 12."

"Yeah, but you are typically in regular attendance except for the last few weeks." "Well preacher…I'm getting ready to die," Bob admitted.

"That's what I came to talk to you about. Have you made peace with God?" The Reverend sat in the chair next to him.

"Not sure that I ever can make that step, preacher. God has not given me the time I needed," Bob stated as a matter of fact. He was not bitter about his condition, just very disappointed.

"Well, God works in mysterious ways…" the Reverend started.

"I knew you were going to say that." Bob interrupted him. "You guys always use that phrase every time something happens that you cannot explain."

"Do you believe in God"? Reverend Michaels asked.

"You know, I'm not sure," Bob stated. "I was brought up as a Catholic and I used to believe, but then the hypocrisy of that church drove me away. Your church seems a lot different. It makes more sense to be a Protestant, I think."

"Well, I am glad to hear that." The Reverend started again, smiling; "Sometimes miracles do happen you know. Our prayer group has seen some fantastic reversals through prayer."

"Not this time, Preacher. I appreciate the effort, but I am getting worse every day and I don't have much time left." Bob started to sob. He typically would not cry in front of someone, but he suddenly felt a wave of emotion come over him. "Sorry there, preacher," he apologized wiping his eyes, "I guess I was feeling a bit sorry for myself." He wiped a tear away. The only place Bob thought he would go to if there was an afterlife would be full of fire and brimstone.

"That's OK. God will be with you during your journey, you just have to accept him." The Reverend stated. "If you accept him, he will meet you along the way and guide you." He moved closer and put his arm around Bob's shoulder. "Why don't we share a prayer?" he asked.

Bob agreed and they said a prayer. Bob figured it couldn't hurt. He was more into scientific explanations of phenomena instead of attributing everything to God. Afterwards they had sandwiches and soft drinks. The preacher left after talking to Sarah about the things happening in the church.

Sarah was happy that he had agreed to talk to the preacher. "Did he help you at all?" she asked.

"That was nice. He is a good preacher. I enjoyed our little talk." Bob told her. Maybe there is something about faith after all. He had ignored the church most of his life, maybe that was why God was punishing him. Still, it did not hurt to pray, although he doubted that prayer would help him now.

CHAPTER 14

*R*ON PRITCHARD PARKED HIS *red Corvette in the lot next to the student union as always. It was almost six o'clock and he had arranged to meet Sue at the door of her dormitory. He was wearing his standard khaki pants and blue shirt but had thrown on a dark blue sport coat. He knew of a great little Italian restaurant downtown and wanted to take Sue there for dinner. As he walked toward her building, he thought about the time he had been injured. He probably should have stopped to talk to the girl. He would have, except he was in so much pain that he could not think straight. He was totally concentrating on getting to see the trainer so that his ankle could be looked at. As he entered the locker room, all of the guys were hitting him on the back and celebrating his winning catch. He was not friends with most of the guys but tried to be friendly. They knew he was a loner, never joining the other jocks at parties, drinking illegal beers. They respected his ability as a receiver but thought he was a weirdo.*

He walked up to Fredrick Hall and went in the front entrance. The dorm was a red brick building built in the sixties. This dorm used to be for girls only, but was now used for both men and women. They were segregated on different floors but that did not prevent the inevitable co-mingling. It was six o'clock. He looked around and saw her coming down the stairs. Joan was with her.

"Hi," he said to them. Sue looked fantastic. She was wearing a black cocktail dress that reminded him of the girl in the movie 'Pretty Woman'. She had on dressy shoes but they were not high heels. If he had to describe them, he would say they were half-heels. She had a white shawl over her arm, taking it along in case the restaurant had air conditioning. Her purse was very small, also black.

Joan was dressed in her usual T-shirt and cutoff jeans. "I had to see if you were actually going to show up," Joan said, noting his attire with approval.

"Well, I try never to stand anyone up," he said, still looking at Sue. She was downright beautiful. "Well, you kids have a good time," Joan said as she started back upstairs.

"She is a little motherly, isn't she?" Ron asked.

"We have been close friends for years and we sort of look after each other." Sue said as she smiled at him. "Where are we going?" she asked.

He wanted to impress her with the restaurant but did not want to tell her just yet. "It's a surprise," he said as he opened the door for her.

They walked past the student union and toward the parking lot. As they neared his car she said, "Wow, now that is a nice car," not realizing that the red Corvette convertible was his.

They started to walk past it but then he turned toward the passenger door side and opened the door for her.

"This is yours?" She was amazed as she got in and sat down.

"Yeah, it's my summer car. It's no good in the winter though, and I have to garage it," he said, matter-of-factly. "400 horsepower is great if you have to move fast or get out of a jam quickly." He was proud of the car, he called it 'the Beast' but it sure was fun to drive.

"Better put on your seat belt," he said as he got in and strapped in himself. "This thing wants to go fast, but I'll try not to frighten you."

They drove to the middle of the city, the traffic was light, but most of the rush hour crowd had gone home already. He pulled into one of the posher restaurants in the city. "Anthony's" was one of the best Italian restaurants in the city. He pulled up to the valet parking and handed the attendant the key. Ron opened the door for Sue to get out. She was looking with wide eyes at the establishment. She had heard about this place but had never considered going there.

"Be careful with my baby," he told the attendant who was used to fancy and expensive cars. "Sure," the attendant said as he got in and pulled away from the curb with a squeal of tires. "Isn't this place expensive?" Sue asked turning toward him.

"It's ok. They have great food here." He had wanted to impress her a little bit. He had made reservations and a table was ready for them. The restaurant was decorated in Roman style architecture. There were a lot of red and purple motifs on the walls. Most of the

tables were already filled with people. A soft Italian love song was playing in the background. Normally he would have ordered wine but he knew that Sue was under age so he ordered an iced tea. She had water with a lemon wedge. They looked at the menu. She was shocked at the prices but he said to order whatever she wanted. He had not spent much money this week so he had accumulated a small reserve. He could always use his charge card and pay for it later. She ended up ordering Shrimp Alfredo; he settled for Chicken Parmigiana. While they waited for the food he began to ask her about her life.

"My mother and father got divorced when I was really young," she started. "I can't remember my father; he left my mother and moved away with some other woman." She was frowning. "I guess he never cared about me, he never wrote or visited us." She fidgeted a bit. "My mother had to go to work to support us. A couple of years later she remarried and then had a set of twin boys with my step-father. My two half-brothers got all of the attention." She had been ignored by her parents most of the time and had learned to take care of herself. She was thin and homely in high school and most of the boys ignored her or picked on her mercilessly. She had made some money baby sitting and started to take karate classes. Her mother did not approve of her taking karate but her mother always seemed to have money to pay for the lessons. From karate she gained confidence, and the exercise training sort of made her blossom into a physically fit pretty girl. In her senior year a lot of the boys started to take notice of her, but thought she was an easy mark. One day one of the big football players came up behind her and grabbed her breasts. In a matter of seconds, he was face down on the floor and she was standing over him holding his arm in an awkward position that made him beg for mercy. He never tried that again and since it was done in the hallway full of students everyone saw it. She was called into the principal's office but since the boy had not registered a complaint, they let it go.

After that, the word got around school and most of the boys would not even attempt to talk to her. She did not even have a date to the prom, but stayed home babysitting her maniac brothers while her parents went out. She did have a few dates but usually the boys her age were only interested in getting her in bed. She and Joan became great friends and discovered that they were both planning to go to the same college. Since both of her parents were working, Sue's mother had managed to save a college fund for her. In addition to that, she had gotten a scholarship due to her straight-A grades in high school, which helped pay her tuition. So, she and Joan had decided to room together in the same dorm. Her friend Joan had tried to interest her in a couple of blind dates but after the first one was such a complete disaster, she had told Joan no more. She had really never gotten over her crush on Ron and she found most of the boys her own age were very shallow with no interest in relationships and they had only one thought in mind and that was to have sex. When she found out Ron was at the same college, she had set out to get him interested and then drop him as an act of revenge. Now, however, she found that she really liked him. He was somewhat handsome, reserved and was more mature, unlike the other boys she had known.

He asked her if she was going steady with anyone and she responded that she was not dating anyone in particular. She then asked him if he was dating anyone. He replied that he had a girlfriend last year but they had broken up, so he wasn't seeing anyone in particular either. She smiled at that.

The food was excellent and they both decided to have cheesecake for dessert. Afterwards he paid the bill with a credit card and they walked to the entrance. Ron was so happy that she was pleased with the meal. He did not want this date to end.

"That was really very good." She walked through the door after he opened it. "Thank you. I haven't been to many restaurants that nice since I was a little girl."

He looked around for the valet. "He must be on break." He looked at her. "You feel like a little walk? They park the cars around the other side of the block." Ron would do anything to prolong the date.

"Sure, Joan and I often go for long walks."

He went into the valet's office. The valet manager was there. "He will be back in a few minutes, sir," the manager noted.

"Just give me the key to the Corvette and I'll get it myself," he asked. Since the manager knew him from previous visits, he opened the drawer and retrieved the key.

"Here is the pass for the gate too." the manager handed him both. "Thanks," Ron tipped him a ten-dollar bill.

They walked down the street. It was getting darker, almost sunset. It was a beautiful night; the temperature was about 75 degrees and there was a slight breeze. Some light clouds were trailing in the sky.

"I love this time of year," he said as he took her hand in his and started to walk down the block. He really wanted to be with this girl. He could not believe someone as pretty and nice as her would not have a boyfriend.

"It is nice," she agreed. She wanted this night to last forever. She was falling for him but not totally sure of his motives yet. She was hoping he was not like the other guys she had dated who only wanted to bed her.

As they turned the corner, a dark figure emerged from the shadows in the alley. He was a scruffy looking man, about 25 years old and about 150 pounds, wearing a dirty shirt and blue jeans. His eyes were bloodshot, obviously he was on drugs. He held a switchblade knife in his hand and stepped in front of them. He turned to Ron. "Give me your wallet, or I cut the girl." He said in a low voice.

Ron was totally caught off guard and froze. He typically carried a small Ruger .380 caliber semi-automatic pistol in his pocket (he had a carry permit) but had left it at home tonight since he had to go on to the college campus to pick her up. The man with the knife moved toward Sue but he was looking at Ron and had the knife pointed at him. That was a big mistake. Ron moved to step between the man and Sue, but she was quicker. She moved so fast it was almost a blur. She kicked the would-be robber in the face, and as he fell back to the ground she grabbed his hand holding the knife, bent it back until he screamed and dropped the knife. She picked up the knife and put her foot on the man's chest with the knife to his throat. All of this happened in about three seconds.

"Ok, asshole, you want to die?" she hissed.

"No...No...please...I'm sorry, honest...I was just kidding, I don't want to hurt anyone," the man lying on his back on the pavement begged.

Ron was astounded. It had happened so fast he could not believe his eyes. How could she do that so fast? He remembered her saying she had taken karate courses but he had not thought much of it.

"Ok. Then beat it before I hurt you." She took her foot off his chest and stood back, still holding the knife and pointing it at the prostrate figure. He had a bloody imprint of her heel on his cheek. He took one frightened look at her and Ron, then got up and ran away. They watched him run down the street as if demons were chasing him. She took the knife, stuck it in a gap between two bricks on the nearby building and bent the knife sideways so that the blade broke off. Then she threw the handle down the alley.

Ron looked at her in disbelief. He was at a loss for words. *"Wow…"* he started. *"How did you do that?"*

"I have a third-degree black belt in karate," she said, slightly out of breath. She looked down at her dress. There was a 3-inch tear in the seam where she had launched her kick. *"Damn. This was my best dress."*

Ron stared at her, not believing what he had seen.

CHAPTER 15

BOB AWOKE AGAIN. HE was in bed. He was astounded at the dream. The dreams were still happening and it was somewhat surprising how real they seemed. He had lost most of the feeling in his legs but was still able to move himself onto and off the wheelchair. Going to the bathroom was a challenge, but he was still managing it alright. Jack had arranged for Bob to have Hospice care and the guy was here to help him take a shower. He could stand on his legs if he could hold on to something to keep his balance. He was having a hard time staying awake now and spent most of the day asleep or half asleep. The morphine Jack prescribed for the pain really made him drowsy. He was still having the dreams though. They seemed to be getting weirder. Must be the morphine, he thought. Sarah was trying her best to take care of him but she really was not able to fully cope with his condition. Bob had given Sarah power of attorney for his health and for their finances. She would be in charge of everything now.

Sarah was unaccustomed to this, as Bob had always been in charge of the finances. She was amazed when she looked at the books. They were in pretty good shape financially. Even after spending a lot of money on the Hawaii trip, Bob still had a considerable financial portfolio. He had often tried to tell her about the stocks and bonds but she did not understand a lot about that stuff. It looked like he had been planning for retirement for a long time. They had a little over half a million saved up in stocks alone.

After Bob took his shower, the Hospice guy left. The male nurse had taken his temperature and his blood pressure and assured Bob that the readings were in the normal range. He wondered what is normal for someone dying of a brain tumor, he thought. After he had dressed and had breakfast, he sat down. He turned to Sarah who was sitting and reading the newspaper.

"Sarah," he croaked.

"Yes dear?" She put the paper down.

"After…afterward you will have my 401K and my life insurance. You should be ok for money." Sarah looked at him, a tear in her eye. "I won't have you though."

"It'll be ok. I don't want you to feel that you if you find someone else… don't hesitate. He should be someone who is kind and will take care of you."

Sarah looked at him. "I don't want anyone else."

"Still, if it happens, I don't want you to feel guilty or anything," he stated. She got out of her chair and ran into the other room, crying softly. Well, that went well, he said to himself. He started to get sleepy again. She had just given him the morphine a few minutes ago. He drifted off to sleep.

CHAPTER 16

ON AND SUE WALKED to the parking garage without any other incidents. She was quiet. He did not say anything either. They got to the Corvette and got in, but he did not start the car. He sensed that she wanted to talk.

Sue sat quietly for a few seconds then spoke looking out of the car, "I suppose you won't want to see me anymore now," she said looking down. "Most boys are afraid of me after something like that."

Ron turned toward her. "Well, I was really surprised, but I really would like to see you again if you let me. I'm not scared of you." He looked at her. "I really like you. I don't care if you are tough. I see a fascinating young lady that I want to get to know better." He started the car and drove to the gate. The gate pass opened the gate and they drove out. "It's still early, you want to go to my place?" he asked innocently.

She was somewhat surprised by his reaction. Also, she was somewhat suspicious of him taking her to his apartment. "As long as you don't get any funny ideas, buster," she said in her tough voice.

"Don't worry about that. I don't want to get kicked in the face." he laughed.

They drove to his place. He parked in the driveway next to the landlord's pickup truck. His apartment was a duplex and he had the upstairs apartment. Apparently, the owner had re-done the upstairs apartment with the idea of renting it out to college students. The house owner had his screen door open and walked out to meet them. He looked at Ron and saw the prettiest girl he had ever seen with Ron.

"Hi Ron." he said, looking intently at the girl. "Hi Matt." Ron responded. "This is my friend Sue." "You know the rules Ron," he said as he eyed the girl.

"Yeah, no problems Matt, I'm taking her back to her dorm before her curfew." Ron noted. "Rules?" she asked as they climbed

the outside stairs to the small porch on the second floor. "Yeah. No overnight guests allowed." He opened the door and let her in.

She looked around the apartment. It was basically a small apartment, with a tiny kitchen, a dining room table, a bathroom and a living/bedroom area. It was not decorated in any particular style. It was just stuff thrown together. The table was well organized as a study desk with a computer and books open with pads of paper with several notes. There was only a single chair for the table and a couch in the room and that faced a small TV. There was a chess set on a sideboard by the window. It looked like a typical male residence.

"This is pretty cozy." she said, sitting on the couch. "So, this is your quiet study place?" "Yeah. You want an ice tea?" he asked, moving toward the fridge.

"No way…It's too late…the caffeine would keep me up all night." She looked at her watch.

"Well, we could watch TV for a while if you want," he said, and went to the TV to turn it on.

"Don't you have a remote?" she asked as he manually changed the channels until he came to a movie channel.

"Yeah, but I lost it somehow." He said as he sat down next to her. A movie was coming on, something about an "Affair to Remember". He did not care what movie it was, he just wanted to be near her for a little while longer.

"Oh, this is one of my favorite movies" she smiled. She wondered when he was going to try to kiss her.

"I can change the channel if you have already seen this." He started to get up. "No…leave it on." She looked at him. He really was trying to be nice to her.

He sat back down and they watched the movie together. He did not try to make any moves toward her. He was the perfect gentleman keeping his hands to himself. She was surprised at this. Most guys would have tried to have her bra off by this time. The movie was sort of sad but had a semi-happy ending. He looked at his watch and said, "Boy it's getting late, I have to get you back." It was already dark. They walked down to his car and he drove her back to campus. She noted that Ron really babied the red Corvette.

"That was a pretty good movie," he admitted to her.

"Most guys don't like those romantic stories. I take it you

hadn't seen that one." She looked at him as he parked the car near the student union. The lot was almost empty now so he parked up close to the building.

"No. I have watched a lot of movies, but I have never seen that one. It looked like an old classic." He opened the car door for her and escorted her back to her dormitory. It was totally dark now and the moon was up, but the walkway was brightly lit by street lights. They held hands as they walked. They stopped at the entrance to her dorm.

She turned to face him. "Well, I had a good time, Thanks."

He came closer. "Can we do this again?" he asked moving his head toward hers but stopping short of kissing her.

"Yes." She said, moving closer so they could kiss. He took note of this and bent down to kiss her.

He expected a small peck and that was all. It was a lot more than that. Her lips were really soft, but when they kissed it was as if an electric shock went through his body. It became very passionate with her arms around his neck pressing closer to him. He wrapped his arms around her and they stayed like that for quite a time. He could feel her breasts pressing against his chest. He opened his eyes and saw hers were closed. He started to pull away. They parted slowly. She was blinking her eyes and obviously had felt the electricity also since she had a surprised look on her face. Wow. He had never felt anything like that with Monica.

"Ok, then, I'll see you in class," he managed to croak.

"Ok," she said, smiling at him. She felt as if she was high. She backed away, still facing him and almost tripped on the first step. "Good night." She turned and entered the dorm.

Ron stood there for a few seconds, wondering what had happened. He had never felt anything like that before with any girl. Then he turned around and went home.

Sue ran upstairs and entered her dorm room, smiling. Joan was waiting up for her.

"You are so late. I was about to call the campus police." Joan looked up from her bed where she had been reading. She saw that Sue's dress was ripped. "Did that guy abuse you?" she said pointing to her dress.

"No, I did that by accident." Sue did not want to give Joan the details of the assault; she would just get upset. "We had a

wonderful time." Sue whirled about the room. "I think I'm in love," she said more to herself than to Joan.

"After one date?" Joan laughed. "Just wait, he will break your heart. They all do, once they get what they want." Joan looked back at her book. She had had some experience with this, more than Sue ever had. She had dated a lot of guys and had been disappointed with most of them. "The real handsome guys are the worst. Once they have achieved what they wanted they will drop you like a hot rock," Joan continued.

Joan thought, the homely guys were even worse. Even before they reached first base with you, they wanted to marry you. She was hoping to find someone in the middle. Someone who was kind and caring that did not want to jump on her on the first date. Those types were as rare as hen's teeth she thought.

Sue wasn't listening. She was so overcome by that passionate kiss that she thought she was in love. She had never experienced anything like that. She could not wait to see Ron again. She hoped her exhibition of fighting skills would not turn him off. The electricity of the kiss was worse than a caffeine high. She was going to have a hard time getting to sleep tonight.

CHAPTER 17

*B*OB WAS FEELING PRETTY good today. The dreams were still vivid but he decided not to tell anyone about them. He definitely was enjoying them. He felt like a pervert, watching two young people enjoying a close relationship. But he had no control over what happened in the dreams. He got into his wheelchair and wheeled into the kitchen. He opened the fridge and got out a water bottle. Sarah had placed a lot of the things he wanted on the lower shelf so he could reach them. Sarah came into the room. "How are you today?" she asked.

"I'm much better today." He wheeled over to see her.

"That's good." She smiled at him. "I'll be in the bedroom changing the sheets."

It was a bright and sunny May day and it had finally warmed up after a long cold winter and spring. He wanted to go outside but there was no ramp for the wheel chair. He finally figured out that he could get out of the wheel chair at the garage entrance, put it on the floor of the garage and then use the railing to navigate down the two steps. He was able to do this but forgot to open the garage door. David had finally moved most of his stuff out of the garage into a storage unit, so the Buick was now parked inside the garage. He could not reach the wall control from the wheelchair. He did not want to call out to Sarah. She probably would not approve of him wheeling down the sidewalk in his wheel chair. Finally, he went over to the Buick and used the door handle to stand up. He opened the door and reached in to get the garage door opener. He was leaning too far and lost his balance, falling to the concrete floor.

Sarah came into the family room and started to say, "I think the Reverend is going to visit again today...," but stopped since Bob was not in his usual place. She looked around. Was he in the kitchen? No. She looked in the bathroom but it was empty also. She started to get worried.

"Bob!" she shouted. "Where are you?" She became frantic. She ran to the basement steps. Did he fall down the steps? No.

No one was in the basement either. She ran up the steps and went to the door to the garage. She opened the door and there he was, sprawled out on the floor. His head was bleeding. She ran to the phone and called 911.

Bob woke up later in a hospital bed. It was a room painted an off-white color, possibly a pearl white. There was a large overhead fluorescent light but it was off. Sunlight was coming through the windows at a high angle. It must be early morning he thought. He tried to turn his head to look out the window but all he could see was a bush outside. At least he must be on a ground floor he thought. He had all sorts of tubes going in his arms and catheters coming out of his abdomen. He was covered with a heavy blanket. He looked over and saw Sarah was sitting in a chair, apparently asleep. What the heck had happened, he wondered. The last thing he remembered was reaching for the garage door opener. His head was bandaged, and was really painful. He found he could move his arms but his hands felt numb. His legs would not move. He looked around his bed. He must be in a hospital. There was amachine next to the bed that was showing his heart rate as a bunch of bumps on an LED display. It looked like it was measuring a couple of other things but he could not tell what they were. The machine was giving a soft beep with each beat of his heart. He looked all around, there should be a call button somewhere. He found it hanging above him on the bed post, almost out of his reach. He was able to grab it but his fingers could not press the button. He finally was able to push the button in by holding it against the bed post.

A pretty nurse dressed in white came in, looked at him and then rushed out again. What the heck, he thought, do I look that bad? About two minutes later the nurse returned with an older man, apparently a doctor. The doctor was a short man, shorter than the nurse, also dressed in a white shirt and dark pants. He had gray hair and a mustache. He had a stethoscope around his neck.

"Well Mr. Parker, you finally woke up." The doctor said. "How are you feeling?"

Bob tried to speak, but at first found he had no voice. Finally, he managed to croak "Ok, I guess. Where am I?"

"You are in the Cleveland Clinic. You have been out of touch for almost a week now." The doctor looked at the machine and then turned to him. "You had a nasty fall and a major concussion. We thought you might not come back to us."

Sarah stirred and looked up. She rushed to his side but did not say anything.

Bob looked at her and said, "I was going to go for a stroll down the sidewalk, Sarah. I am sorry."

She looked relieved "That's ok, we are just so glad you're back," she managed to say. "Someone is here to see you." She walked to the door. In came Lauren, his daughter. "Gee Dad, I thought I had missed getting a chance to talk to you." Lauren was wearing military fatigues but had captain's bars on her collar. She was 32 years old, blond hair and blue eyes. Ron was glad that she had gotten her good looks from her mother.

Bob was very proud of her; she had made a good life for herself. "It's good to see you," he said. "I'm sorry that it isn't under better circumstances." He held out his hand to her.

She took his hand, had a tear in her eye. "They say you aren't going to get any better," she sobbed.

"Yeah, that's alright." He said bravely, "I have had a good life. But I didn't really get much of a chance to spend as much time as I wanted with you. I hear you are engaged." He saw the ring on her finger.

"Yeah, we were hoping to get hitched in September…" She stopped, realizing he probably wouldn't be there.

"Please ask your brother to walk you down the aisle," he said, knowing that September was too far away for him.

CHAPTER 18

*R*ON GOT UP EARLY. *He wanted to see Sue again. He had a quick breakfast and then got dressed, and drove over to the Campus. He parked at the back of the parking lot as he typically did so that no one would park their junker next to his Corvette. He entered the student union and looked around for Sue. She was not there yet so he got an iced tea and sat down on the veranda. Sue came up to him a few minutes later and sat down across from him.*

"Hi," she said meekly. She was dressed in a blue dress that was belted at the waist and had her hair down. "I wanted you to know I really enjoyed our date last night,." she said almost apologetically.

He looked at her. She was beautiful. "I...I wanted to tell you that I really enjoyed it too," he stammered, blushing. "I am hoping we can do that again."

This made her smile. "Yes, that would be nice."

A couple of tables away John Turley was sitting with his pal Reggie Jones. They both looked over at the girl and Ron. "Isn't that guy Pritchard, who was a good receiver for us a couple of years ago?" Reggie asked.

"Yeah. but get a load of the broad he is talking to. She is really something." Turley licked his lips.

Ron and Sue got up to walk to Psychology class. "We need to get the first term paper done, it's due next week." He was really happy that Sue met him in the Student Union before class. She seemed to be happy to see him.

"Have you selected a topic?" she asked.

"Yeah, I read about this Asperger's Syndrome and it is pretty interesting. I may have a slight case of it myself." He was still amazed at how pretty and smart she was. His experience was that the pretty ones were typically aloof and not that smart.

"You think you have a mental disease?" She didn't think he was serious.

"Well, no...but I do share some of the symptoms." He looked at her. She was dressed conservatively in a blue knee-length dress but had white socks and sneakers on. "I hate social gatherings and avoid them as much as possible, I have an intense capability to focus on any problem I am working on, and I can sit and work on puzzles all day." It was one of the reasons he wanted to be an engineer.

"That just sounds like a normal engineering type person," she replied as they got to the classroom and went in. They sat next to each other.

"So, what did you select for a topic?" he asked.

"I have always been interested in paranoia" she looked at him, smiling.

Class was not that interesting but they both took notes and afterward walked over to the veranda at the Student Union. She sat at a near table.

"How about we walk over to the library later to do some research?" She was thinking of a way to get more time with him.

"There is always the internet," he replied, sitting next to her at the table.

There was a computer lab in the student union on the upper floor but it was usually packed with students working on assignments.

"Yeah but I don't have a computer in the dorm. I left my laptop at home since my parents told me it could easily be stolen." She really did not think anyone would take it, but she had always planned on using the computers in the library.

"Ok" he agreed. He would like to spend more time with her and a walk across campus to the library would give them more time together. They were getting ready to leave.

Rick Bass, the top assistant coach for the football team, walked out of the Student Union and looked at the sparse crowd sitting outside. He was looking for girls to invite to the Friday night fraternity party. He spied Sue talking to Ron. She was a knockout. He was the faculty advisor for the Tau Psi Omega Fraternity on campus. He would typically invite several young girls to attend fraternity parties since it was always hard to get a good party going without any women.

He walked over to the table Sue and Ron were sitting at.

"Hello," he started, looking at her and then noticed who she

was sitting with. "Pritchard?" He couldn't believe it. That guy was a natural football receiver and really could have helped the team if he had if not quit.

"Hi coach." Ron reluctantly responded. Rick Bass had been really upset when he left the team. Rick Bass was one of the reasons Ron quit the team. The man treated everyone like shit. There also was something slimy about him that Ron couldn't quite place either.

"You still at this college? I thought you had transferred." Rick Bass had a way of getting the guys on the team on the defensive.

"No, just getting ready to graduate." Ron was hoping he would just leave them alone.

"How come you weren't on the team last year?

"You know I hurt my ankle. It still bothers me." Ron lied a little bit.

"Are you going to introduce me to your friend?" Rick was really interested in this one. She was obviously a freshman and therefore probably not too experienced with guys. This really excited him.

"I'm Sue Conner." Sue looked at the man. He was probably in his thirties, had brown hair in a crew cut and wore what appeared to be a jogging outfit with a headband and everything. He was not very attractive and had mean eyes.

"Well, I'm Rick, Rick Bass, the assistant football coach at the college." God, he thought, she is a real looker. He just had to get her to the party." Look, I'm in a hurry here but I want to give you an official invite to the party this Friday at the Tau Frat house." He fished out a gold printed card from a pocket and handed it to her. It gave the address of the frat House and the date and time of the party. "It is one of the traditional ways of welcoming new students to the college. I am sure you won't want to miss it. It is one of the most prestigious parties of the semester." He gave a big toothy smile.

"Why thank you." She smiled back. "Can I invite my dorm roommate Joan?" she asked.

"Why Sure, the more, the merrier." He fished out another invite card. Hey, this start looked really promising. "You don't have to bring him though." He pointed at Ron. "He is a quitter and a lot of the Tau boys are real football players." He walked off whistling. This was one party he was not going to miss.

"You aren't thinking of going, are you? That guy is bad news." Ron looked at her.

"Come on. It seems like a neat way to meet people." She looked at the retreating coach.

"Well, I don't trust that guy. I have heard some bad rumors about him." Ron was trying to dissuade her. They got up to walk to the library which was across the campus.

A few tables away football players John Turley and Reggie Jones had watched the invitation with some interest. Rick had invited the pretty girl to the party. This could be his chance to get to her. He was in the Fraternity.

Ron and Sue talked about the term paper and how to approach their respective topics. Technically the library was a college library but it was open to the high school students as well since it was located directly across from the local high school. It was about a ten minute walk from the student union. Adjacent to the library was an elementary school and it had a fenced in playground right next to the library building parking lot. The highway next to the elementary school was lined with large oak trees on the side by the school, just up to the edge of the playground.

Sue stopped to look at the kids playing in the playground. *"It looks like they are having fun. Do you like kids?"* she asked innocently.

"I think so. I was an only child so I never got to play with a brother or sister." Ron never understood why his parents had not had more children. He never had much experience with younger kids, so he wasn't really sure if he liked children.

"It's summer, don't they have summer vacation?" He asked.

I think that today is the last day of school here."

"Wow, look at that row of oak trees. They must be almost four feet in diameter." He pointed to the trees just on the other side of the playground.

"Yes. They are beautiful, but I heard the city council wants to cut them down." She remembered listening to the local news on TV.

"Well, that's a shame," he replied.

They went in and started their research. After a couple of hours, they both had enough material to write their papers. *"Make sure you write an original paper,"* he warned her. *"The college uses a super computer to check for plagiarism."*

"Thanks, that's good to know." She appreciated that he knew about things like that. She would never copy someone else's work, but she would warn Joan about it. She got all of her information written down in notes but he took out a couple of books to take home and review.

Her cell phone rang. It was Joan.

"Where are you? I thought we were going downtown to do some shopping." Joan was wondering why she was late.

"I'm sorry…We were at the library doing research for the term paper and lost track of time." She hung up, got up and gathered her things. "I have to go," she said to Ron.

"Ok, I will go with you. We probably should have driven over here in my car." He also got up to leave. "Can we get together later? Maybe go over our notes or something?" He escorted her to the front door of the library.

"How about tomorrow? We don't have Psychology class on Wednesday." She was walking fast back to the campus.

"Ok, that sounds good." He tried to keep up with her. She had a larger stride than most girls. She was only 3 inches shorter than his 6-foot frame, taller than most girls. He was amazed that she was perfectly proportioned; she could have been a fashion model if she wanted to.

CHAPTER 19

BOB LAY AWAKE IN his bed. Sarah had moved him to a nursing home where he could have 24-hour nursing care. He was almost totally paralyzed now. He could still move his arms and his head but had lost all control of his lower body. He could no longer control his bowels, so they had him hooked up with catheters. Sorry state of affairs, he thought to himself. He hated that he could no longer take care of that by himself. He felt he was a burden on the nursing staff who were paid to look after him. Marty had stopped by to see him once and was shocked that Bob was so bad off. He realized why Bob had quit the job now. When asked how the engineering project was going, Marty praised Joe Ross who had taken over for Bob. The project was running smoothly and it looked like they were only going to be behind schedule by two months. Bob was glad that Joe had stepped up. Joe could have taken over sooner but he had always let Bob do the hard work, watching carefully and remembering how Bob did things.

The dreams were continuing but he did not know why they were so vivid. What was the purpose of the dreams? He wondered. He had read once that dreams were the product of your subconscious. Like a warning or something. What were the dreams warning him of? He was basically half dead and could not do anything about things anymore. He was left by himself for long periods of time, but Sarah came to visit him for an hour every day. She would talk about things she did that day, people she saw and typically ran out of stuff to talk about after a few minutes. He would ask her about things in the house that he had not gotten around to fixing. She had hired a handyman who was taking care of a couple of items. She had also hired a landscaper to mow the lawn and trim the bushes. Her brother Tom was coming to visit for a few days. That would be nice. Her brother was a deadbeat who had been a parasite on Sarah's parents until they died. He always had some sort of scheme or plan that he wanted Bob to invest in. But then he moved away and found a low paying factory job in the next nearby state. This was after Bob had told him in no uncertain terms that Tom could not live with them. But Bob held no power over him now. He just hoped that Sarah would not start giving her brother some of his hard-earned money. She would need to use their savings to live on and he told her that. She had agreed with him and said she would not do anything like that. Her brother was very persuasive though, and Bob doubted that she could resist her brother for very long.

Dave and his pregnant wife brought little Susan to come to visit him in the nursing home. Little Susan had turned eight and had grown almost an inch taller. They had stayed and chatted for a couple of hours. Liz was happily pregnant, and was not having the typical morning sickness she had experienced with little Susan. Susan was really sad to see her new Grandpa in such a sorry state. She told him she wanted him to get better so they could play shuffleboard or chess again. He said he would like that. Afterward he cried a bit, knowing that he probably would not see Dave and his family again. The nurse came in to check on him and gave him some medication. He fell into a fitful sleep as the drugs started to kick in.

CHAPTER 20

*S*UE AND RON HAD *finished their term papers and printed them out on Ron's computer printer. It was early afternoon and he decided to ask Sue out again. "Since we are done early, what do you say to dinner and a movie?" he asked as she was packing up her stuff to go.*

"Sure, why not." Sue replied. She was wearing a blue blouse and a tight pair of blue jeans. The blue jeans really emphasized her figure. "I need to get back to the dorm to clean up."

"Ok, I can drive you over." It was raining lightly and he had the convertible top in place on the corvette. They ran down the stairs to his car and managed not to get too wet. The Corvette was not really good to drive on wet roads. The rear wheel drive and four hundred horsepower were a bad combination if the road was slippery. He was very careful and got her to the student union ok. He gave her his umbrella after they stopped and she paused before getting out of the car.

"Do you like me Ron?" she asked in a low voice.

He was surprised at the question. He turned to her." I like you very much, Sue. I would like to keep seeing you as long as you let me." He smiled.

She leaned over and they kissed. It was again electric to him and he tried to embrace her but the seat belt held him back. She quickly broke it off and opened the door. "See you later?" she opened the umbrella getting out.

"I'll pick you up at six," he shouted after her as she ran in the rain.

He went back to the apartment. Showered and dressed in his regular khaki pants, shirt and blue blazer. It had stopped raining but it was cool for a day in early July. The roads were dry at last but he kept the top up on the convertible. It was cloudy and overcast and looked as if it might rain again. He drove to the campus and parked in the parking lot behind her dorm.

He met her at the dorm entrance again. This time Joan did not escort her down to the main floor. They walked to his car, talking about the weather. This time they dined at a different small bistro downtown. He parked the Corvette in a parking garage and they had a short walk to the restaurant. She was wearing a frilly blue blouse with buttons down the front and white slacks. She carried a small white sweater with her purse, in case it turned colder. They ordered dinner and talked about the term papers. They both ordered the chicken salad since it was a house specialty. She had read his paper and thought he would get an A for sure. Hers was shorter and not as detailed but he said it really looked good. Afterward they walked down the street to the movie theatre. It was playing some old classic starring Katherine Hepburn. He thought if it was a classic, maybe she would like it. He had never heard of this movie and she could not remember it either, but they both knew Katherine Hepburn was a big star. He paid for two tickets and they went in. The theatre air conditioning made it cold and she put on her sweater. The movie was about some Grecian women mourning and was terrible. He fidgeted in his seat. The show was terrible. He was not sure he could stand it. They looked at each other after about 20 minutes of suffering and she said, "do you want to leave?"

"Yes, please." They got up and walked out.

"God, that was terrible," he said when they got back on the street. "I am so sorry." "That's all right. I didn't know what it was either," she consoled him.

"I will have to make it up to you." He walked down the street, holding her hand. My God, he thought. She will think I'm an idiot. He knew he should have checked out the reviews before going to that film.

She thought, good. That means he will have to ask me out again. She was falling for Ron and hoped he felt the same way about her.

They got back to his car and drove back to the campus. He parked at the student union. It was still somewhat early, so she said, "Would you like to come up and see my dorm room?"

"Sure…don't they have a curfew?" He remembered his days in a similar dorm.

"Yeah, our floor has to be clear of visitors by 10:00 PM. That gives us just under two hours," she said, smiling at him.

"Ok then. I don't want to get you in trouble." He followed her up the stairs. The building only had four floors but it was unfortunate that she was on the third floor: there was no elevator. The odd floors were for female students, the even floors were for the male students. Obviously, there was some possibility of cross pollination with this arrangement but each floor had a floor monitor who tried to keep some sense of order.

He had to sign in as a 'visitor' and they went to her room. It was a small room, just large enough for two beds, a couch and a desk with two chairs. It also had two closets and they even had a small bathroom area with a shower stall. A small TV was on a shelf next to small refrigerator.

"Wow. You even have your own bathroom." He was amazed at how nice the dorm room was.

"That's one of the reasons Joan and I came for the summer semester, we got our pick of the dorm rooms." She looked around but Joan was not in. *"Can I get you something?"* They did have a small refrigerator. *"We don't have much, but I think there is a Coke we could share."*

"You sure the caffeine won't keep you up?" He asked.

"It is decaffeinated."

"Ok...sure, why not." He sat on the couch and looked at their posters. Apparently, Joan was a fan of hard rock groups with several posters on her side of the room. Sue's side had a single picture of small, tropical Island with a sail boat and clouds in the distance. The island had three palm trees growing on it but otherwise was very small.

She brought over the Coke with two straws and sat next to him on the couch. It was a medium sized couch, so three could just sit on it comfortably. She sat close to him and shared the Coke. He put his arm around her. Somehow the Coke got placed on the floor and they began to kiss. He started to unbutton her blouse but she pushed his hand away.

The door opened; it was Joan. *"Oh, hi you two"*, she had a bag of what appeared to be some snacks and drinks. *"You guys want some chips?"* she asked, totally aware that she had broken up their necking session.

"Hi Joan." Sue replied, happy to see her roommate. *"We were just celebrating completing our term papers for psychology."*

"Yeah, I could see you were celebrating." Joan said with a smirk.

"Maybe I should leave?" Ron was hoping to spend a bit more time with Sue on the couch but did not want an audience.

"No, stay. You don't have to leave just because I'm here." Joan walked over and sat down on the other side of Ron on the couch. *"We are all friends here. What did you kids do tonight?"*

"Just dinner and a movie." Sue said, getting up to get some chips. *"Excuse me a minute."* She went into the bathroom, closing the door behind her.

Joan turned to Ron. *"Are you treating her nice?"* in a low stern voice.

Ron was surprised at this. *"Yes, I think so. She is the most wonderful girl I have ever met."* Ron blushed a bit.

"Well ok. But if you hurt her…" Joan growled, looking at him.

"Believe me, the last thing I want to do is hurt her." Ron looked up as Sue left the bathroom. She stopped at the snacks and brought a bowl of chips over for them to share. She had turned on the little TV but it just looked like one of those stupid reality shows. After about a half hour, Ron got up to leave. Sue escorted him to the door.

"Sorry about the movie," he said looking into her eyes.

"It's ok. Maybe we can try again another time?" She smiled at him. He turned to leave but she stopped him and they kissed goodnight. It was a short kiss; Joan was watching.

He made it down the stairs and headed back to the parking lot. He felt elated. *I really like her a lot,* he thought to himself. *He never had felt this way with Monica. Monica would get upset easily over small, insignificant things and he could never understand it. Towards the end of their relationship Monica told him he was a loser and terrible in the sack. She had a way of making you feel miserable.*

CHAPTER 21

BOB WOKE UP AGAIN. He looked around the room. It was empty except for a couple of chairs, and a hospital monitor that was recording his heart beat and oxygen level. He was almost totally paralyzed now. He could see and hear and sometimes talk but could not move his arms or legs. There was a tube in his nose, he was unsure if it was for food or oxygen. They were probably feeding him intravenously, he suspected. His left eye was blurry and he could not clear it by blinking. So, this must be the end, he thought. Maybe better to just get it over with. Maybe he could ask them to overdose him with morphine to just end it. Jack had said maybe 6 months. It was only his fourth month. The thing in his head must have grown to be enormous by now. Sarah still stopped by every day to see him. She was being faithful to the end. How did it go, 'till death do us part?' He wished it was over, did not consider what he was experiencing as living.

Bob wondered why he could still think normally. The thing in his brain was wrapped around his cerebellum and was invading the cerebrum, but obviously had not yet invaded the frontal lobe where most of the personality and thought processes occur. At least that is what Jack had told him. If they had operated months ago he probably would have ended up as a paraplegic like he was now. Bob's decision to just let it run the course had allowed him at least some time for the Hawaiian vacation. He had really enjoyed that vacation. He knew Sarah was happy to finally see Hawaii. She had talked for years of wanting to go there on a vacation but he always had some sort of work project that was on a critical schedule so he never had the time. They did take a couple of short vacations, and a 3-day cruise in the Bahamas. When the kids were young they drove to Washington DC for a few days and visited the Smithsonian. They had a weekend visit to Gettysburg; a short trip to Dayton to see the Air Force Museum. Once they had all flown out to Las Vegas and rented a car to go to California to see the

Giant Redwood trees and came back through Death Valley in the middle of August. The kids hated that. It was 117 degrees in the shade and he could not use the air conditioner since the car would overheat. So, they had several small vacations but never much time for anything else. He regretted it now, but of course it was too late. His life was over and he wished he had spent more time with his family.

The Reverend Morton had stopped in to see him again. Bob had asked him if Protestants had last rites like in the Catholic Church. The Reverend said they did not do the ritual like the Catholics. The Reverend asked if he would like a Catholic priest to come and visit. Bob said no, he did not need that. Then he and the Reverend said a few prayers together. Bob mostly did this so that the Reverend would feel appreciated. After all, the man did travel all the way over to see him, and he probably had a very busy schedule. Bob did not think there really was an afterlife, but what the heck, it did not hurt to say some prayers. If there was a heaven maybe he would be welcomed. After all, he had never really done anything bad in his life, tried to be a good provider to his family and never strayed away from Sarah for another woman, even though he had had several opportunities to do so.

CHAPTER 22

IT WAS THURSDAY. RON and Sue had turned in their term papers and were leaving psychology class. The midterm exam was next week. Ron was thinking maybe they could have a study session to review the material.

"Are you really going to the party at the frat house tomorrow?" He walked with her down the hall. Joan was walking with them, listening to their conversation.

"Yes, I think it might be fun." She smiled at him. "Do you want to go with me?"

"Well, I don't normally go to frat parties but I guess so." He grimaced. A lot of the football players would be there and he definitely was unpopular with them for dropping out of football. But if he was there with Sue it might not be that bad.

"Ok then. Can you pick us up around eight?" She meant herself and Joan.

"Joan is going with us, too?"

"Yeah she said she would not want to miss it."

"The Corvette only has room for one passenger. I'll have to get my winter car out." The Jeep Wrangler was in his paid garage. He did take it out occasionally in the summer but preferred the Corvette when the weather was warm. The frat house was located off campus and was a bit too far to walk.

"Ok, see you then." She walked off with Joan. They were always chatting about something. Little did he know that most of the time it was about him. Bob drove over to his garage and parked the Corvette. He kept the keys for both vehicles on one key ring that he always carried. The Jeep was a few years newer than the Corvette but still had more miles on it since he used it more months during the year than the Corvette. It was red colored just like the Corvette. For some reason he always liked red cars. It started right up and he drove home to the apartment. He spent some time that night studying for his Hydraulics class midterm.

CHAPTER 23

*I*T WAS FRIDAY. RON *parked the Jeep in the parking lot and walked to the dorm. He was dressed in his typical khaki slacks, white button-down shirt and blue blazer. He did not see any reason to wear a tie to the party, so he didn't. The girls were waiting for him. Sue was dressed in a low-cut striped blue blouse, white skirt that ended just above her knees and white shoes. Joan was slightly more conservative in a short sleeved red dress that was ankle length but was belted at the waist to accentuate her figure.*

"Wow, you girls look terrific," he said as they walked toward the parking lot. Sue held his hand as they walked. "You look pretty good yourself."

Joan smiled at him, "We really need to get back before 10 o'clock. We have a lot of studying to do this weekend for midterms."

"Yeah, you wouldn't think they would have a big party like this just before the midterms." He agreed.

The girls were both surprised at seeing the Jeep. "I thought Sue said you were a sports car enthusiast." Joan approached the vehicle. "I'll get in the back, so you two lovebirds can have the front."

"This vehicle will go through any type of snowy weather." Ron bragged as he opened the doors on the passenger side for both girls.

"Wow, he is a gentleman too." Joan remarked as she got into the back seat. Sue just smiled; she knew he was showing off a bit.

They drove over to the Tau Frat House and parked in the lot behind the house. The parking lot was large, but already almost full of different vehicles. The house was huge, at least three stories tall, painted white. The large Greek letters TψΩ were prominently displayed above the doorway. As they walked up to the door, a pledge opened the door for them but asked to see their invitations. Sue and Joan showed theirs but Ron didn't have one. The pledge hesitated but Sue said "he's with me." The pledge was taken aback by seeing the two very pretty girls and said it was ok.

They entered into a large 'Great Room' that was filled with about 40 people. There was a huge fireplace on one side of the room, with what appeared to be a bar on the other. There was a large keg of beer at the bar and several bowls of snacks. A pledge was serving beer in clear plastic glasses. There were a few couches and chairs along the outside of the room but the center of the room was bare. There were a few potted plants along the outside wall between the couches. The ratio of males to females in the room was about two to one. Soft music was playing in the background. It sounded like the Beach Boys.

Joan groaned. "Don't they have any good rock music?" she hissed.

Almost immediately, a short guy wearing a 3-piece gray suit came over to them. "Hello, I'm Jerry Baker, vice president of Tau Psi Omega. Please make yourself at home and enjoy the party." He could not take his eyes off Sue. She was by far the most beautiful girl in the room. They walked over to the bar area. Jerry followed them trying to engage Sue in conversation.

Richard Bass, the assistant football coach, looked up from the sophomore girl he was talking to and saw Sue and her companions enter. Shit! She brought that Pritchard guy with her. This might complicate things. He walked over to Shawn Taylor, the starting quarterback on the football team.

"Shawn, I need you to run interference for me. That Pritchard guy is over there. I need you to distract him for a while." Rick jerked his head toward the trio.

"Pritchard? Hey, he was that real good receiver we had a couple of years ago." Then he saw the girl with him. Wow, she was a looker. He looked knowingly at the coach and said, "Ok I can do that."

John Turley saw that Pritchard had arrived with the pretty girl. He needed to get Pritchard to back off so he could get a chance at the girl.

Shawn Taylor walked over to Ron, put his arm around him. "Hey buddy, long time no see. You got to meet a couple of guys over here." He pointed to a group of guys wearing football jerseys in the corner. Turley grinned at him and figured he would get Ron in an argument and then put him down. Then he could make a move on the pretty girl.

Ron looked at Sue with a sad look on his face. He did not want to leave her side just to talk with some jocks.

"Go ahead and talk to your friends. Joan and I can fend for ourselves," Sue said seeing the crowd in the corner. Ron reluctantly went with Shawn to talk to the football guys. He did not like leaving her unattended in this pool of barracudas.

Rick Bass walked to the bar and got two beers. He was wearing a two-piece suit and a tie tonight. He discretely removed a small bottle and poured some of it into one. He took a drink out of the other one to make sure he did not mix them up and walked up to Sue and Joan. Jerry looked at him and saw Rick give him the thumbs up signal. Jerry immediately transferred his attention to Joan. He was aware of Rick's reputation with girls and was not going to interfere since Rick was a football coach and the fraternity advisor. "I am so glad you could make it." He gave Sue the once over. She had on a short skirt, open toed white shoes. No pantyhose. Wow. This is going to be easier than I thought he said to himself. He gave her the glass of beer.

"I'm not 21," she said, offering it back to him.

"Hey, this is a private party. You don't want to be a party pooper. Just have one, it will make you relax." Yeah, she will relax alright, he thought. He looked at the clock. After about 10 minutes she would be putty in his hands.

"It does look like a nice party," she said as she reluctantly accepted the beer. "Ok."

He watched as she took a small sip. Yuck, she thought to herself, this stuff is terrible. Her palate was more accustomed to sweet soft drinks or tea. She smiled at him, trying to be nice. "So, what's with all of this," she pointed to all of the paddles nailed on the wall.

"Oh, those are used in the pledging ceremonies. Everyone has to make a paddle and we give out merits for creative design, demerits for poor designs." He moved closer, trying to look down her cleavage without being too obvious.

"How come some paddles are larger with several letters on them?" she asked innocently.

"Oh, those are records of pledge classes that made it into the brotherhood." The letters are the pledges initials." He replied. "Hey, I got to go talk with someone, I'll be right back."

She smiled as he left. She thought he was a bore, but harmless. She walked over to the bar and grabbed a handful of snacks. She looked to see if there were some soft drinks but could not see any. She looked around the room. Ron was still with his football friends but he was looking over in her direction. It appeared that some heated discussion had started and Ron now had his back to her. Their Psychology instructor was over there too and was telling a story or something about football. She simply smiled and turned to walk back toward Joan who was sitting on a couch talking to the guy named Jerry.

Rick Bass walked over to talk to Jim Taylor, the President of the Fraternity. After getting his attention, he asked: "Which is the Rose room tonight?" Rose was the code word for an open bedroom that consenting adults could use for sex. Rick took a look at Sue. Her glass was empty. He figured he had about five more minutes before the drug took effect. He had to get her away from her friend.

Jim looked at him hard. This guy was insatiable. Every time they had a party he would take some young lady upstairs. As ugly as he was, Rick seemed to have a way with the ladies. "The white room at the end of the hall," Jim said looking at the girl he had seen Rick talking to. Wow, she was a looker. How was this guy so successful? What was his secret?

"Thanks." Rick winked at him and went to the bar to get a couple more beers. He returned to Sue who was sitting on a couch next to the other girl, Joan. Jerry had been sitting next to them but got up to go do something when Rick came over. He sat next to Joan, giving each girl a beer. Hope you are having a good time," he said watching Sue carefully.

"By the way, which dorm are you staying in?" he casually asked Sue. "Oh, Joan and I are in Fredrick Hall, near the Student Union."

He told them that the Tau Frat house was basically made up of most of the football jocks on campus. He talked on and on about the football season. Sue was getting bored with him and was getting slightly drowsy. She yawned.

Rick took this as a sign that the drug had taken effect and asked Sue if she would like to see the Trophy room.

Sue got up and said ok. He guided her over to the stairs. "I have something I want to show you. It's really interesting." He whispered to her as he looked around to see if anyone was watching. Jerry was back talking to Joan and Ron was still with the football group in some sort of argument. The coast was clear so he guided Sue up the stairs. They walked down the hallway. At the end of the hallway was a room with a rose taped to the door. He opened the door and led her in and quietly locked the door behind him. It looked like a standard bedroom. Sue turned toward him with a funny look. Where were the trophies? He pushed her down on the bed. He lifted her skirt with one hand exposing her white cotton panties as he started to undo his pants with the other hand.

Rick had done this several times before. After a couple of drinks, he would select the prettiest and most innocent looking girl at the party and pour some GHB into her drink. That stuff made them zombies, and he would take them upstairs for some quick sex. The best thing about it was they did not remember anything about it. So far, the only time he almost got in trouble was the time that a sophomore nursing student got pregnant. The only thing was, she could not remember when or who she had had sex with. The frat guys knew he usually scored at the frat parties but did not know his secret. There was always one room open upstairs reserved for consenting adults that he could use. He would then take the girl back to her dorm after he had dressed her. It always worked like a charm.

Rick had grown up with an abusive mother. She had berated him on everything he tried to do. So, he generally stayed with his father who was a coach of a high school team. Rick was too skinny to play football but he paid attention to how his father coached the team. This eventually paid off for him as he became a coaching assistant and eventually an assistant coach.

He had a brief affair with a girl in college but she thought he was disgusting and told him so. Ever since then, he'd had an intense hatred for women and smart college girls. They were all lousy and treated him badly. So, he got even with them by screwing them when they were partially unconscious.

CHAPTER 24

BOB WOKE UP WITH a shock. The girl in his dream was in trouble and there was nothing he could do about it. Up till now everything was going pleasantly in the dream. Now it had taken a darker side. He wondered if the tumor was causing the dream to change so drastically. Was he hallucinating the whole story because of the tumor?

He was almost totally paralyzed now. He could hear people talking but could hardly form words of speech. His left eye was totally gone but he still could use his right eye. Something was wrong with his sense of smell. He used to be able to smell the antiseptic aroma when they cleaned his room but now, nothing. He could not move his head anymore, was totally numb from his neck down. He was having trouble breathing so they had hooked him up to a ventilator. He was still having the dreams. He wished he could have warned the girl in the dream but he had no control of the dream. It was as if he was watching a movie inside his head. Sarah still visited him every day but he could not respond to her anymore. The doctor had told her that he was still alive but was not sure for how much longer. He heard the doctor ask her if she wanted the machines keeping him alive turned off. She began to cry and said no, please keep him alive. He was disappointed at that. Why not let him go? This must be costing a fortune. His health insurance probably was picking up some of it. They had signed up for extended disabled care insurance years ago but that should be running out soon. Sarah's brother Tom had visited one time and came over to Bob and looked down at him. He said, "I guess you can't chase me away now," he grinned, and laughed.

He just wished it would end. It was terrible hearing people talk to him and not being able to respond. The respirator was keeping him alive. He hoped that the thing would break down so he could end this meaningless existence. He had never really discussed this with Sarah. He probably should have signed one of those DNR papers when he had the chance. If there was a God, he prayed for this to end.

He wanted to stay awake as long as possible. He did not want to see the pretty girl get ravaged by the bad man. He could feel himself drifting off again. He fought it for a while but soon gave up and drifted off to sleep again.

CHAPTER 25

*R**ON HAD BEEN SURPRISED** when Shawn Taylor came over and greeted him warmly at the party.*

"Ron, old buddy, how are you doing? There are some guys over here I want you to meet." Shawn pointed him toward some guys wearing football jerseys.

Ron looked at Sue. He did not want to leave her side.

"Go ahead and talk to your friends. Joan and I can fend for ourselves." She and Joan continued to walk to the other end of the room.

Shawn was explaining to the other players, most of them juniors, how good a receiver Ron was. One of the older guys, a senior, remembered him and asked how come he quit the team? Ron explained that he had injured his ankle at the end of the year and just didn't think he could help the team anymore. Actually, he quit because he did not like assistant coach Bass and wanted to spend more time on his coursework at the college. He didn't tell these guys that since they wouldn't understand. They continued to talk to him for a while. He was surprised that Shawn was so friendly; he had run into him on campus the year before and Shawn appeared to be upset that he had dropped out of football. "We need a good receiver; we could use you." Shawn had proclaimed before walking away mad. Gary Johnson, his Psychology teacher joined the group. He started to argue about this year's team with a couple of the players about the training program. Ron tried to back out of the conversation.

Ron was finally able to break away from the football jocks and looked around the room. He did not see Sue anywhere. Maybe she went to the restroom? He walked over to where Joan was sitting, talking to Jerry Baker on the couch. They were talking about movies they had seen.

"Have you seen Sue?" he asked, interrupting them.

Joan looked up at him. "She was just here a few minutes ago. She was talking to that football coach guy." Joan scanned the room but could not see Sue. Jerry did not say anything, just looked at the floor.

Ron was getting worried now. That asshole Bass was a slime ball, and he had heard some bad things about him. He walked around the room. Neither Sue nor Bass could be seen. This could be really bad. He was just about to go upstairs when he saw Sue coming down the stairs. He met her at the bottom of the staircase.

Sue looked at him. "You were right about that Bass guy. He just tried to rape me." Ron looked at her. "Are you alright?" His anger was showing. He looked upstairs as if to go up.

"Yes, I'm ok. But Ricky boy will not be rejoining the party soon. I kicked him so hard in the nuts he may have a hard time walking for a week." She yawned. "Ron, please take me back to the dorm. I am really tired."

When no one was looking she had poured the remainder of the beer Rick gave her into one of the potted plants. She really did not like the taste of beer.

They gathered up Joan who insisted upon giving her phone number to Jerry before leaving. "Are you sure you are ok?" Ron was concerned since she was so tired.

"Yeah...Just...fine," Sue leaned on him as they walked to the Jeep. He told Joan about the attempted rape and what Sue did to Rick.

Joan asked her if she needed anything, concerned that Sue was starting to slur her words. "Nope. But don' ever go with that Ricky guy, he is not verrry nice."

Joan looked at Ron and Ron looked back at her. "I think he may have drugged her." He was obviously angry. When they got back to the dorm, Ron more or less carried Sue up the two flights of stairs to her room. When they were inside, he put Sue on her bed and she kicked off her shoes and closed her eyes and fell asleep.

"What are we going to do?" Joan asked, meaning about the attempted rape.

Ron looked at Sue and then at Joan. "I guess she could fill out a complaint, but he might fill out a complaint that she assaulted him. Let her sleep this off and she can decide tomorrow." Ron moved toward the door.

"It serves him right. I hope the guy is permanently damaged." Joan was covering Sue up with a blanket.

Ron looked down at Sue and still had some residual anger. He should have protected her better. He said good night to Joan and left. He figured he might have some unfinished business to complete with Rick Bass about all of this. He drove to his apartment. He was so angry he couldn't sleep. He thought about going over to the campus police to report the incident but it was late and he was tired. It appeared to him that Rick Bass may be the one who was attacking all of the young girls. He needed more evidence. He would talk to George Coleman tomorrow to tell him what had happened.

CHAPTER 26

ROBERT WAS AWAKE AGAIN, but he was not sure that he really was awake. He now had no contact with the world around him. He could not feel anything or move anything. It was as if he was floating in a cloud. There was some pain but he was not sure where it was coming from. Maybe he was already dead he thought. But should there be pain? He wondered if this was the afterlife. He had heard stories of people moving towards a light when they had a near death experience. He could not see any light. There was just nothingness.

"Doctor, can you tell if he is still alive there?" Sarah asked, concerned.

The doctor was the nursing home doctor and he had seen plenty of cases like this. "Well, his heart is still beating and there is still brain activity. I would say that he is in a coma." The doctor was looking at the monitor that recorded Bob's heartbeat. The steady thrum of the ventilator as it pushed oxygen into Bob's lungs and the steady low beeping of the monitor were the only other sounds in the room.

"How long will he be like this?" She clenched her hands together.

"It is hard to tell. Could be a day, could be a couple of weeks." The doctor looked at the woman. The man on the bed was her husband, the only man she had ever loved and she did not want to let him go. There was nothing they could do for him. He wanted to disconnect the ventilator and end the man's misery but Sarah would not allow it. He could not do it without her permission. He needed her permission to pull the plug. It could not last much longer, he thought.

"I would consider recommending that you stop the ventilator and let nature take its course." He counselled Sarah.

"But he still has brain activity." She stated. "So, there is a chance he may recover from the coma, right?" she asked.

"Yes…It is a possibility. I can understand your feelings toward your husband," he replied.

"As long as the insurance continues to pay, we wait," she stated. She did not care for this doctor. "OK," he responded, and turned to walk out of the room.

Sarah was not going to give up on Robert. She felt that with enough prayer, God would respond and bring him back to her. She sat down on the chair by the bed and took out some knitting she was working on.

CHAPTER 27

*R*ON GOT UP EARLY *and skipped breakfast. He needed to visit Sue to see how she was doing. He got in his car and drove over to the dormitory. He wanted to know how Sue was recovering.*

Sue was dressed in jeans and an old shirt and sitting on her bed when Joan let him in.

"How are you feeling today?" he asked Sue as he came into the room and sat next to her and held her hand.

"Well, I have a slight headache, but otherwise I'm ok." Sue replied.

"I wanted to know if you wanted to press charges against that guy at the party." He knew his buddies on the campus police department would want to know about this. This could start a scandal for the assistant football coach.

"I remember kicking him really hard, but after that everything is kind of blurry. It was sort of a reflex, actually. He pushed me down on a bed and started to undress me." Sue looked at the floor. There was nothing to be ashamed of, but she still felt foolish for getting into that type of situation. She was almost too embarrassed to talk about it.

"Well, I heard that the assistant football coach had a bad accident at the Frat house and had to be taken to the hospital." Joan informed them. Jerry had called to tell her.

"Good, I was planning on visiting him." Ron growled.

"If they took him to the hospital, maybe they had to amputate?" Joan smiled.

"Well, there is a small chance that he might claim that Sue assaulted him. I think you ought to get your complaint in first." Ron was looking at Sue but she was blushing.

"I feel so stupid." Sue started to cry. "I don't want anyone to know."

"Don't feel bad. I think he drugged you with a date rape drug." Ron was remembering how sleepy she became after she came down

the stairs. "I am surprised that it did not affect you more after than it did.

"He gave me a beer to drink. But I hate the taste of beer. I took one sip and then when no one was looking dumped it into one of the potted plants," she confessed.

"That probably saved you from being raped," Ron concluded. "I think I will go over to see Rick at the hospital." He got up to leave.

"I am so sorry." Sue was remorseful. She was more upset that Ron probably thought she was such a naïve, ignorant, stupid girl. He probably would not want to date her now.

"Don't be. You were a victim." He started to walk to the door.

He was still mad, but controlled, as he left the building. He drove over to the campus hospital. Since the college had a full nursing program, it contained a hospital on campus. It was a small hospital, only two stories high but it had a full emergency room and surgical ward. He parked and walked to the entrance. He inquired at the desk what room coach Bass was in. The girl at the desk told him and he walked upstairs to the patient ward.

He walked into the room. Coach Bass was lying in bed and had an IV in his arm. "Hello, Asshole" Ron started.

"Pritchard, you bastard. Your little bitch almost ruined me," Coach started.

"Well, you aren't going to be so well off after they charge you with attempted rape." Ron looked down on him. "They won't want you to be a coach anymore."

"Hey, she attacked me." Bass complained.

"Yeah, after you put drugs in her drink and tried to rape her." Ron smirked. "We are having an analysis of the drug being done right now," Ron lied.

"Hold on, hold on..." Bass looked at him intently. "I can't stand that type of publicity." The college dean would insist that he be fired.

"Then resign and leave the campus and we won't prosecute." Ron had an evil look in his eyes.

"Also, if you leave, you won't run into me in some dark alley when you aren't expecting it. What she did to you will seem like nothing when I get done with you." Ron fantasized catching him in an alley with a baseball bat.

Richard Bass could see Ron was not kidding. He did not doubt that Ron meant it. He could probably get some of the guys on the team to maybe rough Ron up, but if word got out he was raping girls they might beat him up instead. "Ok. I will leave as long as you don't tell anyone." He was thinking of leaving anyway, had an offer of a coaching position at a junior college a couple of states away. There were always ways to find and score more stupid young females.

"Then you better do it soon or I will have no choice but to press charges. I have some friends in the campus police department and they would really love to get their hands on the guy who has been drugging and raping coeds," Ron bluffed.

Rick knew he had no choice. "OK, as soon as I get out of here."

Ron left the hospital. He felt a little bit better but would have felt a lot better if he beat the shit out of the guy. He would have to try to cheer up Sue. He hoped she would still want to date him.

He stopped outside the hospital and had a thought. If Bass got away clean, he would start preying on more young girls. Ron couldn't let that happen. He felt he had to do something even though he had promised not to do something to Rick.

He walked over to the Campus Police office. George was sitting at a desk filling out a report on traffic violations.

"Hi George."

George looked up. "Ron. How are you? What brings you to see us?"

"I just heard about an attempted rape at the Tau Frat House last night. I thought you might be interested." Ron was smiling at him.

"Really! Well tell me all about it." He pushed the paperwork aside.

"I understand some coed was drugged and somebody tried to have sex with her but she kicked him real hard in the nuts."

"Do you know who it was?"

"Rumor has it the guy was taken to the hospital here on campus."

"Wait a minute…you don't mean Coach Bass?" He remembered patrolling by the hospital when an ambulance arrived and Rick Bass was taken into the emergency room Friday night.

"Could be. An enterprising policeman could check the guy's closet in the hospital and maybe find a vial of date rape drug in his

pocket." Ron suggested.

"Wow this could be a big scandal." The dean of the college would not like that, George thought. "How did you hear about it?"

"I was at the party and happen to know the girl who was drugged." "Well, I need probable cause to do a search warrant."

"The girl involved doesn't want the publicity." Ron said firmly.

"Maybe the rumor is enough to let me talk to him." George got up and put on his patrolman cap.

"Well, you didn't hear it from me, ok?"

"Sure. But I can talk to the Frat guys to see what they say happened."

"Thanks." Ron walked out of the police office. He hoped they crucified the guy. Ron couldn't stand the thought of letting Rick go somewhere else to prey on more young girls. He felt bad about lying to Rick about not saying anything but he could not just let him go free.

CHAPTER 28

*B*OB WAS DRIFTING AGAIN. The only way he could determine if he was awake or asleep was that the dreams stopped when he was conscious. These periods were getting shorter and shorter.

The doctor was watching his chart. He could see that there were periods of low brain activity followed by periods of relative activity. He figured that Bob was in a coma. Still, the wife did not want to pull the plug yet.

Although the man had given power of attorney to his wife, he had not signed a 'Do Not Resuscitate' form. The nursing home was supposed to continue servicing this guy until he died of natural causes. As long as the wife continued to keep going he would do as she wanted. The doctor made some notes on the medical chart at the foot of the bed and left.

CHAPTER 29

IT WAS TUESDAY. RON had spent the weekend studying but had made an effort to stop to see Sue both on Saturday and Sunday. She was somewhat quiet and reserved, obviously still somewhat upset about what had happened. She did not want to leave the dorm, so he had not pressed her to. He had not seen her on Monday but was hoping to see her in class today.

Ron walked into the student union and ordered an iced tea. He walked out to the veranda and saw that Sue and Joan were sitting at a far table with that guy Jerry from the Frat house. He walked over and joined them. Sue was wearing a gray shirt and an old pair of blue jeans. She had her hair pulled back in a ponytail and was wearing glasses. Even wearing old clothes with no makeup, she looked really beautiful, Ron thought.

"Hello," he started. He looked at Jerry who was obviously upset. Joan had just told him what had happened to Sue. Ron sat down with them. Sue looked at him but did not smile.

"I am really sorry." Jerry looked at Ron. "I should have told you that Rick had taken her upstairs." "You knew about this?" Ron's voice was getting a little bit angry.

"Well, I knew he usually scored at these parties but I didn't know he was drugging girls. All the Frat guys usually stayed out of his way."

Ron nodded, "Ok, I can see where you might not know about the drugs. One thing that puzzles me, how did he get the girls out of the Frat House once they were semi-comatose?" Ron was calming down a bit.

"There is a back stairway that leads down to the kitchen. The back door to the parking lot is just off the kitchen. One time I was in the kitchen getting snacks and I saw him come down, carrying a girl to the back door. I asked him if he needed help, but he told me the girl had had too much to drink and he was taking her home. I never really thought too much about it." Jerry confessed.

"That explains why some young girls are found asleep at the doorstep of their dormitories by the campus police department." Ron noted.

"Well, I am really sorry about this. I did hear this morning that the assistant football coach resigned and was leaving for a different college." Jerry sounded fearful of Ron.

Joan leaned over and put her hand on Jerry's. *"You didn't know, don't feel bad."* It was apparent that Joan and Jerry might be becoming an item.

Ron looked at his watch. It was almost time to go to Psychology class. *"Can I walk with you to class?"* he asked Sue.

"Sure, if you want to." She was hoping that they still had a connection. They got up to leave. Joan stayed behind with Jerry. Sue was holding her books close to her chest. She was still feeling low about what happened at the party.

"You know…I still owe you a movie." Ron started, hoping to cheer her up. *"Can you break away from your studies tonight?"* he asked.

"You sure you still want to go out with me?" She asked meekly. She had been afraid that Ron would not want to date her anymore.

"More than anything. I think there is a good picture playing over at the multi-theatre. We won't go back to the one down town." He was hoping to lift her spirits. *"See you about six?"*

"Ok." She smiled at him. Maybe he still liked her.

A few tables away John Turley sat with his buddy Reggie. He had heard what had happened to the coach. If this girl was a karate expert or something, he would have to be careful.

Ron and Sue got to class. Their graded term papers were handed out. Ron looked at his, He got a 'B+'. Sue showed him hers, she got an 'A'. Ron was at a loss to explain why he did not get an A but was happy that she did. Apparently the instructor liked shorter essays without as much detail.

They took the midterm test. Ron thought it was easy and breezed right through it. When he looked up from the test, Sue was already handing hers in. How could she do it faster than he did? He checked a couple of more answers and then walked up to turn his paper in.

Gary Johnson looked up as Ron turned his paper in. *"I heard you had a run in with Rick Bass?"* he said smugly.

Ron was taken off guard. "We just had some words is all," he said defensively.

"Well, the idiot had it coming to him. I really did not like the way he treated some of the players." He looked intently at Ron. "He quit the team this morning."

"Sorry if it hurts the team." Ron turned to go.

"No. it left a coaching position open. I was offered that position, so it worked out good for me." Gary smiled.

Ron turned back. "Well, I think that will be an improvement for the team." Ron smiled back at him. He walked outside. Sue and Joan were waiting for him. He walked with them back to the Student Union.

"Don't you have another class?" he asked Sue.

"Yes. It starts in about 15 minutes. I suppose I should go." Sue walked off. Joan told her she would follow in a couple minutes. Joan sat down with Ron at a table.

"Is she ok?" He asked Joan.

"Yes. I shouldn't be telling you this, but I should warn you, she thinks she is in love with you." Joan looked at him hard. "If you intend to hurt her, I will be very upset."

"Don't worry. I think I am falling in love with her too. But don't tell her that, " Ron confessed.

Joan smiled. "Well, she is young and naïve about some things."

"I would protect her if I could. But she seems to be able to handle herself fairly well. I see you and Jerry are maybe…" He left it open.

"He is a nice guy. Not too bright but nice. We are just acquaintances." Joan assured him.

"Well maybe we could double date sometime?" Ron offered, figuring it would be good to get Joan on his side.

"I would like that." Joan smiled. Maybe Ron was ok after all. She hoped so for Sue's sake. "Well, I have to go to class too." She ran toward the Economics building.

Ron was elated to hear that Sue might be falling in love with him. He felt the same way about her. She was three years younger than he was, but she seemed so much more of a vital, vibrant woman than Monica had ever been. They had not known each other very long so he was cautious about getting too involved. But he felt that they had more than a physical attraction for each other.

It appeared to be something much deeper than that. He found that he wanted to be with her all of the time.

John Turley and Reggie got up from their table and followed Joan. They did not do anything, just watched her entering the economics class.

CHAPTER 30

*R*ON PICKED SUE UP *around 6:00. They went to the small bistro again and had a couple of specialty salads that Sue really liked. She was wearing a blue blouse with a white skirt and was still wearing glasses and had her hair in a ponytail. She was not using any makeup but Ron did not mind. He thought she looked beautiful. They made small talk, not really discussing the events of Friday. Afterwards they went to see a new release movie that was about a woman social worker who was working in Africa to help starving children as a civil war was raging. It was not really Ron's type of movie but Sue seemed to enjoy it. He suggested that they stop by his apartment and she agreed.*

"Did you like the movie?" he asked as he drove the Jeep back to his place.

"Yes, I thought she was a real hero." Sue noted. She was surprised that Ron selected that show, she knew that most guys liked action movies. Her brothers had taught her that.

"Well, I read a review of that one and it sounded interesting," he confessed. Actually, he had seen that particular actress in several movies and really liked watching her. When they reached his place, the lights were out downstairs, the landlord and his wife must be out, Ron thought. He escorted her upstairs and they sat on his couch.

"Would you like something to drink?" he asked.

"Just some water please." She did not even want to think about drinking alcoholic drinks for a while. He brought her a bottle of water, but he had a beer.

"I like beer," he said, apologizing. He sipped the beer while she took a drink from the water bottle. "That's ok. I don't think I'll have one of those for a while." She blushed.

He sat next to her and they started some serious necking. He kissed her hard and she responded. He moved his hand up her leg under her skirt but she pushed his hand away. It was a subtle notice to him that anything more would have to wait. After a while he broke off and turned to her. "I want you to know that I am falling for you. I would like to go steady with you." He felt funny saying that but was not sure she was ready for anything serious yet.

"I feel the same way about you," she whispered. She wanted him more than ever but did not want to move to the next step yet, either. She kissed him again. "I think I love you." she whispered.

Wow, Ron thought. This is too good to be true.

She looked at the chess set on the sideboard. "Do you play chess?" she asked.

"Well, I was city champion in my senior year of high school." He blushed.

"But you weren't in the chess club at high school?" she asked. She had joined chess club and had no trouble beating all of the boys in the club.

"No. I always had football practice." He looked at her and smiled. "You want to play a game?" "Set it up," she said enthusiastically.

They sat at the table with the chess board. He tried the standard Queen Pawn Gambit since not many people knew how to answer it. He found that she did know the answer and soon had him pinned down. He struggled defensively to stop her offense, but she always had another move and it surprised him. Finally, he gave up and surrendered. He saw she would checkmate him in another three moves.

"Wow. Where did you learn to play like that?"

"My grandpa taught me to play when I was young. Later I played a lot in the chess club at school." "Well, you should get rated by the chess federation. You are really good." He was very impressed.

"I never thought much about it. It is an easy game to play." She said, hoping she had not bruised his male ego.

"Well, I guess I should get you back to the dorm. It's getting late," he said reluctantly. "Yes." She got up and straightened out her skirt.

"Can I cook you a meal sometime this week? He wanted another excuse to bring her to his place.

"You can cook?"

"Well...I can make a respectable spaghetti dish," he confessed.

"That sounds good to me. How about on Thursday?" she offered.
"It's a date." He smiled.

He took her back to the dorm. He really liked this girl a lot. He wanted to be with her and make love to her but that could wait. He could wait until she was ready. He would never force himself on any girl. Girls were magnificent and amazing creatures and he just liked being with them. The physical size of the male body to the female body obviously dictated that males would be the aggressor, but he had always lived by a code that if the lady was not interested then he would not push the issue. He had an affair with Monica, but she never really seemed to want him for the long term. He was just somebody she could use while she looked for something better. Sue appeared to be totally interested in him and that excited him much more than Monica ever had.

CHAPTER 31

"**D**OCTOR, IS HE STILL alive?" Sarah asked the attending physician. "Yes, he is hanging in there but he definitely is in a coma. Dr. Debra Miller was sorry that Sarah was losing her husband. The other doctor was not here today.

"Is there any chance he will ever wake up again?" The medical costs were starting to mount up. The long-term disability insurance was almost totally gone.

"There is a possibility." The doctor said reluctantly. She was not a proponent of euthanasia. She was deeply religious and felt that God would end a life when it was necessary. In this case she doubted that it would be much longer but she could not tell that to the wife.

"All we can do is wait and see." The doctor said. "Yes," Sarah Agreed.

Bob, of course, did not hear any of this. He was totally unresponsive to the world outside his body and just kept on dreaming.

CHAPTER 32

RON PICKED UP SUE at the dorm on Thursday night and brought her to the apartment. He cooked a spaghetti dinner with a salad and bread. She was wearing the sexy black dress that she had worn on their first date. He noticed that she had stitched up the rip in the seam. He was in his typical khaki pants and white shirt. He did manage to get some spaghetti sauce on it, but did not care. She was kidding him about it, but he told her it was a cook's preference if he wanted to decorate his shirt. He also had offered her some red wine although he was not sure that she would drink any. The spaghetti and meatballs turned out ok and Sue was laughing at his jokes. He offered her some wine and she tried it. It turned out she liked wine. So, they ate the meal and then later they transferred to the couch.

"You should take that shirt off and soak it before that stain sets," she told him. "Are you trying to get me undressed?" he said, jokingly.

"Would that be so bad?" she teased.

He took off the shirt and hung it on a chair by the desk. They started to neck and he was amazed at her passionate kissing. This time she let his hands explore her body. She was becoming aroused. He knew that he did not want to force anything but he was getting aroused himself. She could tell that his body was becoming ready. He was hoping that the wine he gave her had not released her inhibitions past where she wanted to be.

"Wow," he croaked. "We should probably cool it before something gets out of hand." "Would that be so bad?" she whispered.

"No. But I want you to be sure," he whispered. He didn't want her if the wine made her careless. He had to ask "Are you a virgin?"

She paused, looked at him and then said "Yes."

He pulled away from her. This was a completely different situation than he imagined. She was nineteen years old and still a virgin? He had to reevaluate the situation. If she was a virgin, he would have to think in terms of a permanent relationship. Her first time should be special, not a quick slam bam and thank you ma'am, let me take you home. He could not do that to her. Not that a permanent relationship was a bad idea. He really thought he loved her but was not ready to formulate any thought of marriage yet.

"Uh...we better get going, it is getting late." He got up and went to the closet to get another shirt.

She was puzzled. She had finally worked up the nerve to have him make love to her and he had backed away. She was disappointed, but in a sense she was relieved. She had fought off other boys in high school who just wanted to bed her and forget her. Ron obviously was unlike those boys.

"Ok," she said and got up to go.

They went downstairs and got into his jeep. He started the car but did not put it in gear.

He looked at her. "Do you think you could be happy married to an engineer?" he postulated.

Sue looked at him with adoring eyes. "My grandfather was an engineer. He made a pretty good living. But he died when I was really young."

"Well, I have to finish college, find a job. It's a lot of time before I can get to that point." Ron put the car in gear and backed out into the street.

"It is good to have a plan." She agreed, smiling at him. Did he just propose to her? She did not think so. She could follow his line of reasoning.

When they got to the dorm, he walked with her to the entrance. They stopped and he kissed her again. It was a long passionate kiss and passing girls snickered as they entered the dorm.

"I will see you later?" Ron asked. "How about we go to the park on Saturday and have a picnic? We could invite Joan and Jerry to go with us." He wanted to keep his promise to Joan about the double dating.

"Ok." She was happy to go with him anytime now. He had the perfect opportunity to take advantage of her and didn't. She entered the dorm and went to her room on the third floor. Joan was in the room, watching their small TV.

"How did the date go?" Joan asked, turning off the TV. Sue wanted to tell her. "We almost made love tonight."

"Really. You had to fight him off?"

"No. I wanted to do it but he stopped when I told him I was a virgin."

Joan had long suspected that Sue had not crossed that line but they had never discussed it. "Are you kidding me? All guys want to get a virgin. That is like the 'numero-uno' thing for them."

"Why do you think he backed off?" Sue inquired.

"Well, he must think you are special. Some guys, the good ones, are like that. It sounds like he must really love you."

"You think so?" Sue was hoping this was true.

"I think you got him hooked. All you got to do is reel him in." Joan replied, hugging her.

Sue thought about this. She wasn't going to college to get a husband. She intended to get a degree and become an Art teacher. But she was in love and it was hard to think of a future without him in it.

She told Joan about the picnic and wondered if Jerry would agree to it. Joan said it was a great idea and called Jerry to tell him he had to go to a picnic this weekend. Joan was obviously in control of their relationship.

CHAPTER 33

*R*ON, SUE AND JOAN *were back in class. The graded midterm exams were handed out by Gary Johnson. He said he was in a hurry today and gave out the next chapter to read and then he had to leave early. Since their instructor had been appointed to the top football assistant coach position, he had a lot more things to do on his schedule.*

"Wow," Joan said. "We get out early today. What did you get on your Midterm exam? I got an 85, a solid B."

Ron looked over at Sue's paper. Damn. She got a 96! He only got an 88! "Wow, Sue, you must really be smart," he proclaimed.

"I always have gotten A's," she said. She was puzzled why she missed a question. Looked at the question and realized it was a trick question that could have two or three different answers.

"Well. We have some time to kill before the next class." Joan got up and gathered her things. Sue said "Want to go to the student union for a coke?"

"Sure." Ron got up, putting the paper in his notebook. "Come on Sue. I'll treat you." "Ok." Sue and Joan got up and followed him out.

Ron got next to Sue and said, "Sorry about last night. I almost went too far."

"That's alright" she said, smiling at him. She realized that he respected her. The wine sort of put her in the mood but he did not take advantage of her when he could have.

They were sitting on the veranda. Sue and Joan were each drinking a Coke but he reverted to an iced tea. They were discussing the assignment and Ron was about to ask Sue if she had considered the picnic he had discussed. They could go to the City park by the lake. He was wondering if Joan and Jerry would join them. He started to talk about having the picnic when someone came at him from behind. It was Monica, a medium-height red headed girl wearing a black frilly blouse and tight-fitting black leather pants. She put her arms around him.

"Hello lover boy," Monica cooed as she bent down and kissed him on the lips. "What…" he pulled away from her, stunned.

Both Joan and Sue looked at them, wide eyed.

"Come on with me and let's go have some fun!" Monica exclaimed as she pulled at him. "And get away from these children." She looked at the two freshman girls with some malice.

"Monica…?" Ron was just realizing who it was. "What are you doing here?" He stood up, was somewhat surprised. "I thought…" He started to say as she kissed him again.

Sue could not believe her eyes. The man she was in love with was kissing this other woman. She got up and turned to leave. As Joan and Sue got up and left the table, Sue looked like she was going to cry. Jerry was walking to the table to join them when the two girls ran by him. He was puzzled at first but then he saw Ron arguing with some good looking redhead.

CHAPTER 34

SARAH SAT IN THE room with Bob. The only sounds were the ventilator as it pushed air into her husband's lungs and the heart monitor that beeped lightly with every heartbeat. She did not know what to do. She had talked to the Reverend Morton about the situation and he said she should let God determine Bob's fate. He said he had heard of people who had awoken from a coma after several years. He said it was not right to pull the plug on Bob. Jack Simms had told her just the opposite. That Bob would never come back and prolonging the inevitable was just cruel. She tended to believe Jack but could not bring herself to end Bob's life. She had been praying for him to recover and still hoped he would.

She believed in the power of prayer and that if she prayed enough God would answer. She sat down and took out her knitting. What had started out to be a scarf was turning into a blanket.

Bob still drifted in and out of consciousness, he did not understand what was happening to him. He felt like he was floating on a cloud somewhere. The dream was getting complicated. It looked to him that the boy and girl had a good relationship going until this other woman appeared out of nowhere. He was eager to see what would happen next. He wondered to himself, do other people in a coma have dreams like his? He started to drift off again. He wondered if they were putting drugs in his IV.

CHAPTER 35

*R*ON HAD STOOD UP *and faced the woman. "Monica...I thought we were done." Ron looked at her harshly. They were both standing by the table recently vacated by Sue and Joan. Ron looked for Sue but saw she and Joan were running toward the exit.*

Monica smiled at him. "Yeah, but it did not work out with Stan." Stan was the guy she had left him for. Stan had grown tired of her and her frequent temper tantrums.

"Why did you come to me?" Ron was still somewhat in shock.

"Well, you were fun to be with, driving that fancy sports car of yours, going to the best restaurants. You are sort of boring in bed though. By the way, I am pregnant. It could be yours', you know." Monica was lying about the pregnancy but she was sure that would bring him back under her control. She was too selfish to ever want to have a child and used birth control pills religiously to insure that would never happen.

Ron was shocked. They had sex a few times, but he had always used protection. He could never satisfy her it seemed. Finally, about the time she broke away from him he had realized she was just using him and had no real feelings for him.

"I can't be with you. I love someone else." He pushed her away. "And I know it's not mine if you are pregnant!"

"How can you be so sure?" She asked rather smugly.

"Look. If you want to run a paternity test I will agree to be tested. But otherwise, don't bother me anymore," he shouted.

Monica was shocked. Ron had always been a pushover and tolerated her control of their relationship. Now all of a sudden he had grown a backbone? "I thought you loved me." She pretended to start to cry.

"I did once, but not anymore." He turned to look for Sue and Joan but they had left the student union.

"I suppose you are in love with that cute little child?"

"She is more of a real woman than you will ever be," he spit back at her.

That comment really hurt. She moved forward and slapped him hard across the face.

He backed up a couple of steps. He staggered slightly and raised his fist to strike her back but then lowered it. "Thanks," he said as he walked away.

She grabbed the ice tea container on the table and threw it to the ground. "You can't talk to me that way!" she screamed after him. A lot of people saw this demonstration. Jerry Baker was one of them. She continued to scream, "You're a Loser." at him as he walked away. Everyone on the veranda was staring at them as he retreated.

Ron's cheek was red from the hard slap Monica had given him. He left the Student Center walked over to Fredrick Hall and climbed the steps to the girls' room. He knocked on the door. Joan answered the door but when she saw it was Ron, she tried to slam it in his face. He prevented that by putting his foot between the door and the door jam.

"We don't want to see you!" Joan screamed, trying to get his foot out of the door. "Let me talk to Sue, Please." Ron calmly pleaded.

"She doesn't want to talk to you." Joan hissed.

"It's not what you think. I don't even like that woman." Ron attempted to open the door again but Joan pushed it back.

"If you don't leave, I'm going to call the Campus Police." Joan threatened. "Ok. Ok. But this is all one big misunderstanding." Ron pulled back as the door slammed shut. He stepped away. The Hall monitor walked up to him and told him to leave at once or she would call the police. Dejected, he walked down the stairs and out to the parking lot. He started up the Jeep and drove it to his garage where he kept the Corvette. He changed vehicles and took the Corvette out on the thruway. Driving this car always calmed him down but this time he was really mad and pressed the accelerator all the way down. He started passing all of the cars on the road. He looked at the headsup display and saw he was going over 120 miles per hour. He slowed down. No sense in getting a speeding ticket tonight he thought. He got off at the next exit and turned around. He drove home at a sedate 10 miles per hour over the speed limit. After he got home he took out his phone and tried to call Sue. It went right to her voicemail. He left a message, trying

to explain to Sue that he did not care for Monica anymore and although they did have a fling a year ago, it was all over now. He had no feelings for the redhead and hoped she would understand.

"Well, there goes any plans for the weekend," he whispered to himself. He really felt bad now. He knew he was falling in love with Sue but now she would probably despise him. He walked to his desk and tried to review his assignment for the hydraulics class but could not concentrate. He went to the refrigerator and got a beer. He drank it down and then got another. That was the last one. He would have to go get some more. He grabbed the car keys and ran down the steps. He backed the Corvette out and squealed the tires taking off at high speed.

Back at Sue's dormitory Joan tried to console Sue. Sue would not talk to her, just sat in the corner crying. She saw that he tried to call her on the cell phone but did not answer it. How could he like that other crude woman? Was he dating both of them at the same time? Somehow it did not seem to be something Ron would do. Maybe she was wrong about him. Maybe he was just playing with her?

There was another knock on the door. "If he's back I'm going to call the police." Joan groaned as she got up to see who was at the door. It was Jerry, the boy she met at the frat party. She let him in, pleased that he remembered her dorm room number.

"Hi, Jerry." Joan greeted him. She stood in the doorway and blocked his view of Sue crying in the corner.

"Boy, you guys left before all the fireworks happened." Jerry exclaimed. "What do you mean?" Joan was curious.

"I was just about to join you at your table when that redhead grabbed Ron. After you left, he told her he was in love with someone else and to please leave him alone. She started screaming at him and hit him so hard I thought he was going to fall down. I thought he was going to hit her back but he just stood there and turned and walked away. She had a real hissy fit and started throwing things."

Sue was listening to Jerry's story and stopped crying. Maybe he really did not want the redhead? She took her phone and listened to his message. It appeared to her that she had misjudged him about the other woman. But why didn't he ever tell her about that bitch? She tried calling him back but there was no answer. She desperately needed to talk to him now.

CHAPTER 36

*R*ON WAS OUT OF *beer but wanted another. He drove the Corvette a couple of blocks from his apartment to a small tavern. He parked in front and went inside. He sat down at the bar and ordered a beer. He noticed a group of women sitting at a table near the front window. They appeared to be a lot older than the college girls he was used to seeing. The bartender was friendly. Ron put a twenty on the bar and ordered another beer. He was depressed and wondered if he would ever meet another girl like Sue.*

Ron was midway into his third beer when one of the women got up and walked up to the bar and sat down next to him. She was a platinum blond and wore a low-cut one-piece tight silver colored dress that ended about two inches above her knees. She had a sparkling necklace. She had on a lot of makeup. The other women at the table were watching them carefully.

"Hello." She smiled at him. "My name's Betty."

"Hi. I'm Ron." He looked her over. Maybe my luck is staring to change he thought. She was older but he was lonely and probably had lost Sue for good. Damn that Monica. The group of women looked like the local talent. He wondered what her price tag was.

"You wanna buy me a drink?" she asked, still smiling.

"I guess so. What would you like?"

She motioned for the bartender. He brought a martini one over and placed it in front of her. "She always drinks martinis." The bartender said as he took the twenty and walked to the other end of the bar.

"Is that your red Corvette parked out there?" she motioned at the car parked in front of the tavern. "Yes," he said "It's my summer car."

She sipped the drink as she looked at him. "Maybe you would like to take me for a ride," she said, not meaning a car ride.

"Well...sure, we could go for a ride. You like sports cars?"

"Not what I meant. You want to go to my place?"

"Well maybe..." He stopped talking as she pulled out a pack of cigarettes and a lighter and prepared to go with him.

"Excuse me. I have to get rid of some of this beer." He said as he got up and walked to the Men's room. Her being a smoker was an immediate turn off for him. He emptied his bladder and washed his hands. He had drunk about five beers in the last hour. He would have to be very careful driving home. He could already feel the buzz. Instead of walking to the bar where the blonde was sitting he walked to the door and left. There was a funny look of puzzlement on the blonde's face as she watched him leave.

He drove carefully back to the apartment and parked in the driveway next to his landlord's pickup truck. He managed to stagger up the stairs and into the apartment. It was still early but he took a shower and went to bed.

Ron woke up the next morning with a throbbing headache. He groaned as he rolled out of bed. Too many beers he thought. His cheek still had a vague outline of a handprint where Monica had hit him. It was Friday again but he did not have any classes today. He was hungry, not having any supper last night other than beer. He decided to walk down the street to a small diner where he sometimes ate. After a large ham and cheese omelet with home fries and a large glass of orange juice he began to feel better. He had turned off his phone yesterday so he decided to turn it back on. There were four messages from Sue. She probably never wanted to see him again. Rather than listen to her saying she never wanted to see him again, he put the phone in his pocket, paid the waitress and left to walk back to his apartment. He did not want to talk to anyone today, just rest up and maybe study for the hydraulics test.

When Sue could not reach him by phone she began to get worried. She had to confirm what Jerry had said even if it might hurt. Since it was Friday she did not have any classes so she put on her walking shoes and walked to his apartment. The red Corvette was in the driveway so he must be home. She climbed the stairs and knocked but there was no answer. The door was not locked. She looked around and decided she would open the door to see if he was home. She went inside. Ron was nowhere to be seen although the bed looked as if it had been slept in. She turned to leave. She closed the door and started to walk down the steps *when she saw him approaching on the sidewalk. She stopped at the bottom of the stairs sat down and waited.*

Ron turned the corner and walked up the driveway. He was still depressed so he was looking down and did not see Sue siting there on the bottom step until he was almost at the stairs.

"Oh…" He looked up and recognized her. She was wearing a bright pink blouse and blue jeans. She had her contacts in rather than wearing glasses.

"Hi," she said, trying to be casual. "I thought we needed to talk."

"Yeah…I'm really sorry about yesterday. I should have told you all about my affair with Monica last year. I just did not think it was important. I didn't want you to think bad of me because I was with her for a while. She doesn't mean anything to me, honest." He looked at the ground.

"I heard that you told her off and that she hit you." "Yeah." He blushed, "It was nothing."

"Jerry said he thought you were going to hit her back but that you didn't."

"I can't hit a girl," he said, looking at her. This was true; his moral code would not let him hit a member of the female sex except if one was actually trying to kill him.

"I tried to call you…but you didn't pick up." She was holding her phone.

"I figured you were going to tell me that you never wanted to see me again and I didn't want to hear that." He pulled out his phone.

"Well, I was worried about you so I came over to see you." She looked him in the eye.

"I'm glad you did. I was still hoping to go on a picnic in the park with you this weekend, maybe with Joan and Jerry."

"Jerry said that he heard you say you were in love with someone else?" She blushed a bit.

"Yes…I did say that. I suppose it's true. I'm afraid that I am falling in love with you." He looked at her, clasping his hands together. "And I was pretty sure that Monica had ruined that between us."

The look of relief on her face gave her away. "I love you too." She stepped up and kissed him. Ron had a wave of relief come over him as he kissed her back.

CHAPTER 37

*B*OB WAS AWAKE AGAIN. At least he thought he was. He really could not tell anymore. He had regained partial hearing in his left ear. He heard the swishing noise of the respirator and some muted voices in the background. He tried hard to concentrate on the voices but it was no use. He could not even grunt anymore. The dream was almost constant now. He figured that he must be drifting in and out of a coma-like state. He was hoping that they would turn off the machines that were keeping him alive. What he was could not be called living. He was sure that Sarah would not let him continue to suffer. He started to drift off again. He wondered again if they were giving him drugs.

CHAPTER 38

*I*T WAS SATURDAY. THEY were at the City park. Ron had sprung for the food for the picnic and Joan had gone to the store to purchase it. Ron and Jerry were throwing a Frisbee back and forth about 20 yards from the picnic tables. The girls were setting up a meal on one of the picnic tables.

"I have to thank you for filling the girls in on what actually happened." Ron quietly told Jerry. He could not have predicted that Jerry would tell the girls about his fight with Monica.

"I figured I owed you one after what happened at the party." Jerry replied, catching the floating disk and flipping it back to Ron.

"Well, I am in your debt." Ron caught the disk and threw it back. "Maybe you could put a good word in for me with Joan?"

"I think she likes you, Jerry. Just don't screw it up." "I'm not very good with girls." Jerry admitted.

"Just be honest. That's all they want. If you are kind and thoughtful, that also helps." He threw the Frisbee back.

"Hey you two...food's ready." Joan shouted at them.

They stopped the Frisbee play and walked over to the table. There was fried chicken, potato salad, baked beans and a lettuce and tomato salad. They had lemonade and iced tea to drink. Ron loaded up on the chicken and baked beans. He noticed Sue had a small piece of chicken and some of the lettuce salad. She noticed his look and explained "I never did like baked beans."

"Well, I love them." Joan exclaimed.

Ron walked over to the blanket Sue had put on the ground and sat down. He had grabbed some ice tea. Sue joined him while Joan and Jerry sat at the picnic table. It was partly cloudy and not too hot. The temperature was in the high 70s. "It is a perfect day for a picnic," Sue said when she sat next to Ron.

"This was a wonderful idea."

"I thought you might enjoy getting away from the dorm for a while," Ron said between bites of fried chicken.

"We only have 3 weeks left in the semester." Sue picked at her salad. *The Summer Semester was shorter in duration than the typical semester.*

"Yeah, we both have to write another term paper and then there are finals." Ron was not too concerned. He was carrying a solid B average in both classes. He probably would not make the Dean's list this semester, but he was getting closer to graduation. Three more courses in the Fall Semester and he was done. He would submit his resume to the aerospace company and hopefully get a starting position in engineering. He had it all planned out. But now he had to fit Sue into his calculations. He knew she wanted to finish college and become a teacher. But he did not want to lose her. So, he could continue to court her through the fall semester but then they would have to make a decision about their relationship. He could see himself proposing to her but it might not fit into her plans to get married until she was done with college. He wondered if he could wait an additional three years. What if she grew tired of him as Monica had and drop him for someone else? He'd had his heart broken once before. He did not want that to happen again.

"We have two weeks off between semesters, what do you plan to do?" She asked Ron casually. *"I suppose I will stay at my apartment. I don't have any other place to go."*

"You ever think about going back and visiting our home town?" she asked. *"Not really. I don't have anyone back there anymore."*

"Well, you could come home with me. My parents would love to meet you." She didn't want to push it. Her manic twin brothers were in middle school and normally tried to make her life miserable. If he was there with her she would have an excuse to get out and have some fun. Her brothers maybe would leave her alone if he was there or at least might be distracted by this older man. She also wanted to see how he would react in that environment. Her parents would definitely be surprised if they drove up in his Corvette. Maybe now they would pay more attention to her.

Good God! He thought. Meet her parents? I have only known this girl for five weeks and she wants to take me home to see her parents? He wondered if there was a nice way to get out of this situation.

"Well...I suppose. I could maybe drive you home and stay for a day or two," he managed, trying to cut down the exposure

time without disappointing her. "I don't want to be a burden on your family," he added. He pictured driving up in the red Corvette. He wondered if her father would be impressed.

"That's great," she exclaimed, and snuggled up next to him. They had finished eating and were lying back on the blanket, looking up at the passing clouds. Joan and Jerry went for a walk along the stream that meandered through the park.

Sue decided to attack. She rolled over onto him and they kissed. "You don't think I'm being too aggressive, inviting you to my house?"

"Well, it was unexpected, but it could be interesting," he managed to say. "Do you think I will get along with your dad?" He knew some fathers were really possessive about their daughters.

"He is my step-father and he never really cared much for me. My parents are more interested in my two idiot brothers."

"Well, at least you have a family," he said remorsefully.

They kissed for a while and then had to get up and clean up their picnic mess. Ron wondered if their relationship was moving too fast. Joan and Jerry returned. It really looked like Joan was falling for Jerry. After they packed up, Ron drove them back to the campus in his jeep.

CHAPTER 39

*B*OB WAS STILL IN a coma. Sarah still stopped by to see him every day. This time her brother Tom came with her. They sat in the room and listened to the ventilator continue to breath for Bob. Tom could not understand why his sister did not pull the plug on Bob. The guy was dead anyway, why prolong it?

"This is costing you $400 dollars a day. You could be investing that money." Tom started. "I have a buddy who has the inside line on a good stock. If you give me ten grand, I could double it for you in six months." Tom was pushing hard. His sister had access to a lot of dough and he needed cash badly. He had gambling debts to pay off and did not really care how he got the money. His sister was typically naïve about life but she had married well. Now that she was going to come into some money he should be able salvage some of it.

Sarah looked at Tom and finally realized that what Robert had been telling her about her brother was true. Tom was a parasite and a loser. He kept losing money in all sorts of get rich schemes. She did not say anything, just got up and left.

Tom looked at the ventilator apparatus. Maybe if he turned it off when no one was looking it would free his sister from making a decision. If Bob were gone, she could stop paying this place. The money she would save might end up in his hands. He looked around to see if the nurse was around. He did not see her. He walked over to the device but did not know how it worked. If he touched the wrong thing it might sound an alarm. Finally, he decided he would remove the tube from his mouth. He tugged on it but it was placed pretty firmly.

"What are you doing?" Jack Simms walked into the room.

"Oh, nothing. I thought this was loose but it appears to be ok." Tom stood back. "Are you one of the family?" Jack asked.

"Yeah, I'm Sarah's Brother."

"Well, don't be messing with that stuff." Jack looked at him.

This must be the deadbeat brother-in-law that Bob had told him about. "Where is Sarah?"

"I think she stepped out to get a coffee or something." Tom started to retreat to the door.

Jack just looked at him as he left the room. He wondered if the brother-inlaw was trying to do something bad here? He checked the chart and the readings. Everything was normal.

CHAPTER 40

*R*ON WAS STILL USING *the Jeep. He had invited Sue, Joan and Jerry to go with him to "Anthony's" Italian Restaurant for dinner. Sue was concerned about the cost to Ron. Ron had merely told her that he had gotten his trust fund check and wanted to celebrate. Ron drove over to the student union where they agreed to meet. He parked the Jeep and walked toward the student union. He saw George Coleman walking toward him in his police uniform.*

"Hi George," Ron said as he approached. "What's new?" He stopped to talk.

"Hello Ron. It appears you were right about Rick Bass. When I questioned him about the drugs he wouldn't admit anything but I could see he was lying. The guys at the Tau Frat house backed up your story. It appears he has been doing young girls for quite some time now."

"So...what are you guys going to do about it?" Ron asked.

"Well, we did not have any hard evidence on him without the witness. I understand that he has since skipped town."

"That's too bad." Ron was hoping they had other evidence without involving Sue.

"I think I should warn you...Rick said he was going to get even with you for turning him in. I pretended that I did not know what he meant, but apparently he believes you informed us."

"Oh boy...Well, I can't help that. At least he won't be preying on any more girls here." Ron said, shaking George's hand before walking away. This was disturbing. He did not know what Rick might do but it probably wouldn't be nice. He thought of Sue. Rick probably would like to get even with her for what she did to him. He walked to the student union with a faster pace.

Joan and Jerry were waiting for him at the entrance to the Student Union. Ron looked around for Sue. She was nowhere in sight.

"Have you seen Sue?" Ron asked Joan.

"She said she would meet us here. I am surprised she isn't here. She left the dorm before I did." Joan looked around.

"Maybe she had to go back to the dorm?" Jerry asked. "No. we would have passed her," Joan said, irritated.

"Well, she must have really done Mr. Bass some real damage. I saw he was limping around with a cane." Jerry said.

"You saw Bass?" Ron exclaimed.

"Yeah, he was limping between the dorm and the Student Union when I went up to get Joan." Jerry explained.

Ron took out his phone and tried to call Sue. It went right to voice mail. Then he called George. "George, Jerry said he saw Bass near Sue's dorm," he said as George answered.

"Is she the girl who put him in the hospital?"

"Yes. Maybe you should get over here." Ron was starting to worry. He turned off the phone. "What's the matter?" Joan asked.

"I think Rick Bass is going to try to hurt Sue." Ron pushed past her and started running towards Fredrick Hall. Joan and Jerry followed him.

CHAPTER 41

SARAH WAS VISITING BOB again. She was not going to give her brother Tom any money and had told him so when they had returned to her house. He flew into a rage and stomped out of the house, got into his old Chevy and drove away.

She was feeling vulnerable. Except for her children she was alone. Bob was still technically alive but God only knew for how long. She looked at Bob on the hospital bed. She wished he would wake up so she could talk to him. The reverend came in and greeted her.

"Sarah. How are you holding up?" Reverend Morton sat down next to her. "I don't know how much longer I can take this." She started crying. "Ok. Let's say a prayer. It might help." He replied.

They sat together and prayed for a while. The preacher did not understand why the praying group had not been successful in helping Bob. Typically, they had had a high success rate. Maybe this was God's will. All he could do was to continue to console Sarah as much as he could.

CHAPTER 42

*R**ICK BASS WAS HAVING a hard time walking without a lot of pain. He had a cane with a silver handle and was using it to limp down the sidewalk. He was heading for Fredrick Hall. He wanted to get the bitch that had almost crippled him. The doctor said he would be back to normal in a week or so but he was filled with anger. Because of her he had to resign his job and leave town. He knew the police were looking at him for all of the campus rapes. He was wearing a baseball cap and had dark glasses on but that would not fool anyone who knew him. He was heading towards Sue's dormitory when he saw Sue walking toward the Student Union. He quickly ducked behind one of the large evergreen bushes that lined the sidewalk between the dorm and the Student Inion. He hated her with all the vengeance he could muster. She was walking right towards him! He looked around, hardly anyone was nearby. He could ambush her before she could kick him again!*

Sue was happy. She was back together with Ron and she was getting good grades. Life was good. She had detoured to a small campus shop behind Fredrick Hall to get some money from an ATM. She knew Ron intended to pay for the dinner out but she wanted some extra cash just in case. She was wearing a full-length blue dress with a sash belt and blue sandals. It was a bit dressy but they were going to that fancy restaurant again. She wanted to get to the Student Union to meet with Ron and tell him that she had called her mother and they said it was ok if she brought a guest home with her during break. The extra bedroom was available and they would clean it up before she arrived. Her brothers were at summer camp now so the house would not be crowded. She had texted his picture to her mother and hinted that she was in love with a wonderful boy.

She was walking past Fredrick Hall and about halfway to the Student Union. Her phone rang. She stopped. The phone was in her purse. She fumbled with the purse but could not get it out in time to answer it. She saw that it was from Ron. She went to the messaging but he did not leave a message. That was strange. She was opening her purse to return the phone when she saw movement behind her with her peripheral vision. She turned to look and got hit on the side of the head with Rick's cane. She went down in a heap as darkness swallowed her.

"There bitch." Rick stood over her. "I should take you somewhere and screw your eyes out, but I am a bit off my game right now because of you." Now he only had to get the Pritchard guy. He started to limp away, leaving her sprawled on the sidewalk. The side of her face had a cut and she was bleeding.

Ron had left the Student Union and was running down the sidewalk toward Fredrick Hall when he saw what had happened to Sue. Rick Bass was moving away quickly but Ron started sprinting towards him. Rick turned and saw Ron coming. He knew he could not move fast enough to get away so he turned with the cane. It was a special cane. He twisted the handle and drew out a sharp sword about a foot long from the base of the cane. Ron did not register that Rick had a weapon. He only saw Sue lying prostrate on the ground bleeding and he became furious. He literally saw red as he charged Rick. Although he had been a football coach, Rick Bass had never actually played football. He held the sword up expecting to stab Ron when he came close. Ron had played football and knew how to tackle. He launched himself at Rick and hit him around the knees as Rick stabbed down. Ron felt a stinging in his left shoulder. They went flying backward and Ron heard the satisfying crack of Rick's leg as it broke. Rick dropped the sword and was in real pain as he felt his leg break. The collision knocked the wind out of Ron. They landed on the lawn and both struggled to get up. Ron got to his knees and summoned all his energy to punch Rick in the face as hard as he could, and Rick went down, knocked out. Ron got up slowly, trying to regain his breath. As he stood he heard the sounds of sirens. He turned to go back to Sue and saw Jerry running toward him. Joan was kneeling next to Sue. George Coleman and another officer ran up to Ron.

"Please call an ambulance." Ron panted as he bent down trying to catch his breath. "He hit her pretty hard."

George looked at him and at Rick Bass on the ground. "Looks like you got him." The other officer walked over to Rick and put handcuffs on him.

Ron staggered a bit. He was bleeding from a wound in his shoulder.

An ambulance pulled into the parking lot of the nearest dormitory. Two paramedics got out and rushed over to where Sue was.

The ambulance paramedics loaded Sue onto a gurney and rushed her to the ambulance. She was unconscious and bleeding badly from the head wound. Ron wanted to go with her in the ambulance but the cops wanted him to stay for questioning, so Joan went with her. Jerry had seen most of the action so he stayed to verify Ron's story. Once the cops saw that Rick Bass could not walk they called another ambulance.

George picked up the sword. It had blood on the edge. He walked up to Ron holding the sword by the tip with a gloved hand. "It looks like he got you."

"Wow. I didn't even see that." Ron had finally caught his breath. He opened his jacket. His shirt showed an expanding blood stain coming from his left shoulder.

"I need to call an ambulance for you." George inspected Ron's shoulder.

"No. It's just a scratch. I'm ok." Ron inspected his Blazer. "Damn. He ruined my coat." "Well, we got him for assault if nothing else." George walked with Ron.

"The girl he hit, was that the one he almost raped before she kicked him?"

"Yeah. I saw him hit her. Her name is Sue, Sue Conner." Ron was worried about Sue. He had to get to the hospital to see her. His hand was starting to swell up where he had hit Rick Bass.

"I was coming out of the Student Union and I saw Sue looking through her purse when Rick came from behind and hit her. I ran toward them. When he saw me, he stopped and turned with the cane he had. When I got close enough I tackled him," he explained as George took notes.

Jerry basically gave the same story. He was too far behind Ron to help but he had seen what happened. After both Ron and Jerry had given their statements they were released by the police. George was concerned about Ron's shoulder wound but he knew that Ron wanted to go to the hospital.

"While you are over there, get that wound looked at." He said

as Ron and Jerry ran to the parking lot. They immediately got in Ron's Jeep and drove to the Hospital.

When they got there, they rushed to the emergency room. Joan was there, sitting outside of the ER, crying.

"How's Sue?" Ron asked Joan, concerned.

"They have her in there, working on her." She pointed to the ER entrance. "Ron, she is hurt pretty bad."

"I should have killed that guy when I had the chance." Ron whispered to himself.

"Hey, she is a strong girl, she can pull through this." Jerry tried to console Ron. "Boy, that was some tackle you made. You should be on the football team."

A nurse came out and asked if they were with the girl that got injured. They all replied yes, that they were her friends. "Are any of you her next of kin?" the nurse asked.

CHAPTER 43

SARAH WAS SITTING IN the hospital chapel, praying for Bob. Jack Simms entered and walked up and sat next to her in the pew. He was surprised that Bob was still alive.

"Sarah. How are you doing?" Jack asked.

"I'm ok, I guess. I just wish this had never happened. We were so happy together." She realized that Bob was never coming back.

"Well, he had a good life." Jack was already talking about him as if he was gone. "Things like this happen. Sometimes I think they happen to the wrong people but only God determines these things."

"The reverend was telling me that sometimes miracles do happen if we pray hard enough." She looked down.

"I hope you are right." Jack looked at her. He had seen the MRI and the huge spider type tumor that was in Bob's head. It would have to take a big miracle to make that go away. The best thing would be to pull the plug on the respirator and let him go peacefully. Bob had been one of his best friends and he hated that this had happened. His clinical mind told him that Bob was already gone, and there was nothing more anyone could do about it.

CHAPTER 44

*R*ON RETURNED TO HIS *apartment. He slowly removed the blazer and shirt. He had a 2-inch cut on the top of his shoulder but not very deep. The blazer had absorbed most of the blow. It had already stopped bleeding. He put a bandage on it and washed up. He put on a new shirt and decided to go over and visit Joan at the dorm.*

Ron drove back to the dorm and went up to the dorm room. Joan was there with Jerry. Ron was obviously depressed. Sue's parents were driving down tomorrow and he had to face them. He felt it was his fault since he had basically led the cops to investigate Rick Bass. Maybe if he had stayed silent and let the bastard leave town quietly, this would never have happened. But then the bastard would have started preying on other young girls elsewhere. Now her parents would want to know what had happened to their little girl and he would have to tell them. At least Rick Bass was going to go to prison, hopefully for a long time.

He looked at Sue's poster on the wall. It showed a tropical scene with clouds in the background, a sailboat and a small island with three palm trees growing on it. "That sure is a nice picture."

"Oh, Sue told me about that. When she was young, she got to go on a cruise to Hawaii with her parents and grandparents and that poster always reminds her of that." Joan explained. " She always said it was the best time in her life."

"Wow. I have never been to Hawaii." Ron studied the poster.

CHAPTER 45

*R*ON GOT UP EARLY *and was at the hospital early, walking up to the patient ward. He saw a middle-aged couple talking to a doctor dressed in a white lab coat. He approached them. The woman turned and saw him. She recognized him from a picture Sue had texted her, telling her about this wonderful boy she had met at college.*

"Are you Ronald?" she asked. She was wearing a conservative gray pants suite. There was a remarkable resemblance to Sue.

"Yes. You must be Mrs. Conner?" Ron asked.

"Well, I used to be, but I was divorced and re-married." She appraised him. He was in his typical khaki pants and white shirt with a blue blazer.

"How is she doing?" Ron asked, concerned. "They wouldn't let me see her last night since I wasn't a relative."

The doctor took notice of Ron. "As I was just telling her parents, she is resting peacefully. She has had a major concussion and a slight fracture of her cheek bone. She should be ok, but we need to monitor her for a subdermal hematoma."

"Can I see her? Ron asked.

"Yes, but she is unconscious. We have given her drugs to keep her asleep to allow her brain to heal." The doctor looked to the parents. "She may be unresponsive for a few days yet."

The mother looked at Ron. "She called me and told me quite a lot about you. You must be pretty important to her."

Ron looked at the mother. He could see where Sue's beauty came from. He thought about how to tell her about their relationship but decided to tell her the truth. "Yes. I am in love with your daughter." Ron admitted. He did not care to keep that from them.

Her father took notice of Ron for the first time. "You have only known her for a few weeks, how can you possibly be in love with her?"

"Actually, we have known each other from high school." Ron exaggerated a bit.

"You are what, a senior in college? What are your plans when you graduate?" the father asked.

"I'm an engineering student. I am hoping to get a position with an aerospace company where I was an intern last year." Ron looked at the man. He was in his late forties, dressed casually with tan slacks and a grey sports shirt.

"That sounds pretty good. My father was an aerospace engineer." He looked at Ron with a better appreciation. "I understand that she was attacked by one of the football coaches and that you were involved?"

"Yes. Coach Bass had been drugging girls on campus and raping them. Sue was one of his targets but she foiled his attempt and he later attacked her when she wasn't looking. I managed to prevent him from escaping before the police got there." Ron tried to summarize it as concisely as possible.

"The police officer we talked to said that you attacked an armed suspect and broke his leg."

"Yeah. I wanted to kill him after I saw what he did to Sue."

"Too bad you were not with her to prevent the attack. I understand you were injured in the fight. The police officer I talked to was concerned that you were seriously injured." The father said.

"I was rushing to warn her when he ambushed her. The guy cut me, but not that bad." Ron looked at the floor.

"The police officer said you could have been killed."

"I didn't see the weapon. I just rushed him and tackled him." Ron was uncomfortable telling the story. The father was right, he should have been with her to protect her. Ron turned to the doctor. "Can I see her please?"

The doctor looked at the parents. "I guess so. You all can go in and see her."

They all went into Sue's room. She was in a hospital bed. The right side of her face was bandaged and she had an IV in her arm and an oxygen mask. The doctor said that she was in a medically induced coma.

The doctor noted: "She did regain consciousness for a short time after we brought her in. That is a very good sign. We did not see any sign of a subdermal hematoma in the MRI but we are being on the cautious side. She is a healthy and fit young lady so she should have a full recovery."

"Thank you, doctor." The mother said. The father left the room with the doctor, leaving Sue's mother and Ron alone. They sat in the chairs next to the bed.

The mother looked at Ron. *"You said you were in love with her. What are your intentions?"*

Ron thought for a second. Should he be bold and tell her everything? He decided to be truthful with the mother. *"I want to marry her. But I know that she wants to finish college and become an art teacher. So, I'm not sure how all this will work out."* Ron looked at Sue.

"Have you had intimate relations with my daughter?" Sue's mother asked.

Ron looked at the floor. *"We almost did."* He explained that Sue initiated an attempt but he had not taken advantage of her.

Her mother looked relieved. *"Well, I know that she loves you. She as much as said that when she called me last week. These things work out in the long run. I am surprised she got hurt. She has a black belt in Karate."*

"He was hiding behind some bushes; she did not see him in time." Ron explained. *"I was running toward them as fast as I could but could not get there in time."* He looked down at the floor.

"I thought I heard that you broke the man's leg?" She looked at him.

"Well, I hit him low and as hard as I could. I wish I had killed him for what he did to Sue."

"He is in custody now?"

"Yes. The Police have him locked up. They put a splint on his leg, but he is behind bars."

They sat quietly next to the bed for a few minutes. Then the mother got up to leave. She looked at Ron who was holding Sue's hand with his eyes closed. A tear was on his cheek.

"Please look after my little girl." She whispered in his ear before she walked out of the room.

CHAPTER 46

*R*ON WAS SPENDING *A lot of time in the hospital. He would leave to go to class but then would return to sit next to Sue's bedside. The nurses were concerned that he was not eating or sleeping much. Sometimes Joan would join him for a few hours. The doctors had taken her for a follow up MRI and did not find any bleeding in her brain, so she did not require brain surgery.*

After three days the doctors stopped the drugs and waited for her to wake up. She continued to sleep. Ron would read and re-read the psychology chapters to her that they were studying, hoping she might absorb some of it. On the fifth day, Sue stirred in bed. Ron was at her side, holding her hand. She started to open her eyes and looked at him.

"Where am I?" she managed.

"You're at the Campus Hospital, Sue. You were hit on the head." Ron smiled at her, glad to see that she was back.

She looked around the room. Then she looked at Ron. "Who are you?" she asked.

CHAPTER 47

*T*HE DOCTORS HAD CALLED Sarah to come to the nursing home. Robert's vital signs were slowing. They were afraid he might not last the day. Sarah came and sat near her husband's body. He looked lifeless but was still breathing. The doctors wanted to know if they should disconnect him from the respirator. Sarah said no, not yet.

Dr. Jack Simms visited her at the nursing home. He had an idea and wanted to talk to Sarah. He sat next to her in Bob's room.

"Sarah, how are you doing?" he asked.

"Bob seems to be getting worse day by day," she observed.

"Sarah…I would like to try an experimental drug on Bob." He started. "It might not help, but I don't think it would make him any worse."

"I thought you said there is nothing you could do," she looked at him.

"Well, this is something new and it has not gone through much testing. Another doctor heard about Bob's condition and suggested it to me. It is sort of a chemotherapy drug but we do not have it approved yet. I am going out on a limb here, but he was one of my best friends…If you want to try it," he said in a low voice.

"I don't know…but if you think it would help?" she pleaded. "We don't have much to lose by trying it," he tried to reassure her.

"Well, ok. Let's try it." She seemed relieved that at last there was something that they could do for Bob.

"Ok. I will talk to the house physician here. He is already getting a saline solution intravenously; we can simply add it to that." He got up to go find the doctor. They would start the treatment right away. He did not think it would help at this late stage but it gave him a sense of purpose to try to help his friend.

CHAPTER 48

*R*ON WAS IN A *conference room in the hospital sitting with the doctor and Sue's parents. They were listening to the doctor. Sue did recognize her parents but did not know what had happened to put her in the hospital. She had no memory of the assault or anything from the past five weeks.*

"It is not unusual in some cases of a bad concussion that the patient experiences some memory loss. It will typically return in a few days or it can sometimes take months," the doctor explained.

"Should we take her home?" her mother asked.

"Actually, I would suggest letting her go back to class, she may recover her memory quicker in her most recent environment." The doctor stood up. "I can release her tomorrow, if that's ok."

Sue's father stood up. "That sounds good doctor; I need to get back to work so we will be leaving tomorrow."

Ron stood up. "Joan and I will make sure she gets back to her dormitory ok." "Yes, it's good that she is around her friends," the doctor agreed.

The next day Joan and Ron visited Sue to check her out of the hospital. Joan brought a change of clothes for Sue who immediately recognized Joan and they began to talk. She did not take any notice of Ron who went to the nurse's station. The Doctor was there with the paperwork signed by her parents. To check her out, the Doctor said a wheelchair was required to leave the hospital. Ron asked the nurse where to get a wheelchair.

One of the nurses that had been taking care of Sue while he sat next to her bedside for five days turned to him. "It looks like your girlfriend is ok." She took him to where the wheel chairs were stored.

"Yeah, Thank God." Ron said.

The nurse looked him in the eye. "I had a talk with her this morning. She wanted to know who you were. I told her that I thought you were her boyfriend since you hardly left her side while she was unconscious."

"She doesn't seem to remember me." Ron said lowly.

"She will remember. I wish I had a boyfriend as handsome and dedicated as you are." Ron took the wheelchair from the nurse and returned to Sue's room.

"I don't need a wheelchair; I can walk ok." Sue said getting off the bed. She had already changed into the clothes Joan had brought. The evening dress she had been wearing in the attack had blood on it and would need cleaning.

"Hospital rules say you have to use a wheelchair." Ron told her, smiling.

"Your name is Ron?" Sue asked. She was mildly interested in why he was helping her. *"Yes. Ah…we were…dating before your accident."* Ron looked at her hopefully.

"Well. Ok then." She got in the wheelchair and Ron wheeled her to the elevator. Then he pushed her chair to the entrance and to his parked his Jeep. He helped the girls into the Jeep, and then took the wheelchair back to the hospital entrance.

Sue and Joan were chatting away as if nothing had happened to her. Joan was filling her in on her relationship with Ron.

"You really don't remember him?" Joan asked while he was away.

"He looks familiar and is very sexy looking." Sue admitted. *"I can't believe I would be lucky enough to have him for a boyfriend."*

"Well, you were telling me you were in love with him before your accident." Joan was struggling with Sue's memory loss. At least she remembered that they were roommates.

As Ron returned and started the Jeep, Sue was studying him very closely. They drove over to the parking lot near Fredrick Hall. Although Sue could walk just fine, Joan and Ron got on each side of her going up the stairs to her dorm room, holding her hands.

"I'm not used to being babied so much," Sue complained as they entered her dorm room.

"Well, we have class tomorrow and you have missed a whole week." Joan lamented. *"So, you need to rest up and be ready. There are only two weeks left in the semester. We have to finish a second term paper."*

Sue sat on the couch as Joan went into the bathroom.

"Yeah," Ron chipped in. *"We need to do some research for the term paper."* *"Ron."* She looked at him seriously.

"Yes?" He sat down beside her.

"My mother talked to me earlier today before she went home. She told me that you were planning on marrying me." She studied his face intently.

"Well, that was before you lost your memory." He looked at her. "I was going to ask you but only if you wanted to. I know you want to finish college, and now..."

"The nurse said you spent every day at my bedside."

"I was hoping that you would come back to me." Ron said sadly.

"Well, give me some time. I need to get my head straight, ok?" Sue looked at him intently.

"Sure," he said. "I have to go." He stood up. She stood up also and like a reflex, lifted her face to him for a kiss. He hesitated and she blushed.

"See you in class?" he said awkwardly.

"Ok." She watched him leave. He did look very familiar. He was definitely nice looking and nicely dressed. She wondered if they had been intimate. They must have been if he was already talking about marriage. She wanted to be with him, she knew that much.

CHAPTER 49

*S*UE, *JOAN AND RON were back in psychology class and the instructor gave a quick quiz. Because of his new duties as top assistant football coach, he now had to spend more time with the team. He told his class that he did not have enough time remaining in the semester to review another term paper so he cancelled it and decided to give a quiz instead. It was based upon the material in the last few chapters that Sue had missed. Ron felt bad about that. He had read the chapters to her when she was in a coma, but doubted if that would help her. Maybe this time he would score higher than she did.*

Sue looked at the questions and knew all the answers. It was as if someone had placed the material in her head without her studying it. She was amazed and zipped right through the test. She looked at Ron sitting next to her. She remembered that he used to sit next to her. She still wondered if they had been intimate. He certainly was good looking. And he said he loved her. It then occurred to her that he was the football player in high school who had ignored her. She had a huge crush on him then and now it appeared that he was in love with her. But he did not play football now. He said he was an engineering student. She remembered something about a red sports car. It was slowly coming back to her in bits and pieces.

After they had handed in their papers, Coach Johnson asked Ron to stay behind a minute. Ron turned to Joan and Sue and told them he would see them later. He walked up to the coach.

"I heard what happened to your girlfriend." The coach looked at him. "I had no idea that Coach Bass was that bad. I feel bad for you, but at least you took him down. I heard you tackled him when he was trying to stab you. That took a lot of guts."

"To be honest with you, I was seeing red at the time and lost control. I was going to get him no matter what," Ron confessed.

"Well. I am sorry that the girl missed the chapters we tested

on today." The coach relented, "but she had a solid 'A' going into this test so she should be ok."

"Well, we still have the final." Ron said.

"Yeah, that's in ten days. Maybe you can be her study buddy." The coach smiled.

Ron walked out of class. He hoped she did ok on the test. It was multiplechoice so she probably guessed at some of the questions and got them right. He walked to the Student Union and looked around but could not see Sue or Joan. He knew they had an economics class so he figured that is where they went. He got an iced tea and walked out to the veranda and sat down.

Police Chief George Coleman walked up to him and sat down. "Hello George, what's new?" Ron asked.

"Well, everything is back to normal. We haven't had any more girls drugged lately. I guess we have you to thank for that." George admitted.

"When is Bass going up for trial?" Ron asked, knowing that he was a key witness. "Believe it or not, he confessed and took a plea deal with the prosecutor."

"He pleaded guilty?" Ron was astonished.

"Yes. The sentencing trial will be in a few weeks." "Is he out on bail?" Ron was getting concerned.

"Yeah, but he is laid up with a broken leg, thanks to you." George replied. "Why, are you afraid he will do something?" George did not like the way Ron was getting upset.

"He might," Ron gasped. He could not let Sue get hurt again.

"Don't worry. He is under house arrest; he has a radio monitor ankle bracelet on his foot. If he leaves his apartment, we will know about it." Although that was reassuring, Ron had heard that people had disabled those types of devices. Rick Bass was not stupid. He probably could figure it out.

"Still, I don't feel safe if he isn't behind bars." Ron looked dejected.

"Ok, come with me back to the office, I will give you something," George smiled. Ron got up and followed him. He was curious as to what George wanted to give him.

They walked to the Campus Police office. George dug through a drawer and came up with an auxiliary police badge. "This allows you to carry your pistol on campus. Please don't abuse this privilege." George looked at him. "I trust you since you are one of the good guys." He made Ron raise his hand and swear that he would uphold the law to his best ability. George knew that Ron had attended a seminar on law enforcement for a term paper for one of his social studies courses so he knew a lot about police procedures.

"Wow. OK. Thanks, George." The badge was pinned to a leather folder. He put the badge in his pocket. It felt good that he could now carry his weapon on campus legally. He thought he would go and check on Sue.

He said goodbye to George and walked over to the economics building. There would not be too many classes going on in summer semester. He entered the building and walked up to the second floor. A class was going on in the second room he looked into. He saw Joan and Sue sitting together in the classroom. There were about 20 people in the class. He was relieved. He could not be her bodyguard 24 hours a day, however. He walked back to the Student Union.

Coach Johnson was grading the psychology quick quiz papers. He got to Sue's and was amazed. She had gotten every answer correct. She could not have been cheating, since she had the highest grade in the class, 100%. What gives? The two people on either side of her only got grades in the low eighty percent range. He knew she had been in the hospital, so she could not have studied the chapters he assigned. Maybe she had studied all of the chapters in advance. That must be it. She must be one smart student.

CHAPTER 50

*R*ICK BASS WAS IN *his apartment, sitting on his couch looking at the weapon. It was an old 9-millemeter Berretta handgun. He had loaded the magazine and checked the action. It looked to be fully functional. He had gotten it from his uncle many years ago, but had never fired it. He had watched enough shows on TV to know that if you were close enough to the target you could not miss. He was surprised that the cops had not found the weapon when they searched his apartment. He had it hidden pretty well. There was a loose board in the utility room floor that could be raised and had a small recess below it. These campus police were not very thorough he surmised. All cops were dumb. He felt that he could outsmart them every time.*

He had paid the bail for the assault charge. He knew that they wanted to pin the rapes on him too, but the girl did not want to be a witness. But still, she might change her mind. So, he really needed to eliminate her. That would prevent her from ever testifying. He knew she lived in Fredrick Hall. If he was able to sneak up on her once, he should be able to do it again. He made a garrote out of some piano wire and masking tape. All he had to do was slip the wire around her neck and it would be over. At least he had damaged the bitch that had kicked him so hard. He heard she was in the hospital in a coma. He hoped she would never wake up. If she was still in the hospital, he could easily sneak into her room and choke her. She was another reason why he hated women. She had kicked him so hard he was almost crippled. He did not understand why the drug had not affected her as it had previously effected other girls. Maybe if she was still in the hospital, he could sneak into her hospital room and pour some of the GHB into her IV and just screw her in the bed. He knew from experience that the night nurses only checked each room about every four hours. After he was done with her he would simply strangle her.

Maybe the girl was still at the hospital? He fished out his phone and dialed the hospital. He asked about Sue's condition and said that he was her father. The nurse on duty replied that Sue had checked out of the hospital two days ago. Damn. Another lost opportunity. He would have to stake out her dormitory at night.

He knew his DNA was not on file or they might have arrested him for all of the rapes he had committed already. He had to be careful not to let them get a sample of his DNA. So far he had been lucky. Now if he killed the girl witness and that bastard Pritchard he figured he would be free of the rape charges. He would pay the fine for the assault and move out of town.

The police had put the ankle monitor on his left leg since the cast on his other lower leg was too large for it. He looked at the device. It had a battery and a green LED light showing. If he moved more than 100 feet from the GPS setting it would send an alarm to the police station. He got a hacksaw from his toolkit and removed the blade. If he could get it between his leg and the leather strap that was locking the device to his foot, he could get free. He had some unfinished business with that Pritchard bastard. Pritchard would be easy to find. He drove that fancy red sports car. Wherever that car was, Pritchard would be pretty close. He knew Pritchard could beat him physically but the pistol would give him the advantage. He would have a perfect alibi, since the ankle monitor would show that he had never left his apartment.

CHAPTER 51

*R*ON WAS AT THE *girl's dorm talking to Sue and Joan about forming a study group for the psychology class. Jerry was there but he wasn't in the psychology class. He wasn't taking any summer course work, but typically lived at the Frat house year-round. He was only interested in being with Joan. They were becoming close friends. Ron thought that there was some romance going on between them.*

Sue was watching Ron carefully. Things were starting to come back to her. She was remembering that they'd had some dates, but not the details. He seems like a really nice guy, she thought. How could I be so lucky to attract him? She still had a bandage on her cheek. She had removed the bandage once to look at the cut. She was going to have a small scar about an inch long in front of her right ear. She wondered if Ron would think she was ugly with the scar. Ron seemed to be spending a lot of time with them lately. He was often apprehensive. When they were in the Student Union after class he would be looking around a lot, trying to be aware of some danger. I wonder what he is worried so much about. The guy that attacked her was under house arrest, she thought.

They had stopped talking about psychology. Sue turned to Ron. "Why don't we go to the Dairy Queen and get a milkshake?" she asked. She could see that Joan wanted to be alone with Jerry.

"Ok. That sounds good." Ron got up and they left the dorm room. He was holding her hand. "I was hoping to ask you out for a date but didn't know if you wanted to go out with me again," he explained as they walked down the stairs.

"You can ask me out anytime." Sue smiled at him. She was starting to remember that they had kissed several times.

They walked to the parking lot. He had the Corvette today. The top was up since it looked like it might rain. He opened the door for her and she got in. Then he went around to the driver's side and got in. They sat in the car for a minute.

"Ron, I am going to have a scar on my face." She looked at him for a reaction.

"That's ok. It will add to your beauty, give it some character." He smiled at her. "What flavor of milkshake do you like?" He asked. Sue was relieved. Apparently he did not care about the scar. "I always go for chocolate." "Me too." He started the car and they drove to the Dairy Queen just off campus.

As they were enjoying the milkshakes at the Dairy Queen, he asked, "How about we double date with Joan and Jerry. We never got to the restaurant the night of your accident."

"That sounds good. The restaurant we were going to, is it the same one we went to before?" She was starting to remember more details. "Wasn't that the night the mugger tried to rob us?"

"Yeah. You were awesome. Before I could pull my gun out, you had him on the ground. It was a good thing since I actually left my gun at home" Ron confessed.

"You carry a gun?" Sue asked. She was not alarmed but suddenly curious. "It's ok, I have a carry permit," he explained.

"Can I see it?" she asked.

"Ok, but not in here. I'm not supposed to take it from concealment unless someone's life is in danger." He had taken the NRA test and had passed it easily. The background check done by the Sheriff's department showed that he was a model citizen, had never gotten in trouble with the law. The FBI check also cleared him to carry a weapon.

When they were back in the car, he removed a small pistol from his side pocket and showed it to her. It was a small Ruger LCP .380 caliber semiautomatic pistol. It was only 5 inches long and a half inch wide. He could carry it in his front pocket and nobody could tell he had it. It only held five rounds but he kept one in the chamber so it was ready to fire anytime. It did not have a safety so he had to be careful with it. The trigger pull was high, about six pounds so it really was not so bad to carry it safely.

"It's so small," she said as she looked at it. "Is it loaded?"

"Yes, it wouldn't be much good if it wasn't. It's only for self-defense, it's not very accurate past ten feet," he explained.

"Are you allowed to carry it on campus?"

"Well, not normally. But since what happened to you, George said I could carry it." "Who is George?" She asked.

"He is the Campus Police Chief and a friend of mine." Ron put the weapon back in his pocket. "He kind of deputized me for the short term." He showed her the badge that George had given him. It said he was Auxiliary Police.

"Oh," she replied. Apparently there was a lot more that she did not know about Ron. But it was reassuring that he was a member of the police and could protect her if need be. Typically, she relied on her karate skills that she had perfected in taking lessons for eight years.

"You don't mind that I carry it?" he asked. "No. It's ok. I trust you."

"Don't worry. I have never had to use it, and probably won't ever have to."

CHAPTER 52

ROBERT WOKE UP. HE actually opened his eyes and could see again. The heart monitor next to him started beeping louder as his heartbeat increased with a surge of adrenalin. He turned his head. Sarah was sitting in a chair with her eyes closed, probably napping.

"Sarah!" he tried to say her name but it came out "Garha!"

She looked up immediately. "Robert! You're back!" She pressed the call button for the nurse. The nurse came in. "He woke up!" Sarah exclaimed.

The nurse took one look and rushed out to get a doctor.

"Sarah, you've got to warn them!" he tried to say but it came out as: "Gara bugonna tarnem!" He was frantic. He had recognized who Sue's parents were in the dream. He had to warn them about the bad guy with a gun.

The doctor came in. "He woke up!" The doctor came over and started to check out his vital signs. "Well, this is a good sign!" he exclaimed to Sarah.

"Burgonna arn im." Bob exclaimed. He couldn't hear what he was saying but he thought he was talking ok. The effort was exhausting him though, and he closed his eyes.

Neither Sarah nor the doctor could understand him. "What is he trying to say?" Sarah asked.

"I don't know, but it sounds pretty important." The doctor was writing in his chart. "I should call Dr. Simms immediately," he said as he walked out.

Sarah stood next to her husband. She held his hand and started crying. Maybe it was a miracle. The prayer group had been meeting twice a week and she had joined them. Maybe the new drug he was being given was fighting the tumor. She certainly hoped so.

Robert fell back into a fitful sleep.

CHAPTER 53

*R*ON HAD TRADED THE *Corvette for the Jeep. This time he parked near Fredrick Hall and went up to the girls' dormitory room. He was taking no chances this time. He was going to personally escort everyone to his car. He knocked on the door. Jerry opened it and let him in.*

"Hi, Ron." Jerry looked happy. He had just asked Joan to go steady with him and she had agreed. He was wearing his 3-piece grey suit again. Joan looked radiant in a bright green dress and a pearl necklace.

Ron looked around the room for Sue. She was just coming out of the bathroom. My God, she looks beautiful, he thought. She was wearing the frilly blue blouse and white skirt. She did not have the bandage on and he could see the cut on her cheek. It had not quite healed yet and there was some blue bruising around the cut. When she saw Ron, she put her hand up to her cheek to hide the cut.

"You look beautiful." He exclaimed as he walked over to her. He took her hand, "Shall we go? I have reservations at the restaurant for 6:30." They all followed Ron out the door.

They got to the restaurant on time. Both Joan and Jerry were impressed with 'Anthony's.' They sat down and Ron ordered a bottle of wine. Joan and Sue both looked at him.

"We are under age." Joan whispered. Jerry was 21 so he didn't mind.

"Not so loud," Ron cautioned them. "A little wine won't hurt you. The owner knows me and he won't card you, I promise." Both girls looked more mature than their years but not by much.

They had a wonderful meal. Jerry and Joan talked to each other in low tones and Ron concentrated on Sue. Sue drank a little of the wine but not much. She was remembering drinking some wine at his apartment the night they almost made love. She was cautious about it this time. Ron knew that when carrying a weapon, a person could not become inebriated so he only had one glass. Jerry on the other hand, had three or four glasses and was getting tipsy. Joan was careful to just drink water. She intended to remain totally sober. Ron paid the waiter and provided a large tip. They left and waited for the valet to bring the Jeep around.

"I should have paid for some of that." Jerry said. He was slurring his words a little.

"Tell you what. Next time you can pick up the tab." Ron smiled at him. Jerry was a nice guy. He was glad that Joan was getting along well with him.

As they drove home, Jerry started to fall asleep in the back. Joan tried to shake him awake but he started to snore. "We have sleeping beauty back here." Joan said, somewhat irritated.

They drove over to the Tau Frat house to drop off Jerry. Ron pulled into the parking lot and pulled up close to the back door. He parked the Jeep and went around the car to get Jerry. Jerry woke up as Ron pulled him to his feet.

Ron helped Jerry out of the jeep. "Think you can make it inside?" Ron asked.

"Huh...Oh yeah". He looked back at Joan. "See you tomorrow?" he asked Joan, embarrassed that he had fallen asleep. He had never drunk wine before and was amazed at how it had affected him. He was only used to beer and it did not have the same kick that the wine did.

Joan looked at him and smiled. "Sure, see you tomorrow, lover." She was obviously disappointed. Jerry blushed a bit and turned to Ron. "I think I'm going to be sick," he whispered.

"Here, I'll help you to the door. You don't want to puke in front of the ladies." Ron helped him walk to the door.

"You sure are a swell fellow." Jerry told him as he entered the Tau house.

Ron went back to the girls waiting in the Jeep. "He'll be ok with some rest." Ron said. Joan was slightly upset. Ron figured that she might have had some other plans with Jerry tonight. Sue was glad that Ron did not drink as much wine as Jerry. Ron still appeared to be sober.

"I'll take you girls back to the dormitory." Ron started the jeep and drove over to Fredrick Hall. "I am sure that Jerry will be ok tomorrow."

Ron pulled into the dormitory parking lot, parked the Jeep close to the building and then opened the doors for the girls. He escorted them into the building and up to their room. Joan made some excuse to go see another girlfriend on the same floor to tell her about the restaurant and so that Sue and Ron could be alone.

As they pulled into the parking lot, they did not notice a person waiting in a darkened green car near the entrance. Rick Bass knew that Ron was visiting Sue at the dormitory. Rick was waiting for a red Corvette to come by. He had the Berretta pistol in his hands. Getting the ankle bracelet off was easy and he could put it back on so that nobody could tell it was cut. He did not pay attention to the Jeep. He was waiting for a red Corvette. He was determined to pay back that bastard Pritchard for hurting his leg.

Ron sat next to her on the couch. "Sorry about Jerry. I should have cautioned him about the wine. It has a lot more kick than the beer they have at the Frat house."

"It's not your fault. We all had a good time anyway. The food there is amazing." Sue moved closer to him. She wanted him to kiss her but he was still not sure she remembered him totally yet. Finally, he leaned over to her and they kissed. It was electric to both of them, just like the first time. She pulled him closer but in doing so rubbed against his shoulder.

"Oww." Ron broke off the kiss.

"What's the matter?" she said in a husky voice.

"I'm sorry." He had his hand to his shoulder. "I sort of got cut when I took out the guy that hurt you."

"Can I see?" She was curious. Slowly she unbuttoned his shirt far enough to expose his shoulder. She saw the bandage. "Does it hurt a lot?"

"Not really. They wanted me to go to the hospital but I took care of it myself."

She removed the bandage. It had not yet fully healed. It was still a raw open cut. "Did you put antiseptic on it?" she asked.

"I don't think so." He didn't think it was that bad. He had gotten hurt much worse when he had played football.

"Well, I need to re-do this." She went in the bathroom and came out with a small first aid kit. She put antiseptic on the wound and re-bandaged it. He never said a word although she knew it must have hurt when she cleaned the wound. Typical male reaction— men can't show pain in front of a woman, she thought.

Ron re-buttoned his shirt and got up to go. "Thanks." The bandaging of the wound had sort of killed the mood.

Sue was not going to let him off that easy. "I don't suppose you would like to cook me another dinner?" She wanted to get him alone in his apartment.

He turned to look at her. "Sure, we could do that." He was surprised. He wondered if her memory had fully returned. "How about we get together on Tuesday, after classes are over?"

"That sounds wonderful." She smiled at him. They walked to the door. He turned around and they kissed again. This time she was careful not to touch his shoulder.

Ron walked down the stairs and out to the Jeep. It was getting dark. The days were starting to get shorter now that it was August. Ron was happy again. I think she still loves me he thought. He wondered what he would cook for her this time. He could not do the spaghetti thing again. He made a mean meatloaf but that was not something for a date night. He figured probably grilled steaks and a salad. He got into the Jeep and drove out of the lot. As he passed the car parked near the entrance, Rick Bass looked at him and recognized Ron Pritchard driving the Jeep out the exit.

"Son of a bitch," Rick said as he started his car. "He done changed cars on us." He said to no one in particular. The Berretta pistol was in his lap. He started his car and put it in gear.

CHAPTER 54

*D*R. JACK SIMMS EXAMINED Robert carefully. His vital signs were improving. He had talked with Sarah and found it hard to believe that Bob had returned. He was unresponsive now but the other doctor insisted that he heard Bob trying to talk. It was garbled but sounded like he was excited about something. Jack knew that terminal patients sometimes in a delirium said unusual or bizarre things. It was remotely possible that the experimental drug was starting to work. He noticed that Bob's hair was starting to fall out. He would have to make a note of that for his doctor associate who suggested the treatment.

Sarah was sitting in the room. "He did try to talk to me." I distinctly thought he said 'Sarah.'"

"Well, that is something." Jack sat down next to her. "I honestly thought he was fading away, but he appears to be improving." Jack could not understand it. Maybe they should do another MRI.

"It's a miracle." Sarah started to cry. "Our prayer group has been meeting twice a week to pray for him.

Jack had nothing to counter that. Maybe the power of prayer was stronger than he thought. Or the new drug was helping. Time will tell, he thought. He was amazed that the experimental drug appeared to be working already.

"Well, let's not get our hopes up." He stood up to leave. "We will continue to check his progress."

Sarah was convinced that the prayer group had reversed her husband's disease. She could not wait to tell Reverend Morton. He had told her all along that the prayer group was able to create miracles.

CHAPTER 55

*R*ICK BASS WAS HAVING *difficulty driving his car with a cast on his right leg. By the time he had pulled out after Ron, the Jeep had turned the corner and was out of sight.*

"Damn it." Rick hit the steering wheel with the heel of his hand. He made the turn and sped towards the traffic light at the end of the block. The Jeep made it through on the green but the light had turned yellow and then red as he approached it. He had to stop as he saw the taillights of the Jeep fade in the distance. He could have run the red light but a Campus Police car was at the intersection. He did not want them to catch him violating his house arrest. One of the things he was really counting on was the alibi that house arrest would provide him. He would get Pritchard but he would still look innocent. Rick drove around a bit and then had a thought. He couldn't take the chance that someone would see him during the day near her dormitory. He remembered that Jerry was now helping Pritchard. Jerry had probably warned Ron that he was near her dorm the day of the assault. The guy was a damn traitor.

Maybe he should concentrate on the Pritchard bastard. He was counting on the fact that the ankle bracelet would provide him with an alibi if he shot Ron.

He reluctantly drove back to his apartment. He had a garage suite that allowed him to hide his car when he was home. No one would notice if his car was missing since it obviously would be in the garage. He looked around the neighborhood. No police cars were near, so he pulled into the garage and closed the overhead door. No one had seen him leave or come back. He went into his apartment. He decided he would go out again in the morning and stake out the Student Union parking lot. He realized that Ron parked his car there frequently. He would wear a baseball cap and dark glasses. If he stayed in the car, it would be more difficult to identify him. If he did have to move around, he would hide the cast by putting on some baggy workout pants. He checked the weapon. It was ready to fire. He put the safety on and put it on his coffee table. He had checked the magazine and it was loaded with 9 bullets. That should be enough to kill that bastard Pritchard. He reassembled the ankle bracelet on the off chance that the police would stop and check on him. They were so stupid and probably relied on the signal from the ankle bracelet.

CHAPTER 56

*R*ON GOT UP EARLY, *got dressed and went to the diner down the street for breakfast. Then he drove the Jeep to the Student Union. Since he had the Jeep, he decided to park closer to the front of the lot instead of toward the back of the lot as he did when he had the Corvette. He did not pay any attention to the car three spaces behind and two spaces to the right side of him. He grabbed his books and got out of the Jeep.*

Behind him, Rick Bass aimed the pistol out of his driver side window. He lined up the sights on Ron's back and pulled the trigger. Nothing happened. He tried again, nothing. "What the hell?" he muttered. Then he remembered that the safety was on. He moved the toggle to fire and looked for Ron. Ron had already walked out of his line of sight. "Damn." He considered trying to go into the Student Union but he could not move very fast with the cast on his leg. Also, if someone recognized him he would be in trouble. Well, one thing was for sure, Ron would have to return to the Jeep eventually. He could wait.

Ron got an iced tea and walked out to the veranda. He found an empty table and sat down. He did not have hydraulics class today. The instructor had given them a take-home Final Exam and he had already worked out most of the problems. So, he only had psychology class today. He was hoping that Sue and Joan would join him. He could have texted them but decided not to. It was relatively cool this morning, unusual for early August. The girls would probably have to have their sweaters on to sit out on the veranda. The weather forecast said it would get warmer later and that there was a chance of thunderstorms. Time for class was approaching. He gave up on meeting them so he walked over to the psychology building and went to the classroom. Joan and Sue were already sitting in their seats. They were talking animatedly about something. He sat down next to Sue.

"Hello," he said to them.

They stopped talking and turned to him, smiling. Joan said "I want to thank you for treating us to that wonderful restaurant." She appeared to be over her irritation of Jerry drinking too much wine.

"It was my pleasure to treat such lovely ladies." He poured the compliments on. He was thinking about what he was going to prepare for Sue tonight. He was still thinking maybe steaks. He had a small grill that he could use on his porch to cook a couple of small steaks. He needed to stop by the market on the way home. A nice green salad with tomatoes would go well with that. And he thought also, of course, a nice bottle of Cabernet. He wondered if Sue would be in a romantic mood.

Gary Johnson handed out the graded tests. Ron was surprised. He only got an 82%. He did not think that the test was that hard. He had read the chapters to Sue in the hospital but had not really studied for the test. Joan was very happy; she got an 85% and showed it to them. She was carrying a solid 'B' in this class. Sue got her paper and she had a perfect 100%.

"Boy, that was an easy test." Sue exclaimed to Ron and Joan's amazement. Joan and Ron looked at each other. It was not that easy, Ron thought. How did she get all of the answers right without studying for the test?

After class, the three of them walked to the Student Union. Joan was asking Sue about the test. "I just seemed to know all of the answers." Sue replied.

Jerry came up to them. He looked much better than he had after the restaurant. "Hi guys. How about I treat you all to milkshakes at Dairy Queen?" he asked, falling in beside Joan and looking at her for some sign of forgiveness.

"The girls have another class, don't you?" Ron turned to them.

"Actually, we are done with Economics Class except for the final next week." Joan looked at Sue who nodded in agreement.

"Well, ok then," Jerry motioned to them. "We can go in my car. I'm parked over by the dorm." Jerry had parked over by Fredrick Hall.

"Hey, my Jeep is a lot closer." Ron noted. They were only steps from the Student Union parking lot. He had no idea someone was lying in wait to ambush them with a deadly weapon.

CHAPTER 57

BOB WAS BECOMING CONSCIOUS again. He looked over and saw Sarah watching him. He needed her to warn them. The man in his dream with a gun was going to shoot the kids. "Sarah," he croaked. This time it came out properly. He had regained his power of speech.

Sarah rushed over to his bedside. "Yes Robert, I'm here."

"You gotta…you gotta warn them. Please warn them." He managed to get the words out.

"Who, Robert? Who do I warn?" she asked, puzzled about his wanting to warn someone. He struggled to stay awake. "Got to warn them…in great danger."

Bob fell back into a deep sleep. The effort to talk was exhausting, almost too much for him.

Sarah became alarmed. What was he talking about? Was it something he remembered from work? Or was he suffering from some sort of dementia? At least this time she could clearly understand what he said. She took out her cell phone and dialed Jack's number. She was lucky, he was on break and answered her call. She told him what Bob had said.

"Wow. He was actually talking to you?" Jack could hardly believe it. "Yes. He clearly called me Sarah. He looked right at me."

"What do you think he meant?"

"He wants me to warn somebody, but did not say who." She was worried. "Do you think it is something about the project he was working on before he retired?"

"It could be. Or it could just be some sort of dementia." Jack tried to reassure her. "He has been away from that program for almost five months. I doubt if it is about that."

"Well, I can't think of anything else, so maybe you are right." She calmed down.

Bob was fast asleep. He was entirely bald now. The drug was apparently having some effect on him. Or was it the power of prayer that was bringing him back? Sarah did not care. He was improving and that was all she cared about for now. Still, she was puzzled about the warning. He wanted her to warn somebody about a great danger.

CHAPTER 58

*R*ICK BASS WAS WATCHING *when the four of them came out of the Student Union building. He saw it was the two girls, Ron and that traitorous Jerry from the Frat house. This was great. He could get all of them at one time. He aimed for Ron first. He fired. BANG. The Berretta kicked back in his hand. He had not practiced shooting the weapon and was surprised at the kick back in his hand. Since he was not practiced in shooting, however, he jerked the trigger instead of squeezing it. The result was that the trigger pull shifted the pistol aim off the target slightly to the right and the round missed Ron by about four inches, putting a hole in his back window. Ron saw the bullet strike the window just before the loud gunshot report. He reacted quickly and ducked behind the front of the Jeep.*

"Get down!" he shouted to the others.

Sue and Joan had frozen with the gunshot. Jerry grabbed them both pushed them in front of the Jeep. The second round broke the mirror on the passenger side next to Jerry. He also hurriedly scooted in front of the Jeep, unscathed.

"What is going on?" Joan screamed.

Two more rounds punctured the rear window and came out the windshield.

Sue didn't say anything, just crouched low in front of the Jeep. She closed her eyes. She was terrified. This couldn't really be happening.

Ron told Jerry, "Call 911." Jerry got out his phone and dialed the police.

Ron took out his small pistol. It was ready to shoot but he did not know where the bullets were coming from except they were from the back of the parking lot. He looked under the Jeep to see if he could see the legs of the shooter. He could not see anybody. The shooter must be in one of the cars. Rick was frustrated. The damn weapon was not hitting what he wanted. The pistol also kept ejecting the empty shells through the window on to the ground.

One shell actually came back and hit him in the eye before it popped outside. He thought he might have hit one of them but they were hiding behind the Jeep. That's not fair, he thought. He would have to get out of the car and approach them to get a better shot.

Ron popped his head up and looked to see where the shooting was coming from. He spotted the dark colored sedan about four spaces behind him and to the left. A flash and another bang as a bullet imbedded itself in his left rear quarter panel confirmed that the shooter was there. Ron aimed the small .380 pistol. It would be practically useless at this range and he only had five shots, but at least he could return fire. Maybe the attacker would be scared off. He aimed carefully and shot off two rounds at the dark car. His ears were not accustomed to his shooting a weapon without hearing protection and he winced in pain.

"Holy Shit!" Rick Bass said to himself as one of Ron's shots struck his windshield. "He's shooting at me!" This was not how it was supposed to be. He didn't want to get shot. He started the car and backed up quickly, hitting a vehicle behind him. He put the car in gear and squealed his tires as he turned out of the parking lot. He could hear sirens coming from far off. He sped down the block and turned into the first side street he came to. In his rear view mirror, he saw a police car with flashing lights rush past the side street going toward the Student Union. That was close, he thought. Got to get back to my apartment and get the ankle bracelet back on.

George Coleman was in his squad car and pulled into the Student Union parking lot with his siren blaring and lights flashing. He came to a stop by the red Jeep. Ron Pritchard put his weapon on the ground and held his hands up so the policeman could see that he wasn't holding a weapon. George got out and saw the damage to the jeep and that there were people huddled in front of it.

"What's going on?" George had his service revolver drawn and was looking in the obvious direction that the shots had come from. "Is anyone hurt?"

Ron looked at the girls and Jerry. Everyone seemed to be ok. "I don't think anybody got hit. George, some maniac started shooting at us from over there." Ron pointed in the general direction where the dark sedan had been parked. "He left in a big hurry when I returned fire." Ron pointed to his weapon on the ground.

George looked at the tiny .380. "You use that thing for a gun?" He walked to the area where Ron had pointed. He saw several shell casings on the ground. He used a pen to pick one up. "This is a 9-millimeter. You guys are very lucky no one got hit." Another police car pulled into the parking lot. A couple of more cops came over to inspect the damage to the Jeep. When Ron indicated that the shooter had backed into the SUV parked behind it, they went over to look at it.

"There is definitely some dark green paint on the front of this SUV. He must have hit it pretty hard," the other cop, Andy Hall, was saying. George counted five 9mm casings on the ground. He figured they probably could get fingerprints off of some of them. One of the other cops was interviewing the two girls and Jerry who confirmed Ron's story. A small crowd was gathering at the front of the parking lot. One of the cops went over to disperse them.

George walked over and picked up Ron's small .380 pistol. "I have to confiscate this for the report. I can get it back to you tomorrow, OK?"

"Sure." Ron replied. "I don't think I hit him at that distance. I think he heard the sirens and ran away."

"You know, you ought to get a decent piece to carry." George remarked. "This thing is probably only good for about six feet."

"Yeah, but nobody can tell I have it," Ron objected. "I do have an old Browning High power in a drawer at home."

"That's more like it. Did you qualify with it?"

"Yeah, I used that one when I took the carry permit course." Ron replied. "It is pretty large for concealed carry though."

"You should get a shoulder holster. You usually wear a blazer anyway." George suggested.

"Ok. Maybe I will try that." Ron admitted. He remembered that he did have a shoulder holster somewhere in his closet.

The Jeep was in no condition to be driven. One mirror and both the windshield and back window were ruined. Ron called the Triple-A service number to get it towed to a repair shop.

Both girls were in shock, hugging each other. Ron turned to Jerry and said "You did good, getting them out of the line of fire."

Jerry looked at Ron. "Yeah, but you scared him away with your gun." He seemed to be more impressed with Ron.

George came over to them. "Did either of you get a license plate number?"

"No." Ron replied, he had been too busy dodging bullets to take time to look at the license plate. Jerry looked down. "It didn't have a front license plate, but I think I recognized the car."

George looked at him. "Whose car was it?"

Jerry looked up with a frown. "It looked a lot like Coach Bass's car."

George looked at Ron. "You better go get that Browning for protection. I would hate to see you get shot by some maniac."

"Yeah. You suppose it was Rick Bass?" Ron asked him. "Who else has a reason to shoot at you?" George asked.

"Well, I did break his leg. I probably should have killed him then."

"No, you wouldn't have done that. You aren't a killer." George turned to Andy and said, "Looks like we need to get over to Mr. Bass's residence to check on him." He and Andy walked over to their police cruiser and drove away.

CHAPTER 59

*R*ON LOOKED AT HIS *Jeep. It was a mess with the front and back windows starred with bullet holes. He turned to Jerry. "I guess we will have to use your car." As if nothing had happened.*

Joan and Sue were still very upset. "Someone tried to kill us." Joan was crying hysterically. "Sue, are you ok?" Ron asked her. She flew into his arms and started to cry.

"I guess we will go to the Dairy Queen some other time," Ron told Jerry. "Let's get these girls back to their dorm."

"Yeah, that's a good idea," Jerry replied as Joan leaned on him.

They managed to return to the dorm without any more incidents. After the girls were safely in their room, Ron turned to Jerry. "I need a ride to my garage." Ron sort of figured that having steaks with Sue that night was out.

Both girls were too shaken up to want to go out.

Jerry agreed to give him a ride in his late model Kia. They drove to the garage in silence. Jerry was still somewhat in shock from the near death experience. He was really amazed that Ron could be so calm. Jerry dropped him off at his garage to retrieve the Corvette.

"Boy, that's a nice car you have there." Jerry was impressed.

"Yeah, but it gets lousy mileage." Ron was looking at Jerry's gray Kia. "Well, see you around." Ron turned to get in the Corvette. Jerry drove back to the Frat House and Ron returned to his apartment. He was tired from all of the excitement but his adrenalin level was still high. He did not expect to be shot at and he did not like it. When he got back in his apartment, he dug out the Browning High-Power pistol from his closet. He had some 9-millimeter cartridges some place. He dug around some more and found a box of ammo. He sat on his bed and took the Browning out of its case. It was an old weapon but was still functional. He removed the magazine and checked the spring. It was still good. The magazine could hold 12 rounds but he knew from experience

you should never fill a magazine to its fullest capacity unless you planned to shoot immediately. It could sometimes jam the magazine spring and fail to feed the next round to the firing chamber. He opened the cartridge box and loaded 10 rounds in the magazine. Then he checked the action on the pistol. It worked just fine. He dug out some gun oil and oiled the slide. He inserted the magazine and put the weapon at half-cock which meant the weapon would not fire unless the user thumbed the hammer back all the way. The gun was now loaded and ready. The gun was just too bulky to put in his pants and he did not have a pancake holster for his back, so he slipped it under the bed pillow for now. He would have to look for the shoulder holster if he intended to take it with him.

The campus police showed up at Rick Bass's apartment. George Coleman was with Andy Hall. They knocked on the door and Rick let them in and asked what they wanted. George noted that the ankle monitor was still on Rick's left foot.

George asked' "Have you been here all day?"

"Sure. I'm not allowed to go anywhere." Rick pointed to the ankle monitor.

They asked to look at his car. He took them out to the garage. The car was missing. "Oh my God!" Rick exclaimed. "Someone has stolen my car!" A small motorcycle was parked near the back of the garage.

George was not impressed. "You want to fill out a stolen car report?" he asked. "I guess so. I haven't used that car for almost a week so I am not sure how long it has been gone."

George looked at Rick's hands. "We need to take a test here." He motioned to Andy to open a bag with some soft white sheets in it.

"What's that?" Rick asked suspiciously.

"Oh, don't worry. It's called a paraffin test." Andy took the white malleable sheets and pressed Rick's hands in it. He then put them back in the bag.

"What does that do?" Rick was curious.

"It is a standard test for GSR." George said casually. He walked to the door. The Andy was writing information on the specimen bag. "We will be back. Don't go anywhere." They left.

I wonder what GSR is? Rick pondered. He had ditched the car about a block away and had walked home, reassembled the ankle monitor just before the cops came. You could not tell it was cut unless you knew where to look. His alibi should still hold up. He still had to figure out how to get that Pritchard guy. He would be more careful next time and lie in ambush like he got the girl.

Andy turned to George in the patrol car. "You think he was too stupid to wash his hands?"

"Well, he didn't have much time to before we got there. So, there is a chance. Funny he did not know that GSR stands for gunshot residue. Be sure you don't lose that evidence bag." They would take it to the lab in town for analysis. They also had collected the five spent cartridges and there were definite fingerprints on them. Since they had Rick's fingerprints from when they booked him for assault, they could easily check this.

"I bet if we look around the neighborhood we will locate his car."

CHAPTER 60

SARAH WAS ON THE phone to Marty at Bob's old workplace. "Marty, Bob kept on saying 'Got to warn them' over and over. I am not sure, but it could have been something to do with his work."

"Ok. Thanks Sarah. I doubt it has anything to do with his old project. He hasn't been here for five months and we finished that job a few weeks ago." Marty reassured her.

"Well, ok. I just thought you should know." Sarah hung up the phone.

Marty was not one to dismiss a warning like this so quickly. He called Joe into his office.

"Joe. I want you take out Bob Parker's notes on the turbine mechanism and just review them. "Marty, I finished the qualification on that project several weeks ago." Joe Ross complained. "Just do it." Marty replied, dismissing him.

"Ok. You're the boss." Joe walked out. Jesus! He thought. As if I did not have enough to do. He went back to his desk and took out the folder. He went through several notebooks. He didn't see anything that was unusual. He was getting tired of this useless assignment but thought he would look at the FMEA. He took out the Failure Modes and Effects Analysis that Bob had worked on before he left. He was breezing through the 30-page document when he saw an annotation on the drive shaft. Bob had put a red question mark on that part. What the heck? He had not seen that before but he had assumed that the FMEA was ok because it had been released when Bob was still here. He knew that the customer had increased the maximum thrust load, but that was after Bob had left. We looked at the entire system and everything looked ok, he thought. He went over to Henry O'Toole who did the FEA (Finite Element Analysis) stress analysis.

"Henry, did we check this drive shaft part out with the new loading values?" He asked.

"Is that from the turbine job?"

"Yes."

"The system was checked out thoroughly, Joe."

"I know, but could you just look at the drive shaft?"

Henry sighed, stopped the program he was working on and opened up the turbine mechanism. He selected the drive shaft and pulled it up. "Look" he said "It is all green. A slight stress riser on the chamfer but it is within the limits." Joe was relieved. The he looked at the loading diagram. "What load was applied?" Henry checked and said it was at nominal 85% load. "What is it at the new max load condition?" Henry started to manipulate the program inputs. He could not find that particular file. That was strange.

"This will take a few minutes." Henry said, wondering why that particular load diagram was not already in the computer memory. At least the part was already meshed. All he had to do was increase the load level. It took a while but the new load image came up on screen. "Oh shit." Henry said. The diagram had turned red with excessive stress way past the yield limit of the material at the chamfer. "I thought I ran this condition." He pleaded. "We have a problem."

"Can we use a stronger steel with a higher heat treat?"

"Joe, it's made of 4340 steel and already at the maximum Rockwell-C level."

"Can you see if we can fix that part within the available envelope?" Joe was getting upset and starting to sweat.

"I will get right on it." Henry turned back to the screen.

"Goddamn it," Joe said to himself as he walked away. How did the mechanism pass the acceptance test? He went to look at the project log book. He was satisfied that it had passed the ATP until he saw the Revision letter on the acceptance test. It was at Revision level 'B'. The new maximum conditions were at Revision 'C'. Oh Jesus, we may be in trouble, he thought. He went to the test engineer, Don Higgins.

"Don, did you run this test?" he showed him the ATP sheet. "No. I see Larry's stamp on this. Why? It passed ok."

"Look at the ATP revision." Joe stressed. "It looks ok to me." Don said. "Look it up in the computer." Joe was getting upset. "Shit." Don said when he saw the ATP version at Rev 'C'. "How come I didn't get a memo on this?" "We talked about it in the weekly coordination meeting last April." Joe noted.

"Was that when I was on vacation?" Don asked. "Crap. Larry must have used an old copy."

Joe wasn't listening any more. He ran back up to engineering and looked for Henry. Henry was at his desk running more FEAs. He asked Henry if the part could be fixed.

"Hey Joe, the current shaft won't pass but if we increase the diameter about 60 thousandths and put a large radius where the chamfer is it will pass and still meet the envelope." Henry smiled.

"OK. Get a drawing changed and we will rush it through sign-off." Joe was relieved. "Hey, that's not my job..." Henry complained.

"Just Do It!" Joe shouted as he headed for Marty's office.

He burst into Marty's office. Marty was on the phone and motioned for Joe to go away. "Marty!" Joe shouted, "This is important."

Joe covered the phone and looked at Joe. "I'm talking to the customer. They are starting the Turbine Qualification test tomorrow."

"Well then, tell them not to exceed 85% power or it will fail!" Joe shouted. "What? Are you crazy?"

"No. Bob had found a weakness in our drive shaft. It will not make 100% of the new max power. I don't know how he knew it, but he must have suspected something was wrong. Then the lab guys ran the Acceptance Test to the old revision." Joe was pleading.

"Shit." Marty slumped in his chair. He looked at the phone and started to explain to the customer that there was a problem. Damn, he thought to himself, Bob saves our butts even on his deathbed.

CHAPTER 61

GEORGE COLEMAN WAS BACK at the Campus Police office. He was sitting at his desk waiting for a call from the Lab. Andy Hall walked up to him. "I just got a report on the fingerprints on the spent shell casings. We have a partial match to Rick Bass."

The phone rang. It was the Lab. Yes, the paraffin they had collected had definite GSR. Jessie, the police secretary came over to George's desk. "It looks like the city police found Rick Bass's car on a side street within walking distance of his apartment." She handed him the report. "The windshield had a bullet hole in it."

"Well, I think that is more than probable cause to get an arrest warrant." George said. He motioned to Andy. "Let's go pick him up." He asked Jessie to call a judge and get a search warrant.

Andy and George took George's patrol car. He called the city police and gave them the update on the evidence they had. The city police said they would send a backup car for them. They got to the place where Rick Bass's car was found. There was definite evidence of a rear collision. George took note that there was a bullet hole in the windshield. Ron did get a round on target. He was amazed that that small little pistol could hit something at that range. They drove over to Rick's apartment. A city police car and two officers were waiting outside. George and Andy got out of their car and walked up to the door. George's phone rang. It was Jessie and she said that a search warrant had been approved. She could have it sent right over.

They knocked on the door. There was no answer. Andy looked at George.

"I'm not going to wait." George told the other cops. "I guess we have to break in."

One of the city cops walked over to his car and brought out a battering ram device. He approached the door and then broke it open. George and Andy entered with their guns drawn, not knowing what to expect. They did a quick scan of the apartment. No one was home. Andy motioned for George to look at the kitchen table. The ankle monitor was on the table. Next to it was a cartridge box of bullets with several bullets missing. They were 9-millimeter, the same as at the campus shooting scene.

"It looks like he may be armed and dangerous." Andy noted.

"Yeah, looks like you are right. But how far can a man with a broken leg get on foot?" They looked at each other and then went into the garage. The small motorcycle was gone.

George turned to Andy. "Put out an All-Points-Bulletin on that bastard. I bet he is headed toward the campus."

Rick Bass was having some difficulty driving the motorcycle with a cast on his leg, but was managing it. He had looked up the street address where Ron Pritchard in the Campus Website which he still had access to his computer.

Website which he still had access to in his computer. One had to list your address if you lived off campus and were a full-time student. It was just a matter of having clearance to get into that database. Since he had been the Assistant Football coach and a part time geography teacher, he still had that clearance. The campus secretary had not canceled his clearance yet.

This time he was not going to fail. He had intended to ride to his car and ditch the bike, but he saw a police car there and decided he was still in the clear. Stupid cops would still think he was in his apartment with the ankle monitor on. He had re-loaded the berretta and had stuck it in his waist band. He did not intend to miss this time. He had to find a place to hide out until it got dark. He drove to the city park.

CHAPTER 62

SARAH WAS BACK HOME, trying to figure out what to have for supper. Typically, Bob did the shopping and planned the meals. She merely cooked them unless he cooked on the grill outside. The phone rang. "Hello," she answered.

"Sarah, it is Marty. Thanks for giving us the warning. Bob had flagged a bad part in our assembly before he retired, but no one here followed up on it." Marty sounded relieved that the customer was not upset. They were going to postpone the test while a replacement shaft was being manufactured. The program was already four months behind schedule but that was typical for this type of development program.

"Well, I'm glad we could help." Sarah was surprised.

"How is he doing, anyway?"

"He was unconscious again today but his vitals are improving." Sarah was still thinking that the prayer group was responsible for Bob's change in condition. She wanted to talk to the Reverend Morton to see if they could continue the prayer group's effort.

"Well, when he wakes up again, tell him we found the problem. He may have just saved a multi-million-dollar program." Marty was actually happy. If the turbine had failed, it would mean the loss of a lot of sales dollars for the company. Since he was a major shareholder, he would have taken a huge personal economic loss.

Sarah was relieved. So, Bob, even in a coma could still worry about fixing a major problem at work. She thought her husband was remarkable. Now if she prayed a bit harder, she thought, maybe he would make a recovery.

CHAPTER 63

SUE AND JOAN HAD recovered from their scare. They felt safe behind the locked door of their room. They had changed into their pajamas. It was still early, but they were both exhausted from the morning's incident. Joan was still impressed that Ron had been able to drive their attacker off with his pistol. She did not know that he was allowed to carry a gun, but Sue said that the campus cops apparently let him. Sue told Joan that he was an auxiliary policeman with a badge and everything. Joan told Sue that she was lucky to have Ron for a boyfriend. "He seems to be about perfect. And he wants to marry you?"

"That's what he said." Sue had almost totally recovered her memory. She almost felt that she did not deserve someone as good as Ron. He was almost too good to be true. She had not known him long enough to be absolutely sure of him, but she did not think that she wanted to live without him in her life. She was totally in love with him and trusted him. He was good looking, smart, courteous, had good manners and apparently was not poor. He had a constant income and ambition to be an engineer. She knew that her grandfather had been an engineer and had made good money. It was too bad that her grandfather had died when she was so young.

"Are you going to marry him?" Joan asked. "Well, he has not made an official proposal yet."

"What will you do if he does propose? You still have four years of college to complete." "I don't know. I want to continue college, but I can't think of him not being with me."

"Just because you are married, it doesn't mean you can't continue college." Joan was thinking she would probably be Sue's bridesmaid.

"Do you think he would wait for me if I asked him too?"

"Girl, the way he looks at you, I think he would do anything you asked." Joan fell back on her bed. "Yeah but if that Monica girl comes back..."

"After what Jerry told us, I don't think you have to worry about her." "How are you and Jerry getting along?" Sue asked, also lying on her bed.

"You know, he is really a nice guy. I think he wants a relationship. I was planning on seducing him the other night, but he got drunk on all that wine." Joan looked at the ceiling.

"You mean go to bed with him?"

"Girl, I know you haven't tried it, but it sure is a lot of fun. That is, if you get the right guy. You need to find out if they are kind lovers and still respect you afterwards." Joan looked at Sue. "Some guys will simply want to do you then forget you. You want to stay away from that type."

"Yeah, but how can you tell?"

"Well, if he is already talking about marriage, then I think you are ok. I can tell that he already respects you a lot."

Sue thought about that for a while. Maybe she needed to go all the way with him and see how he reacted. If he really loved her, she would find out if they would have a chance at a permanent relationship. Then she remembered, they were supposed to have dinner this night. She got out her phone and texted him; 'I wish we would have had dinner tonight. Can we try again for another night?' She waited for a response.

He texted back, 'Sorry about what happened today. Yes, I definitely would like to try again. How about we try for Friday night?'

She quickly responded; 'Ok. It's a date' She put a heart emoji at the end of the message. She would have to wear something sexy to try to get him in the mood. What if he got her pregnant? She had started the birth control pills when she came on campus at Joan's insistence. She had been on them now for almost two months. They should be working by now, she hoped.

It was early evening. Rick Bass stopped the motorcycle. He was in front of Ron's apartment. He got off the bike and walked it up the driveway silently. He parked the bike on the outer side of the red Corvette so that it could not be seen from the apartment. He took out the weapon and made sure that the safety was off. He wondered if Ron was living in the upstairs or downstairs apartment. Probably the upstairs apartment. A lot of people near campus had remodeled their upstairs to be off campus apartments to pull in some extra money. It was almost 8 o'clock. He knew from experience that college guys did not stay inside on warm summer nights. Ron would come out to go somewhere. When he did, he would walk to the sports car and Rick would get him. He walked over to the edge of the garage and stood there, watching. He made sure that the weapon was ready and that the safety was off. At point blank range he was sure he would not miss. He was getting impatient. If Ron did not come out soon, he would have to walk upstairs and get him when he opened the door. He was tired of waiting. He finally decided to climb the stairs and shoot the bastard when he answered the door.

Ron looked in the fridge. No beer. He also would have to get supplies for Friday. He looked at his watch. Darn. The food mart would be closing. He would have to go tomorrow. He thought about going to the nearby tavern to get a beer, but that woman in the silver-colored dress might be there. Heck with it. He lay down on his bed and closed his eyes. He was amazed at how calm he had been when the shooting had started. He really wasn't trying to impress the girls, he thought. His engineering mind naturally assessed the situation and tried calmly to find a solution. If that first round had hit him, things would have turned out a lot worse. He had always faced danger cautiously but with some amount of self-control. He really was exhausted and the adrenalin high had left him tired. He fell asleep. There was a sudden knocking on his door. Ron started to get up. He thought about the pistol but left it where it was. He walked to the door.

CHAPTER 64

*S*ARAH WAS TALKING TO Reverend Morton. "He actually woke up and talked to me." She was telling the reverend.

"That's good news Sarah."

"I think the prayer group is working." Sarah said.

"You may be right. God does work in mysterious ways," he said. They talked about continuing the prayer sessions.

Her brother Tom was staying at her house temporarily. He had apologized for his behavior before and she had let him in. He was hiding from the mob as he had lost about 25 thousand dollars in gambling at their hidden casino. At first, he won a lot of money but then started to lose. He knew he should have stopped when he was losing but he figured his luck would return and kept using credit to win it back. Finally, they would not give him any more credit and wanted their payback. He said he would raise the money but knew he did not have it. His only hope was that his sister would bail him out. Maybe if she gave him some money he could run from the mob. He had friends in Florida that would hide him for a while until he could figure out what to do.

CHAPTER 65

*R*ON OPENED THE DOOR. George Coleman was standing there. "You might want to come out and see this."

Ron stepped out onto the porch. He saw the blinking lights of two police cars in the road. Matt and his wife Becky were already standing at the edge of the driveway. Ron walked down the steps, following George. Two policemen had a figure kneeling on the ground with handcuffs on. The figure on the ground had a baseball hat and wore dark glasses. George walked up to the figure and removed the hat and glasses. It was Rick Bass. There was a semi-automatic pistol on the ground.

"It looks like he was going to ambush you Ron," Andy Hall said as he pulled the figure to his feet. Ron walked up to Rick. "What the hell are you trying to do?" he asked.

"You turned me in, asshole. You broke my leg." Rick hissed.

"We had a warrant for his arrest and had patrolled the campus without seeing him. That's when Andy suggested that we drive by and warn you this guy was armed and on the loose." George watched Andy take Rick to the patrol car. "When we saw the motorcycle in the driveway, we called for backup and snuck up on him. He didn't offer any resistance."

"Wow." Ron had missed another close call. "Let's not tell my girlfriend about this," Ron pleaded.

"Sure, it's no problem." George said smiling. "He won't get out on bail this time. Not for attempted murder and a shooting on a college campus."

"Good to hear." Ron said.

"Geez Ron. We don't need all of this excitement." Matt, his landlord said.

"It's all over now, Matt." Ron turned to go back upstairs. As the police were departing, Matt and his wife went back inside. Ron had a thought. He got into the Corvette and drove over to campus. It was already about 9:30 PM. He parked near Fredrick Hall. He went in and the Hall monitor looked at him.

"It's almost closing time, buddy." She said.

"I will just be a minute." Ron walked over to Sue and Joan's door and knocked. "Who is it?" Joan called through the door.

"It's just Ron."

She unlocked the door. He saw she was in her pajamas.

"I'm sorry. I didn't want to disturb you, but I wanted you to know that the police caught the shooter from this afternoon."

"Oh...ok, thanks." Joan replied. Sue came to the door. She was wearing pajamas too. "Come in for a second, Ron." Sue stood back to let him in.

Ron entered. Joan retreated back to her bed. Sue put her arms around him and they had a long passionate kiss. He could tell she had nothing on under the pajamas. They were sort of shear and did not leave much to the imagination. He was starting to get aroused but he backed off.

"I...I guess...I will see you on Friday," he managed. "We need to study for the Psychology final." She purred.

"Yeah. We should do that." He backed through the door. "It is near closing time, I should go." He turned to leave but stopped to look at her again.

"Maybe tomorrow?" she asked.

"Sure. That sounds good. I'll text you." He left, closing the door slowly behind him. "Wow, that was pretty passionate." Joan smiled at her. "I think I might have excited him just a little bit," Sue replied as she locked the door and returned to her bed.

"I am surprised he didn't just jump on you right there on the floor." Joan joked. "He is too much of a gentleman to try that." Sue got into the bed.

"Well, I could tell he didn't want to leave. You definitely have him." I guess I will find out Friday, Sue thought as she pulled the covers up. I will try to seduce him and see what this sex stuff is all about.

CHAPTER 66

RON LEFT FREDRICK HALL and returned to his car. Wow, Wow, Wow, he thought. Sue is really in love with me. He could hardly concentrate on driving the car. She had gotten him all worked up. He returned home. A strange car was parked in his spot. He parked behind it. He walked up the stairs to his apartment. A figure was sitting on the top step. It was Monica. She was wearing a black trench coat.

"Where have you been lover? Pronging your child girlfriend?" she sneered. "Monica, what are you doing here?" Ron was not happy to see her.

"I thought you might want a toss in the hay for old times' sake." She opened her coat. She did not have anything on under the coat. Ron was shocked. Why was she doing this? She was very beautiful, but in a different way from Sue.

"Why are you doing this? We are through for good." He managed to blurt out.

"Come on Ron...you don't want that little girl when you can have a woman." She leaned towards him.

Ron did not know what to do. He definitely would love to quench his lust with her, but then she would be in control again and that would ruin what he had with Sue. He saw only one solution. He turned around and went back down stairs and got into the Corvette. He backed out and squealed his tires as he left.

Monica was puzzled and frustrated. She thought about going inside and waiting for him to return only to find her naked in his bed. No guy could resist that she thought. Oh well. She finally gave up and went down and got in her car and drove away. His loss, she thought.

Ron was definitely aroused by Monica but he did not want to lose what he had with Sue. He pulled out and headed for the interstate. He got on the interstate and drove until he found an all-night truck stop. He parked the car in the area for automobiles and went into the restaurant. He sat down at a table and picked up the menu.

An attractive blond waitress came over. "What'cha want honey?" She had seen him walk in and he did not look like a trucker.

"Can I get a cheeseburger and an iced tea?" He looked at her. She was really cute he thought.

"Sure thing." She smiled at him, noticing he had no wedding ring. She walked away. She was wearing a short skirt and a pink blouse with a light green apron.

Three truckers came over and sat at a booth behind him. They were swearing and cussing. Apparently they were in a convoy transporting something across country in three trucks. The cute waitress walked over to their table. They started to flirt with her but she apparently was not interested. She asked for their order and they gave it to her, still making lewd comments about her. Ron turned to look at them. Any one of them would outweigh him by about fifty pounds. They were almost middle aged but looked tough. They saw him look and one of them sneered, "Are they letting little kids in here with the men?"

Ron ignored the comment and stopped looking at them. He definitely did not want to tangle with these caveman types. Luckily, a couple of state troopers came in and sat at the table next to him. The truckers stopped talking and whispered in low tones.

"Is that your red Corvette out there?" one of the cops leaned over and asked Ron. "Uh…Yes. That's mine." Ron smiled at them.

"Nice looking ride." The other cop said. He looked at the other cop and whispered something to him.

Then he turned to Ron. "Someone phoned in to our office the other night that a similar red Corvette was speeding on the highway, going over a hundred miles an hour." The cop looked at him. The pretty waitress walked over to the troopers' table to take their order.

"Couldn't be me. I work with the campus police at the college." He lied, but then showed them the badge George had given him. The waitress looked at him.

"Well. OK then. Sorry to accuse you," the first cop said. The truckers heard this exchange and stopped talking.

"Did you hear about that shooting at the college today?" the first trooper asked him.

"Yes. I was there." Ron did not want to say that he was the target. "But the shooter was apprehended this evening."

"Well, that's good to hear," the second trooper noted.

The waitress appeared relieved that the troopers had come in and whispered something about the truckers at the other booth. Both cops looked over at the truckers but did not say anything. She went back to her counter.

The waitress brought over his burger and ice tea. "Are you a cop also?" she asked him in a low voice.

"Well, not really. I just help out the campus police when I can." He blushed. It was a little white lie but what the heck.

"I get off at midnight. You want to get together?" she whispered.

"Wow. Ah...I would really like to, but I have to get back to the college." He managed. "Can I maybe have a raincheck?" He didn't want to turn her down and make her mad.

"Ok." She smiled at him and walked away.

What is it tonight? He thought. Every girl I run into wants to bed me. He finished the cheeseburger, paid up and left a hefty tip.

The two state patrolmen were standing over talking to the three truckers who had been making the lewd comments. Ron figured it was a good time to go.

He headed back to his apartment. When he got there, Monica's car was gone. Good, he thought. Maybe she will get the hint and leave him alone. He was half afraid that he would find Monica in his bed naked. He would have a hard time not responding to that.

He climbed the stairs after parking the car, and entered the apartment. He looked around. No one was inside. He went to the bed. The browning pistol was still under the pillow. He locked the door, brushed his teeth and went to bed. It had been a long day and he was exhausted.

CHAPTER 67

SARAH WAS AT THE nursing home with Robert. They still had a respirator on him. She was hoping that he would wake up again and talk to her. The nursing home doctor had said that he had slipped back into a coma. The Reverend Morton was still working with the prayer group. He really believed that the prayer group was providing a miracle. Sarah had told him of the warning that Bob had given about the engineering project and that Marty, the Engineering Vice President was sure that Bob had saved their program. Reverend Morton was impressed by this but he told her that God had allowed Bob to make the warning, a sure sign that it was indeed a miracle. Sarah was praying again, hoping that he would talk to her again.

Dr. Jack Simms had previously argued that they should let Bob die but now was an advocate of the new experimental drug. She was now convinced more than ever that Bob would recover. Jack Simms did not push the issue, but he had seen the MRI, and the thing inside of Bob's head was probably not going to go away, no matter how hard they prayed. He did not have anything against prayer, but the reality was that Bob was going to die and probably very soon unless the new drug really started to shrink the tumor.

Sarah's brother Tom had been bothering her for money again. He said he was desperate, and finally told her that he had lost money to the Mob in gambling and that they were going to beat him up. He actually got on his knees and begged her to help him. She had no choice but to write him a check for 10 thousand dollars. She could not bear to see her little brother hurt. That sort of depleted the checking account. She would have to start drawing funds from Bob's 401K savings. The long-term disability insurance had run out and now the health care cost was hurting more. She did not know if her brother was lying to her or not. She hoped not. Either way, that was the last of the money her brother would get from her. He was an adult. He should be able to provide for himself.

Tom was happy. He got some of the money he needed to pay off the gambling debt but he still needed another fifteen thousand. The ten thousand would however let him buy an airplane ticket to Florida where he could hide out. He would figure something else to do once he was safely away from the mob. Yes. It was going to work out. He had some contacts in Fort Lauderdale that would help him in his new existence. He wondered if he should change his name. He needed to return to his place to get his stuff. He would buy an airplane ticket on the way.

CHAPTER 68

RON GOT UP EARLY and completed his last hydraulics assignment. All he had to do now was hand it in. It was a take-home test which allowed use of the textbook to try to solve the problems. The problems were tough but he thought he had most of them correct. He texted Sue to see if she wanted to get together to study for the Psychology Final. She texted back that she would be ready in about half an hour. He responded by asking if they should go to the library. She agreed.

He called the auto repair shop to find out about the Jeep. He got an estimate for replacing the back window and windshield. The passenger side mirror required replacement also. Insurance would pay for the glass replacement but he had to pay for the side mirror. He verbally agreed on the cost and asked when it would be ready for pickup. They said it would be ready by Friday morning.

He got ready and grabbed his laptop, Psychology book and a notebook. He had on his normal khaki pants, blue shirt and blue blazer. He looked in his closet and had dug the old shoulder holster out of the closet and had it on under the blazer. He took the Browning pistol and put it in the holster. It was heavy on his left side which had the cut in his shoulder, but he figured he could get used to it. After what happened yesterday he did not want to be caught unprotected again. It was true that Rick was in jail, but Ron was just paranoid enough that he felt better having the gun than being without it.

He drove over to see Sue at Fredrick Hall and met her at her dorm room. She was dressed in a short blue skirt, a frilly white blouse and white sandals. Joan was busy and decided not to join them.

"Hi," he started.

"Let's go," Sue said, leaving and closing the door.

They went down the steps to the entrance and walked to his car. They got in the car but he did not start it.

"What's the matter?" she asked.

"I need to be honest with you." He started again. "When I returned home last night, Monica was at my place." He looked at Sue. "She tried to seduce me but I turned her down."

"I thought you were through with her." Sue frowned looking down.

"I thought so too. But nothing happened. I don't want to have any secrets from you." "She is a pretty woman," Sue looked at him. "How could you resist her?"

"It was not easy, but I am in love with you." He blushed.

"Well, thanks for telling me." She leaned over and kissed him lightly.

They drove to the library. As he parked the Corvette next to the fenced-in playground, he asked "No kids at the playground?" The huge oak trees were still lining the road. Apparently the city had not gotten around to removing them yet.

"It's still summer vacation. They don't go back to school until next week," she responded.

They went into the library and found a quiet table away from the crowd where they could study. They would read a chapter and then quiz each other on it. After a couple of hours, they got tired of this and she suggested they go get a milkshake. He was tired of studying also, and agreed. They left the library and walked to the car. Before he could open the door for her she turned and faced him. He stopped and they embraced. He kissed her and she responded by putting her arms around him.

"Hey what's this?" she encountered the bulge under his left arm.

"Ah...it's something I wanted to have with me after what happened yesterday." He opened the blazer and she saw the Browning in his holster.

"Wow. You are prepared today," she said as he closed the blazer. "Yeah. I don't think I need it, but it just feels better to have it."

"Psychologically speaking, you are a paranoid." She smiled at him.

"Maybe so, but I don't want to take any chances. It's better to be prepared."

They got in the car and drove to the Dairy Queen. They had their chocolate milkshakes and he drove back to her dormitory.

"Boy, we drove all over town and nobody took a shot at us," she teased. *"True. Good thing they didn't. I was prepared,"* he kidded back at her.

He escorted her back to her room. "See you in class tomorrow?" he asked.

"Yes. This test should be a breeze." She had invited him in. Joan was not in the room.

"By the way, how did you do so well on the last test? You did not get to study for it." He leaned against the doorframe.

"I don't know. The information was in my head. Just like someone had put it there," she replied. *"I remember reading those chapters to you when you were in the hospital."* He looked at her.

"Really?" She looked back at him. *"It must have helped somehow."* She drew him close and they kissed again. They both felt the sexual tension rising. She was tempted to ask him to stay but was not sure when Joan would return.

He reluctantly turned to leave. *"See you in class."* He smiled, closing the door. He was not sure he could resist her much longer. He wanted her first time to be special.

CHAPTER 69

*R*ON WAS UP EARLY *and went to the food mart. He got four steaks, salad makings, a six pack of beer and a good bottle of Cabernet. He figured he would invite Joan and Jerry over too. He got back to the apartment and put the stuff in the refrigerator. His phone rang. He answered. It was Sue.*

"How are you doing?" she purred.

"I just got back from the store to get stuff for tomorrow night's dinner."

"What are we having?" She asked.

"I thought I would grill you a steak."

"That sounds good."

"Do you want to invite Joan and Jerry too? I have extra steaks," he asked casually.

"I think they have other plans." She lied. She wanted to be alone with him.

"Ok. See you in class?"

"You bet." They both hung up.

CHAPTER 70

SARAH'S BROTHER TOM ARRIVED at the apartment that he shared with a friend. He had just purchased an airplane ticket to Miami and still had over 9,000 dollars in his pocket. He was going to pack up and get out of town. He opened his door and immediately two hefty guys grabbed him from behind.

"Hey, what gives?" he shouted.

"Shut up or I'll break your arm," the voice behind him said.

They marched him to the kitchen and forced him to sit in a chair, then taped his arms to the chair. He looked at them. It was Big Tony and Little Richie, enforcers for the local Mob.

"You owe us 25 Grand, where is it?" Big Tony asked menacingly. Big Tony was about 300 pounds and six foot tall. He was almost bald but typically shaved his head. He was wearing a white polo shirt and dark pants with a brown blazer. Little Richie was not little. He was a musclebound 250 pounds and also six foot tall. He was dressed similar to Big Tony but had a crew cut, tattoos up and down his arms and a nasty scar down the side of his face.

"Look, I told Louie I would get it this week, honest." Tom was starting to sweat. "Well, where is it?"

"I got some of it with me, almost ten grand." He head bobbed to indicate his pocket.

Little Richie dug the envelope out of his pocket and looked in it. "Yeah he's got some of it," Little Richie hissed. His voice box had gotten crushed in a fight and he always talked in a hoarse whisper. "Hey, look here, a ticket to Miami, leaving tonight."

"Going to skip out on us?" Big Tony growled.

"No, no…I was going to see a friend in Florida. He owes me a lot of money. I was going to bring it back, honest." Tom was sweating more now.

"Who is your friend? Why can't he just wire the money? Tony asked.

"Look…he is…he…is on the lam from the authorities. He won't go near a Western Union." Tom stuttered. "That's why I have to go get it from him. He is good for it, honest."

"I don't think Louie will buy that," Little Richie whispered.

"If we kill him now, we still got the 10 Grand," Big Tony said. "Where did you get the 10 Gs?" Richie asked.

"From my sister, she has over a half million dollars. Look, I can get more from her and then pay her back when I get back from Florida." Tom was trying to think fast.

"What do you think?" Big Tony asked Richie who obviously was the brains.

"I don't know…the 10 Grand is a good down payment." Richie noted. "But maybe we need to convince him and his sister to fork over the rest. Give him some chin music." Richie stood back as Tony put on a glove and then started hitting Tom in the face.

"Ow. Please stop," Tom protested. Tony did not stop but started to hit him harder. "Noooo…Please." Tom screamed. Tony hit him again and again.

After about five minutes Tom passed out and his face was all bloody. "Good enough?" Tony asked.

"Yeah, that will give him something to think about." He put the envelope of cash and the ticket in his inside coat pocket. They turned and walked out.

CHAPTER 71

*R*ON, SUE AND JOAN *were in the psychology class and the Finals were just being handed out. They all dug into the packets and started to write. Ron thought this isn't too bad. Most of the questions were on the stuff he and Sue had studied at the library. He noticed that Sue was buzzing through the questions much faster than he was. She was already on page three and he had just started page 2. How does she do that? he wondered. This was a timed test. About half way through the test time Sue closed her packet and walked up to Coach Johnson's desk. She put the test down and turned to walk out. She was the first person finished with the test.*

"You're done already? Gary asked.

She turned back. "It was sort of easy." She smiled at him. Then she walked away. Gary Johnson was still amazed at this girl. She must have a very high IQ, he thought.

Ron was still struggling with the test. Joan finally finished and handed in her packet. She then walked out. She had agreed to meet Ron and Sue at the Student Union after the test. There were about five minutes left when Ron finished and turned in his paper. He tended to be thorough and always checked his answers one more time before handing a test in. He was pretty sure he had done pretty well. After he turned it in, he walked to the Student Union.

As Ron got to the Student Union, he looked around for the girls. Then he saw them, sitting at a table. Two burley football players were sitting with them, trying to talk to them. Ron walked over to the table. One of the football players, John Turley, looked up at him and recognized him. He said "Get lost Pritchard," he said in a very menacing voice.

Ron looked at Sue who could not move since one of the guys had his huge hand clamped on hers. She looked up at Ron with a helpless look on her face. Joan was sitting there looking at the confrontation with a look of horror on her face.

"Get away from my fiancée." Ron growled.

The other football player, Reggie, looked up and said, "She doesn't have a ring on."

"It's true, we are engaged, and he just hasn't given me the ring yet." Sue said in loud voice.

"Well, well, well." Turley stood up. "Suppose I show her who the better man is?"

Ron looked around. The crowd on the veranda had gotten quiet. Everyone was looking at the confrontation. "You don't want to do this." Ron replied. The guy had about 60 pounds over him, but he would probably be slow. If he hit him hard and fast he had a chance. If the big guy started to wrestle him he had no chance.

"Let's you and me find out," the big man took a step forward.

"Wait." Ron put his hand up. The big guy stopped. Ron took off his jacket revealing the pistol in his shoulder holster. He took the holster off and set it on the table with his badge and jacket.

"You're a cop? The big man took a step back.

"Sort of." Ron turned to face him. In the background behind the football players, he saw George and Andy walking toward them.

"I don't want no trouble with a cop." The big man knew that policemen were trained in self-defense and he did not feel like losing some teeth.

"What's going on here?" George and Andy were in their police uniforms and approached the group.

The other football player, Reggie, stood up. "Nothing, officer, we were just leaving," John Turley remarked. He grabbed Reggie by the arm and they turned and walked toward the entrance.

George looked at Ron and the girls. "Looks like I am always saving your butts."

"I was going to handle it." Ron walked over to the table. He put on the shoulder holster and jacket. He turned to George. "I suppose you want this back." Ron handed him the badge.

"No. Keep it for now. You are almost graduated and you have been a great help to us." George and Andy both smiled at the ladies and walked away.

Joan was in partial shock. She had no idea that Ron was carrying such a big pistol in a shoulder holster. She was amazed previously when he had returned fire at their attacker with the small pistol. Now it appeared that he was really a part time cop?

*Ron sat down at the table. "Why were they bothering you?"
Ron asked.*

*"We were just sitting here talking about the test when they
came over and sat down with us about a couple of minutes before
you came. They suggested that we should go out with them and
celebrate finals being over," Sue tried to explain. "We did nothing
to encourage them."*

*"I didn't know you were an official police officer." Joan
remarked.*

*"Well, not really, but George and I are good friends." Ron
tried to explain. "So, we are engaged?" Sue questioned him with
a sly look on her face.*

*"I couldn't think of anything else to say," he pleaded. "Hey,
you want to celebrate the end of finals?" he mockingly asked her.*

*The girls got up and they walked toward the entrance. "We
could go get a milkshake, but I can only fit one passenger in my
car. The Jeep is still in the shop until tomorrow."*

*Joan looked at them and replied "You guys go ahead. I'm
going back to the dorm."*

*Sue looked at Ron and said "I'm not in the mood for a
milkshake. How about we go for a walk?" "Ok." They walked
toward the tree park south of the Student Union.*

They walked over to his maple tree.

"This is where I sometimes sit and meditate," he told her.

*"It is a nice quiet, shady spot." She proclaimed, sitting down
under the tree. He sat next to her. They sat there quietly for a
while. "Do you really want to marry me?" she asked quietly. "We
haven't known each other very long."*

*"Well," he began," you are by far the smartest girl I have ever
met; you are beautiful, gentle and kind. You are sexy as all get out.
And you can kick the heck out of a mugger," he replied. "What
more could a guy want?" He smiled at her.*

*"I need to finish college." She looked at him, a tear going
down her face. His compliments really touched her. "It's going to
take almost four years."*

*"I want you to," he declared. "I need to finish college myself
and then get a job. I really should not ask you to get married until
I can support you in the manner I want to."*

"I don't want to lose you." She looked down.

"If I give you a ring for a pre-engagement, will you accept it?" he asked. He had a small box in his hand.

"Is this an official proposal?" she gasped, looking at the box.

"Yes. Will you marry me?" he opened the box. A single solitaire diamond ring was in it. He had had this for quite some time. It had belonged to his mother. He almost gave it to Monica before she showed her true colors. In some ways he was naïve about love, but he knew that he wanted to be with Sue for the rest of his life.

She started to cry. *"Ok. Yes."* He put the ring on her finger.

"That belonged to my mother." It was a modest, half karat single diamond on a white gold ring.

She leaned over and kissed him. *"It's beautiful."* She buried her head in his neck. *"Can we wait until I am out of college?"*

"Whatever you want; I will never ever tell you what you can and cannot do. If you want to be with me, then that is alright. If you decide to go a different way, I will understand." He looked into her eyes.

"I thought the guy always had to be in control?" she asked.

"Any relationship has to have some give and take. If we cannot agree on something then we should try to compromise. If our careers pull us apart, then we will have to decide to cross that bridge then." He held her hands. *"Up until then, you will have my love if you want it."*

"Yes. I want you. Forever and ever." She smiled at him as a tear ran down her cheek.

CHAPTER 72

*T*HE POLICE OFFICER WAS talking to Sarah. He had pulled into her driveway, knocked on the door and asked if she knew a Tom Lewis. She said, yes he was her brother. She was wondering what trouble he had gotten into now.

"He was beat up pretty bad, lost some dental work. The guy he was sharing a house with came home and found him. He was strapped to a chair, unconscious. We found your address in his wallet and figured we better check it out."

"He's in the hospital?" she asked.

"Yes, the paramedics were concerned that he might have some brain damage." "Thank you. I'll go to the hospital."

The police officer turned to go but turned around. "Is he in some sort of trouble?"

"He said he owed some money to the Mob. I gave him some money. I was hoping that was all he needed." She exclaimed.

"Well, it sounds like this was a warning. The next time we will probably find him floating in the river."

Sarah went back inside. This can't be happening, she thought. Her little brother was mixed up with the Mob and they were probably going to kill him. What can I do? She would have to pull some money out of the IRA to pay off his debt. She got ready to go to the hospital.

CHAPTER 73

SUE WAS BACK IN the dorm. She showed Joan the ring.
"Wow, good for you!" Joan was excited. "And he hasn't bedded you yet? That is really unusual. Guys don't even buy a car without a test drive," she exclaimed.

"Well, tomorrow he is cooking dinner for me at his place." Sue hinted. "By the way, he was going to invite you and Jerry over too, but I told him you guys have other plans." Sue looked at her friend intently.

"That's ok. Jerry did ask me to go to a movie. It looks like we are busy," Joan smirked. "Now that the semester is almost over, are you heading home?" Sue asked.

"Yeah. My brother is coming up to pick me up early next week. Do you need a ride home?

Sue smiled. "No, I have invited Ron to stay at my house for a few days, He is going to drive me back."

"Wow. Wait till your mother sees that ring."

"Yes. But maybe things are happening too fast..." Sue paused.

"Nonsense. I could see you two had some definite chemistry about you. He is definitely a good catch. I hope I get that lucky." Joan smiled.

"He is so understanding and gentle. He says he won't try to control me. He wants me to finish school." Sue sighed. "He intends to pursue an engineering position at an aerospace company."

"That is unusual," Joan agreed. "Do you two think you can have a longdistance relationship?" "I hope so," Sue said hopefully.

CHAPTER 74

*R*ON WAS COOKING THE *steaks. He had picked up Sue at Fred rick Hall and had driven back to his apartment. He was amazed how she looked. She was wearing a frilly sleeveless white blouse, a short black skirt and had black fishnet stockings on with black mid heel shoes. Her blouse was almost transparent and she was not wearing a bra. She did have the engagement ring on. He could hardly cook, thinking about her. She was inside preparing the salad and setting the table while he was on the porch with the small propane grill.*

"Almost done?" she asked through the screen door.

"About another two minutes. You said you like your steak medium?" "Yes."

That was ok, since he liked his medium also. He was finding several things they had in common.

He turned the steaks one more time and cut one to see that it was a hot pink inside. "Steaks are done," he called as he put them on the platter and turned off the grill. He brought them in and set a steak on each plate. They were simple T-bone steaks. She had the salad already on the table. He went to the refrigerator and got the wine. "You want some wine?" he asked.

"Sure. That sounds good." She was smiling at him.

He looked at her. She had been flirting with him ever since he picked her up.

He opened the wine and poured two glasses. They ate the steaks and salad. She asked for more wine.

"You don't want to drink too much. It'll go to your head like with Jerry," he cautioned her. "Ok, just a little bit," she said softly. She drank it down.

"Well, it's still early. You want to do something?" He couldn't take his eyes off of her. She was so damn beautiful.

"Yes." She got up and walked over to his bed. "You care to join me?"

"Ahem." he gasped. *"I thought you might want your first time to be something special."*

"It will be if you come over here and join me," she purred. *"You have to see if I am worth this ring."* She held out her left hand to him.

He could not fight the urge anymore. He came over and they kissed, a long, passionate kiss. She let him undress her. She lay back on the bed. *"I'm new at this, you will have to tell me what to do."*

"OK." He got undressed and joined her.

CHAPTER 75

SARAH WAS AT THE hospital, talking to the doctor. "He got quite a beating. His nose is broken, his jaw is fractured, he has lost a couple of teeth. His left eye is swollen shut. I think his attacker must have been right-handed." The doctor was reading from the chart.

"Will he recover?" she asked.

"Well, no one really ever recovers from this type of beating. The wounds will heal but his spirit will probably be severely diminished."

"Can I see him?" she asked.

"Yes, go ahead. He may have trouble talking, we had to wire his jaw shut." The doctor pointed to the room.

She walked into the room. She was horrified at how her brother looked. He was sedated but awake. His nose and the left side of his face were bandaged. He was looking at the ceiling with his one good eye.

"Tom." She tried to get his attention. He looked at her and then away. "Tom, can you hear me?"

He grunted and looked back at her. "Who did this to you?"

He started to cry. A tear crossed his cheek. "I'm so sorry." He managed to slur. "Why?" she asked.

"I am a worthless piece of trash." He turned to the wall. "Tom. Can you tell the police who did this to you?" she asked.

"No, they will kill me if I do." His words were slurred but she could make them out. "How much do you owe them?" she pressed.

"It doesn't matter, I'm not worth it." He was still crying. "How much?" Her voice was raised slightly.

"About 20 Grand," he whispered.

CHAPTER 76

*R*ON WAS DRIVING SUE *back to the dormitory. Sue looked at him with adoring eyes. He had been so gentle with her, stopping often to kiss her. Then it got into a much faster pattern and then they were done. He had cuddled with her afterwards. She thought she had a climax, but it was so sudden it was almost a shock. He had used a condom. She had never seen one before but understood how it worked. She had two younger brothers whose diapers she had changed so the male anatomy was not new to her. He told her he loved her afterward. They had reluctantly parted and dressed so he could take her back to the dorm. He had asked if she was ok. She had replied by kissing him again.*

"Can I see you tomorrow?" he asked. He wanted to be with her now all of the time. "That would be nice," she said. She wanted him again already.

"We could get married right away and you could stay in school," he started. "You still want me after the test drive?" she teased.

"God, yes. You are the most important thing in my life now," he answered honestly. "So, I can keep the ring?"

"Please. Don't joke about it. Yes...I want you. I want you to keep the ring."

They arrived at the dormitory and kissed again in his car. Then they got out and he escorted her to her door. She turned to him," I do love you, Ron."

"I know. I love you too." They kissed again.

They parted. She went in and he walked away. She saw Joan sitting on her bed reading. Joan looked up and saw her.

"You did it!" Joan exclaimed.

"Yes, how did you know?" Sue looked at her.

"Well, you still have the engagement ring on and you have that dreamy smile on your face. How was it?" she was curious.

"It was just beautiful." Sue sighed, "He was so gentle and caring and boy, that was fun." "Sounds like you got one of the good ones." Joan smiled at her.

"He wants to get married right away." Sue twirled around the room. "Wow. You two have got it really bad." Joan said.

CHAPTER 77

SARAH HAD MADE TOM tell her who to give the money to. It was some unsavory underworld person connected to the mob. Sarah had withdrawn the amount from her IRA account and was prepared to make the payoff. She then asked Jack if he would accompany her since she was unsure of these types of people. Jack could not do it but said he would look into an acquaintance of his. He knew a man who was familiar with the underworld figures. He was a private detective named Michael Kramer. Kramer was a big man, almost 6 foot, 4 inches tall. Jack knew he was an ex-marine and an excop. Kramer had come to him to ask him to please operate on his mother. After reviewing her case, other doctors did not want to operate since they believed she probably would not survive the operation. Jack Simms thought
she might do ok with a new type of procedure and agreed to do the operation. Kramer's mother survived the operation and returned to a normal life. Kramer was so happy that he told Jack if he ever needed any help he could call on him. Jack had never thought about it until now. He went to his office and sorted through some business cards. He found the one Kramer had given him. It had a picture of a chess piece on it, a white knight. The writing underneath said 'Private Investigations' and a phone number.

He called Kramer who answered on the second ring. "Michael, this is Doctor Simms from the Cleveland Clinic. How is your mother doing?" Jack asked.

"She is great Doc, how are you doing?" Kramer replied. Kramer knew he wasn't calling about his mother.

"I'm doing fine. I was wondering if you could do a small favor for me?"

"Ah, ok, sure. What do you need?" Kramer was hoping it wasn't something he didn't want to do.

"I have a friend whose wife's brother is in debt to the mob. Her brother could not pay off his gambling debt so they beat him up pretty badly." Jack explained.

"What do you want me to do?"

Jack could sense some unwillingness in Kramer's voice. "She wants to pay off the debt but is scared to go by herself. Her brother is in the hospital and cannot do it himself."

"Can't her husband make the pay off?"

"Her husband is in the hospital, dying of a brain tumor. We do not expect him to live out the month." Jack explained.

"Oh. I see why you are asking me now. So she has the money? Is it in cash?" "Yes."

"Well, if all she needs is an escort, I suppose I can do that for her." Kramer agreed. Jack made arrangements for them to meet.

She met him at a coffee shop. She saw him come in, a heavyset man in his forties, about 275 pounds. He was wearing a brown plaid suit, white shirt with a red tie. Obviously, fashion was not his main strength. He looked around the room and saw her sitting alone in a corner. He walked over to her table and sat down.

"You are Mrs. Parker?" "Yes."

"I am Kramer." He looked around the room, obviously trying to be aware of any threats. "How do you know Jack Simms?" She was curious.

"He operated on my mother, fixed her up good when all the other doctors said she was a hopeless case. I owe him for that." He looked at her.

"Well, ok." She struggled to find the right words. "My brother owes a lot of money to the syndicate. They beat him to within an inch of his life."

"Ok. How much are we talking here?"

"Tom said it was 20 thousand." She said in a very low voice. "Whew…that is a fair amount." He whistled softly.

"I want to pay it off but I don't know how to be sure they will leave him alone." "Who is the guy he owes it to?"

"Tom said that it was someone named Louie at the Caribbean Cocktail Lounge, downtown." "Yeah, I know that crowd. I am surprised they didn't kill him."

'They beat him pretty badly; I can't just let them kill my baby brother. I have the money, but I'm afraid to go there by myself," she said softly. He leaned over to hear her better and she saw he had a gun in a belt holster. "Is that a weapon?" she whispered.

"Don't worry. I have a permit. You got the cash on you?"

"Yes." She patted a pocket of her coat. "Do you want to see it?" "Not here. Ok, let's go and make the payoff."

They got up to leave. He escorted her to his black Mercedes parked in the lot. They drove downtown. Along the way he turned on the radio. It was set to a classical music station. She was surprised that a rough character like Kramer would have such a nice car and listen to classical music. He must be much more refined than he appears, she thought.

"Do you mind if I smoke?" he pulled out a big black cigar.

"I wish you wouldn't. Those things make me sick." She replied in a subdued tone. She had no idea where this strange man was taking her. She had a lot of money in an envelope in her coat pocket and she was feeling very unsure of this whole situation. She wished it was over and that she was back in her safe quiet house.

"Ok, no problem." He concentrated on driving. She was a very attractive lady. She was a little bit older than him but she still was what he would consider a lady. "I think I heard something about your husband dying or something?"

"He has a brain tumor and the doctors say he will die. I am praying that he won't," she said in a low voice.

"I am sorry to hear that."

They got downtown and he took a few side streets away from the main drag. There she saw the Caribbean Cocktail Lounge, a sort of run-down looking bar with neon signs in the windows. They parked in a lot next to the bar.

"Ok, give me the cash." He held his hand out. She hesitated.

"Don't worry, I will pay off the debt. If you walk in there by yourself they will shake you down," he told her.

"Ok," she reluctantly handed over the envelope.

He opened the envelope and thumbed through the cash. He found a hundred-dollar bill and removed it and put it in his pocket. "That is for my carrying fee. They won't miss one C-note." They got out of the Mercedes and walked to the door. He opened it for her and they entered. It was somewhat dark inside and it took a few seconds for her eyes to adjust. She followed him to the bar and sat down on a stool next to him. There was a half nude girl dancing on a small stage in the corner to some old rock music. Three or four patrons were watching the girl strip.

"Barkeep." He motioned to the bartender.

A real ugly little man in a ragged black suit wearing an apron came over and asked what he wanted to drink.

"Bring me a beer." He put a twenty on the bar. "And tell Louie someone is here to see him." "Nobody here by that name." the little guy said.

"Just do it little man. We have something he wants."

The ugly man walked away and picked up a phone at the end of the bar. He talked for a minute and scooted away.

Kramer looked around and saw big Tony at a near table. He was the bouncer today, watching the patrons who were watching the girls undress on the stage. He happened to look in Kramer's direction and stood up.

Sarah saw the rather large bald man came over and sit next to her. "What are you doing here Kramer? Who is the dame?" Big Tony said, looking at Sarah.

"Big Tony, long time no see." Kramer turned toward him. "I have to talk to Louie."

"Well, you can talk to me and I will relay the message." Tony had his huge hands on the bar. "Nope." Kramer said. "My business is with Louie." "Don't push it too far, Kramer." Tony growled.

A back door opened and two men came out and walked over to them. One of them had tattoos up and down his arms and a terrible scar on his cheek. The other was a dark Negro that was dressed in a black 3-piece suit, black shirt, white tie and shiny black shoes.

"Kramer. What is this about?" the black man hissed.

"I understand a guy named Tom Lewis owes you some money." "Could be, I am not sure I know a Tom Lewis."

"Well, this is his sister, Mrs. Parker." He motioned to Sarah. "She wants to pay off the debt but doesn't want any more trouble." Kramer leaned back, his jacket was open, showing the weapon in its holster. His hand was near the holster.

"Hey…nobody wants any trouble." The black man took a step back.

The tattooed man reached into his jacket but did not pull anything out. He folded his arms to hide that he was holding something in his jacket.

"Well, that's good, because Mrs. Parker just wants this all to end." Kramer stated. "Sure, sure we can do that. You got the payment?"

Kramer fished the envelope out his pocket and handed it to Louie. "It's short a C-note as my finder's Fee." Kramer whispered.

"That's ok. We are all friends here." The black man opened the envelope and thumbed through the contents. "It looks like the debt is all paid off." He smiled. He motioned for Tony to join them and handed him the envelope "Put that in the safe," he told Tony.

The other man with a scar looked hard at Kramer. "Maybe me and you will have a face off sometime," Little Richie spat. He took his arm away from his jacket.

Kramer looked at him. "Any time you feel lucky." He growled.

"Not today, Richie." Louie hissed. The three of them turned and headed for the back door. Kramer did not say anything.

Kramer turned to the bartender. "I didn't get my beer, but you can keep the twenty as a tip." "Come on, let's get out of here," he told Sarah.

"That's it?" she asked.

"Yeah, they don't give receipts." They headed toward the door. Once outside, Sarah felt a lot better. "Thank God that is over. Thank you." "Yeah, just hope your brother is smart enough not to gamble here anymore."

CHAPTER 78

*S*UE DECIDED TO GO *over to the Student Union to see if her final grades were posted. The semester was officially ended and they had three weeks off before the fall semester started. She also had to register for her next classes. Registration did not start for another two days so she postponed returning home until after registration. She had already talked with her advisor and knew which classes she wanted to sign up for. Two would be exciting, one was Art History and the other was Modern Art. She also had to take chemistry, which was not as exciting. She was hoping that Ron could help her through that. He had gotten a 'B' in that course. She was walking out to the veranda when she saw Monica Martin sitting at a table by herself. She debated about turning around but decided it was time to meet her face to face. She walked over to Monica. Monica looked up and saw her.*

"Monica..." Sue started.

"You!" Monica stood up and put out a clawed hand towards Sue's face.

Sue grabbed the hand as she was trained to in Karate and turned the hand so that the pressure point made Monica fall to the ground on her knees.

"Owwww...that hurts." Monica moaned.

"Are you going to be calm, or should I break your wrist? Sue hissed. "Ok, ok, ok. I give up. You win."

Sue let go. "Now let's talk." Sue motioned to the table.

Monica got to her feet rubbing her hand. "Where did you learn to do that?" "I have a black belt in Karate. Do you need another demonstration?" "No. Once is enough." She reluctantly sat down.

"Ok then. I want to talk to you about Ron," Sue started.

" You are ruining it. I was going to get him back." Monica was still massaging her wrist. "Well, you are too late." Sue showed her the engagement ring.

"He gave you the ring? That was going to be mine but I screwed it up." Monica looked at the ring. "He said you broke up with him months ago for someone else." Sue looked at her intently.

"Yes. I thought Stan was so much more exciting, but I was wrong. He dropped me for someone else." Monica looked down at the table. "Ron was kind and gentle. I thought he was really boring, but now I see I was wrong."

"Well, he is in love with me now. You have to back away."

"Yeah, I got the message the other night. I went to his apartment totally nude under my coat and he took one look and walked away. Not many men could have done that. He must really love you."

"I heard he saw you but he did not give me that detail," Sue related.

"That's just like him. He is not like most guys. He's humble and doesn't brag about himself. I heard he was involved in a shooting the other day here on campus. I wanted to find out what that was about. That's why I was here. He typically sits out here before class."

"Classes are over now." Sue looked around. The veranda was almost deserted. "Ron was shot at by a crazy guy and he returned fire with his pistol. But no one was hurt."

"He's carrying a pistol? I didn't know that."

"Yeah, it turns out he was working with the campus police to put away a rapist." Sue explained.

"Did they catch him?"

"Yes. You'll probably read about it in the paper." Sue looked at her. "I don't read the paper much." Monica was looking at the table top. "How did you two ever meet?" Sue was curious.

"I never went to college. We met in a bar near campus one night and he took me for a ride in that fancy sports car of his. I thought he might be entertaining for a while but he is really sort of boring. We were together maybe a month or two, that's all. I guess he is pretty smart though, getting a degree in engineering."

"Well, he has asked me to marry him," Sue looked at her. "You are so young. What are you, 18?"

"Actually, I will be 20 next spring." Sue was thinking that yes, she was a lot younger than Ron or Monica. Maybe she was being naïve about marriage?

"Well, you are lucky to have him. I won't bother him anymore," Monica said remorsefully. "I would like us to be on a friendly *basis, if that is possible," Sue put her hand on Monica's. "Yeah sure. Just don't use that karate stuff on me again."*

"I won't. Just don't try to attack me again."

"I'm sorry about that. I don't know why I did that. I have a terrible temper and I never seem to be able to control it."

Just then Ron walked out onto the veranda. He wanted to see if Sue was there. He had run into Joan and she said Sue was going down to the Student Union to find out if her final grades were posted there. He spotted Monica and Sue talking. Oh-oh. This could not be good. He walked over to their table.

"Hi," he said meekly.

Monica and Sue looked up and saw him.

Monica spoke up first. "Ron, I am sorry about the other night. I should not have surprised you like that."

Ron was shocked. Monica was apologizing for something? That was not in her nature. "That's ok. But you should know that I am with Sue now."

"Yeah, I understand that now." Monica looked down at the engagement ring. "I hope you guys have a happy life." She got up to go. A tear was at the corner of her cheek.

Sue got up too. "You take care," she said as Monica walked away.

"What was that all about?" Ron asked when Monica was out of hearing distance. "We were trading notes on you buddy." Sue looked at him sternly.

"She was telling you about how boring I am?" He looked back at her. "Yup." Sue turned and kissed him.

"Well then. Ok. Did you look at your final grades yet?"

Yeah, I got A's in both Psych and Economics," she said as if that was her typical standard. "Darn. I only got 2 B's. I must have been distracted by something," he confessed.

"Well, you better do better next semester if you intend to graduate," she teased. "Tell you what. I will take you out to dinner to celebrate."

"Not cooking at your apartment?"

No. but we could stop there afterward if you want," he said with a big smile. "Gee, that sounds nice."

CHAPTER 79

*S*ARAH WAS BACK AT the nursing home. The doctor told her that it looked like Bob had fallen back into a coma after almost being awake for a couple of days. She was hoping that he might recover, that the prayers were doing something. Now he just lay there with the respirator doing his breathing. She sat in his room, thinking. She had taken her brother home and was nursing him back to health. Her brother Tom had become a changed person. He no longer argued with her about anything. He just sat there, depressed all of the time. She was worried that he might commit suicide. He did not ask her for money anymore. He told her he had given up gambling for good. She asked him if he might try to find a job. He had replied that he would as soon as he was better. She thought about the situation. She hated to admit it, but maybe the beating was for the good if it improved his behavior.
Maybe she would be able to live with her brother if he got a job and started to pay his own way.

She had talked to Jack Simms and explained that the Kramer guy had fixed the problem. Now her brother was free to live his life. She was curious about Kramer though and asked what Jack knew about him. Jack could tell that she must have liked Kramer. He told her that he was an ex-marine and ex-cop who made his living now as a private detective. Jack wanted to know how Robert was doing. Sarah was sad now that Robert was in a coma. She asked Jack if there was anything he could do to help. He did not want to give her false hope but said maybe they could try higher doses of the experimental drug to see if it would help.

CHAPTER 80

*R*ON PICKED UP SUE *at her dorm room. Joan had somewhere to go with Jerry, possibly to visit the rose room at the Frat house. Sue looked radiant. She was wearing a red dress with a blue scarf and red sandals. Ron of course, was in his typical khaki pants and blue blazer. Ron had gotten the Jeep back but had parked it in his garage. He was driving the Corvette tonight. Sue was strangely quiet in their walk to his car. Ron wondered what was bothering her.*

"Everything ok?" he asked.

"Yes. I have been thinking about us."

Oh-oh. Ron thought, something is bothering her. "What's the matter?" he inquired. "Do you think I am too young for you?"

"No. Most marriages have a slight age differential. I have heard that the optimum age differential is 7 years." "That's not what I meant." She looked at him. "I am basically inexperienced in the aspects of love. You have had previous experience. I have not." She had dated a few boys in her senior year of high school but never considered these experiences to be the same as what she was experiencing with Ron.

"Look. It doesn't matter. What matters is what is in your heart." He stopped as they neared the car. "I want you. That is a fact. If you have any doubts, I can wait. If you decide things are not right between us, I will understand. I want you to be happy and I hope it is with me."

"I love you. I want to be with you. But I want to finish college. Can we wait until then to be married?" she asked.

"I will do whatever you want." He was being honest.

"I need to know if you want children."

Ron had to pause and think. He did not have much experience with small children. "I never really thought about it much, but yes. I want children. I think you would be a beautiful mother."

"Do you mind if they are raised as Protestants?"

"Sure. I am not really affiliated with any particular religion so whatever you chose is fine by me."

"You don't ever do drugs?"

He had to pause again. He had tried some grass once but found it clouded his mind. He did not want to do it again. "No. I can't concentrate on my engineering and do that stuff."

Sue smiled. "Those were all the right answers."

"I passed the test?" He smiled back.

"Yes." She reached for him and they kissed.

They went to dinner at Anthony's again to celebrate and then later stopped at his apartment. One thing led to another and after necking for a while they ended up in his bed again. It was pretty much as wonderful as the first time. "I could get used to this," Sue said afterward.

"I hope you enjoy it as much as I do." Ron replied. He looked at her nakedness. She was absolutely perfect and beautiful, even without clothes.

"I never knew love could be so beautiful," she sighed.

They got up and showered together in his small bathroom. They teased each other and then helped towel each other off.

They returned to the bedroom to retrieve their clothes. "Are you sure you can put up with me?" She teased. "Well, I do love you and want to marry you."

"You don't mind waiting for four years?" She watched him get dressed.

"No. If that's what you want, then I can wait. I just hope you don't get tired of me or we grow apart." He watched her as she got dressed.

"I won't let that happen." She looked at the ring on her finger.

"You never know what might happen. But I will remain faithful to you as long as I live." He meant every word. "If you want me to," he added.

"I want you to. We will grow old together and raise a family," she said. "I will teach art and you will become a famous engineer."

"I hope you are right." He laughed. He was concerned that maybe they were rushing into too much commitment, but he was happy with her and she appeared to be happy with him. For him, everything was dependent upon finishing college and getting the engineering job. If he could not support her properly he would not be able to marry her. It gave him a terrible incentive to complete college.

CHAPTER 81

SARAH WAS AT THE nursing home again. The doctor wanted her to understand the situation. Bob was failing. His blood pressure was low, his kidneys and liver were both failing.

"I don't think he has much time left." The doctor told her. "His heart is still beating though." She stated.

"Yes. His heart is still going and his brain waves are still there. He is not brain dead. We are giving him medication to improve his situation, but I wanted to tell you that I think he may have a week or less time left."

Sarah took the news calmly. If this is what God wanted then she would accept it. "Well, we have been praying for him." She looked at the floor.

"It never hurts to pray," he admitted, "but I wanted you to know he is failing fast." The doctor was still administering the experimental drug but after some initial success it did not appear to be helping much. He did not approve of using experimental, unproven drugs, but in this case he did not think he had to worry about possible side effects. The patient was clearly dying.

Sarah was hoping that Jack Simms might still come up with some sort of treatment for Robert. She knew it was a longshot but maybe her prayers would come true. She called Jack on her cell phone.

"Hello, Jack?"

"Sarah. What is it? How is Robert?" Jack asked.

"The doctor here says Bob may only last another week. Are you sure there is nothing more we can do?"

"Sarah, we can increase the dosage of the experimental drug but I am not sure it will help." "Yes please. Hurry though." She was getting desperate.

CHAPTER 82

*S*UE WAS PACKING *A small bag to take with her when she went home. It was Sunday morning. She typically would go to the church on campus on Sunday but decided she wanted to see Ron instead. There was not much storage space in Ron's Corvette, but she figured she could wear stuff from her closet at home. They originally had planned to leave on Sunday but now that had changed to Monday. Sue had to check in with the campus dormitory facility on Monday to reserve her dorm room for the fall semester. She also had to register for her classes. Ron had already pre-registered, one of the perks for seniors.*

Ron had asked for her address so he could put it in the Corvette's GPS. She said that was not really necessary but he liked to use that function when he was traveling. She only lived about 100 miles from campus so it was only about an hour and a half drive.

Joan's brother had arrived and Joan had left with him. Since they were reserving the same room, she did not have to pack up everything and just took one suitcase.

"You have fun during the break," she had told Sue with a wink as she left.

It had been a weird semester. A lot of things had happened, some good, some bad. She had met the man she was going to marry, had been assaulted, almost raped, and shot at. She hoped the next semester would be more boring. At least she had started with a 4.0 GPA by getting two A's. The best thing that had happened to her was Ron. When she first came to the college her goal was somewhat vague, get a degree in Art Education and find a teaching position. Now her plans were all centered on Ron and what he was going to do. He was very supportive of her getting the degree and continuing with her plans, but she was half afraid his career path might separate them for long periods of time. That could be hard on their relationship. It had all happened too suddenly, but she was happy for now. She did not mind the long engagement. The chances of her meeting a better match for a mate were very slim. He was, as they say, almost perfect.

Her phone rang. She picked it up. It was Ron.

"What time do you want to leave tomorrow?" he asked.

"The dormitory office opens at 9 AM and I have to register for classes, so let's plan about noon?" She was unsure how long it would take if the office was very busy.

"Ok. That sounds good. We can get lunch on the way." He always liked to stop at a Bob Evans restaurant since their food was usually good.

"That gets us to my house around 2:30 PM then. My parents might still be at work. We might have my bedroom to ourselves for an hour or so." She was already trying to plan how they could be together alone.

"What about your brothers?"

"School started on Friday. They won't get home from school until 4 PM. They were at camp for two weeks but are back at home now."

"Well ok. I will see you at your dorm between 11:30 and noon." "What are you doing today?" she asked.

"Not much really. Checking the car to make sure it is ok for a small trip, maybe adding a coat of polish."

"You want me to come over and help?" she wanted to see him. "Sure, I suppose so." He agreed. He wanted to see her too.

"Ok. I can walk over; it isn't that far."

"Ok. There is a small diner down the street. I will buy you lunch if you help. It isn't a fancy place but they do make good cheeseburgers."

"I'm on my way." She hung up and hurriedly found an old pair of jeans and an old blouse. These should be appropriate for washing and polishing a car, she thought. She put on a pair of sneakers, tied her hair back in a ponytail, and grabbed her purse. She left the dormitory and walked the eight blocks to his apartment. She saw him looking under the hood of the Corvette.

"Is everything ok?" she inquired as she walked up to him.

"Yeah, I was just checking the oil. The beast is ready for a road trip."

They started to wash and polish the car. With both of them working on it, it did not take long. "It really is a pretty car," she said when they were finished.

"Yeah, I really like this car. It has a lot of power. It can go from zero to sixty in 4 seconds." He stood back looking at the vehicle.

"Wow, that is pretty amazing." She threw down her polishing rag. "Hey, someone promised me a lunch."

"Ok. You want to wash up first?" he pointed upstairs.

"Yeah, I probably should." She started to the apartment. He followed her up the stairs. While she washed her hands in the bathroom, he took a pitcher of iced tea out of the fridge and took a long drink.

"You want some tea?" he asked.

"Sure." She moved over to him. She turned to him and they started kissing.

"You sure look beautiful," he said.

She took him by the hand and led him to the bed. He took the hint and then they were in bed together again. They did go get lunch at the diner down the street but it was much later than he expected.

"I think I have created a monster," he remarked when they eventually got to the diner. "You are complaining?" she asked.

"No, but I think I better start taking some vitamins if I am going to keep up with you." He smiled.

She was famished and ate two cheeseburgers. He only had one. "You better eat more if you are going keep up your strength," she teased.

After they were done eating, they walked back to the apartment. "I will drive you back to the dorm," he said.

"Yeah, that's the least you can do." she teased him again.

When they got back to the dormitory parking lot, she asked, "Do you want to come up? Joan already left and I am all alone."

"Well to be honest, I am a bit tired," he dodged. "Come on. I won't attack you again," she promised.

"Ok. I guess I can for a while." He got out and they walked to the dormitory. There was no hall monitor now that the semester was over and most of the students had gone home.

They got to her room and relaxed on the couch. "So, your parents are expecting us tomorrow?" he asked.

"Yes. They have the spare room all ready for you. It is right next to my bedroom."

"Well, that's convenient."

"I thought you might think so." She moved towards him and they began to kiss. One thing led to another and they ended up in her bed.

"You lied to me," he teased her afterward. "We ought to cool it for a while. You are wearing me out."

"I suppose so," she agreed. She really liked making love with him. Now that she had tried it, she couldn't get enough of it.

"Your parents are going to want me to make an honest woman out of you. They may insist on a shotgun wedding," he teased her.

"They don't have to know." She hugged him.

"Oh, they will know. Parents are pretty smart you know." He wondered how this arrangement was going to work out.

"Well, we are engaged," she protested. She looked at the ring on her finger.

"That's true. But parents are sort of funny about these things." He kissed her shoulder.

"Well, I am not going to worry about it." She yawned. "I am going to take a nap," she said drowsily. She closed her eyes and rolled over on the bed.

He took this as a hint and got up and dressed. Wow. This girl is fantastic. He thought. How could he be so lucky? She was beautiful, smart, sexy and very pleasant to be with. She did not complain about things and did not tell him to do things. He definitely could see being married to her. He left the dorm room and locked the door behind him as he left. He walked down the stairs. As he walked out of the dorm, he saw George Coleman walking by in his police uniform.

"Hi, George." He turned to catch up with him. "Ron. What are you doing over here?"

"My girlfriend hasn't left for the break yet, we are going to go to meet her parents tomorrow." Ron smiled.

"Wow, that sounds like it is getting pretty serious." George had seen Ron's girlfriend; she was a very attractive young lady.

"I guess so. I have asked her to marry me." Ron was still smiling.

"No kidding. Good for you." He was very happy for Ron. He knew Ron had been very depressed after his break up with

Monica. "I guess this might interfere with our card games."

"Actually, it shouldn't. She wants to wait until she completes her degree here." "Aren't you about to graduate?" George asked.

"Yes. But that just means I have a head start to get a job to be able to support her," Ron replied. "That's a good thing," George remarked.

"Well, it should be pretty quiet here for a couple of weeks." Ron noted as he turned toward the almost empty parking lot.

"Yeah, we have had more than enough excitement here with you this semester," George agreed. They shook hands and went in different directions.

Ron got in his car and returned to his apartment. He was tired, but needed to take a shower. Afterward he hit the sack. Tomorrow was going to be a long day and he wanted some rest. He thought about Sue. How could he be so lucky to find a girl like her? She was perfect in every way. He had not set out to find a wife, it just sort of happened. Now he was happier than he had ever been since his parents' accident. He wondered if her parents were going to like him. If they didn't agree to the marriage it could complicate things. He had already met them when she was in the hospital. But now they were engaged to be married and that could make things different. He wondered what it would be like to be part of a family again.

CHAPTER 83

BIG TONY HAD BEEN given the money to put into Louie's safe. As he put the cash into the safe, he saw an old deposit slip that Sarah had inadvertently not seen when she grabbed an envelope to put all the cash in. He pocketed the slip and closed the safe. Later he reviewed the deposit slip. It had Sarah and Robert's name and address on it. Big Tony thought to himself, why not go and see if he could shake some more money from the money tree? Richie and Louie did not have to know about it. He waited a week and then found an excuse to leave the bar to run an errand by himself.

Tom, Sarah's brother was feeling morose. The threat to his life was gone but he was a changed person. To be strapped to a chair helpless while someone almost beat you to death was a humiliating experience. He vowed that he would never let himself get in that position again. He knew he owed his life to his sister and now he was determined to pay her back somehow. He was healing slowly. The doctors had said his jaw would heal in a few more weeks. Until then he was subsisting on milkshakes and liquid food. Sarah had been nice to him and let him stay at her house while he got better. He had never realized just how good his sister had been to him. He intended to not disappoint her again.

Sarah had gone to see Robert again. He understood now how much Sarah loved Bob. She was praying for him every night and went to see him every day. He wished now that there was something he could do to help, but it was too late. Bob was going to die and no amount of prayer was going to save him.

At least he could do some housework for her while she was gone. He straightened up things, took out the trash and washed the dishes. There was a knock on the door. He went to answer it.

"Hello shit head." It was Big Tony standing in front of him. He was alone. "What do you want?" Tom was suddenly terrified.

"Just stopped by to see how you were doing. Is your sister here?" Tony knew that Tom's sister had money. Tony was wondering if he could shake some loose for himself. "Mind if I come in?"

Tom was scared. He did not know what to do. He knew he could not defend himself against this big gorilla.

"Big Tony." A voice behind Tony made him turn quickly. It was Kramer walking up to the door. "What," Tony said, but then saw the .38 caliber gun in Kramer's hand pointed at him and froze. "I believe we have paid off all of the debt." Kramer hissed.

"Yeah, ok. Right. I was just stopping to see…"

"You came on your own. I knew you would." Kramer interrupted him. Kramer had parked his car down the street, figuring that someone would come calling sooner or later.

"Hey Kramer, there's no need to be so nasty." Tony was suddenly very friendly but did not take his eyes off the weapon.

"If I tell Louie you are freelancing, he will cut your thumbs off." Kramer looked at Tom and figured that he was Sarah's brother.

"Look. I will back off. No reason to do that."

"Then get out of here before I change my mind." Kramer motioned with the gun for him to leave. "And don't come back or I will hear of it and tear you apart."

Big Tony did not want to go against Kramer. He had heard some nasty things about Kramer and knew he did not threaten lightly. He had heard Kramer had taken out three guys in one incident all by himself on the east side of town.

"Ok. I'm out of here," Big Tony more or less ran to his car in the driveway. He got in and drove away.

Kramer holstered his weapon and looked at Tom. "He was going to try to pry more money from your sister."

"Who are you?" Tom was puzzled but relieved.

"My name's Kramer. I helped your sister pay off those goons. You must be the brother." "Yes. Well, I am sure glad you happened to be in the neighborhood." Tom was very relieved. "I like your sister. It's too bad she has a brother that gets her in trouble."

"Hey, it's not like that anymore. Honest," Tom protested. Who the hell was this guy?

"I sure hope you learned your lesson. Your sister deserves better from her own family." Kramer looked around. He knew Sarah had left earlier. He had been watching the house for a couple of days now. "Is she coming back soon?"

"She went to the nursing home. Her husband is dying. He has this brain tumor." "Yeah, I heard about that. With all that going on you had to make her life worse?"

"Hey, I didn't know it would turn out this way." Tom felt uneasy, hoping this guy would go away.

"Well, you better straighten up. If I find out you are going to screw up again I might just rough you up myself." Kramer was bluffing but the kid brother didn't know that.

"Yeah, sure. I don't intend to get in trouble again…honest." Tom was looking down at the ground. If this guy was tough enough to scare Big Tony, he didn't want to offend him.

"Well, Big Tony won't be back. He knows Louie won't tolerate that kind of stuff." Kramer started to leave.

"Thanks anyway." Tom called after him. Tom was stunned. He had just been scared shitless by Big Tony when this other big guy comes along and saves him. Sarah must know some good people, he thought.

Kramer walked away thinking this kid is a loser. He will get in trouble again. He got in his car. Maybe he should stop by the nursing home and see the sister.

CHAPTER 84

IT WAS MONDAY MORNING. Sue woke up early had a good shower, then had some cereal for breakfast and got dressed. A simple pair of tan slacks and a white blouse would be good for today. She slipped her sneakers on and prepared to go over to the Campus office. It opened at 9:00, so she left early and was there at 9:05. She went to the Campus Dormitory Office first. There was not much of a line. After showing her ID and filling out some paperwork she succeeded in continuing her dorm room reservation for another semester. She had to forge Joan's name on the document, but Joan wasn't going to complain.

Then she got in line to register. There was a line but it did not take long since it was early in the morning and a lot of the students typically registered in the afternoon. She had had a conference with her advisor early last week. She already knew which classes to sign up for. She was going to take basic math, Chemistry, and two Art classes. She would not get any Education classes until winter semester. She was hesitant about taking Chemistry but it was a requirement. She figured that Ron could probably help her with that class. So now she was free to leave. It was 10:30. She considered calling Ron to let him know that she was ready to go, but he probably was doing something and she didn't want to appear too eager. He said he would be at her dormitory at 11:30, so he would. She went back to the dormitory. She should clean it up so that there was no mess awaiting her return. There was stuff in the fridge that needed to be thrown out. She did some housekeeping chores and then left the dorm room with her bag and small purse. She would wait for Ron by the entrance.

She sat on the steps outside and waited for him. She wondered how her family would react to adding him to the family. She looked at the engagement ring. It was so beautiful. She didn't know much about being a wife but figured she would do ok with Ron. He was easy going and compassionate. He would have patience with her, she felt. She had noticed that he never seemed to get angry, but instead would look for a solution for any problem that arose. She looked at her watch. He should have gotten here by now. She was eager to get started.

CHAPTER 85

SARAH WAS WITH THE doctor in Bob's room. The doctor had just told her that Bob was failing and would probably not last the day.

"Are you sure?" She asked.

"His heart has started to become erratic. The pattern shows a constant deterioration." The doctor was sad. He knew that Sarah was hoping for a miracle but it just wasn't happening.

"The brain waves are decreasing also as less oxygen gets to his brain." The doctors were pumping pure oxygen into Bob's lungs with the respirator, but the blood flow to his brain was slowing gradually. His blood pressure was dropping slowly.

"We could administer adrenalin, but that would only give him a short boost." The doctor was hoping that Sarah would accept the fact that Bob was going.

"So, there is nothing more we can do?" she asked tearfully. "I don't think so."

"Can I stay with him for the final minutes?" she asked.

"Of course. When the heart monitor stops beeping then it is over." The doctor walked over to the nurse waiting outside.

"Stay with her for the final minutes." He told her as he walked away. They had increased the amount of the experimental drug that Doctor Simms had prescribed but it did not appear to have any effect.

Sarah waited with the nurse but Robert's condition did not change. It just stayed constant. She started to pray again, please let him live.

CHAPTER 86

*R*ON GOT UP EARLY *and dressed in his usual attire of tan pants and blue shirt. He had packed lightly, had a small bag with about 3 changes of clothes and underwear. He threw in his one remaining good blue blazer. He knew the trunk of the Corvette would not hold much. He hoped Sue did not pack a lot of things. Still, she was a woman and they tended to need a lot of stuff. He hung up the shoulder holster and the pistol in his closet. He did not anticipate needing it in his old home town visiting her parents. It would just tend to complicate things. Her father might object to a stranger in the house with a gun. He put the auxiliary police badge on the desk. But then thought, it might come in handy if he got stopped for speeding, so he put it in his wallet. George had not yet returned his small .380 pistol, so he would be defenseless for a while. It would be uncomfortable for him to not have anything, so he grabbed a large pocket knife and put it in his pocket. He walked to the diner down the street and had a plate of eggs and sausage. He felt better after eating. He walked back to the apartment. He did some minor house cleaning, changed the bed sheets and took the laundry downstairs to his landlord. He knocked on the door and Matt opened it.*

"How are you doing Ron?" Matt smiled at him.

"Pretty good. Can Becky do a load of laundry for me?" He had an agreement with them that allowed him to get laundry done once or twice a month.

"Sure, I don't see why not." Matt took the basket.

"By the way, I am going out of town for a few days. I'm going to meet Sue's parents." "That sounds serious Ron. Is she that good looking brunette?"

"Yes. I have asked her to marry me. We are engaged." Ron smiled.

"Well good for you. Every guy needs to settle down with a good woman." Matt looked over his shoulder towards Becky. "I

hope you are as lucky as I have been. Do you plan to keep the apartment?"

"Yes. I have one more semester of school to finish up and then I will look for employment. I am hoping to work at the same company where I was an intern last summer."

"That is a pretty far drive, isn't it?" Matt questioned.

"Yeah but I want to stay close to campus since Sue will be here another four years getting her degree, Ron explained.

"So, are you getting married right away or going to wait?" Matt wanted to know if he needed to rent out the upstairs again. It was really too small for a married couple.

"No, she wants to wait, so she will be staying on campus while I keep the apartment."

Ron said good bye and went back upstairs. He looked at his watch. It was 11:00, still too early to pick up Sue. He did not have anything really left to do but kill a half hour. Then he spotted the reference material that he had gotten from the library. He should take that stuff back and turn it in. He had had the reference books too long, and probably would need to pay a fine. He could drive south of campus to drop off the books and then drive north to pick up Sue. They were ultimately driving north to her parents place anyway.

Ron loaded up the books, grabbed his small travel bag and walked down the stairs. He stowed his bag in the trunk and then put the reference books into the passenger seat of the Corvette. It sometimes was a bother that he could only have one passenger seat in the car, but it was worth it to be able to drive such a magnificent Beast. The car looked really sharp after they had polished it yesterday. He got in the car and pulled out onto the street. He drove south toward the library. Since the elementary kids were back in school now he had to pay attention to the 20 MPH school zones.

He was thinking about how today was going to go. He wondered if the parents would be against the marriage. He had met them at the hospital when Sue was hurt but he really didn't get a good read on how they felt about his relationship with their daughter. The father had been impressed with Ron as an engineering student, something about his father being an engineer. The mother had been more reserved and was obviously relieved when she found that they had not been having intercourse. That had all changed now. Sue and he were lovers and he was not ashamed of it. If two people really love each other, a marriage certificate is just a piece of paper. Besides, he had asked her to marry him and she had accepted his ring. He hoped they would approve.

Ron turned down the street to the library. He had the radio on. It was a beautiful sunny day, perfect for early September. The trees had not started changing color yet. As he drove closer to the library he could see lots of children playing in the playground. It must be getting closer to noon, he thought. He suddenly became aware of a semi-trailer truck moving left of center in the road ahead of him. He could see that the driver had slumped forward, and the truck was apparently out of control. It was heading right for the playground full of kids.

CHAPTER 87

SARAH SAT WATCHING THE monitor of her husband's heart. The nurse sat beside her, holding her hand. Suddenly Bob's body arched up and he screamed "Gaaaa." He then fell back down. The nurse ran to his side, wondering what was happening. The monitor was visibly showing a better heartbeat. His breathing increased.

"Is it…is it over? Sarah sobbed, starting to cry.

"No, he is actually getting better." The nurse looked at her watch it was

11:15 am. She made a note of it on his chart. Then she rushed out of the room to get a doctor.

Sarah had hoped and prayed for a miracle. Could he really be getting better? Maybe Bob was coming back to her.

If he was improving, there was still hope.

The doctor came in and checked his vital characteristics. "I can't believe it. He is getting better." He made some furious notes on the patient chart and started to walk out of the room. "I have to call Dr. Simms." he said as he left.

Sarah walked over to Bob and could see the abrupt change in his breathing and heart beat on the monitor. It must be a miracle she thought.

CHAPTER 88

*S*UE WAS WAITING ON *the steps of the dormitory. She looked at the time. It was already noon. Ron should have been here by now. It was not like him to be late. She took out her phone and dialed his number. It went straight to voice mail. That was unusual. He either did not have his phone on or the battery must be low. Ron never kept enough messages to use up all of his storage space; he almost always deleted them right after he heard them.*

She continued to wait but started to get hungry. What could be taking him so long? Finally, she gave in and started to walk to Ron's apartment. It was only about eight blocks away, and she made good time. She watched the traffic on the road to make sure she did not miss him if he drove by. It would be hard to miss a bright red Corvette.

He better have a pretty good excuse, she thought. As she walked, a fire truck went bye with its lights flashing and siren blaring. That was followed by a police car, its siren on also. Something must have happened she thought.

As she finally got to his apartment building, she did not see the red Corvette in the driveway. She walked over to the steps. Maybe he had driven to her place by another route? If he was at her dorm he would have called her cell phone. She took the phone out and checked but she had not missed any calls. She ran up the steps and tried to open the door. It was locked. She looked in the window but the apartment looked empty.

Sue was puzzled. He was not answering his phone and was not home. Where could he be?

Matt opened the door downstairs. He had heard footsteps on the stairs and walked outside to check. He saw the pretty brunette looking in the window of the apartment.

"Miss, are you looking for Ron?" he asked.

"Yes, I was supposed to meet him today. We were going to..." she stopped when she saw the sad look on his face.

"Please come down here…you better see what is on the TV." Matt pointed inside.

She went into his house. There was a wide screen TV in the family room. There was a news bulletin on the TV. The screen showed all sorts of emergency vehicles with flashing lights.

The announcer was speaking "…apparently the truck driver had a heart attack and died. His vehicle was out of control and heading right for the playground. Several of the teachers on the playground said that if that red Corvette had not sped up and hit the truck, it would have definitely killed a lot of kids. Unfortunately for the driver of the Corvette, the tractor trailer jack-knifed when the Corvette diverted it into the big oak tree and the tanker trailer crushed the Corvette. The driver of the Corvette would have had to be going pretty fast to divert the truck from the playground into that large oak tree. I guess you can say the driver of the Corvette was a real hero."

Sue looked in horror at what looked like what was left of Ron's red Corvette. She fell to her knees on the carpet. The visible rear license plate was Ron's. She remembered noting the number when she was polishing the car the day before.

"Noooooooooooooooooo," she wailed as tears streamed down her face.

Matt's wife Becky knelt down beside her and put her arms around her. "Please, let's sit over here," she motioned to the couch. As they sat on the couch Sue started crying into her shoulder.

The announcer on the TV said "It does not look like the Corvette driver could have survived that crash," as the camera panned over what was left of the red Corvette. The tractor trailer had jack-knifed back across the road when the truck had impacted the large oak tree. In doing this it had slammed into the side of the Corvette. Several firemen were working on the car, trying to pry what was left of the Corvette driver from the car.

Sue didn't want to watch but she couldn't take her eyes off of the screen. If there was a chance of seeing Ron, she didn't want to miss it. The screen changed and went to the weather forecast. Sue was in shock. The one person she had fallen in love with was probably badly hurt or dead.

CHAPTER 89

THE DOCTOR LOOKED UP from his examination. Bob was definitely getting stronger. His heart beat was higher, his lung function almost normal. The doctor was puzzled since he was told by the neurologist that Bob had a major brain tumor that was about to kill him. When he checked the brain scan, Bob appeared to have stronger brain waves. How was that possible? Perhaps the new drug was having an effect after all.

The doctor ordered another MRI to be taken. He explained to the wife that they had to see the tumor, to see what was really going on. She reluctantly agreed, knowing the cost of the test was high. But she had to know if he was improving. She was hoping it would come back that the tumor in his head was gone.

CHAPTER 90

*S*UE WAS ON THE couch with Matt's wife Becky. Matt approached Sue. She was still crying but it had diminished to an occasional sob. He felt helpless, wanted to do something for the girl. "Ron might have survived that crash," he told her. "We should drive over there to find out."

Becky gave him a hard look. "I'm not sure that's a good idea," she told her husband. She did not think that the poor girl would be any better off seeing the dead body of her lover. That could be too traumatic for such a young girl.

Sue looked up. "Yes, I want…I want to…to go. Can you take me?" she said between sobs.

Matt realized why his wife was disapproving but he was also curious. "Come on, we can go in my truck."

They got into his truck and they drove the four miles to the accident scene. Sue was not paying much attention until they got close to the street the library and school were on. The police had blocked off the road to the library, so they had to park the truck on a side street and walk toward the accident. They got within about fifty feet of the accident. A policeman saw them approaching and motioned them back.

"Can't go any closer folks, sorry, you will have to go back." The police officer was Andy Hall and he suddenly recognized Matt and the girl looked like Ron's girlfriend. "Oh, I'm sorry." He held them. "Wait here, I will see if someone can talk to you." He ran toward the crowd of paramedics and firemen.

Sue looked at the accident. There was a body on the ground, covered with a blanket. An ambulance van was backing up toward the body. Some paramedics got out and put the body into the van. Sue started to cry again. Was that Ron, she wondered?

The firemen were dousing the scene with water. The tractor trailer had been filled with gasoline and they were not taking any chances of possible fire and explosion. The Corvette was barely recognizable as a car, the front end had been demolished and the trailer had impacted it on the driver's side. It appeared that the firemen had to cut the top and the door off of the Corvette to get to the occupant.

Andy Hall came back with another man wearing a fireman's uniform. George Coleman was with him also.

The man in the fireman's uniform asked "You two know the driver of the Corvette?"

Matt answered first. "Yes, I am his landlord. That looks like Ronald Pritchard's car," he pointed to what was left of the Corvette.

George confirmed, "Yes it was Ron Pritchard." He had a sad look on his face when he looked at Sue.

The fireman added, "We had to cut him out of that car." Sue looked up from her tears and said "I am Ron's fiancée."

The fireman spoke up. "Well, I can tell you he was still barely alive when we pried him out of the vehicle. He was in really bad shape. The paramedics thought he was dead but he was still breathing. The ambulance left with him for the hospital about ten minutes before you got here." Both the fireman and George figured Ron was dead by now, no one could live through that type of crash.

George came up to Sue. "Come on, I can take you to the hospital." He still had a sad look on his face. He remembered talking to Ron the night before and how happy Ron was to be marrying this girl. He led her over to his police cruiser and opened the door for her to get in. He knew that she was in for a hard time accepting Ron's death. Why does this always happen to the good people? he thought to himself. Being a cop, he had seen a lot problems and distress. This time it was different, Ron was a good friend of his and the guy had everything to live for. Especially now that he was engaged to this pretty girl. Why would he sacrifice himself? He did it to save some school children he didn't even know. George thought it was the most selfless act he had ever seen and probably no one except Ron would have done it. Sue didn't say anything. There was still some hope that Ron might live. She was holding on to that hope. George drove through town with his flashers on but without a siren.

"Does Ron have any family in the area?" George asked her.

"His parents were killed in an accident when he was in high school and he was an only child," Sue recited from memory. "He

lived with his grandmother after that but she died later," Sue told him. "I don't think he has any family left."

"That complicates things." George wondered who the hospital would notify if he has no family. "I think I am the only one he has now," Sue stated.

They pulled up to the hospital and he parked the police cruiser in a no parking area. "Come on, I'll go with you," he told Sue. They got out of the car and walked to the emergency entrance. He left the flashers going. She looked back and wondered why he did not turn them off.

They walked into the emergency area. It had a double set of doors. There was a hospital guard by the second door and he wasn't supposed to let anyone into the emergency area. He stood back when he saw it was a policeman.

George walked up to him. "Did a guy just come in here from a traffic accident?" "Yes, but you can't go in there."

"Well, this is his wife. And we need to know how he is doing."

The guard looked at the girl. She looked really young, but very pretty. "Ok. Stay here and I will see if I can get someone to come out to talk to you."

George looked at Sue and said: "If you want to know how he is doing you have to be a family member or his wife."

"Ok." Sue agreed. As long as they did not ask to see a marriage certificate she could pretend to be his wife.

They waited for about ten minutes. Then a nurse came out and looked at them. "Are one of you the next of kin for Ronald Pritchard?" she asked, looking at the girl.

"Yes, I am." Sue said meekly.

"Ok, come with me." She said and led Sue and George into a small room off to the side of the central nurse's station in the emergency room. "Wait here. I will have the doctor see you. He is very busy at the moment." She drew a curtain across the door. They sat in the two chairs in the room.

George felt that he had to say something. "I was talking to Ron last night as he left your dorm." He started. "I have never seen anyone so happy. He was telling me that he was going to marry you."

"Yes." She held out her hand with the engagement ring to show him. "We were going to drive to my parent's house to share the good news today." Her eyes started to tear up again.

They waited in silence for a while. Then George started again. "You know, Ron is one of the finest people I have ever met on campus. He is honest, hardworking and a true friend. You really could not find a nicer guy."

Sue appreciated the description but she had already come to the conclusion that he was all of that and more. "I know," she replied. "Why did he do this?" She asked herself out loud.

"I think he probably saved a lot of kids today. It was the most unselfish thing I have ever seen anyone do. He is a true hero." George's voice cracked slightly as he fought not to cry.

"I suppose so," Sue agreed. But why did it have to be him?

George's radio squawked and he had to answer it. He listened for a minute and then said "Ok, I'll be there in a couple of minutes." He turned to Sue. "I have to go." And then he walked out.

Sue sat in silence. She started to pray for Ron. Please let him live. Please let him live.

CHAPTER 91

SARAH WAS WAITING FOR the doctor to return. They had brought Bob back from the MRI about 15 minutes ago. He was no longer hooked up to the respirator since he was breathing on his own now.

The doctor walked into the room finally and sat down next to Sarah. She looked at him with anticipation.

"Well, I suppose it is good news. The tumor has shrunken quite a bit. We don't understand why but it appears that your husband is getting better."

Sarah could not believe her ears. "Will he keep getting better?" she asked.

"It's too early to tell, but it is possible he will regain some capacity." The doctor did not want to give her too much hope. According to all his experiences as a doctor this man should have died by now. Perhaps the experimental drug that Doctor Simms had provided was making the difference. He would have to update his notes if they wanted a record of the drug reaction.

"Thank the Lord," Sarah said quietly. She had hope that Robert might get better. The prayer group was proving to be effective. She looked at Bob. He appeared to be peacefully asleep.

"Do you think he will come out of the coma?" she asked the doctor.

"Well, he might. I have never seen anyone be so close to death and then come back so strong." The doctor was telling her the truth. He had to go about his rounds so he started for the door. He turned to Sarah and said "Maybe all those prayers helped."

CHAPTER 92

*S*UE WAITED PATIENTLY FOR *the doctor. Finally, a man pushed back the curtain and entered the room. He had on an operating smock. There was blood on his smock. He sat down next to Sue.*

"Are you here for Ron Pritchard?" "Yes. I am his wife," Sue lied.

"Is your name Sue?" he asked.

"Yes," she responded. How did he know that, she wondered?

"Good. I am Dr. Reynolds. Your husband was in really bad shape when he was brought in. We had to operate immediately. His chest was basically crushed with several ribs puncturing his lung. That is what we just got done repairing. He was lucid for a minute before we put him under. He kept saying your name over and over. He was bleeding internally pretty badly but we were able to stabilize him for now. His right leg is basically shattered. He also has a bad concussion. He is in ICU right now. He did regain consciousness for a minute or so. He kept asking for 'Sue'. I assumed that would be you."

"Will he live?" she asked, her voice trembling.

"I would say he has a 50-50 chance. But he is young and strong, and we can hope that there are no further complications." The doctor did not want to give her false hope but he knew from experience to be truthful about his diagnosis. The boy was in really bad shape. He was not sure that they could save the leg even if he did live.

"Can I see him?" she pleaded.

"Probably not yet. I will check with the Intensive Care staff to see if they will agree to let his wife see him." He saw the diamond ring on her hand. She looked too young to be a wife, but you never knew these days. She sure was a very pretty girl the doctor thought to himself.

"Can I wait here?" she asked? Tears were still streaming down her cheeks.

"Come with me, I will take you to a waiting area." The doctor looked at her with sympathy. So young and so vulnerable he thought.

They walked down a hall to a room with some chairs and couches. A couple of people were huddled on a couch on the other side of the room. A TV on the wall was on.

"There is a coffee machine and snacks by the sink." He pointed to a small kitchen area. "Please help yourself." He made sure she sat down, and turned to leave.

"Thank you," she said meekly.

"You are most welcome," he said. He really wanted the boy to survive for this girl. From what the paramedics told him; the boy had crashed his car intentionally to save a group of school children. If anyone deserved to live it was him. An announcement on an overhead speaker said "Doctor Reynolds to the ICU, Code Blue." The doctor said I have to go and hurriedly left to go to the Intensive Care Unit.

Sue sat there for a few minutes. She was still hungry so she got up to look and see what was by the kitchen. There were some protein bars. She found a tea bag and a plastic cup, poured hot water into it and returned to the couch. The TV news was on and showing the crash scene again. The TV person was interviewing a teacher from the playground.

"What did you see?" the reporter asked.

"Well, we were all out on the playground and I was watching my group when I saw that big truck start to come right at us. I sort of froze, did not know what to do. Then that red car accelerated and hit the front of the truck turning it toward the tree. It was a terrible crash." The teacher was a middleaged brunette with glasses on.

"So, the driver of the red car deliberately hit the truck?"

"Yes, I heard his car roar and leap into the path of the truck. I hope he lives, but I doubt if anyone could survive that crash." She started crying. "Thank God he did it. There were several children in the path of that truck."

The picture transferred to the TV reporter. "It appears as if the driver of the red car saved a few lives today by self-sacrifice. The driver was taken to the hospital but there is little hope that he will survive. This is one of the most heroic acts I have ever witnessed.

This is Jeb Meyers of TV 7 reporting." The camera panned back to what was left of the red Corvette.

Sue sat there. She started to pray again. Her phone rang. It was her mother. "Are you coming home today?" her mother asked.

"Momma..." Sue moaned, but then started to cry. "Ron is badly hurt...they don't think he is going to make it."

CHAPTER 93

*D*R. JACK SIMMS WAS sitting with Sarah in Bob's room. He had looked at the MRI pictures and could hardly believe what he saw. The tumor had shrunk slightly. Bob was getting better. The experimental drug must be working. It was still too early to hope for a complete recovery but it was progress.

"He appears to be getting better," he told Sarah. "Thank God." Sarah was optimistic.

"We will have to wait to see if the new drug continues to work," he told her. "You think it is the new drug that is helping?" She asked.

"I have no other explanation."

"Well, we have been praying for him. The Lord is saving him for me," Sarah stated.

"You may be right," Jack conceded. He was not about to dampen her faith in God. He really thought it was the new drug doing it though. He wished he had known about this drug months ago. Perhaps Robert would have made a complete recovery if he had known of this drug when they first discovered the tumor. He doubted if Bob would make a full recovery. Besides, it really did not hurt anything to pray. Still, the change in the tumor was remarkable. He would have to let his friend who had recommended the drug know that it did appear to work.

CHAPTER 94

IT WAS ABOUT MIDNIGHT when Dr. Reynolds came back to see Sue. As he entered the room Sue rushed to him. "How is Ron doing?" she pleaded.

"Please. We had to operate again. He was drowning from all of the blood in his lungs. He died on the operating table…"

Sue collapsed and fell to her knees, "No…No…" she moaned.

"Wait…" He grabbed for her arms, "We were able to bring him back!" They had to use a dose of adrenalin and used an electric shock to restart his heart. "He is still in ICU but he has stabilized somewhat." Ron had lost a lot of blood but they were giving him transfusions as they operated. Dr. Reynolds was very tired from the long operation, but after they had finally stabilized the patient a second time, he remembered that the boy's wife was still in the waiting area.

Sue was relieved. "Can I please see him?" she pleaded.

"If you want to see him, you can now, he is out of post-op and is in the Intensive Care Unit," he said to her. She nodded yes and followed him down the corridor. They got into the elevator and went up a couple of floors. Sue realized that they were at the city hospital and not the Campus Hospital. She did not notice when George drove her here. She was crying and in shock at the time.

They got off the elevator and walked through a door that the doctor opened with his badge. He led her down the hall to a room and they went in. A nurse was doing something with a machine that was hooked up to the body in the bed.

"He almost did not make it. His heart stopped when we were working on his chest wound. We had to restart it. But then he seemed to recover," Doctor Reynolds explained. "He has a strong spirit."

Sue was not really paying attention to the words; she was looking into the room. Sue looked at Ron. She gasped. He had the left side of his face bandaged and there were tubes going in his nose and in his arm. There was a hump where his right leg was. She turned toward the doctor.

"His leg...?" She asked.

"We have a pressure cast on it right now. It was broken in three places, a compound fracture. We may operate on it tomorrow to try to save it. We couldn't do it today because his internal bleeding has to stabilize before we give him any of blood thinners necessary when working with a broken femur. Often blot clots will occur that can cause a massive heart attack or stroke when that bone is broken."

"But you can fix it?"

"If you give us permission to operate on it we may be able to save it. I'm afraid that if it is too bad we may have to amputate it." Doctor Reynolds looked at her. He wanted her to know the hard facts. "Please. Please try to save the leg," she pleaded.

"Ok. It looks like he may live if he doesn't develop any more complications. You never can tell with these types of cases. I suggest you go home and get some rest."

"No. I will stay right here if you let me." She wanted to be near Ron if at all possible.

"Ok. I will ask the head nurse if she can bring a cot in here for you." The doctor could tell that she needed to be near her husband. Apparently they had not been married very long. He hoped they were not on their honeymoon. He had watched the newscast on the news after the operation about the boy and planned on giving him the best treatment due a true hero.

The doctor talked to the head nurse. She was adamant about not letting the girl stay with the patient.

"We don't allow that in the ICU," the nurse exclaimed.

"Look, this is the kid that sacrificed himself to save a bunch of school children. His young wife wants to be near him. I really think we can bend the rules a little in this case."

"Well, OK, but it's on your responsibility," she finally agreed.

The nurse backed down. Doctors in a hospital were like gods and she knew better than to argue with him about this. He could have her transferred to a much worse ward. She went and found a cot in the off-duty nurse's lounge and took it into the room. She looked at the poor girl standing near the patient with tears coming down her face. Her attitude softened some and she asked her if there was anything she could get her.

"No. I just want to be near him," Sue replied. She sat on the cot and watched Ron quietly.

A few hours later George Coleman stopped at the hospital and asked about Ron. The woman at the desk told him that Ron was in the Intensive Care Unit. She did not know what his status was.

George walked over to the elevator and took it to the third floor. He did not have a passkey to get into the Intensive care unit but asked a passing nurse to let him in. She looked at his police uniform and hesitated but then opened the door for him. George walked through the ward, being careful not to disturb anyone. He finally came to the room that had Ron's name on the door placard. He peaked in and saw Sue sitting there, her hand holding Ron's. He backed away. At least he is still alive he thought. There still might be hope that he will live. It would be a real miracle that anyone could survive that crash. He went back downstairs and out to his patrol car. He got into the car and sat there. The stress of the day began to get to him. He started to cry. He stopped himself. A police chief can't cry, he said to himself. He started the car and drove back to the campus.

CHAPTER 95

SARAH WAS VISITING BOB again. This time her brother Tom accompanied her. He did not say much just sat there with her. The nurse came in to check his vitals.

"He is improving." She told Sarah. "His liver and kidney functions are back to normal and I got a reaction when I tested his autonomous nervous system."

Sarah was very happy to hear this. Her prayers were finally being answered.

Tom was happy for her. He did not understand much of what the nurse said but it sounded like good news. He was at a loss for what to do with his life. He did not really have much education. How was he to survive? He could get a repetitive boring factory job but that was what drove him to try to make money gambling. Maybe he could go to the community college and learn a trade. Only he did not have the money for that and he was not about to ask Sarah for more money. He was depressed. He was a burden on his sister and wanted to contribute to her wellbeing somehow.

Sarah sat there and took out some knitting and started to work on it.

Tom was stuck here with her until she decided to go back home. He started to think about his life. He had checked out the local community college but he knew right away he was not going to fit in with all those young kids. The college did offer night classes for adults but the curriculum did not appeal much to him. He did not see himself as a welder or as a repair electrician. He never did well in high school, barely passing enough courses to graduate. He had basically gone from one menial job to another, never finding his niche. He had tried drugs and booze and that was basically his life. He started to gamble and would typically win occasionally if the game was honest. He had made the mistake of going to the club run by the syndicate. At first he won a lot but then started to lose.

After a while he figured the games were fixed, but by then he was in debt too far to back out. He thought about his friends in Tampa. They sort ran their own syndicate. If he could get in with them he probably could make some good money.

CHAPTER 96

*T*HEY TOOK RON INTO the operating room at 8:00 the next morning for the leg operation. Sue was exhausted. She had sat up all night watching Ron lay there unconscious. She was told to go to the waiting area again. This time she ate a couple of protein bars and had some more tea. Thankfully the TV was off. No one else was in the room and she was very tired. She was about to fall asleep when a man came into the room and walked up to her.

"Are you Mrs. Pritchard?" he asked.

At first she did not respond, confused by the question. "Ah... Yes, I am," she finally said.

"My name is Jeff Tyler." He sat down next to her. "I work for the engineering company where Ronald Pritchard was an intern last summer. We heard about his accident and I had to come to see him." Jeff was about 45 years old and wore a black suit, but without a tie. "I was his manager." he stated.

"Yes, I think Ron told me about that. He was hoping to get a position with your company when he graduates later this year." Sue responded.

"Well, we thought he was an extraordinary young man and would make an excellent engineer. I had not heard that he had married," he said looking at her ring finger.

"Well to be honest, we are only engaged." Sue admitted. "Ok. I understand. They said you were his wife?" he asked.

"He has no next of kin, so I told them we were married," she whispered. "Well, no matter. We still want to hire him. How is his health insurance?"

"I believe he had something from the university, but I don't know the details." She looked at the floor.

"Well don't worry about it. My company will pick up the expenses based upon the circumstances." "Why?" she asked.

"Our vice president had a nephew on that playground and he sent me to take care of the hero." "That is very thoughtful. Please thank him for me." Sue blushed.

"Is there anything that I can do for you?"

"I'm waiting for him to come out of surgery. If you want to pray for him I would appreciate it," she said, yawning.

"You look tired," he said. He noticed that she was an extremely attractive young girl. His heart went out to Ron for finding such a lovely creature. "Why don't you take a nap and I will watch for the doctor when he comes?"

"You probably have a very busy schedule. I don't want to hold you here," she said. "Nonsense. I drove all the way here and checked out of the office for the day." "Ok. I am tired." She curled up on the couch and fell asleep.

He looked at her and thought, boy, if I was 20 years younger, I would give Ron a run for his money for this one. She was the prettiest girl he had seen in a long time. He got up and turned on the TV but kept the volume low so as not to disturb her.

CHAPTER 97

SARAH WAS IN BOB'S room, praying for him when suddenly he stirred. She got up and rushed to his side. He groaned and tried to move his arm. She pushed the nurse call button.

"Bob. Bob, can you hear me?" she asked.

Bob thought he heard someone calling his name but it was far away. He groaned again but then fell into a deep sleep.

The nurse came in and looked at him. "Is everything alright?" she inquired. "He moved and groaned a couple of times. I thought he might wake up but now he is silent again."

"Well, maybe he is getting better." The nurse was hoping he would recover. She had watched this woman come and visit every day and knew she was dedicated to her husband. She picked up the clipboard and made a notation. Then she checked his pulse and blood pressure. "His pulse is strong and the pressure is in the normal range again."

Sarah sat down again. She was convinced that the prayer group was creating a miracle.

She took out her knitting and started to knit. She did not like staying at the nursing home all of the hours she was but if Bob woke up, she wanted to be here.

CHAPTER 98

*S*UE HAD SLEPT FOR *about an hour when her mother entered the room. Her mother looked around and saw Sue on the couch next to a middle-aged man.*

"You must be her mother." Jeff Tyler stood and addressed her. The resemblance to Sue was amazing, he thought. Her mother was wearing a conservative blue pants suit.

"I am Sue's mother," she said. "Who are you?"

"My name is Jeff Tyler. I work for the engineering company that hopes to hire young Mrs. Pritchard's husband." He could see that the mother was very attractive also.

"They're not married yet, I don't think," she said.

The conversation woke Sue. She looked up. "Mom," she cried as she got up from the couch and hugged her mother. "Ron's in the operating room. They say he might die," Sue sobbed.

Her mother had finally seen the newscast about Ron Pritchard and had hoped it was all a mistake until she called her daughter and found out it was Sue's Ron. The news was making him out to be a hero who saved countless children from being killed. She was impressed with the boy but knew her daughter was going through a difficult time, so she had driven down to see Sue.

"He's still got a chance, right?" her mother asked, looking at Sue. "Yes, but it is all so horrible. He might die or lose his leg," Sue rasped.

"Ok, but let's think about being positive." Her mother tried to reassure her. Her daughter was near hysteria, but that was probably natural after what had happened.

They sat down on the couch together, hugging each other. Her mother noticed the engagement ring on her daughter's hand. "That's a nice ring you have," she observed.

"Yes. It was Ron's mother's ring. She died in a car accident when he was in high school," Sue whispered.

"Well, this young man must be something special," the mother remarked.

"He is. He is the nicest, smartest and most considerate man I have ever met," Sue started. "And I am deeply in love with him, momma."

"I remember talking to him when you were in the Campus Hospital. He seemed like a real nice person and he said then that he hoped to marry you. I assume you have been intimate with him?"

Sue looked at the floor. "Yes, we have been lovers. I don't think I can live without him."

Her mother looked at her poor daughter. "Well, let's pray that he survives the operation." She closed her eyes.

A woman dressed in white with a clipboard came in and walked up to Sue.

"You are Mrs. Pritchard?" she asked.

Sue looked at her and said "Yes."

"Well, we have insurance paperwork that needs to be addressed."

Jeff Tyler stood up. "I can take care of that for you. Let's go to your office to discuss it." They walked out of the room.

Her mother looked at her. "You are already married?" she asked.

"No. I lied about that. They asked for his next of kin and he doesn't have anyone. He was an only child and his parents are gone. So, I stepped up and told them that we were married or they wouldn't let me see him," Sue explained.

"Oh. I understand now." Her mother now realized that her daughter was completely committed to Ron.

"I saw the newscast about the accident. They are saying if he had not sacrificed himself several children would have been killed," her mother related. "He must be a special person to do that."

"Yes. That is the kind of guy he is. That is why I am in love with him." Sue closed her eyes, starting to drift off to sleep, sobbing lowly.

Sue's mother looked at her little girl. She had grown up a lot since starting college. She hoped that the boy would live and spare her daughter more anguish. Why is it that the good ones always die young? She was glad that he had asked Sue to get married. That showed that he was responsible for his actions. Why would he sacrifice himself to save some children? He must be a very caring person, she thought. Not many people would do what he did.

CHAPTER 99

S ARAH WAS IN BOB'S room. He stirred and she walked over to his bed. "Bob?" she asked.

Bob did not open his eyes. He started to mumble and then said clearly "My leg, my leg. my leg hurts." Then he went back to sleep.

The nurse came in and Sarah told her what he had said.

The nurse went over and examined his legs but they both appeared to be fine.

"I don't see any distress here." She said after checking him over. "I think he is delirious."

Sarah was not so sure. If he could talk even a little bit then he must be getting better. The prayers were working, she thought.

CHAPTER 100

*G*EORGE COLEMAN ENTERED THE *waiting room in his police uniform. He walked over to Sue but saw she had fallen asleep. "Are you her mother?" he asked.*

"Yes." Do you want me to wake her?"

"No. Let her sleep. She stayed up all night next to his bedside." George noted. He confessed that he had snuck into the ICU ward and had seen her sitting near Ron late last night.

"Do you need to talk to her?" Sue's mother asked.

"Actually, I just wanted to see how she was doing. Ron Pritchard is one of my best friends and I know he is in love with her."

"You know Ron?" she asked.

"Yes. He just helped us put away a rapist that has been terrorizing the college campus."

"Really? I thought he was just an engineering student."

"Well, he is, but he is also a member of the Auxiliary Campus Police." George replied. "He is also about the best student on campus. He has made the Dean's list four semesters in a row."

"It seems everyone thinks he is superman." the mother remarked.

George looked at her. "Well, he's not superman, but he is probably the best person I have ever met. How many people would charge their car into a runaway semi to save some children? I doubt if he even hesitated to do it. He took a 3300-pound vehicle and diverted a 30,000-pound semi-tractor rig into a large oak tree. I calculate he must have been going close to a hundred miles an hour to have that much momentum."

"He does seem to be pretty remarkable," the mother admitted.

George sat down next to her. "According to Ron, he thinks your daughter is someone special."

"I've always thought she would be successful in anything she tried to do."

*Her mother started to cry. "I hate to see her struggle with this."
She looked down at Sue. "You said he is your best friend?"*

*"Yes. we met on campus a couple of years ago and he helped
me graduate and that led to me getting selected to the campus
police force." George smiled as he remembered. "He is the type of
guy that goes out of his way to help people."*

*"Maybe that is why he tried to kill himself saving those
children." Sues mother noted.*

*"Well, Ron is a strong guy. He should pull through this. All of
the fire department and police in this town are praying for him."*

*They sat quietly for some time. Then the door opened and
the doctor came in. He walked over to Sue. "Miss?" he asked.
Her mother nudged her and Sue woke up. The tracks of her tears
were still on her face. She had a hopeful look in her eyes as she
recognized the doctor.*

"Yes. Is he alright?" she whispered.

*"Well, the good news is we were able to save the leg. It was
a clean break. We had to pin the bone together and he won't be
walking on it for a few months but he should regain full use." The
doctor hesitated.*

*"The bad news is he appears to have a subdural hematoma
and we may have to perform brain surgery." The doctor hated to
tell the young girl this but thought she should know the facts.*

*"Oh no." Sue started to cry all over again. "How bad is it?"
the mother asked.*

*"Well, it's hard to tell. We have him going for an MRI right
now to get a better picture of the situation. I'm sorry, but I can't be
sure how bad it is until we get the test results." The doctor looked
at Sue. "He is a strong and healthy young man. He survived three
surgeries already that most people would not have lived through.
Don't give up hope." The doctor turned to leave.*

*George walked with him to the door. "Doc, everyone on the
force is pulling for him. Do your best," he pleaded.*

*"Don't worry, I have contacted the Cleveland Clinic and asked
for their best Neurosurgeon to come here for the operation."*

CHAPTER 101

*B*OB WAS IN A deep sleep. He would wake up for a few moments and then fall into sleep again.

He was breathing on his own. For some reason he was regaining the feeling of his extremities. He felt as though he had ventured too close to a precipice and was now coming back. He wondered about the dream. He had experienced the crash in his dream and felt the pain that Ron had. He wondered if Ron had died since he had no feeling from him recently. The other parts played on in his head. He figured he must be delirious.

He woke up again. He looked over and saw Sarah sitting next to him, reading a book. "Sarah," he said evenly.

She was startled and looked over to him. "Yes Bob?" she said, almost not believing that he was actually talking to her.

"Please tell David I have to talk to him." "You want to talk to your son?" she replied.

"Yes. I need to talk to him about the future. I have seen the future." "What do you mean?" she inquired. What is he talking about?

"I saw what is going to happen. He needs to know." Bob was tiring rapidly.

"Ok. I will call him to see you." She figured it was best to humor him. He must be hallucinating due to all of the drugs.

"Good. I need to talk to Jack also." He whispered as he started to fall back to sleep.

She looked at her husband. What was he talking about? She dialed Jack's number but he did not answer. He must be in surgery or something, she thought. She was about to dial her son's number but remembered that he was on a business trip to the west coast this week. I will tell him when he returns, she told herself.

CHAPTER 102

*D*R. *JACK SIMMS WALKED into the City Hospital. He had been contacted by Doctor Reynolds to perform a critical surgery on a boy that apparently had sacrificed himself to save a bunch of school children. He had seen the news footage and hardly believed that anyone would do what that boy did. He checked in at the information desk and got a visiting physician badge. Then he walked up to the ICU ward and asked to speak with Dr. Reynolds. A nurse told him that Dr. Reynolds had pulled three straight shifts and was in the Doctors' lounge taking a nap. He asked for directions and walked to the Doctors' Lounge. He walked in and saw a couple of interns eating their lunch. He asked for Dr. Reynolds. They pointed to the adjacent bed room. He went in and found Dr. Reynolds lying on one of the cots, apparently asleep. As he turned to leave, Dr. Reynolds sat up.*

"Are you looking for me?" he said groggily.

"You are Dr. Reynolds? I am Dr. Simms from Cleveland."

Dr. Reynolds got off the cot and immediately walked over to him extending his hand for a handshake. "Yes. I have heard of your good work."

"Well, I was asked to come here for a very delicate operation. I assume that was you."

"Yes. We have to try to save that boy. He deserves the best doctor we can get." Dr. Reynolds walked out of the lounge with Jack and headed to the ICU.

"Is it true that he saved a bunch of kids from getting killed?" Jack Simms asked.

"Yes. I saw the news footage. It was amazing. The MRI pictures look really bad. He needs a brain operation, and frankly, I am not that good about this type of surgery." Dr. Reynolds opened the door to Ron's room.

Jack looked at the boy on the bed and then looked at the MRI images. "I see what you mean." Jack suddenly felt very old. He was due to retire last year but had held on for another year due to a promise he made to an old friend. "The way this pressure is building up we should operate immediately. Tell the nurses to prep him ASAP."

"Ok. Do you want to talk to his wife first?" Dr. Reynolds asked. "Yes, we should do that. Is she in the hospital?"

"Yes. She is in the operating room waiting lounge. Come on, I'll introduce you." They walked down the hall though security doors and into the waiting room.

As he walked up to the girl on the couch sitting next to her mother, he was struck by how pretty she was and strangely enough somewhat familiar. "Hello," he said to her; "I am Dr. Simms. I am about to operate on your husband."

Sue looked up at him. He looked somewhat familiar, maybe at a long-ago family gathering or something? He was fairly old man with gray hair and a bald spot on the top of his head. He was wearing a business suit, not a surgical outfit.

"I am Ron's wife. What operation does Ron need?" Sue was all cried out and she looked very tired.

"He has a bad subdural hematoma. We have to release the pressure on his brain or he will die." Jack Simms gave it to her straight. He did not think there was much time to argue about this.

Sue's Mother said, "Well then let's operate." Sue nodded in agreement.

Dr. Reynolds replied that he would get the paperwork for them to sign as Dr. Simms took the hand of the girl. "I will do my best for him." He reassured her.

"Thank you Doctor," was all she could say. He turned to leave and headed for the OR.

Sue's mother was remembering something. She had met this doctor before, but when was it? Then it occurred to her. He was at her Father-in-law's funeral.

CHAPTER 103

BOB WAS AWAKE AGAIN. It was dark, probably night, he thought. He wondered why he was feeling better. Were they giving him a drug that was fighting the tumor? A nurse came in to do her nightly duties of emptying his catheter bags, give him a quick cleaning and change his bed pads. She turned on a low light so she could see what she was doing. He had been developing bed sores so they would alternately move him on to his side to relieve the pressure on his backside. He still did not have complete control of most of his body. He opened his eyes to look at her. She noticed this and stood back.

"Are you awake?" she asked. "I think so." He replied.

"I thought you were in a coma." She exclaimed.

"Yes, I guess so. I think I have been asleep for a long time." "So, are you feeling better?" She looked at his chart.

"I'm not sure. But I seem to be. Can I get something to eat? I am really hungry," he asked.

He had been getting most of his nourishment from a bag that was filled with a liquid mixture of proteins and carbohydrates that was gravity fed into a tube that went to his stomach. The nurse looked at the feeding bag and saw that it was empty. After checking the chart, it appeared that the day nurse had not replaced the bag with a new one.

"Can you chew?" the nurse asked.

"Well, I can talk so I guess I can chew," he replied.

"Let me remove that feeding tube and I will get you something from the cafeteria."

"I have a craving for chicken noodle soup." He wanted to taste something. His mouth was dry with no saliva. "Can I have a drink of water?" he asked.

The nurse went out of the room and came back with a bottle of water with a straw. She adjusted his bed so he was in a sitting position. He could not hold the drink so she held it for him as he sucked in the wonderful cold water.

"I can't seem to move my arms," he complained.

"Well, you are at least awake." She had been taking care of this patient for weeks and had never seen him awake before. "Maybe the feeling will come back as you get better."

"I hope so. What is your name?"

"I am Nora," she replied. She was a short middle-aged, blond woman wearing her typical white nurse uniform. She did not mind the night shift. She was divorced and had no one to take care of at home except her three cats. The night shift was typically quiet since most of the patients were asleep.

"I need to talk to Dr. Simms. Can you leave a message for him to come and see me?" he asked.

"I can leave a message with the head nurse at the Nurse's station."

"Thank you."

"I will go and see if I can get some soup for you." She left the room. He tested his body. It appeared that his neck, eyes and mouth worked ok but there was basically no feeling in the rest of his body, although he was definitely hungry. I wonder if I will be a paraplegic from now on. That was not a pleasant thought but it was better than being in a coma. Again, the dreams had seemed extremely vivid. When he was with Ron in the car and it hit the semi-tractor rig he had felt Ron's pain and it was intense. Now he had no contact with Ron and wondered if Ron had died. That would be terrible for Sue. He could understand why Ron had crashed the car to save the children, but was amazed that anyone would do that. It was basically suicidal. The kid had so much to live for and he sacrifices himself? Bob thought, wow, I could never have been that brave. And he was amazed to think that all of this was probably all happening in the future. Based upon his mental calculation it was 11 years into the future. Or was it really just a figment of his disease-damaged brain? He did not know. There was no way to confirm it either way.

The nurse returned with a bowl of soup. She spoon fed him slowly. It tasted wonderful, he thought. Afterward the nurse asked if he was cold.

"I don't know, but probably," he responded.

She covered him with another blanket. Then she left him. He was tired after talking so much and now with the warm soup in his stomach he felt drowsy.

He did not want to fall asleep. He was afraid he might not wake up again. But eventually he did fall back to sleep.

CHAPTER 104

*D*R. SIMMS AND DR. Reynolds were in the operating room with Ron. It was a complicated operation requiring the cutting open of Ron's skull and repairing the blood vessels that were leaking into his brain. The operation took about 4 hours since there was more than one blood vessel that had ruptured. After both doctors were satisfied that the repairs were successful, they replaced the skull fragment and closed the wound.

As they left the OR, Dr. Reynolds turned to Jack Simms. "Wow. There was a lot of damage. You were masterful in there. Do you think he will be ok?"

Jack Simms looked at him. "We did the best we could. Now it is up to him."

"There was some brain damage I think. Do think it will be significant?" Doctor Reynolds asked.

"I don't think it was that severe, but it is a good thing we went in there otherwise he would be dead by this time tomorrow," Doctor Simms noted. He walked into the scrub room.

Jack cleaned up and then went down to the visitor's lounge see Ron's wife, the young girl. As he walked in Sue stood up and rushed to him. "Is he alright?" she pleaded.

Jack took her hands in his and said, "We were able to repair the damage but we cannot be sure that he will not have some brain damage. All we can do now is wait and see."

"But he has a chance?" Her eyes were starting to tear up.

"He has a damn good chance. He is a healthy young man and we did the best we could for him."

"Thank you, Doctor," she said looking at the floor. She went over to the couch and sat down next to her mother.

Jack Simms was about to leave when the girl's mother came over to him. "You are Jack Simms, aren't you?"

"Yes. You look familiar. Do I know you?" he asked.

"We were both at my father-in-law's funeral. You were one of

*the pallbearers I think," she said. "That would be Bob Parker?"
he said, "About 11 years ago?"*

*"Yes. I am Liz Parker, Dave's wife. Susan is my daughter." She
looked at Sue.*

*"My god! What a coincidence." He was astounded. "Bob
Parker was one of my best friends. It was too bad the way he died."*

*"Yes. My daughter was really upset when he died. They were
really close and they only knew each other for a short time."*

*"Well, you can reassure her that we did the best we could to
save her husband," he remarked, shaking her hand.*

*"Well, she is engaged to Ron but they haven't been married yet.
She just told them that since he has no next of kin." Liz whispered.*

*"Oh...I understand." He looked at the girl. She was a very
beautiful girl and had a diamond ring on her left hand. He hoped
that everything worked out for them. "Well, take care. I have to go
and check on the patient." He turned to go. As he walked back to
the ICU he started thinking about what Bob Parker had asked him
on his deathbed.*

CHAPTER 105

*B*OB WAS AWAKE AGAIN. It was morning; sun was coming through the window blinds. The day nurse came in and was surprised to see him sitting up in the bed. She asked if he wanted something to eat. He said yes but that he was unable to feed himself. She went away and came back with some oatmeal. She spooned it into his mouth and he would swallow. He did not care much for oatmeal but it would at least help with the hunger pangs. He disliked not being able to feed himself but had no choice. After he was done, she took his vitals and made annotations on his chart. He waited, awake for a while, thinking of the dreams. Jack Simms finally showed up.

"Well, I see you are awake today," he said as he came in and saw Bob sitting up. "Jack, it is nice to be back. I feel as if I have been on a long journey," Bob started. "Apparently the experimental drug I have given you has had a good effect," Jack said. "What drug? I thought you said there was nothing that could stop the tumor."

"This is really experimental stuff that a colleague of mine told me about. It is brand new. But it seems to be helping you," Jack explained. "Also, your wife's prayer group seems to think that they can produce a miracle."

"Well, I am glad to be able to talk to you. You are a few years younger than I am, correct?" Bob asked.

"Yeah, a few years, why?" Jack asked.

"When do you plan to retire?" Bob was very serious.

"I don't know. Angie and I figured I would go to 65 and then retire to the country somewhere." "That would be about 11 years?" Bob asked.

"Yes. I guess so."

"Can I ask a big favor of you?" Bob looked into Jack's eyes. "I suppose so." Jack was curious about what Bob wanted.

"Can you postpone your retirement one extra year?" Bob was starting to cry." There is something important that you have to do for me."

Jack looked at Bob. Was he being delirious again? "What is it?" he asked.

"I know you won't believe this, but you have to operate on a special young man in 12 years. You are the only one who can save him." Tears were running down Bob's face.

Jack could see he was very serious. "Ok. But how do you know this?"

"Whether you believe this or not, I can see into the future." Bob was getting very tired. "Please, I am begging you."

Jack did not understand why Bob was saying this. He decided to go along with the request. "Ok, sure, Robert. I will do as you ask."

"You promise?"

Jack smiled "Sure. I promise."

"Good. Thanks." Bob closed his eyes; he was falling asleep again.

Jack realized that Bob had drifted off. He wondered what this was all about. It was a strange request but an extra year of surgery wasn't that bad. He had set his original retirement goal with the hope he had enough saved up for retirement. An extra year would just ensure that he had enough. He wondered if there was anything to Bob's request. Bob really seemed to believe that he could see the future. He would have to tell his doctor friends that the new drug did shrink the tumor but had some unusual side effects.

CHAPTER 106

*S*UE WAS SITTING NEXT *to Ron's bed in the ICU ward. Ron now had a solid cast on his right leg which was elevated slightly off the bed. He had a large bandage on his head and a bandage on the left side of his face. He had several tubes going in and out of him. He had an oxygen mask on. There was an electronic monitor next to the bed which showed his heart rate and blood pressure. The monitor was silent but would make an alarm if the readings went off scale. It appeared that the readings were normal. The nurse had told Sue that for now Ron was on medication to allow his brain to heal. A nurse was checking his oxygen levels and making notes on the chart as Dr. Reynolds walked into the room.*

"How is he doing?" he asked the nurse, who handed him the chart. "He appears to be almost normal," the nurse said.

"Well, that's good." Doctor Reynolds performed a couple of checks himself. "Will he recover?" Sue asked the doctor.

Dr. Reynolds sat down next to Sue. "He has a very good chance now. Dr. Simms from Cleveland basically saved his life during the operation. I am not sure I could have performed that surgery as well as he did. But we can't tell for sure yet. His vitals look good but that could change anytime."

"Oh. But so far it's good, right?" she asked. Sue was very tired. She had been at the hospital three straight days without a shower or a change of clothes.

"You should go home and get some sleep." Doctor Reynolds suggested. "He won't be awakening for a day or two. You need a break."

"Ok. My mother is down in the waiting room." She got up to leave.

Dr. Reynolds escorted her back to the waiting room. Her mother was sitting there, watching the TV.

Sue's mother looked up and asked "Is he doing ok?"

Dr. Reynolds looked at her. "He is in a drug induced coma for now. We need to let his body try to repair itself. You need to get this girl fed and rested." he said, gesturing at Sue.

"OK. Thank you, Doctor." Sue's mother took Sue's arm and they walked to the exit. Her car was in the parking lot.

"Do you want to go to our home?" She asked her daughter. "No. Can you take me to my dorm?" Sue replied.

"Sure. I always wondered what your dormitory looked like anyway." They got in the car and drove to the campus.

"How did Ron look?" she asked her daughter.

"Oh Momma, he is in such bad shape...he is all covered with bandages and they have tubes going into him all over." Sue was all cried out or she would have started to cry again.

"Well, at least he is still alive. That should give us some hope."

Sue's mom took her to the dormitory. The place was almost deserted. Almost everyone had left for the three-week break between semesters. She was amazed at how nice Sue's room was. It was, she thought a very comfortable apartment, even if it was on the third floor. After Sue had showered and changed clothes, her mother took her to a fast-food restaurant to get something to eat. They were sitting there eating burgers and fries.

"So, it looks like Ron is going to be OK?" her mother asked.

"Dr. Reynolds seems to think he might make it now." Sue was eating but was still dead tired. "Are you still planning to marry him?"

Sue looked at her mother. "The accident has not changed anything. I still love him." Sue replied.

"He may be a different person after the brain surgery." Her mother wanted to prepare Sue for the worst possible outcome. "Sometimes something this traumatic changes a person's personality. He may be a completely different person than what you know now."

"He stayed by my side when I was in the hospital. He even tolerated my loss of memory. He didn't give up on me," she pleaded. She had no intention of giving up on him.

"Ok. But he may have changed. Not everyone can go through what he has and come out the same," her mother said. They ate the rest of the meal in silence. Afterward her mother dropped Sue off at the dormitory and drove back home.

Sue climbed the stairs. She entered her room. Joan was back. Joan ran to her and they hugged. "I had to come back after what happened to Ron." Joan was crying.

"He has been terribly injured," Sue filled her in. "They didn't think he was going to survive but the doctors managed to pull him through."

"I heard that he saved a lot of kids on that playground."

"I guess so. But he nearly killed himself doing it." Sue was looking at her bunk. "I need to rest. I have been at the hospital for the last three days."

"You better get some sleep." Joan could see Sue was exhausted. Sue walked over to her bunk and got in and fell asleep immediately. Joan covered her with a blanket. Then she called Jerry.

"How are you doing?" she asked.

"Oh, ok, but I'm just hanging at the Frat house." He was glad to hear from her. "How was your visit back home?"

"It was too short. I had to come back for Sue when I heard what happened to Ron," she explained.

"Yeah, I heard he was in serious condition and not expected to live," he said sadly. In the short time he knew Ron; he had become good friends with him. Ron was a real standup guy; he did not bullshit you like most of the Frat guys.

"Well, Sue just returned from the hospital and says he may make a recovery." Joan whispered, trying not to disturb Sue.

"Wow. That's great news." Jerry began to cheer up. "How about I come over to see you?"

"Well, she is sleeping right now, she is exhausted. But I can meet you in front of the building if you want to go get something to eat." Joan suggested.

"That sounds good. See you in about 15 minutes?" he replied.

"Ok." Joan hung up. She looked at Sue. This had been a very weird semester with everything that had happened. If college life was going to be like this all of the time, she did not think she could take it. She had to admit that most of it had revolved around her roommate. Poor Sue had had a rough first semester. Joan would prefer to have a boring time for the next semester. As far as Sue's relationship with Ron, she was amazed at the type of guy he was, willing to sacrifice himself for some children. According to Sue,

he was kind and caring and apparently pretty smart, also. She was happy for Sue. She hoped that he survived and that they would have a happy life together. She got ready and went down to meet Jerry.

CHAPTER 107

SARAH ARRIVED AND SAT down next to Bob. Bob was apparently asleep. The nurse told her that Bob had a long talk with Doctor Simms in the morning. Sarah was sure that the prayer group was making a miracle occur. According to Doctor Simms, Bob should have died weeks ago. She wondered if the experimental drug was also helping.

Michael Kramer entered the room and sat next to Sarah. "How is he doing?" he asked.

Sarah was shocked to see the private detective. "He is improving. What are you doing here?" "Just checking in with you to see how the brother is doing."

"Tom is planning to attend the community college and learn a trade," she remarked. Actually, she was glad to see the man. He knew his way around and seemed very competent.

"Well, that's good news," he noted. Although Sarah was a few years older than he was, Kramer felt that she was very attractive and he liked her. For her sake, he hoped that her husband made a full recovery. He didn't believe that the brother was going to do well at the college. He was too old and once a loser, always a loser. He planned to protect Sarah from whatever her brother would try to do next.

"Aren't you pretty busy?" she asked, wondering why the man was here. She had to admit that he was an attractive man.

"I am sort of in between things right now." As a private detective, business usually involved following a wife or husband that was cheating on their mate. Once and a while he had to deal with the bad side of society but he was confident in his abilities. Right now, he was not busy.

"Well, it is nice to see you again." She replied. "Tom has changed his ways; he is no longer gambling."

"That is good." He did not believe this, but let it go for now.

They sat there in silence for a few minutes. He got up to leave but handed her his business card. "Just in case you need me, give me a call."

"Thank you. I will," she blushed a bit.

Kramer left the room and walked down the hall. He would check on the brother discretely just to make sure. The husband looked like he was on his deathbed. Kramer doubted that he was getting better.

CHAPTER 108

SARAH WAS IN BOB'S room. Bob would periodically wake up, talk for a few minutes and then fall back asleep. He could not move his arms or legs but was able to swallow small amounts of food and sip water through a straw. His vital statistics were being maintained near normal. He was able to breath on his own but they had a tube connected to his nose to provide oxygen. Bob had asked if his son Dave was going to visit. Dave was still on his business trip in California but would return home in a few days.

Sarah kept hoping that he would get better but he seemed to be stuck as a paraplegic. He did talk to her for short periods of time but it seemed to make him very tired. At least Bob wasn't in a coma anymore. The last time Dave had visited him, Bob was in a deep coma with no hope of recovery. She knew the doctors were puzzled at his partial recovery. They attributed it to the experimental drug. She knew it was the power of prayer that had brought him back, or at least she believed that.

"Sarah?" Bob spoke.

She went to his bedside. "Yes dear?" "Can I have some water?"

She lifted the water bottle with a straw to his lips and he drank a few swallows. "Thanks," he whispered.

"How do you feel?" she asked.

"I feel as if I am floating in a pool of water. I have almost no feeling below my neck," he stated as a matter of fact. He did not feel sorry for himself. He just wondered if he was going to get better or worse. He had already lived longer than Jack Simms had predicted.

"Is David coming soon?" he asked. "I need to talk to him." "He is traveling but should be here in a couple of days." "Oh." He closed his eyes.

"You will get better," Sarah reassured him. But he had already gone back to sleep. She knew that her prayers were being answered.

CHAPTER 109

*R*ON HAD BEEN IN *a drug induced sleep for three days when the doctors thought he should wake up so they could test him. They had placed him in the MRI machine after the brain surgery and everything now looked normal. The leg bone was set ok and the rib punctures to his lung were no longer bleeding. Now they needed to ask him how he felt and run tests on his memory and reflexes, so they stopped the drugs in the hope that he would wake up. He did not wake up.*

Sue had slept for the better part of a whole day. She woke up hungry but there was nothing to eat in the dorm room. Joan had gone out with Jerry so she got dressed in a pair of slacks and a T-shirt. She put her hair up in a ponytail. It showed off the scar near her ear but she did not care. She started to walk down the stairs to the exit. George Coleman was just outside the dormitory entrance as she approached the door.

"Hello Sue. I was just coming to see you," George started. He was wearing his police uniform. "Hi, George." Sue replied. She was still somewhat tired but glad to see Ron's police buddy.

"I was wondering how you were doing."

"I'm ok. Just going to get something to eat and then maybe catch a bus over to the hospital."

"You need a ride? My patrol car is in the parking lot," he quickly said.

"That's nice of you, but you don't have to do that." She knew policemen did not have time to ferry people around.

"It would be my privilege to give the fiancée of my best friend a ride." He smiled at her.

"Ok. Thanks." She gave in and they walked to the police car.

"Where do you want to go to eat?" he asked as they got into the police car.

"That little diner down the street from Ron's apartment has really good cheeseburgers," she hinted.

"Sounds good to me," he replied as they pulled out of the parking lot. "I must thank you. You have been very kind."

"It's the least I can do for the future wife of a hero," George kidded.

"I don't think of him as a hero. He is my love, the center of my heart." She was serious.

"I think he feels the same way about you."

"Why do you think he did it? Hitting the truck, I mean," she asked.

"I believe he saw what was going to happen and just did it without thinking of himself." George theorized. "Anyone in a car without that much power would not have had the chance to divert the truck. They say he must have been going close to a hundred miles an hour at impact." He had seen the wreckage of the Corvette. There was not much left of it. The Corvette was basically a huge motor on wheels and that motor came into the passenger compartment upon impact. He was really surprised that Ron had survived. In a crash like that there were typically no survivors.

"Wow. How did he survive?" she wondered out loud.

"All I can think is that God spared him for his selfless act," he postulated.

They arrived at the diner. She went in with him and they sat down at a table. The waitress rushed over to give them menus. She was always happy to see police officers in her café. They typically did not come in with pretty girls though. The girl looked familiar. She thought that she had seen her with the guy that was in the crash by the playground.

"Weren't you in here with that Ron guy last week?" the waitress asked. Sue looked up. "Yes. He is my fiancée."

"Isn't he the one that crashed the Corvette into that semi and saved allthose kids? Did he survive that crash ok?" the waitress asked, concerned.

George answered. "He is in the hospital, but it looks like he might live."

"Well, I am glad to hear that. Order anything you want. It's on the house." They both ordered a cheeseburger and a coke.

After finishing their meal, George drove Sue to the city hospital. It was about six miles from the college campus, way too far to walk. George parked the cruiser and went in with her. At the information center they discovered that the doctors had had Ron moved out of the ICU and he was now in a postop ward. This was good news. It meant that he was no longer considered critical. They went to his room. It was a double occupancy room but he was the only patient in it. He was still hooked up to a bunch of tubes and monitors. George asked at the nurse's station if the doctor was available. The nurse said she would check to see if the resident was available.

Sue sat next to Ron's bed. He was still unconscious. George sat with her for a while. The doctor came in. He said his name was Dr. Blaine, a young, good-looking African-American man in his late 20's.

"Doctor, how is Ron doing?" Sue asked.

"The doctor looked at the young girl and replied: "He is still unresponsive at this time. We have stopped the sedative treatment and are waiting for him to wake up."

"Is he ok?" George inquired.

"We cannot predict his mental capability but believe he should have a complete physical recovery. He will probably require some physical therapy to return to a normal life."

Sue was relieved to hear this. "Is Dr. Reynolds still monitoring his condition?"

"Dr. Reynolds was monitoring him, but has gone home for some much needed rest." Dr. Blaine replied.

"Ok. Do you mind if I stay here with Ron?" Sue asked.

"I understand that you are the wife?" the doctor asked. Visiting hours were almost over. "Yes, she is." George said as he stood up. He looked questioningly at the doctor.

"Well in that case, I guess you are welcome to stay in the room," the Doctor said, not wanting to have a conflict with a policeman.

George walked out with the doctor, leaving Sue sitting next to Ron. She watched his monitor for a while. Ron was in pretty much the same condition as she had seen him previously. The bandage on the side of his face was smaller, indicating that it had been changed. His head was still bandaged and his right leg still in a cast and lifted off the bed slightly by a system of wires and pulleys. She was still somewhat tired so she put her head back and closed her eyes.

The night nurse came in to monitor Ron's vital statistics and noticed the girl had fallen asleep, so she turned the lights down low before leaving to do her other checks on the floor.

Later, the sun came streaming into the room as the blinds were only half closed. Ron woke up. The first thing he noticed was the pain. His leg hurt, his side hurt, his face hurt and his head hurt. Jesus, he thought. Am I still alive or is this some part of hell? He opened his eyes. He was in a white room. He tried to look around. He saw that Sue was sitting next to him, asleep. He did not want to disturb her but the pain was intense.

"Hello," he croaked. It was difficult to talk with a tube down his throat. His throat was dry. "Hmmm?" Sue started to wake up. When she saw that Ron was awake, she stood up excitedly. "You're back. Thank God!" she said rushing to his side.

"Water?" he managed to croak again.

She looked around. There was no water on his tray. She ran to the nurse's station. The nurse there was busy working on her computer.

"He's awake!" Sue cried. "He wants some water."

The nurse looked up surprised. "There is a refreshment station down the hall." She pointed to her right. She went back to her typing.

Sue rushed and found the station. It had coffee and tea bags. It also had a spigot for hot or cold water. She grabbed a cup and filled it with cold water. Then she ran back to Ron's room. He was still awake. She put the cup to his lips and he drank some of the water. She stood back as he grabbed the cup with his right hand and drank the remainder.

"Pain." He moaned. "A lot of pain."

She reached for the call button and pressed it. A 'DING' sounded out in the hall as the call light came on.

"I was hoping you wouldn't leave me." Sue started to cry. "How long? How long have I been out?" he struggled to say.

"Almost a week." Sue leaned over him as if to kiss him. He closed his eyes. The pain was distracting him.

"My leg?" He noticed it was elevated and he could not move it. "It was broken, but they put a cast on it," she explained.

"The kids in the playground?" he asked, slowly remembering what had happened. "You saved them. No one was hurt," she replied.

"Good." He closed his eyes again.

The nurse entered and was glad that he was awake. He told her that he was in pain and she opened a valve on a second IV that contained morphine. She set it to drip every couple of minutes or so, then said she would get the doctor and left.

"The car?" he asked looking at her for the first time.

"It was totaled. Not much left from what I saw," she informed him.

The medication began to work and he relaxed a little. He looked at her and recognized who it was. "I guess I really messed us up. I'm sorry."

"That's Ok. You survived. That's all that matters." She smiled at him. "My head hurts really bad."

"They had to do brain surgery on you. You had a real bad concussion," Sue explained.

He felt around the left side of his head with his right hand. The bandage was covering the surgery site, but he could tell they had shaved his head.

"Jesus, I must look terrible." He looked at Sue. Sue looked at him and said "You look beautiful."

"I guess our engagement is off." He looked at his leg. "You won't want to marry a cripple." "Oh no. I won't let you get away that easily," she replied.

"I can't go to class like this. I won't graduate in time to get the engineering position." "Oh yes you will, even if I have to push you around in a wheelchair," she said firmly. He looked at her again. "I love you." He said, a tear forming at his eye.

She leaned over to him and this time they kissed.

Dr. Reynolds entered the room. "I hate to break this up but I need to see my star patient." Sue stood back and let the doctor examine Ron. "How do you feel?" he asked.

"A lot of pain," Ron replied. He did not recognize the man but assumed he was a doctor.

"That is understandable, based on how many repairs we made to your body. I suggest that you don't try to kill yourself again for a while. You need time to heal." The doctor took the medical chart at the foot of the bed and read some annotations. "You are getting some morphine to keep the pain in check. I don't want you to try to get up for a while. That leg needs a week or so to start to knit. We

had to put three pins in it." He looked at Ron. "This little lady here has been waiting patiently for you to wake up. I don't want you to mess up your recovery, OK?"

"Ok Doc. Can I at least get this tube out of my throat?" Ron asked. "Yeah. It looks like you can start having solid food. I will tell the nurse." He walked out of the room. "That man operated on you four times. He saved your life," Sue related to Ron.

"Wow. I didn't know. I guess I have a lot to thank him for."

"George has been in and out of here a lot. He gave me a ride in a police car to bring me here." Sue wanted him to know that his friend was concerned for him.

"Where am I?" he asked.

"We are at the city hospital. You were in too bad of shape to take you to the campus hospital." "Oh. What about the driver of the truck I hit?"

"According to what I read in the paper, he had died of a massive cardiac attack," Sue related.

"So, I did not kill him…Good." Ron was starting to really feel the drugs working now. He was slowly drifting off to sleep. Sue let him sleep. He had a lot of healing to do.

She sat next to him and prayed, thanking God for returning him to her.

Doctor Reynolds walked by the room again and peaked in and saw that Ron had gone back to sleep and the pretty wife was sitting there patiently holding his hand. They must really be in love, he thought. The boy was not out of the woods yet, he thought. They had saved his leg but probably should have amputated it. Typically, people with broken femurs developed blood clots that could cause strokes or even death. He hoped it would not happen this time.

CHAPTER 110

BOB WOKE UP AGAIN. His dream had still continued. He wondered how the story would end. He felt the pain that Ron was having. It was not pleasant but it was better than feeling nothing at all, like his body was. Sarah had not come in today. Another guy had. He was a rough looking individual, someone Bob would have been careful not to upset in his old life. He was heavyset, about 250 pounds and looked like he had been in a few fights. He was wearing a brown plaid suit.

"How are you doing?" The man asked.

"I guess I am dying, but it is a slow process." Bob replied.

"My name is Kramer. I am helping your wife and brother-in-law out of some trouble." "What kind of trouble?" Bob asked.

"Your brother-in-law got caught losing a lot of money to the Mob gambling. He owed the money to the Mob and since he couldn't pay them, they beat him up pretty bad, so your wife forked over the cash to pay them off," Kramer recited.

"Where do you come in? How do you know Sarah?"

"Jack Simms asked me to help out as a favor to him. I helped your wife pay off the debt. I thought you should know about it." Kramer sat down in the chair next to the bed.

"I didn't know. Sarah didn't tell me about it."

"I think she is ashamed of her brother. She thinks he is going to the community college to learn a trade."

"He is pretty old to go to back to school."

"Yeah. The brother looked into it and then took the tuition money and went to the racetrack and blew most of it."

"No shit." Bob was upset that Sarah was still trying to help her brother. "I figured now that you are awake you might want to know this."

"Thanks. I cannot do much about it though, in my condition." Bob was puzzled why this guy was telling him all this.

"I know. But I like your wife a lot and I don't want her to get hurt anymore." Kramer confessed. "What can you do about it?" Bob was curious.

"Well, I can arrange an accident if you want."

"You would do that?" Bob was becoming anxious about the way the conversation was going. "I can. But she is your wife and she is spending your money." Kramer looked dead serious.

"I cannot sanction hurting her brother." Bob was getting scared now. "What if I arrange for him to leave town for good?" Kramer negotiated. "That might work." Bob was relieved.

"If that is what you want, consider it done." Kramer stood up. "Will you do me a favor?" Bob asked.

"Name it."

"I am going to be dead soon. Can I ask you to look after Sarah? She needs someone strong to lean on."

"I was going to do that anyways." Kramer smiled. "Glad you aren't upset about it."

"No, actually I am somewhat relieved. You seem to be a strong character. But I hope you treat her with kindness," Bob pleaded.

"She is a real lady. I won't ever hurt her," Kramer reassured him. "You can ask Jack Simms about me. He saved my mother in an operation that no other doctor would try. I owe him a lot."

"You are friends with Jack?"

"Well, we are not buddies but I told him if he ever needed help, I was there. That's who asked me to help with the brother-in-law."

"Well, then, thank you. I appreciate it." Bob was getting tired. "There is one other thing." Bob asked.

"What?" Kramer was about to leave but turned to look at Bob again.

"I have this step-grandchild." Bob looked at Kramer with a serious look. "Yeah?"

"She is something special. Her name is Susan. Could you sort of look out for her too?" Bob asked. "I suppose so." Kramer wondered why he was being asked this.

"I would appreciate it if you were sort of a guardian angel for her." Bob asked meekly. "Sure, if I can, I will." Kramer promised.

"Thank you." Bob was relieved.

"So long." Kramer turned and walked out of the room.

Wow. A lot had been going on while he was comatose. He was glad that this Kramer guy was looking after Sarah. She needed someone strong to help her. He wondered how she felt about this guy. He was still wondering when he fell back into a deep sleep.

As Kramer walked down the hall he was puzzled by the dying mans request. He appeared to be more concerned with the well-being of a little girl than he was about his wife being looked after by him. Still, he did like the wife, and if the guy died he might try to get to know the wife better if she was ok with it.

CHAPTER 111

*T*HE FALL SEMESTER HAD *already started. Ron had gotten much better after three weeks in the hospital. He had struggled for the last couple of weeks doing some therapy. Finally, the doctors said he was well enough to return to the college. The doctors were amazed at how fast he had recovered. He had a lot of scar tissue but it looked like he was going to make a full recovery. His hair had started to grow back in from where he was shaved for the brain operation, but he started to wear a baseball cap to hide the bandage. Sue had been with him as much as she could during the recovery period. He missed the first full week of the fall semester but felt that he could still catch up and at least get a passing grade.*

He been looking forward to completing his degree program but now he was in a wheelchair and could not walk, even using crutches. He was glad to be preparing to check out of the hospital. Sue was going to drive his Jeep over and pick him up. He wondered about the hospital bill. Four separate major operations should cost him a significant amount of money. No one had approached him with a bill yet. He had a few thousand in his checking account, but that probably would not even make a dent in his bill. He had let his insurance with the college lapse so it meant he would have a lot of bills to pay off. He was wondering how he would make it up the stairs to his apartment. He sat in the wheelchair, looking out the window. He figured he was going to be in debt for a long time. It was kind of depressing but he could only think of being with Sue. Still, he figured he would manage somehow if she stuck by him. Would she still stay with him if he was heavily in debt for several years?

A man came into the room. He looked over and saw it was the engineering manager of the aerospace company he had been an intern with the previous summer. "Hi, I'm Jeff Tyler. Do you remember me?" he asked Ron.

"Yes. Hello Mr. Tyler." Ron was surprised to see the man. He was hoping to eventually work at the same company after he graduated.

"Well, we were wondering when you can start at our company." Jeff remarked as he sat in one of the bedside chairs.

"I sort of had an accident. I'm not sure if I can graduate on time now." Ron was despondent.

"Well, there's no rush. Take your time. I have a paper for you to sign." He handed Ron a paper. It was pre-dated a week before his accident.

"What is this?" Ron asked.

"It says you were an employee of our company just before your accident. We need it for insurance purposes." Jeff smiled.

"What does this mean?" Ron was confused.

"Our company is picking up your hospital bill. You are officially an employee once you sign the paper. Your title is only an engineer level 1, the lowest grade in engineering, but you can negotiate for a higher level once you graduate."

"Why would you do this?" Ron was astounded.

"We see a great potential in your possible contribution to our company." Jeff explained.

"I am very happy to join your company, but I don't deserve all this." Ron studied the paper. It looked real. Why would they do this for him?

"Let us worry about that. From now on you are a new hire, but on leave to finish your education."

"Wow. Thanks so much." Ron signed the paper and gave it back to Jeff. *"I don't know what to say."* Ron was amazed at this good luck.

"Just finish your degree, but don't take too long to do it. I will see you when you are ready to start work. We look forward to you joining our team." Jeff smiled at him and then walked out of the room.

Ron was stunned. Why would they do something that nice for him? He was only an engineering student, not even out of college. He had thrived at the company as an engineering intern but did not think he had made that good of an impression. At any rate, he now had a job secured for when he graduated. That made him smile. Maybe, just maybe everything will turn out ok after all.

He wheeled himself over to the mirror. The cast on his leg stuck straight out so he could not get too close. They had removed most of the bandages from his face but he still had some bandage covering his head. Thank god he had the baseball cap. He saw a 2-inch red scar on his left cheek. That probably happened when the driver side window imploded on him. Well, he and Sue both had matching scars now. His side did not hurt anymore but it was still tender. The pain in his leg had become manageable as long as he did not bump it. His head still had a dull pain but what was worse was it itched like crazy under the bandages.

Campus policemen George Coleman and Andy Hall walked into his room. "I see you are much better." Andy observed.

Ron turned to meet them. "How are things going on campus?" He was surprised to see half of the campus police force this far into the city.

"Everything is pretty quiet since you aren't there now. We thought we would come to break you out of this place." George smiled at him.

"I was waiting on a ride. Sue is supposed to bring my Jeep over."

"I think I saw her by the nurse station arguing about some paperwork." Andy looked out the door down the hall.

Sue came into the room. "Damn. They won't release you until Dr. Reynolds comes over." She exclaimed. "Oh, hi George, hi Andy." She smiled at them.

"I guess I can wait for the doctor." Ron observed. He had a room full of the people he loved most and was going to enjoy it. "The crime rate must be pretty low for you guys coming this far into the city."

Andy looked at George "Didn't you tell him?" "Tell me what?" Ron was curious.

George smiled. "Well, it appears that someone exceeded the speed limit in a school zone and we have to arrest him." He joked.

"You have got to be kidding." Ron exclaimed.

"Nope. There are severe penalties for that." George was trying to look serious. Ron looked at Sue. She was smiling also. What the heck was going on?

Dr. Reynolds came into the room. He was in a business suit, not his typical white operating smock. "Well. How do you feel Ron?" He asked.

"I still have some minor pain but the nurse gave me some pills to take. I guess I feel pretty good. How soon can I get this cast off?" He pointed to his leg.

"It will be about 8 more weeks. Then you may require some therapy." The doctor replied. "Ok then. Can I go home now?" Ron asked.

"I want to shake your hand." The doctor stepped forward.

"I should be thanking you for saving my life." Ron shook his hand.

"It was my pleasure." Doctor Reynolds smiled and then left the room. The nurse came into the room and handed Sue Ron's release papers.

"OK then. It's time to go." Sue said as she got behind Ron and pushed his wheelchair out of the room and to the elevator. The two policemen escorted him, one on each side. They went down in the elevator together. The elevator door opened and there were hospital people lined up on either side of the exit. As Sue pushed him to the door, all of the people started clapping.

"What's going on?" Ron asked. Nobody said anything. As Sue pushed him to the Jeep, he noticed she was parked behind a police car. Behind the Jeep was a fire engine. As Andy helped him into the Jeep, Sue handed the wheelchair to George who put it in the back of the jeep.

Sue got in and started the Jeep. Ron had to put his seat in the farthest back position due to his cast. He just barely fit in the seat. Andy and George got into the police car in front and turned on their flashers. As they pulled out, Sue followed and the fire engine turned on its flashers and followed her. As they drove through the city towards campus, a few people lined the streets and were waving at Ron.

"Please tell me what this is all about?" he asked Sue.

"A few people around here think you are a hero," she explained. "I don't understand." He was puzzled.

"Well, you saved a lot of kids that day. Some people think that was heroic." She was smiling.

"Anybody would have done that."

"No. You were at the right place and time with probably the only vehicle that could have done the job."

"I killed the beast." He meant his car.

"Yes. On the news they made you out to be a hero," She replied. "I'm no hero," he grumbled.

"You are a caring, sensitive person who goes out of his way to protect others," she said. "That may be true but…" he stopped as they arrived at his apartment.

Matt and Becky were in the yard. Sue pulled the Jeep into the driveway. The police car pulled over and parked in the street. The fire truck pulled away and left.

Sue got out of the Jeep and went around to remove the wheelchair out of the back. George and Andy came up and helped her. She got the wheelchair over to the passenger side door and Ron sort of hopped into it. She wheeled him over to Matt.

"About time you got back. I was about to rent out your room." Matt kidded.

"What is that?" Ron pointed to a lift chair that was mounted to the railing on the steps.

"Some police guy had the city engineer hook up that contraption." Matt pointed to the lift chair.

Becky came over to Ron and gave him a hug. "We are so glad you survived." She said with tears in her eyes. He smiled at her and said he was ok.

Ron looked at George. "I suppose I have you to thank for this?" he said pointing to the chair lift.

"It's just temporary. The landlord gave us a real hard time but we finally got him to agree." George laughed. "Why don't you try it out?"

"It would be just my luck to survive a car crash and then get electrocuted by some faulty wiring." Ron joked. He got on the chair lift and turned it on. It slowly propelled him to the top of the stairs. Sue followed him up the stairs. Matt and Becky went back inside. George and Andy said goodbye and left also.

She opened the door and he hopped inside. There was another wheelchair inside by the door so he sat in it. He wheeled the wheel chair over to the window and looked out.

She closed the door and walked up to him, smiling.

"I don't think I will be up to any serious lovemaking until I get this cast off," he said. "Well, we will see about that," she purred.

He was still looking out the window. "I am not sure we should get married. You probably don't want to be engaged to a cripple.

You can give the ring back; I won't hold you to the engagement."

Sue looked at him. "They said you might have some brain damage from the brain operation." She grabbed him by the collar. "Are you trying to back out on me?" she said frowning.

"No…but it may take me several months to get back to normal. I don't want to be a burden on you. You are a young and vibrant woman with her own desires." he looked at her.

Sue was amazed. How could he feel this way after all they had gone through? "Do you still love me?" She asked.

"Well yes, of course I do…but."

"Well then, nothing has changed unless you want it to." She looked at the ring on her finger. "Unless you ask for this back, I am keeping it forever."

He looked relieved. "I was hoping you still wanted to be with me. But I am a wreck right now."

"They say it is for better or worse," she said, smiling." If this is as bad as it gets, I can take it. You didn't give up on me when I got hurt."

"I had to give you the chance to back out if you wanted to. I am still deeply in love with you and still want to marry you," he replied.

She bent down and gave him a passionate kiss. The electricity was still there. "Wow," he said. "By the way…I am now employed by that aerospace company."

"Yeah, I talked to your manager and he said he wanted to hire you."

"So—you already knew!" He was surprised. "I have no secrets from you?"

"No. None at all. But that's ok. You just concentrate on getting better and finishing school. I will be here to help." She smiled.

CHAPTER 112

*K*RAMER WAS AT THE racetrack. He spotted Sarah's brother Tom walking away from the claim counter. Tom had finally won a race and was counting his winnings. Kramer walked up to him and stopped in front of him. Tom stopped, looked up and froze.

"I heard you were going to go to the community college." Kramer growled. "Well, ah…yes…I plan to." Tom was surprised to see him.

"I don't think so." Kramer said.

"Maybe I'll go next semester when I'm ready." Tom managed to talk evenly. "I don't think so." Kramer repeated.

"Why? Why do you say that?" Tom was getting scared.

"I talked to your brother-in-law. He doesn't want you killed, just gone."

"What do you mean?" Tom was looking furtively for an escape route.

Kramer grabbed him by his shirt. "If it was up to me, I would just choke you and throw you in the river. No one will miss you."

"What…" Tom was really getting scared.

"Look. I am giving you a one-way ticket to Tampa. If I see you in town after tomorrow, I will exercise the other option. Do you understand?" He handed Tom a bus ticket.

"Ok, OK…I can do that." Tom stammered.

Kramer reached over and took his winnings. "Gee, this is only about 50 dollars." "I need that." Tom pleaded.

"No. You will just blow it on another race." Kramer put it in his pocket. "You already wasted the tuition money she gave you. You are a real loser."

"I was on a winning streak, honest." Tom complained.

"Keep in mind that I can find you anytime I want to. And if you are not on that bus tomorrow, I will know it." He released his grip on Tom. "Thank your brother-in-law for not letting me waste you. Now get going." Kramer sneered.

Tom walked away as fast as he could. Why was this guy terrorizing him? He had seen that Big Tony was scared to death of the guy. He did have an intention of going to the college but he just couldn't fit in with all those young kids. He did not have any skills except for repetitive factory work that drove him crazy. If he had some money he could do Ok in Tampa, but now he was almost broke. He couldn't ask Sarah for more money. She would be suspicious.

He got back to Sarah's house. She was in the basement doing laundry. Her purse was on the kitchen counter. He walked over and opened it. She had a few credit cards and some cash. He pocketed the cash. It was only about 80 dollars. He lifted one of the credit/debit cards and put it in his pocket. He did not want to take one of her major credit cards. Those were too easy to trace. He went to the room she was letting him stay in and packed a small bag with his clothing and personal articles. There was a glass case in the living room with an old baseball in it. It was autographed by Stan Musial and was probably worth some money. He took it and put it in his bag. He hid the glass case behind some stuff in her curio cabinet. If she did not see it, she would not miss it. He knew there was probably some jewelry on her makeup stand in her bedroom. He went into the bedroom and searched through her armoire. He took a couple of rings that looked like they had diamonds in them. He pocketed them plus a pearl necklace he found. He left the bedroom and headed for the door. Sarah came upstairs and saw him heading for the door.

"Going out?" she asked wondering why he had his bag.

"Yeah, I am going over to a friend's house for a few days. I will see you later." He lied as he opened the front door to leave.

"Ok...Bye." She was puzzled by his response.

As he walked to his old beat-up car, he tried to remember which pawn shops were nearby. He still had the bus ticket and planned to use it. He was scared to death of the Kramer guy. The stuff he took from his sister should provide him with enough cash to get established with his friends in Tampa. He found a pawnshop and parked in front. He walked in. There was an old bald guy behind the counter. A glass shield was between them with a small hole near the bottom of the counter. He could see that the old guy had a gun in his belt.

"What can I do for you?" the old man asked.

"Well, I was going to get married but the girl turned me down so I thought I would get rid of the ring." Tom lied. "I would go back to the jewelry store but I have to leave town in a hurry." He showed the old guy one of the rings.

"Have to leave in a hurry, eh?" the old man knew that he was lying. Here was a chance to make a profit. He took the ring and looked through a loupe at it. It was a good diamond, about a half karat in a 14-karat gold ring. He figured it would go for about nine hundred dollars. "I will give you three hundred in cash for it." He said.

"Hey. I paid more for it than that." Tom lied. "Take it or leave it." The old man smiled.

"Ok. I am in a hurry." Tom agreed. He knew better than to unload everything in one place. He grabbed the cash and walked out the door.

The old man knew it was probably stolen, but he had friends who would fence the ring for him. He would get cheated but would still make a couple of hundred dollars. Not bad for ten minutes of work.

Tom hit another pawn shop on the other side of town and got four hundred for the pearl necklace. He stopped in a store to get some bottled water and went to pay for it with the debit card. "Say, I am short of cash. Can you put some on the card for me.?"

The clerk said "Ok. But our limit is 25 dollars."

"Hey, that's good." Tom pocketed the extra cash. He now had enough to head south. He still had some items to pawn but he could do that in Florida. He headed to the bus station. There was a used car lot next to the bus terminal. He pulled in and parked.

A salesman came up to him. "Looking to buy a good car?"

"Not really. How much will you give me for this Chevy?" Tom asked. "We don't typically buy cars, we sell them," the sales guy replied.

"Well, you can make a good profit on this one. I don't want much," Tom persuaded.

The sales guy looked at the car. It was sort of beat up but he could probably get a couple of thousand for it. The owner looked like he really needed the money badly.

"I will tell you what. I will give you five hundred if you sign it over to us." He would start low and see how high the guy would negotiate.

Tom knew he was getting cheated but he didn't want to miss the bus. He had the title in his pocket and pulled it out. "Give me the money and it's yours," he said.

The salesman was shocked. "Do you have some identification?" He wasn't going to buy a stolen car. Tom showed him his driver's license. The name matched the title.

"OK. Wait here. I will write you a check." The salesman turned away. "No. I need cash." Tom insisted.

The salesman turned back. "Ok. I will see how much we have in the safe." He walked to the office. The sales guy figured the guy must be on the lam from the police or something. He checked the safe. There was about eight hundred dollars in there. He counted out four hundred and fifty. He put another fifty in his pocket and made the paperwork out for five hundred and walked back out to Tom.

"Well, we only had four hundred and fifty in the safe, so I guess it's no deal," the salesman said.

"That's close enough." Tom signed the title and gave it to the sales guy. The sales guy counted out the money and had him sign a bill of sale. Tom signed it without looking at it and gave it back to the salesman. Tom walked away. The salesman smiled at him said "You come back anytime."

Tom walked into the bus station and checked the schedule. The bus for Tampa was scheduled to leave in about 45 minutes. He went to the counter to have the ticket checked. It was a good ticket and the man told him when the bus would leave and the bus number. Tom walked over to the seating area and sat down. He had a little over a thousand dollars now with a couple of more items to pawn yet. He would have to spend some of it on his friends to show he was a successful guy, but when they let him into their organization, he would make lots of money.

Kramer looked through the window and saw Tom sitting waiting for the bus. This was good. He was half afraid that the jerk would not show up. He really wouldn't have killed the guy but felt that if he didn't threaten him he wouldn't leave.

He would tell the dying man and his wife that her brother had decided to go to Florida to look for a job.

CHAPTER 113

SUE MANAGED TO DRIVE Ron to the college in the Jeep for the first day of the second week of classes. Ron and Sue both had all of their classes on Mondays and Wednesdays so that was somewhat convenient. The classes were not all at the same times so it meant that one of them would be in the Student Union while the other was in class. At first the other students were very friendly toward him and greeted him since everyone thought he was a hero. But after a week or so things changed back to normal. There were a lot newer students around now for the Fall Semester.

Ron was in class and Sue was studying quietly inside the open sitting area because it was too cold outside to sit on the veranda. It was late afternoon but she had one more class.

Greg Sommers was a new freshman just starting at the college for the fall semester. He was walking through the student center when he spotted Sue. He had graduated with her last May and was surprised that she was at this college. He knew she had been accepted to several Ivy League schools out east. What was she doing at this university?

"Hello." Greg Sommers said as he sat down next to her. Sue recognized Greg. He was one of the boys she had dated back in her senior year in High School.

"Hi Greg," she responded. She had a couple of dates with him but they never really hit it off. He was somewhat aggressive and tried to get her to have sex with him. She had to basically fight him off. She had begged off on the third date saying she was busy. He took the hint and did not call her again.

Greg was amazed to see Sue. He had a big crush on her in high school. "I didn't know you were attending college here. I heard you had offers from an Ivy League University." He looked at her with considerable appreciation. Maybe they could start dating again?

"Well, I wanted to stay closer to home, and they did offer me a full scholarship here." She answered. The diamond ring on her left hand was openly displayed for him.

"Wow. Is that an engagement ring?" He was surprised. *"Yes. I am engaged to a senior engineering student."*

"When did that happen? I didn't see that at graduation four months ago." He also noticed she had a new scar on her cheek near her ear. He wondered about that. He hoped she was not being abused by the guy she was engaged to.

"I started here during summer semester and met Ron here."

"That was quick. He must be quite a guy." Greg was disappointed. But still it was nice to see someone who he knew at the college.

"He is wonderful." She blushed a bit. *"He has a job waiting for him at an aerospace company when he graduates at the end of the semester."*

"So...you are going to drop out of college to raise kids and stuff?" He was surprised that she would probably give up her scholastic career for some guy.

"No. We have agreed that I will finish my degree here at the college and become a teacher and he will work as an engineer."

"Wow. That sounds like you have it all planned out." He was amazed at the change in her. When he known her, she was shy and reserved. Now she seemed to be full of confidence about her life.

"Here he comes now." she smiled.

Ron approached them in his wheel chair. His leg was mending but he still had the cast on. He managed to cover it up with some baggy jogging pants, but he still had the white shirt and blue blazer on. He still had a baseball cap on to hide his head scar. His class was over so he wanted to see Sue. He saw her talking to a guy at her table.

"Hi," he said as he wheeled up to the table. Jerry was with him and had helped wheel him to and from class.

"It's about time," Sue said as she broke into a wide smile. Jerry sat next to her. *"Who is your friend?"* Ron asked also smiling, glad to see her.

"This is Greg, a friend from high school. Greg, this is my fiancé, Ron."

"Hello." Greg managed. My god, was she going to marry a cripple? he thought. *"Hello Greg. Did you go to South High also?"* Ron asked.

"Yeah, Sue & I graduated together." Greg smiled.

Sue interrupted. "Ron was a senior at South High when I was a freshman. If you remember, that was the year they went 10 and 0 in the football conference. He hurt his ankle in the last quarter scoring the winning touchdown in the final game." Sue was bragging a bit.

"Wow. That's amazing. I remember that play. You got creamed in the endzone but managed to hold on to the ball," Greg said. He sure doesn't look like a football player now, he thought.

"Yeah, that was a long time ago. I don't play football anymore. I'm just trying to finish up my last semester here." Ron noted.

"Sue said you are in Engineering?" Greg asked.

"Yes, I have an engineering job waiting for me at an aerospace firm." Ron was looking around. He wondered if his friend George was going to join him as they had planned for a beer in the downstairs pub.

Joan walked up to the table. "How's it going guys?" Joan asked. Then she noticed Greg. "Hey, aren't you the guy who dated Sue for a while?" she asked innocently. Jerry frowned at her, knowing that was probably not something Ron wanted to hear.

"So, you two dated?" Ron asked Greg.

"Yeah we went out a couple of times." Greg started to blush.

"Well, you let a real good one get away." Ron smiled and looked at Sue.

Joan reached over to Sue. "We have a class in ten minutes, we better get going."

Sue got up and looked at her watch. "I guess so. See you later, darling." She said as she bent over to kiss Ron. She then walked away with Joan and they started their usual chit chat.

"Well, that was awkward." Greg said. Sue was obviously in love with the cripple. He wondered why.

"No. That's ok." Ron looked at Greg. "What is your major, by the way?"

"I am going into a business management curriculum. It seems to be a good field." Greg looked at Ron.

"Yeah, I had to take a business class. They are easy A's compared to engineering." Ron noted.

Jerry could sense a bit of tension between them. "I was a business management student for a year but then changed my major to social studies."

Ron looked at Jerry. "When are you going to graduate?" he asked.

"Well, I am technically a junior but this is my fifth year here. We have a lot of parties at the Frat House and I am taking my time." Jerry blushed a bit. Now that he had met Joan, he was becoming more serious about his studies. He was thinking of a more permanent relationship with Joan and therefore had to get a degree and get a good job.

Just then George Coleman walked up to Ron. He was in his police uniform. "I thought we were going to get a cold one." He was off duty for the rest of the day, and although he still wore the uniform, he could still drink a beer with his friend.

"Well, I got to go. See you around." Ron said as he turned his wheelchair to go with George.

Greg looked at the policeman. He turned to Jerry as they headed for the elevator. "Ron is friends with the police?" he asked.

"Technically, he is a police auxiliary," Jerry said as he got up, thought about going to join them. "That guy is crippled, and Sue is still going to marry him?" Greg asked.

Jerry stopped and turned to look back at Greg. "He's not a cripple. He is a hero. Didn't you see the car-truck crash about seven weeks ago on the news where Ron diverted a semi from hitting a bunch of children on the playground?"

"That's him?" Greg was stunned. "I thought the guy got killed."

"He almost died on the operating table. It took four operations to save his life!" Jerry was almost shouting. "He is probably the best person I have ever known. And Sue is deeply in love with him. They are going to get married."

"Wow. I'm sorry. I didn't know." Greg apologized. He had no idea that the guy was a hero. When he saw the car wreck on the news he could not believe anyone could live through that.

"Ok then. But don't think of him as a cripple. When his fractured leg heals he will be as good as new." Jerry turned and walked away.

Greg sat there and thought for a while. He was amazed that he actually met the guy from that accident and that Ron did not act at all like a hero. He seemed to be a normal guy, although in a wheelchair. He was disappointed in that Sue was now unavailable but maybe he could somehow get back into her good graces and steal her from the cripple. The problem was that she looked very happy to be with Ron. He knew that even good relationships sometimes didn't last. If Ron was graduating and she was staying in school, he could wait for the right opportunity. Maybe he could work his way into being with her as a "friend" and make Ron Jealous. That could create a crisis between them and he would step in and grab her on the rebound.

CHAPTER 114

ROBERT WAS HAVING A relapse. Instead of getting better he felt himself slipping away again. He could still talk but it was getting more difficult by the day. He could just barely chew food again but did not tell the nurse that.

A man came into his room. It was the Kramer guy. Bob looked at him.

"Hello." Bob managed to say. He wondered why the man was visiting him again.

"The brother-in-law problem is resolved." Kramer told Bob. "I saw him get on a bus to Florida. He won't be coming back."

"Good. Thank you." Bob managed to say. He was relieved that Sarah would not have to worry about the stupid brother.

"He hocked some stuff at a pawn shop. I think he stole some of your wife's jewelry." Kramer wondered if he should have done something about that. Maybe catch him and throw him in prison for a few years? But, no the sister would not have pressed charges. So, it was better to take the loss and hope he never came back.

"That's ok as long as he doesn't come back." Bob was having trouble forming some of the words.

"Yeah, that's kind of what I figured." Kramer agreed. "You seem to be getting worse. Are you doing ok?"

"No. I am dying. I'm just taking more time than I thought," Bob mumbled. "Well don't worry about your wife. I will look after her."

"Please, could you also look out for my little granddaughter?" He reminded Kramer. "Her name is Susan and she is very special." Robert managed.

"Don't worry about it. I will do what I can." Kramer reassured him. He wondered what was so special about a little girl.

"Thanks." Bob was losing consciousness.

"Ok then." Kramer hated to see the man dying like this. But there was nothing he could do about it so he walked out of the room. He wondered how long he should wait after the guy died to ask the wife out on a date. He also wondered about the little girl. Why should the grandfather be so concerned about a little girl?

CHAPTER 115

*R*ON WAS FINALLY GETTING *the cast off his leg. It was a Friday and he did not have any classes today. The doctor still wanted him to walk with crutches for another week even though the X-rays showed the femur had healed pretty well. The stainless steel pins in his leg would stay there since the bone had knitted around them. The doctor showed Ron the X-rays.*

"You will probably be able to tell when the weather changes with a dull pain in your leg, but that's pretty normal for this type of fracture," the doctor warned him.

It was about six weeks into the semester and the itching under the cast was driving Ron crazy. "Well, I am just glad to be rid of the thing." Ron appreciated the doctor removing the cast a week earlier than planned. The dead skin on his leg looked disgusting. He would have to take a shower as soon as he got home. He took off his shorts and put on a pair of khaki pants he had brought with him.

"So how is school going for you this semester?" the doctor asked.

"Well, I might not make the dean's list but I am doing well enough to graduate." Ron looked at the doctor. The distraction of having Sue around him had made it hard to concentrate on his studies. At least now she would not have to drive him to and from class. He was carrying a solid B average in his last three classes. He had been surprised that he was getting a partial salary from the engineering firm. It was not much but it was helping to pay his expenses. He was already planning on saving up for another Corvette. The insurance on the old one did not account for a lot since it was such an older model. The official police report stated that he had collided with a truck that was moving left of center. The insurance company argued that the collision could have been avoided but did eventually pay up. So now he had about half of what he needed to buy a good used Corvette. He probably should

be buying a family car now that he was going to eventually get married. Sue was neutral about getting another Corvette. She said that if he wanted one he should get it. She just didn't want him to start crashing into trucks anymore.

The doctor gave him a crutch from the closet. He adjusted the height to fit Ron. "If you use this for a week you can return it to me, there is no charge," the doctor stated. "You can leave the wheelchair here. I will return it for you."

"Thanks, Doc. I appreciate it." Ron turned to leave. As he hop-stepped into the waiting room he saw Sue sitting and reading a magazine. He hopped up to her.

"Ready to go?" he asked as she looked up.

"Well, that's an improvement," she said noticing that the cast was off. She got up and headed to the door, holding it open for him.

"OK." He said as he got to the Jeep. He held out his hand for the keys.

"Are you sure you can drive?" She teased as she gave him the keys.

"I think so." He looked at her. She was still the most beautiful girl he had ever seen. She was wearing a blue halter top with a light blue jacket and a white skirt. She went around to the passenger door and opened it and got in before he could get to it to open it for her. He hopped over to the driver side and got in, shoving the crutch into the back seat. It was nice to be able to drive again. He drove her to her dormitory and dropped her off. They had a passionate kiss in the front seat and he almost suggested going up to her room. But she got out and waved at him as she walked to the dormitory. He drove back to his apartment. He parked the Jeep next to Matt's truck as usual and started to get out when Matt came out of the side door of the garage.

"Hey! You are driving again," Matt greeted him.

"Yes. I finally got the cast off but the doctor wants me to use this crutch for one more week."

Matt was amazed at how quickly the boy had mended. "Did you get your settlement from the car insurance?" Matt asked.

"Yeah, but it is not quite enough to replace the Corvette with a new one. I might have to do some research for a good used one. Hey, we might have a poker game on Saturday." Ron had not asked Sue out Saturday. He wondered if she would mind them

having a poker night. Better to find out if she got upset over things like that now.

"That sounds good." Matt agreed. They had not played cards since the accident. He looked at Ron. "Hey, ah, do you have a minute?"

"Sure." Ron sort of hopped over to Matt using the crutch. He was slowly getting the hang of using it to keep his weight off the damaged leg.

Matt opened the side door to the garage and Ron followed him. Matt turned on the lights. A metallic blue Corvette was in the garage, the same model and year as Ron's old one.

"Wow. You got yourself a Corvette!" Ron was surprised. It was beautiful.

"Yeah, I have been working on it, restoring it. It is almost back in new condition. It is the same model and year as your old one, except it has a removable glass top instead of a convertible. It is an LT3 instead of your old LT2, so it has leather seats, a factory installed GPS Navigation display and the expensive fancy wheels."

Ron sort of hobbled around the car. "Boy, she is a beauty. You must have been working on this for a while."

"Yeah. Pity I have to get rid of it. The wife won't let me keep it." Matt grimaced.

"No kidding." Ron hated that Matt could not keep it. He was already falling in love with the car.

"Yeah. I hope someone who appreciates it will take it off my hands." Matt looked at Ron slyly. "Wow. How much are you asking for it?" Ron inquired.

CHAPTER 116

ROBERT HAD FALLEN BACK into a coma. Sarah and Reverend Morton were sitting in his room.

Jack Simms was examining Robert. "I just don't understand it. He was making such a good recovery with the new drug." Jack made some notes on the chart.

"He still might recover?" Sarah asked.

"It is possible, I suppose, but it sure does not look like it now." Jack put the chart back.

Robert's son David entered the room. "I just got back from my business trip. I understand that Dad wanted to talk to me?" He looked at his mother.

"Yes, he was asking for you, but he is not conscious now." Sarah got up and hugged David. Reverend Morton also got up and shook David's hand. "We will continue to pray for him."

David was disappointed. He had wanted to talk to his Dad, but could not get back in time. He felt guilty for not being here when Bob wanted to talk to him. Maybe his father would regain consciousness and be able to talk to him.

"Do you think he will wake up again?" he asked Jack.

"I don't know. I am increasing the amount of the drug that brought him out of the coma the first time. We do not have anything to lose at this point." Jack looked at Sarah and the preacher. "Probably doesn't hurt to keep on praying. He has already lived two more months than I expected."

Sarah had realized that her brother was not coming back. First he did not come home and then later she saw some of her jewelry was missing as well as the autographed baseball. She thought about reporting a robbery but then decided against it. She could not put her brother in prison. Kramer then visited her and told her that her brother had gotten on a bus bound for Florida. She knew he had some friends there and hoped he would straighten out his life but knew he was probably hopeless. She felt lost, first her husband

and now her brother. Her children were living away from her so now she was basically alone. The thought made her depressed so she had called Reverend Morton and asked him for guidance. The reverend sympathized with her and told her to put her faith in God and everything would come out alright. She hoped he was right.

David and the reverend talked for a while and then they both left. Sarah sat in the chair looking at her husband. The doctors had reinstalled the respirator to help him breathe, and a tube down his throat to assist in feeding him. She was not sure she could endure this up and down status of Bob. They were going to increase the drug dosage, hoping it helped. She would increase her praying also. She took out her knitting and started to work on it.

CHAPTER 117

ON WAS VISITING SUE and Joan in their dorm room. It was Saturday morning and he was explaining that he had a poker game that night and would not be able to take her out. Saturday night was one of the few times where both George and Andy were available to play poker. They were sitting on the couch while Joan was at the table, studying.

"Don't either of them have girlfriends?" Sue asked, irritated. Saturday night was typically a date night.

"To be honest, I don't know. Being a cop makes your schedule difficult and you have to be ready to run off to duty at any time of the day. A lot of girls probably don't tolerate that," he explained. "Anyway, I thought I would take you out to lunch to make up for it."

"Ok. That sounds good to me." She was a little put off by not having Ron on a Saturday night date but it did not really matter that much. He should spend some time with his friends. He would, however, be passing up on some nice fringe benefits she had planned on having with him.

"Well, grab your jacket and I'll take you to lunch," he replied. "Should we invite Joan?" she asked.

He did not say anything but looked at Joan.

"You guys go ahead. I am in the middle of this assignment that is due Monday." Joan noted, seeing that Ron probably wanted to be alone with Sue.

They said goodbye and walked down the steps to the first floor. He still had to struggle with steps with the crutch but they eventually got to the first floor. "I will be glad when I don't have to use this thing." he noted.

She looked at him and smiled. Ron had come a long way in only two months. He opened the door for her and they walked out toward the parking lot. Sue looked around but did not see the Jeep. It was typically parked as near as possible to the door. She was

about to ask him when she saw that they were walking toward a
Corvette.

"Did you get another Corvette?" she asked.

"Well, it was a good deal and my insurance money covered the
cost." He smiled at her.

She walked up to it. It was a pretty blue color and was almost
the same as his red convertible except it had a glass top. "Wow.
This is a nice one."

"Get in. It is the same model as the one I had, only it is in better
shape and lower mileage." He was already proud of the vehicle.

"You aren't planning to hit any trucks, are you?" she teased.
"No. I don't plan on doing that again. Not with you in the car."

She got in the passenger side. He got in slowly. He was still a
little careful with his leg, it was still tender. He moved the crutch
to the back of the hatchback.

"Well, this one has a lot more storage space than the
convertible." She leaned over to him and they shared a passionate
kiss.

"Do you think we will live happily ever after?" she asked him.

"I hope so. We have had enough excitement this past summer
to last a lifetime. I want the rest of our life to be boring as heck,
except for making love to you," he replied. They pulled out of the
parking lot.

"Well, a little excitement would not hurt, at least in the
bedroom," she agreed.

He drove the Corvette down the road. He could see that they
would be happy together. He knew she would become a successful
art teacher and he already had an engineering position waiting
for him. Life was good.

CHAPTER 118

ROBERT WAS AWAKE AGAIN. He could not communicate to the outside world but he thought he was awake. He was happy that Sue and Ron had survived their accidents and wondered why the dream ended so abruptly. Things were changing. He felt as if he was swirling down into a hole. But there was a light. It was far off but he was slowly going toward it. He did not see it with his eyes but it was there. So strange he thought…

Sarah got up late and drove to the nursing home. Lately the doctors were saying that Robert was fading again. Yesterday they said he might not last another day. Even Jack had said that increasing the experimental drug dose did not seem to help. So, she had stayed late but he still held on, so she went home. She was tired so slept later than normal. Now she was on her way to visit him again.

As she entered his room she saw the bed was empty. She looked to see if she was in the right room. Then she walked to the nurse's station. A nurse was sitting there, typing into a laptop.

"Where is my husband?" she asked.

The nurse looked up at her. "Didn't they call you?" she asked. "No. No one called." Sarah was getting worried.

"Well, I'm sorry to have to tell you this but he died last night." The nurse was sorry that no one had called the wife. Someone had screwed up. "Let me get the administrator for you." She started to dial the phone.

For Sarah it was immediate grief. She looked around for a chair to sit down. In a way it was a relief. Bob had suffered so much and now it was all over. She walked down the hall and sat down in the patient lounge. A couple of people were in there working on a jigsaw puzzle. She started to cry but silently. The administrator came into the room and spotted her.

"I am so sorry for your loss," she started. "The night nurse found him unresponsive and not breathing. She called the doctor who pronounced him dead." The administrator was sorry that no one had called her, but apparently the night nurse went off duty and assumed someone else would call the family.

"We did not expect him to make a full recovery." Sarah remarked. "But I thought he might last a little while longer."

"The body has been transferred this morning to a funeral home, the one your husband asked for when he was still conscious." The administrator told her. "If there is anything I can do, let me know. The doctor will fill out a death certificate and we will send it to you."

"Ok, thank you." Sarah had to go to the funeral home to make arrangements. She took out her phone and called Jack Simms. It was early in the morning and he was in his office.

"Yes?" he answered.

"Jack, Robert is gone. He passed last night." Sarah told him.

"Oh…I am so sorry. I did not think he was going to recover from this latest relapse." Jack was saddened by his friend's death but he knew all along there was only one outcome. He had been surprised that the new drug had worked for a while, maybe delayed the death by a month. "If there is anything I can do, let me know."

"Yeah, sure." Sarah terminated the call. Now she had to figure out the funeral arrangements and what she was going to do with the rest of her life. She was not that old, still in her early fifties. Robert had not wanted her to be left alone and had told her to find another husband, but she could not see herself in a dating mode again, not after 28 years of marriage. She left the nursing home and drove to the funeral home.

CHAPTER 119

THE REVEREND MORTON PRESIDED over the funeral service at the funeral home and then later again at the graveside. Robert was laid to rest in an attractive metal casket with wood veneer. Jack Simms was one of the pallbearers, His son Dave was another. Other men from Sarah's church took the other places. It was a windy cold day for the end of August, somewhat unusual for this time of year. At least it was not raining. Robert's daughter Lauren and her fiancé were also able to attend. They had gotten emergency family leave and had flown in from Germany. Some of Bob's old co-workers also attended the ceremony. His old boss, Marty was in attendance. He was missing Bob since the engineering department just wasn't as efficient as when Bob was there. Sarah's brother Tom did not show up. Sarah had gotten a postcard from him about a week ago saying that he was sorry for all the trouble he had caused her but that he was doing ok in Tampa. Kramer showed up at the burial and stood in the background. He was wearing his brown plaid sport coat and tan pants again. He was sort of glad that Robert's suffering was over for he knew it was hard on Sarah to keep hoping for Bob's recovery. It was sort of announced that everyone would return to Sarah's house for snacks and fellowship. Kramer followed the crowd and when he had a chance he walked up to Sarah.

"I am so sorry for your loss," he said to her with his hat in his hand.

"Oh, hello." Sarah was surprised to see Kramer but she was also happy to see him. She really liked him a lot. She sort of hoped that he would somehow feel the same way about her. "You must join us. We are returning to the house for snacks and refreshments."

"Ok. Sounds like a plan." He walked beside her to her car. Her son David was driving the old Buick for his mother. He looked up to see her walking with Kramer. Kramer was a big man. He wondered who this guy was. The guy looked like he weighed almost 300 pounds but he wasn't fat, he looked like all muscle.

David walked up to him. "Hello, I am David, Robert's son," he introduced himself.

Kramer looked at him. "It's nice to meet you. My name is Kramer. I'm a friend of your mother's." Kramer smiled at him.

Kramer knew he had to be nice to the family. "I am a private detective. Your dad asked me to sort of

look after your mom."

"Oh, well, in that case, it's nice to meet you." David was puzzled. Still, it was like his father to worry about Sarah. If his father had asked this guy to watch over her, David doubted that anyone would try to take advantage of her.

They all got in their cars and drove to the house. Sarah had arranged to have a caterer bring some food trays and drinks. All of this was laid out on the dinner table. Everyone was helping themselves to the food as Sarah walked around and tried to be a good host. Kramer bumped into Jack Simms. Jack was happy to see him.

"How is your mother doing these days?" Jack asked.

Kramer smiled at him. "She is doing just fine since you saved her life. She is off with her friends at the casino this weekend. I still owe you for that."

"Hey. It's ok. I was just glad that you could help Sarah with her brother. I have been a friend of the family for years. Robert was my best friend." Jack was genuinely happy to see Kramer. The first time they had met he had been somewhat intimidated by him but now they were good friends.

"Sarah's brother is in Florida. I arranged that for Robert." Kramer said as he bit into a sandwich. "You got to talk with Robert?" Jack inquired.

"Yes. It was when he had made a partial recovery. He didn't want Tom dead, just out of the picture. He also asked me to look after his wife when he was gone."

A chill ran down Jack's spine. Would Kramer really have killed Tom? He knew Kramer had underworld connections, so anything was possible he supposed. "So…Bob asked you to take care of Sarah?" Jack asked.

"Well, I am here for her if she wants me to be." Kramer finished the sandwich.

Jack considered that. Sarah had no one to help her since her family was living so far away. It might be good that she could have someone to help her if she needed it.

Sarah came over to them. She was smiling at Kramer and wrapped her arm around his. "I am so glad you were able to make it" she was looking at Kramer. She turned to Jack. "I want to thank you Jack, for recommending him to me. He was such a big help."

"That's good." Jack was sort of shocked. He had not figured that this scenario would occur, but he was glad that Sarah had someone powerful to lean on now that Bob was gone.

The party was sort of low tone since everyone was sorry to see Robert die. Most of the people present knew that he had suffered quite a lot in the last few months. Liz, David's wife was very pregnant. She was about seven months along and looked like she had swallowed a watermelon. The doctors had confirmed that she was carrying twin boys. Apparently Liz and David had enjoyed the cruise to Hawaii a lot more than they had expected. Little Susan was unhappy about two boys entering her family but knew that she would have to tolerate them. Susan was sorry that her step-grandfather had died. He had been very nice to her and had taught her how to play chess and shuffleboard on the cruise. Robert had noticed that little Susan was small for her age and also very skinny. He had set aside some money for Liz to pay for karate lessons for her. Then he had talked about karate with Susan and had interested her in self-defense. He had let her watch a couple of karate movies and she did pick up an interest. He felt that young girls should be able to defend themselves. Also, Bob knew that the physical and mental training would give her confidence about life. She already was a straight A student in school.

The wake was starting to end and Kramer walked into the dining room to look for some food to snack on.

Susan sat in a corner and was eating a piece of cake. She was dressed in a light blue dress and had her hair in a ponytail. Kramer got a piece of cake and came over and sat next to her. She looked up at him and asked "You like my Grandma, don't you?"

Kramer was shocked at the little girl's observation. He did not think it was that obvious. "Yes I do. I met with your grandpa and he told me to take care of her." He smiled at the young girl. He looked at her again. "You must be Susan."

"Yes. How did you know that?" she was curious.

"Your grandpa told me about you." He could see that she was indeed, special.

"Grandpa Bob was a nice guy. Are you a nice guy?" she asked. She apparently was not intimidated by Kramer's large size.

"Yes. I can be a nice guy." He looked at her with some interest. This little girl was pretty smart.

"Grandpa taught me chess. We had a nice trip to Hawaii together." She looked at the cake and took a bite. "He let me eat all the ice cream I wanted. We played shuffle board on the boat."

"It sounds as if he really loved you." Kramer noted. He was starting to understand Bob's preoccupation with the little girl.

"I really miss him a lot. He told me all about karate and how it was good to know how to defend yourself." She looked up at him again.

"Well, I agree with him on that. Young girls should be able to defend themselves. I know a good Karate Dojo in this area if you want me to take you there sometime."

"That would be super." She smiled wide. "How old do you have to be?"

"Well, some kids start when they are only 5 years old." He knew a good instructor that had taught him some very good defensive moves.

Susan was surprised. "Really? Wow, then I could start right away, I am almost nine."

"Yeah. Well, we would have to talk to your parents about that." He was already becoming somewhat attached to the little girl. "How are you doing in school?"

"School is easy. I get straight A's all the time. It is actually boring sometimes, but I really like Art class." She finished the piece of cake.

"So, you like Art?"

"Yeah. It is really interesting. My teacher lets you draw or paint whatever you want and then tells you how to improve your technique. It is very rewarding to create a good picture."

"Have you ever been to the Cleveland Art Museum?" He asked.

"No, but my mom keeps promising to take me sometime." She looked up at him.

"Maybe I can take you and your grandma there." He looked into her pretty green eyes. There was something about this little girl. He could see what Bob had meant when he said she was something special.

"I would like that a lot." She smiled at him.

"Well, I usually keep my promises so let's see if we can plan to do that."

Kramer got up. As he did, his sport coat opened and Susan saw the pistol in a holster on his belt.

"You carry a gun," she said calmly.

"Yes, I am a detective." He closed his jacket quickly. "I have a permit to carry it." "Do you have to deal with bad men?" she asked.

"Sometimes I have to, but not that often." He looked down at her.

Susan smiled and looked up at him. "You are a nice man. I can tell." Susan got up and walked over to get more cake.

Kramer looked in amazement at her. She was very mature for such a young child.

Reverend Morton came over to talk to Sarah. "I am sorry about Robert, but he is probably in a better place now," he said to Sarah as he shook her hand. "I thought our prayer was working for a while at least."

Sarah looked at the reverend and said: "I know reverend. it just was not to be."

Sarah was saying goodbye to the people as they were leaving. People. Jack

Simms and his wife were among the last to leave. Angie came over to Sarah and hugged her.

"I am really sorry about Bob." Jack confessed. "I tried everything I could to save him." "I know, Jack. He almost made a comeback. It wasn't your fault." Sarah reassured him.

"I am going to miss him; he was my best friend." Jack teared up. He started for the door. "It's ok." Sarah noted. "I am just glad he isn't in pain anymore."

Soon almost everyone was gone except for David and his family who were staying at her house for a few days. Liz was really tired and went upstairs to bed.

Sarah did some cleaning on the dinner table and took some dishes into the kitchen. She noticed Kramer was still here and was helping David clean up in the kitchen. Kramer was washing dishes, David was drying.

"You're still here," she said to Kramer. She was pleasantly surprised.

"Yeah, thought I would help clean up." Kramer smiled at her. Little Susan was sitting at the kitchen table, working on a Sudoku puzzle. He was drying his hands on a dish towel. He pointed at the little girl. "Susan wants to go to the Cleveland Art Museum. How about you and I take her there tomorrow, make a day of it?"

"Yes. That sounds wonderful, as long as it is ok with Dave and Liz." She looked at David.

Dave looked at his mother. "I guess so. Liz is not feeling very well and wants to rest here a few days with her pregnancy." David replied. "I am sure that Susan would enjoy it. All she talks about is art class."

"Well, you and Liz are welcome to stay here as long as you want." Sarah was happy to have the family at the house. It was big and lonely just for one person.

Kramer looked at Susan. She had a big smile on her face. "Good. It's a plan. I will come by and pick you and Susan up at 10:00 tomorrow morning." Kramer was happy. He had just arranged a date with Sarah.

Later Kramer left and David sat alone with his mother in the front room. Susan had gone to bed upstairs.

"Well, that was a long day." David noted. "Yeah." Sarah was tired.

"By the way, Robert arranged to have a fund for Susan so she could take karate lessons." Sarah explained.

"Ok, but I am not sure Liz will go along with that." David remembered that little Susan had mentioned that Kramer had said he could arrange karate lessons for her. She obviously wanted to do it.

"You like that Kramer guy?" David asked. He had to find out what was going on. "Yes. I hope you don't mind. He is a nice guy."

"He seems to be a nice guy. He told me that Dad had asked him to look after you." David noted.

"Really? I did not know that." Sarah was surprised.

"Hey, I am just glad that you have someone to help out." David could see that she was tired but wanted to let her know that it was ok with him that she and Kramer could be together. "He seems to be a real standup guy. Even Susan likes him already."

"Well, I like him too." Sarah confessed.

"Dad would be happy if he knew you had someone to lean on." David said.

"Yes, Bob as much as told me that when he knew he was dying." Sarah replied. "Well, I am happy for you." David got up to go to bed.

"Thank you." His mother replied. She missed Robert terribly but she was excited about being with Kramer. She was very tired and checked the door locks and then went to bed herself. She was looking forward to visiting the museum with Susan and Kramer.

-The End-